FIRE IN THE WASTES

BY

DONALD MORRISON

Published by Dark Forest Publishing

ISBN-13: 979-8-9881141-7-8

First Edition

Printed in the United States of America

Thank you to everyone who has ever read my works. You are the reason I do this.

Thank you to everyone who has ever read my works. You are the reason I do this.

"There are two problems for our species' survival – nuclear war and environmental catastrophe – and we're hurtling towards them. Knowingly."

Noam Chomsky

CHAPTER 1

Warm beer sloshed in a dirty glass, a thin crack running from handle to lip—a scar from years of hard living in the wastes. No bubbles rose to the surface; the beer was as flat and lifeless as the land outside. Along the rim, a faint shimmer marked the ghostly hieroglyphs left by thirsty souls long gone. The man staring into the glass didn't care about the grime, or that the brew inside was likely older than he was. Out here, such things didn't matter. The drink served its purpose.

No one alive remembered the taste of real beer, the crisp bite of carbonation. That was a luxury lost to a thousand cycles past, before the Merge. These days, what passed for beer was closer to mead— warm, flat, and rough, but what it lacked in flavor, it made up for in strength. The last true beer, bottled and labeled, hadn't been seen since the old world burned. Now, folks drank whatever would dull the edge of the wastes, and if it went down without killing you, it was good enough.

The man lightly tapped his thumb against the worn wooden table, the air surrounding him as stale and warm as the half-empty tankard he stared down into. It hovered thick and nearly palpable, filling the saloon that was as vacant as the wastes outside.

Across the dimly lit room sat another who was quietly hunched over their own isolated table. The only indication this patron wasn't dead was the tiny twitch coming from his left shoulder every few moments. Scavenger's tic. One of the early symptoms of sun-sickness. The latter stages of this incredibly common, and more often than not, lethal affliction, were the uncontrollable shaking, shuddered breath and loss of motor functions. Death commonly accompanied this as one of the final symptoms. In the wastes, the sun was just another unchecked box on the endless list of things that offered an average life span of around thirty years.

At another table sat a younger girl. Young and pretty, in a desolate, apocalyptic survival type of way, she was dressed for the wastes, leather pants and vest over a thin, dirty white shirt. She wore a wide brimmed hat, just low enough to conceal the deep worry that was little contained behind her hidden gaze. The girl seemed out of place and scared. But these days, everyone did. The more on edge you were, the longer you lived. Carefree didn't make for a long life in the wastes.

Outside, the wastes simmered beneath a merciless sun, the sky bleached bone-white and empty. A dust devil clawed its way across the barren ground, twisting itself ragged before collapsing into nothing. The heat pressed down like a blacksmith's hammer, leeching the color from the world until everything was the same scorched, brittle shade of rust and ash. Sagebrush clung to life in scattered patches, while the skeletal remains of ancient cactus stood as monuments to things that had died long ago.

A single dirt road, rutted and half-swallowed by drifting sand, ran past the sagging saloon, its wood warped, its tin roof pitted and sun-bleached. The road vanished into the horizon both ways, a promise of nothing but more emptiness. The wastes it crossed seemed to stretch on forever, a desolate canvas painted in dried blood and tarnished copper.

At the front rail, three horses stood tied, their ribs showing through hide stretched thin by hunger and time. Over centuries, beasts had either adapted to the wastes or twisted into something new, warped by fallout and the slow poison of the bombs dropped after the Merge. These three were the lucky—or unlucky survivors: gaunt, hollow-eyed, able to go days without water, weeks if pressed. They couldn't carry much more than a rider and a side bag, but out here, they were worth more than gold. Engines were a memory this deep in the wastes. The only machine that still ran was the battered caravan that rattled along the old tracks between settlements. Everything else was hoof, boot, or the long, slow walk to nowhere—a walk most folks didn't survive.

There were rumors, whispered over cracked mugs, of steam and combustion engines roaring back to life in far-off Europa. But here, in this dead stretch of sun and silence, such things were just stories. Out here, the only thing that moved with certainty was the wind, and the only thing that lasted was the dust.

The man staring down into his glass drew a slow, heavy breath, a scowl flickering across his weathered face as a sudden, unsettling flutter disturbed the stale air above him. He growled, the lines of irritation pulling his features taut. In a single, practiced motion, he swatted at the air over his shoulder.

A small, humanoid creature with wings like a dragonfly darted out of reach, narrowly avoiding the blow. It let out a shrill, high-pitched string of curses—half language, half insect noise—as it shot up toward the ceiling, trailing a faint shimmer of dust in its wake.

"Damned fairies," the man snarled, glaring up as the tiny creature flitted angrily back to its perch on the mantle above the bar. "You gonna do something about that?" he barked at the bartender, who sat behind the bar with a battered paperback in hand.

The bartender looked up, eyes dull, and shrugged with a kind of apathy. "Don't bother me none."

The man at the table grumbled, shooting another glare at the fairy. The little creature met his gaze with equal contempt, then scoffed and turned away, wings buzzing in the thick, smoky air.

The stranger drew a long, steady breath, then reached for the warm glass and knocked back the last of its contents in a single swallow. He set the empty vessel aside and turned his gaze to the window, scanning the sun-bleached world beyond. A flicker of movement caught his eye, but before he could focus, his attention drifted—one last, sidelong glance at the girl sitting alone, careful not to linger. Her hat and boots were sun-faded, her clothes worn thin by the road. She looked like a scrapper, maybe a scavenger, but she carried no iron, and there was a softness to her features that didn't fit either trade. Not beautiful, not really, but there was something about her—sunset hair curling from beneath her hat, a quiet strength beneath the dust and leather. He forced his thoughts away. In the wastes, letting your mind wander in that direction was a good way to end up dead. There were places for that kind of company, but this wasn't one of them.

He shook off the notion, pushed the glass away, and turned to call for another drink—just as the saloon door slammed open, a blast of furnace heat rolling in.

"GOBLINS!" The man who stumbled through the door nearly collapsed, his voice cracking into a ragged scream. "Goblins coming! They're right behind me!"

For a heartbeat, the saloon froze. The man's wild eyes darted to the barkeep, who calmly racked a battered shotgun from beneath the bar. The girl at the corner table jerked upright, fear flashing across her dust-streaked face. The other patron, slumped in a haze of cheap liquor, managed to lift his head—one bloodshot eye twitching as he tried to focus.

"I don't know what's worse," growled the man who'd just wanted to finish his drink in peace, rising from his seat and thumbing the grip of his pistol. "Goblins, or this piss-water beer…"

The newcomer dropped to the floor, pressing his back against the bar, one hand clutching his chest, the other shaking around a rusted pistol. "We're dead," he whimpered, lips cracked and eyes glued to the door that still swung on its hinges.

"You might be," the first man said, glancing at the trembling wreck beside him. "But this ain't my day to die."

He shot a quick look at the girl, who sat rigid, both hands flat on the table, her eyes narrowed to slits beneath the brim of her battered hat, locked on the door.

"How many?" he growled, never taking his eyes off the entrance.

The man on the floor just shook, eyes wide and unblinking. "How many!?" the question came again, louder, sharper.

4

"I don't know!" the frightened man barked, voice breaking. "A dozen. Maybe more."

The first man's brow furrowed. *A dozen?* he thought. *Too few for a proper raiding party. Scouts, maybe?*

His grip on the pistol eased just a hair. Outside, another dust devil twisted past, the wind carrying the promise of violence.

"Well, hell," he muttered, drawing his pistol and striding toward the door.

"They're gonna kill you, mister," the man on the floor whimpered.

"Like I said," came the reply, cold and steady as he thumbed back the hammer. "Not today."

With that, he marched to the door, using the barrel of his gun to nudge it open, ready to meet whatever the wastes had sent his way.

The scalding breath of the wastes slammed into him, heat and dust clawing at his skin. Grit crept into his nostrils, coating them until every breath tasted of rust and bone. He squinted against the glare, eyes stinging beneath the brim of his battered hat. The air moved in slow, blistering waves, brushing past the dead cactus—each creak from their sun-bleached husks a warning spoken by the desert itself.

He pulled a faded bandana up over his nose, the gesture as much ritual as necessity. Off to his right, the sound of metal clinking—thin armor scraping, trinkets rattling on cracked leather—grew louder. Goblins didn't bother with stealth. They didn't have to. Out here, numbers were their only law.

But there was nothing truly strong about goblins. Alone, they were little more than pests—easy enough for a grown man to handle, sometimes even a child. But when they gathered, twenty, fifty, a full raiding party swelling to hundreds, that's when the real danger began. That was the goblins' strength: the horde, the chaos, the certainty of violence.

Standing in the blazing heat, the man listened, measuring the sound. No more than a dozen, he reckoned. Too few for a proper raid. Scouts, maybe. Still, it was strange to find them this far south, away from any known encampment. He let the thought settle, silent and wary, as the wastes pressed in around him.

2

The girl in the bar leaned over her table, eyes sharp as flint, watching through the grimy window as the man outside stood motionless, pistol in hand, the wind tugging at the hem of his battered duster. Each breath she took came in short, uneven bursts, her chest tight with dread. She swallowed hard, watching another dust devil spiral across the dead street before dissolving into nothing.

"What in the hell are goblins doing this far south?" she muttered, voice barely above a whisper.

She tore her gaze from the window and looked to the barkeep, who stood behind the counter with his shotgun cradled in his arms, knuckles white.

"Guess it was bound to happen eventually," rasped the man who, moments before, had been curled beneath the bar. His voice shook as he added, "Better goblins than orcs, I suppose."

The girl flicked a glance at the frightened man huddled at the far end of the bar, then turned her attention back to the stranger outside. He hadn't moved, rooted to the spot as the breeze played in the dust around his boots. The pistol in his hand looked steady, but inside the saloon, the air was thick with fear.

The man stood just outside the battered saloon, boots planted in the dust, waiting as the goblins drew closer. He watched the rising cloud—thin, but telling—marking their numbers. Still, something about it gnawed at him. Goblins had their own lands, far to the north, tucked between the human territories and the shadowed elven woods. They didn't stray this far south, not unless something was pushing them, or pulling them. He couldn't shake the question: what in the hell were goblins doing this deep in the wastes?

He knew he wouldn't get an answer. Goblins weren't much for conversation. You could catch one, try to wring some sense out of it, but they weren't known for brains, and the odds of one speaking human were slim to none. They weren't the scheming sort, either—no hidden motives, no grand designs. For generations, their clans had clawed out a foothold in what eons ago, had been the Dakotas, fighting over scraps and territory, never building much, never changing. They almost never ventured beyond their borders, and only a handful of times in living memory had they been seen this far south, in the scorched belly of the wastes.

The wastes—an endless, blistered stretch of land that once marked the southern edge of the old United States, from what had long ago been called Arizona clear to the long-forgotten state of Texas. Now, it was nothing but a graveyard of sun and silence. Only those with nowhere else to go called it home: scavengers, scrappers, drifters, reapers. Out here, survival was a matter of grit or sheer desperation. The lucky ones carved out a living between orc raids and bandit ambushes. The unlucky simply vanished, swallowed by the dust.

The sun's fury never let up, not even at night. Rain was a memory, lost to centuries. Those who lasted did so by stubborn will or because they had no other choice. Water was precious—collected by evaporators or drawn from the few remaining wells in settlements like Paradise Wells, Serenity, and Corith. Those towns rationed water at a price most couldn't pay.

The wastes were inhospitable, a scorched expanse where hope dried up faster than sweat. But for some, it was still home. For a rare few, it was better than the so-called societies that had risen elsewhere—places like Europa, across the dead sea, where elves and humans had supposedly built something new with magic and machines. Or the Scattered Isles, where outcasts and halflings floated on the bones of drowned cities.

Yet for all the luxuries whispered about in distant lands, the folk of the wastes were their own breed. There was fortune to be found here—old tech, gems, relics of history. Some struck it rich, only to lose it all in a blink. Most scraped by, risking life and limb for whatever they could scavenge, selling their finds piece by piece just to see another sunrise. Every so often, someone would stumble on a treasure trove, sell it for a king's ransom, and dream of leaving the wastes behind. But more often than not, those riches vanished on supplies, or were stashed away for that fabled day when they'd finally escape.

But as the stranger stood, watching the goblin troop approach, he repeated the same words in his head. *This wasn't that day.*

The man watched as the goblin in the lead finally noticed him. The clan banner—little more than a ragged strip of hide—waved atop a crooked pole strapped to the goblin's back, fluttering with each loping stride. The whole pack was coming at a jog, just slow enough to give the man time to steady his nerves and draw a breath. The moment the lead goblin realized a human stood in their path, it slowed, raising a pale green hand. The others caught his scent, and for a heartbeat, the whole troop hesitated—twenty sets of yellow eyes measuring risk and reward. The leader's nostrils flared, eyes narrowing as it weighed the promise of another human ear for its belt against the cost of losing its best scouts. But one man, alone, against twenty? The odds were tempting.

With a shriek, the goblin chief yanked a dagger from its belt and charged, the rest of the pack surging after, howling for blood.

The stranger's pistol was up in a blink, his aim cold and sure. The first shot blew the back of the lead goblin's skull wide open, spraying the three behind with what little brain it had. For a split second, the pack faltered, their momentum stuttering. Then another goblin took up the cry, screaming something guttural in his tongue that roughly translated to: "For glory!" Then the charge resumed.

The man fired again, and again, four more times in quick succession. Five goblins dropped where they stood. In a practiced motion, he thumbed the release on his pistol, catching the spent cylinder as it popped free. His duster swept aside, he slid the gun down to his belt, snapped in a fresh cylinder, and fanned the hammer—six shots, five more goblins down.

The last ten goblins skidded to a halt, staring at the carnage. They nudged and hissed at each other, none eager to be the next to fall. For a moment, the only sound was the wind and the distant rattle of dust. Then, as if by silent agreement, the pack broke—one shot cracked the air, and the goblins scattered, vanishing back into the wastes, their courage spent.

The man stood alone, the hot wind tugging at his coat, smoke curling from the barrel of his pistol. He could have dropped another handful as they ran, but what was the point? A group that small would limp home, spinning tales of ambush and survival. To waste bullets on them would be as pointless as pulling a single thorn from a cactus.

With a soft shake of his head, he calmly slid the pistol back into its holster and turned to make his way back to the saloon.

3

All eyes were on the man as he stepped back into the saloon, the door swinging shut behind him with a pained, metallic creak. The room was silent—soaked in the kind of hush that settles after gunfire. Even the fairy above the bar had gone still, its usual chittering cut short.

The barkeep swallowed hard, never taking his eyes off the stranger as he reached down and pulled a battered jug from beneath the counter, filling a glass that waited atop the bar. He slid the drink across with two fingers. "This one's on the house."

The man smirked, exhaling the dust and adrenaline from his lungs. He made his way to the bar, nodded to the barkeep, and picked up the glass before returning to his table—the same battered seat he'd claimed before the shooting started.

He'd barely settled when the girl from the far table rose and crossed the room, boots whispering over the warped floorboards. She sat down across from him, her eyes sharp and unblinking.

He stared at her for a moment, then lifted his glass and took a slow sip, letting the silence stretch.

She studied him, gaze moving over every scar and line, as if searching for something beneath the grit.

"Can I help you?" the man asked, voice low and even.

"I'd like to hire you," the girl replied, her words snapping across the table like a thrown knife.

"Not interested," he said, setting the glass down but keeping his hand on the handle.

"But I didn't even tell you what for—"

"Not. Interested."

She leaned in, hands edging closer, voice dropping to a hush. "I can pay you."

His eyebrows lifted, a flicker of mock surprise crossing his face. "Still not interested."

The girl exhaled sharply, settling back in her seat. "But you're a drifter. Isn't that what you do? Take dangerous jobs for the money?"

The man's eyes narrowed, a ghost of a smile tugging at the corner of his mouth. "What makes you so sure?" he drawled. "What makes you think you know a damn thing about me or what I do? Maybe I'm just a fella passing through, stopped in for a drink and a bit of shade." He paused, letting the words hang, not entirely untrue. He took a long, deliberate sip from his glass, punctuating it with a sigh that was half mockery, half warning. "You ought to be careful making assumptions out here. Quicker still trying to hire a stranger. That's the kind of mistake gets folks killed—or worse."

He studied the girl across from him, her face unreadable, her stare just as steady. When it became clear she wasn't backing down, he finished his drink in one swallow and pushed back from the table. "Young lady."

"I know where there's an old armory," she said, voice low but steady. "Pre-world. Thousands of guns. Maybe more."

He stopped mid-stride, turning to face her fully. "Pre-world?" he echoed.

"Yes."

"And you said thousands?"

"That's what I said."

He stared at her for a long moment, the silence stretching between them. He drew a slow breath, exhaling through his teeth. "How do I know?"

"Know what?" she asked, feigning innocence.

He shook his head. "Don't play coy. You know damn well what I mean. How do I know this armory even exists? Part of me wants to call bullshit. Everybody's heard the stories about the old facilities. Everybody knows there's no getting in. Plenty have tried."

She hesitated, then chose her words with care. "I know where there's a key."

His gaze sharpened, suspicion and curiosity mingling. "And how'd you come by something like that?"

"My grandfather," she replied. "We're scrappers. Always have been. He found the key cycles ago, left it to my father. We've been working one of the facilities for the last two cycles."

"Scrappers," the man muttered, voice rough as gravel, shaking his head with a bitter smirk. He let the word hang in the stale air, eyes narrowing as he studied the girl across from him. Desperation clung to her like the dust of the wastes—he could almost taste it, sharp and sour. Her eyes pleaded, silent and fierce, but she held herself tight, refusing to let the cracks show. Out here, weakness was just another way to die.

He let the silence stretch, then pushed back from the table with a sigh. "All right. I'll bite."

The change in her was instant—a flicker of hope, a smile that flashed and vanished just as quick. "Really?"

"Yeah," he said, dropping back into his seat. "But first, fetch me another beer. I might change my mind if I sober up too much."

She sprang to her feet, eager as a coyote at dusk. "Sure thing, mister." She hurried off toward the bar, boots whispering over warped floorboards.

He watched her go, gaze lingering on the shape hidden beneath road-worn clothes, then drifting up to the fairy perched on the mantle. The little creature glared back, wings twitching in the smoky gloom.

"Ech," he grunted, shuddering. The fairy spat a string of curses, half-chitter, half-language, before turning away.

Moments later, the girl returned, setting a fresh glass in front of him before slipping back into her seat. He took a long pull, letting the warmth settle in his chest.

"So," he said, setting the glass down, "what's the job?"

She hesitated, eyes dropping to the battered tabletop. "It's my brother," she said quietly. "He was taken."

He smirked, shaking his head. "If he was running his mouth like you, telling folks like me he had a key to the biggest pre-world armory left in the wastes, I'm not surprised." He studied her, reading the sorrow etched deep in her face. After a moment, he sighed, fingers drumming on the mug. "Reapers?"

She shook her head. "No. I don't think so. I'm not sure. I don't know."

He leaned back, voice low. "If it was, this'd be a recovery job. He'd already be dead."

"They can't kill him," she said, voice trembling but stubborn.

He frowned, suspicion flickering across his face. "Oh? And why's that? Never known reapers to keep hostages. Usually, they're just meat—or worse."

"My brother's got a map. Not just any scrap—something old. Pre-world. The kind of thing folks kill for out here. Or at least, that's what they think he's carrying."

The drifter's eyes narrowed, voice low and wary. "Pre-world, huh? Let me guess—this is about the armory? That why they snatched him? Figured he'd lead them straight to a vault full of guns?"

She nodded, jaw tight. "Yes... and no. The map points to Deltron—the weapons cache. But it also marks another place. Something worse than guns. Something that should've stayed buried."

He let out a dry, humorless laugh. "Worse than arming the reapers with a thousand rifles? Hard to imagine. So why was your brother out there, running his mouth? You know what happens to folks who advertise they're holding the most valuable secret in the wastes?"

Her fist hit the table, rattling the empty mugs. "Stupid! I told him we should've gone alone. But he wouldn't listen—kept saying we needed help. So, he rode into Blister Springs, tried to hire drifters. I warned him not to mention the map, but—" She shook her head, anger and regret tangled in her voice. "He told them anyway."

The drifter's gaze was steady—cold. "So, one of those drifters, or someone meaner, overheard. Decided to take the prize for themselves."

She nodded, voice small. "But my brother doesn't have the map."

He leaned in, voice dropping. "That why you think he's still alive?"

She swallowed. "He knows where it is. He won't tell."

The drifter's eyes hardened. "Everyone talks, given enough pain. Even the toughest break."

She looked away, blinking back tears.

He softened, just a hair. "Not saying they're hurting him. Not yet. But if your brother doesn't have the map… that means you do, don't it?"

She met his gaze, defiant. "No. I hid it. Somewhere safe."

A crooked smile tugged at his lips as he sipped his drink. "Smart. So, if I help you get your brother back, you'll just hand over the map and let me ride off into the sunset?"

"We," she said, voice firm.

He raised an eyebrow. "We?"

"I'm coming with you."

He shook his head, voice flat as the wastes. "No. I work alone. I'm not dragging you into hell just to watch you die. You don't know what it's like out there."

She stared him down, blue eyes sparking with something wild. "I know exactly what it's like." For a heartbeat, a flicker of lightning danced in her gaze.

He stiffened, reading the truth in her eyes. His voice dropped to a rough whisper. "Of course. Why wouldn't you be?" He glanced around the saloon, then leaned closer. "Born with it, were you? Witch, or mutant?"

She bristled, voice sharp with old wounds. "Born. My mother, her mother before. It's always been in us. I hate that word—witch. Nothing good ever comes with it. That's old world talk, you know?"

15

The drifter nodded, eyes fixed on the battered tabletop. "Heard tell of witches long before the Merge. Hunted, burned, run out of every corner of the old world."

"I thought magic only came after the Merge?" she asked, voice low.

He shook his head. "No. My mother always said magic's been here since the first sunrise—just hidden, or too wild for folks to use. The Merge just... changed things. Made it so people could harness it, shape it, do more than just whisper to the wind." She hesitated, then added, "There are schools in Europa now. Places where you can learn magic, study it proper."

He raised a brow. "Didn't know that."

"Yeah. My brother and I... we used to talk about going there. To Europa. Just needed the credits." Her voice faltered. "The armory was supposed to be our ticket."

He nodded, understanding. "But now, getting your brother back—that's what matters."

She looked up, fierce. "More than any haul."

He set his mug down, the dregs swirling. "If you don't like being called a witch, what should I call you?"

She straightened. "My name's Anika."

He gave a small, respectful nod. "All right, Anika. Where do we start looking for your brother?"

"Jarek's at the old copper mine, two days east." Her words came out quick, urgent.

He frowned. "Thought you said he was taken in Blister Springs?"

"They followed him from there. Broke into our farm, thinking he'd lead them to the map. I was in Old Port, picking up supplies. When I got back, I saw them dragging Jarek away. He's smart, but too trusting. I tried to warn him..." Her voice trailed off, eyes clouded with regret. "I followed them for two days. Watched them vanish into the mine. That's when I knew I needed help. This was the first place I stopped."

He gave a dry chuckle. "Lucky me."

"If they find out where the map is, they'll kill him." Her voice trembled. "Jarek's all I have left. Mother's gone. Father disappeared months back. He's it."

He leaned forward, voice gentle. "How many took him?"

"At least ten," she whispered.

He nodded, calculating. "Ten's rough, but not impossible. Did you see any more at the mine?"

She shook her head. "No. I stayed up top. Didn't dare get closer."

He gave her a rare, approving look. "At least you made one smart call." He paused, then asked, "You sure he hasn't just run off with the map himself?"

Anika bristled. "He wouldn't. He'd die before giving it up."

He shrugged. "I've seen family do worse for less. But if he's holding out, maybe he's still alive." He studied her. "He's not... like you, is he? Not a witch?"

She shook her head. "No. Just me."

He sighed, finishing his drink. "Well, there better be something worth all this trouble at the end of that map." A heavy silence settled between them, broken only by the faint chitter of a fairy somewhere above the bar. He set his mug down with a soft thump. "I know I'm gonna regret this," he muttered, shaking his head. "Let's go get your brother.

4

Torchlight flickered across the iron bars, shadows dancing along the rough stone walls of the cell. The air was thick with damp and the memory of old earth, but even five hundred feet down, the heat pressed in—heavy, close, and unkind. Jarek sat hunched on the lone bench, knees drawn up, staring out into the dark where the tunnels branched away. He'd lost track of time. Days, maybe. Food had come twice—a stick of salted lizard, a palmful of water in a battered tin cup. No words, just the scrape of boots and the rattle of keys. Voices sometimes drifted from the tunnels, muffled and strange, but never for him.

Now, footsteps echoed closer, slow and deliberate. Jarek straightened, heart thumping. The cell was bare—no bedding, no bucket, just stone and iron and the stink of fear.

A figure emerged from the gloom, robes the color of old blood and dust trailing along the floor. The cowl hid the stranger's face until, with a slow, ritual motion, the figure drew it back. Torchlight caught on a pale, bald head and eyes sunk deep in shadow—eyes that glinted like a rattler's in the dark.

Jarek's voice was small, desperate. "What do you want from me?"

The man studied him in silence, gaze unblinking.

"I didn't do anything. Please. Let me go."

A slow breath, then a voice like a knife sliding from its sheath. "You know why you're here, boy. You know what I want."

"I don't, mister. I swear. Please. You have to believe me."

"I have to do nothing," the man hissed, the words curling in the stale air.

Jarek gripped the edge of the bench, knuckles white. The man cocked his head, listening to some distant sound only he could hear, then straightened, eyes narrowing. "I don't care for games. Give me the map, and maybe I'll consider not feeding you to the goblins waiting below."

Jarek's whole body tensed. "Please. I don't... I don't know anything about a map."

"Don't lie to me, boy. You're only making things worse for yourself."

"I'm not lying..." Jarek's voice broke.

The man's stare didn't waver. He closed his eyes, as if mourning some private loss, then opened them with a sneer. "You went to Blister Springs. Tried to hire help to cross the wastes. Told them you had a map—one that would lead to a pre-world facility, treasures beyond reckoning. I know, because I've watched your family come and go from one of those very same places for a season and a half."

Jarek's eyes went wide, torchlight glinting in their depths.

The man reached into his robes, drawing out a small object, holding it up with a thin, cruel smile.

Jarek's breath caught. "How...?"

The man's smile widened. "Did you think your father was the only soul in the wastes with one of these keys?"

Jarek's gaze dropped, hope draining away.

"I'm not after the guns, or the facility you so carelessly spoke of. I want something else. A place with power far greater than Deltron..."

Jarek's gaze lifted, searching the pale, pitiless face beyond the bars. He couldn't fathom how this man not only possessed a key, but also the knowledge of the old world's secrets—things only his grandfather and father had ever spoken of in whispers. He and his sister had spent weeks in those ancient halls, but never alone, never with the keys. How could this stranger know?

The man's eyes were black pits, cold and bottomless. He leaned in, voice a rasp that seemed to scrape the stone itself. "You want to know what's wrong with this world, boy?" His gaze never wavered, burning with a venom that made Jarek's skin crawl. "Before the Merge, this land belonged to humans alone. And what did they do with it? They tore each other apart—war after war, slaughter after slaughter. They were a plague upon themselves, a species that fed on its own misery."

He took a step closer, the torchlight catching the sharp lines of his face. "Then the Merge came. Corithia bled into this world—elves, halflings, goblins, orcs, the fae. A new dawn, a chance for something better. But did humanity learn? No. They just found new monsters to hate. For the first time, they united—not for peace, but to turn all that violence outward. They hunted us, butchered us, burned us alive. Millions died. The goblin and orc hordes were nearly wiped from the earth. Elves driven north, fairies caged and broken, witches—my kind—hunted and tortured, burned at the stake for daring to touch the wild magic that seeped through the cracks."

A flicker of unnatural light flashed in his eyes, like a storm barely held at bay. "And when they realized they couldn't finish the job, they unleashed the flame. Built their bunkers, chose who was worthy to live, and rained fire on the rest. They called it salvation. I call it cowardice."

He pressed closer to the bars, voice trembling with old fury. "For a thousand years, we've clawed our way back through the ashes. Goblins and orcs forced to carve out scraps of land, elves hiding in the shadows of human cities, halflings chained, fae hunted for sport. And my kind—still hunted, still burned, still spat on in the street. Humanity never wanted us here. They never will. They'd rather see the world burn again than share it."

A screech echoed from deep in the tunnels, the sound of something hungry and patient. The man's lips curled in a sneer. "I'm done fighting for a place at their table. I'm done pretending we'll ever be accepted. I'm done pretending this world will ever be anything but a graveyard for my kind."

He straightened, the torchlight throwing his shadow long and twisted across the stone. "I don't care about the guns," he spat. "Guns are nothing. They're just another tool for the same old hate. No. What

I want is Arcan. The place where the real power sleeps. The place that can wipe the slate clean."

Jarek felt the blood drain from his face, his veins turning to ice. "No…" he whispered.

The man's smile was as thin and cruel as a razor's edge. "Yes. Very much, yes."

Jarek's voice was barely a breath. "How…?"

The man's eyes glittered, full of old wounds and bottomless hate. "Because I've spent a lifetime watching your kind. Because I know what it is to be hunted. Because I know what it is to want to burn the world that tried to burn you."

"How do I know about the Arcan facility?" The man's voice was soft, almost amused. "Like I said—your father isn't the only one with a key. I watched your family come and go, spending days at a time in Belcor. I knew how long it took your father to make it to Outpost and back, or to your homestead. And when he wasn't there, I was. I spent that time at the terminals, reading the old world's secrets, learning the purpose of every facility." He smiled, a cold, thin thing. "You could say, learning their purposes gave me purpose. At first, I was just biding my time—waiting for the right moment to kill your father, maybe you, maybe your sister, and sell the whole place for scrap. But then I learned about Arcan. And the fire." His eyes glinted in the torchlight. "That's when I knew why I'd been drawn here. The one thing I never found, not in all my time in that place, was its location. But then, one of my men told me a young fool was looking for an escort to an ancient facility. Fate, it seems, has a sense of humor."

He let the words hang, then his smile faded. "So, I'll ask you one more time. Where is the map?"

Jarek stared at him, a single tear slipping down his cheek. "No."

The man's face hardened. He drew a deep, gravelly breath, exhaling with a low rumble. "Then I'll send my men to find your sister. Maybe she'll be more agreeable."

"NO!" Jarek lunged at the bars, hands grasping for the robed figure. "NO!"

5

The drifter had spent the afternoon in near silence, answering Anika's anxious questions with little more than a grunt or a nod. But as the sun bled out behind the horizon, he finally broke his quiet with more words than he'd spoken all day. "It's getting dark. We should probably bed down for the night."

Anika's voice was sharp, desperate. "What!? No! We have to get to my brother!"

He shook his head, voice steady as the dusk. "And I think it'd probably do us best to be alive so we can actually do that. Need I remind you of the scouting party I just fought off?" He paused, letting the silence settle between them. "Just... think for a moment. How much do you know about goblins?"

She sat rigid atop her horse, mind racing. Every moment spent not moving felt like a betrayal. "But... my brother—"

The drifter drew a long breath, eyes scanning the purple-orange horizon. "If there's one, there could be more." He paused. "It's already strange, seeing a scouting party this far south. Last thing we want is to get caught in the dead of night by a raiding party." He looked at her, voice low. "So, I'll ask again. How much do you know about goblins?" He swung down from his horse.

Anika hesitated, then answered, "A little. What our parents told us. They're mostly north. Small groups can be scared off, but they're dangerous in numbers. They usually stick to their own areas."

He studied her face, the last light catching in her eyes. "Goblins care about two things: food and territory. And yeah, they usually keep to their own. Unless they're looking to expand. And if they are... then it's strength in numbers. One on one, you could probably take a goblin in a fight. That's why you never see just one. When they raid, there's hundreds. If the territory's big enough, thousands. But what comes first is always the scouting parties. And generally, it's more than one.

So, seeing one this far south? Means there's more." He frowned, gaze drifting to the horizon. "I just... something doesn't sit right."

"What?" Anika's voice was tight with fear as she scanned the horizon herself.

"I don't know." He met her eyes. "Thirty years I've been in the wastes. You know how many times I've seen goblins this far south?" He held up his hand, wriggling his fingers. "Not once."

She stared at his hand, then slowly climbed down from her horse. "You didn't grow up here?"

He gave a short, humorless laugh. "That's your takeaway?"

She shrugged, a little embarrassed. "I'm just trying to get my mind off everything, okay? Just for a moment."

He watched her for a beat, then softened. "No. I didn't grow up here."

For a moment, her worry faded. She'd never met anyone who hadn't grown up in the wastes. "Where are you from?"

He scoffed, as if the memory tasted bitter. "Where did I survive as a kid? Thornbrush."

"Thornbrush?" She found a rock and sat, curiosity momentarily overtaking her fear.

"Yeah. Out west."

Her mind spun with questions. "What's it like? Outside the wastes?"

He scoffed again, settling onto a flat rock nearby. "Not too different than here."

"Then why did you leave?"

He was quiet for a long moment, the hush of the desert settling around them. "My folks died when I was young. Sickness. My uncle took me in. He wasn't a good man."

"Did he hurt you?"

He looked at her, eyes shadowed. "He tried. Once."

"Oh," she said softly.

24

He took a deep breath, exhaling slow. "He liked to remind me how much of a burden I was. Liked to say my mother—his sister—was a whore, that she only got with my father because she couldn't do better. Yeah. He wasn't a good man."

"I'm sorry."

"One day I'd had enough. He came home from the quarry, drunk on swill. Tried to put hands on me. I fought back. There was a scuffle. When he realized I wasn't gonna just take it, and that he wasn't gonna win... he pulled a knife. So, I took out my father's pistol and I shot him."

Anika looked at him, the last of the light casting deep shadows across his face, blending his beard with the darkness behind.

"Punishment for killing is the same there as it is here. Quick drop at the end of a rope. So, I left."

"But couldn't you have explained what happened? You were a kid."

He shook his head. "Killing is killing. Don't matter who's at fault. Or how old they are." He paused. "It's easier for folks to look the other way here in the wastes. Communities are different. They have codes. You don't steal, you don't kill. There ain't no gray area. You live in a community, you live by their code. Out here, there's no one enforcing the code. So, I packed up what I could and headed to the only place I knew they wouldn't come looking. I've been here ever since."

Anika felt a stir of emotions. She'd thought of the drifter as nothing more than a hired gun, but now, as the last of the light faded, she saw him for what he was—a person, battered by the wastes. "You've never thought about going back?"

A smile cracked across his face, a small chuckle escaping. "To what?" He lifted his hands. "Ain't nothing there for me anymore. Nothing except bad memories and a noose."

"I'm really sorry."

"Why? Don't be sorry for me. I made the choices that got me here. I quite like who I've become. I'm comfortable with it. Besides, my sister's brother was an asshole. I'm glad I shot him. Should've done it sooner." He didn't feel entirely that way, but it felt good to say.

Anika stayed quiet, feeling bad for stirring up old wounds.

A quiet stillness edged in. The drifter moved from the rock to a flat patch of earth, pulling a small object from his side bag and placing it under his head. Anika watched, wondering how long it would take her to get used to sleeping under the stars. She was grateful for what she had—a farm, a bed, food. Not much, but comfort, and that was rare in the wastes. She thought of Jarek. "Do you think we're gonna find him?" she asked, voice trembling.

A long silence stretched between them.

"Eventually they're gonna get what they want. Let's just hope we get there before then." He looked up at a single star racing across the sky. "At least we have one advantage."

"Hmph?" she asked.

"We know where they're keeping him."

Anika looked up at the stars, feeling the weight of worry pressing down. Every breath held back a shudder, every shudder a river of tears. It took everything in her to hold her composure. The silence of the wastes pressed in, her thoughts swirling. Then, at the moment she was about to break, she lay down on the ground, curled up, and closed her eyes.

6

Anika blinked awake to the pale hush of dawn, the world still heavy with the ghosts of the night before. The wastes stretched endless and silent, broken only by the silhouette of the drifter standing a few paces off, his figure etched against the bruised horizon. He held a battered spyglass to one eye, scanning the emptiness with the patience of someone who'd spent a lifetime waiting for trouble to come crawling out of the dust.

For a moment, Anika watched him—how he seemed to vanish into the landscape, boots powdered with red earth, duster faded to the same sun-bleached shade as the ground. His wide-brimmed hat cast his face in shadow, leaving only a glimpse of short, sand-colored hair at his neck. In that instant, he looked like something torn from the pages of her father's old pre-world books—a relic of a world that had burned away long before she was born. The ache of memory stung, and she forced herself upright, shaking off the weight of sleep.

"See anything?" she called, her voice rough with dust and dreams.

The drifter lowered the glass, snapping it shut with a practiced flick. "Nothing yet." He studied her, eyes sharp beneath the brim. "You ready to go after your brother?"

Anika nodded, resolve settling in her bones. "I am."

"Good." He glanced east, where the sun was just beginning to bleed over the rim of the world, painting the wastes in molten gold. "We've got maybe six hours before the heat gets bad. We move fast, keep our heads down, and find shelter before midday. How far did you say the mine was?"

"Half a day's ride," she answered.

He nodded. "We'll push hard, rest when the sun's at its worst, and make the mine by late afternoon if we're lucky."

She hesitated. "Why stop at midday?"

He turned, a flicker of curiosity in his gaze. "Why?"

"Why do we have to stop?" she pressed.

He studied her for a long moment, as if weighing her worth. "You said your family's scrappers, right?"

Anika nodded. "Yeah."

"Then you should know—nobody travels when the sun's at its peak. That's a quick way to end up with sun-sickness, and that's something I have no interest in getting. So, when the sun hits ten, we stop. When it hits two, we continue. In the meantime, we'll draw a shade, hunker down, and keep ourselves entertained by waiting." He could see the protest forming on her face, the urge to argue.

Ani knew what midday meant, but desperation had pushed self-preservation to the background. She was willing to risk everything for her brother. But standing there, the drifter's stare steady on her, she felt a tinge of embarrassment. "Okay."

"Yeah. You're damn straight it's okay," he replied with a smirk, turning and starting off.

The hours passed, the air growing hotter, the sun brighter. By the time they stopped for midday, Anika had already used two hydration tablets—more than she'd usually take in a day. "You're not thirsty?" she asked, watching the drifter finish attaching the shade to the second pole.

"Not yet." He paused. "Never could get the knack for those pills. Just don't feel right."

"Hydration tabs?" She frowned. "All they are is a hyper-concentrated form of electrolytes. One pill's like a gallon of water."

"I know what they are. I just don't like 'em. I prefer getting my water the old-fashioned way. Drinking it."

"But what do you do when you're in the wastes? There's no water out here."

"There is," the drifter said, voice low as he rummaged in his battered pack. "You just gotta know where to look. And one of these helps." He pulled out a small, tarnished cylinder, its metal dulled by years of dust and sun. With a click, three thin needles shot out the front, glinting in the harsh light. "Evaporator," he said, turning it over in his hand. "You press it up against anything with a hint of water left—dead cactus, old roots, even a corpse if you're desperate. Sucks out whatever's left. When it's full..." He pressed the button again, the needles snapping back inside. "Handy little storage unit."

Anika's eyes widened. "I've never seen one of those before." She reached out, curiosity flickering, but hesitated as he held it just out of reach.

"Careful," he warned, a crooked grin on his lips. "Works the same on people as it does on plants, if you're not paying attention."

She pulled her hand back, face twisting. "That's... awful."

He shrugged. "Some of the reaper packs carry 'em. When someone dies, it's just more water for the pack. Out here, necessity don't make for rainbows and puppies."

Anika shuddered, eyeing the device with new disdain. "Have you ever...?"

He shook his head. "No. Not to say I wouldn't, if it came to it. Just never had to."

"That's horrible."

"So is dying."

She had no answer for that, and for a moment, the silence between them was as heavy as the heat. "So, what's the plan when we get there?" she asked, changing the subject.

The drifter smirked, tucking the evaporator away. "We'll see when we get there. No sense planning for what we can't see. Could be guards, could be gates, could be nothing but dust and bones. We'll figure it out as we go." He paused, studying her. "Best conserve your strength till then."

Anika let out a frustrated breath. "So that's it? No plan? I thought drifters always had a plan."

He raised an eyebrow. "How many drifters you hired before?"

She shook her head. "You're the first."

He grinned. "Then don't go lumping me in with your stories. I'm just trying to survive, same as anyone."

She scoffed. "You would've let me walk out of that saloon alone if I hadn't mentioned the armory."

He shrugged. "Didn't hurt your chances."

"You're only helping me for the guns. So, you can sell them. That's what this is about. Credits." She paused, a sly smile tugging at her lips. "Drifter."

He didn't flinch. "I ain't too proud to admit it. Out here, risking your hide ought to be worth something."

She pressed on. "Doesn't matter why you're doing it. You took the job for the promise of credits, not even knowing what it was. Drifter."

He looked at her, a little thrown. "Maybe by definition, that makes me a drifter. But I didn't agree until I knew what I was getting into. Let's not twist things."

"Then what are you?"

He shrugged again. "Just another soul trying to make it through the wastes."

She smiled, just a little.

"What?" he asked, suspicious.

"Nothing."

He stared, catching the glint in her eyes. "What?"

"Nothing."

He scowled, but she just grinned wider. "Drifter," she whispered.

He threw up his hands, dust puffing up around him. "Fine. Call me drifter if it suits you." He narrowed his eyes playfully. "I'll just call you scrapper."

She grinned. "I'm good at it."

He shook his head. "Save your energy. You'll need it."

"Whatever you say, drifter."

He almost smiled, then caught himself. It had been a long time since he'd had a conversation like this—longer still since he'd wanted one. For a moment, he let himself remember a different life, a different love, before the wastes had taken it all. "We should be there by mid-afternoon," he said quietly. "We'll watch the mine, see what we're up against. You got a pistol in that bag?"

"Yes," Anika replied, voice soft.

"Good. You might need it." He hoped she wouldn't. "Let's see what we're up against first, then we'll make a plan. Sound good?"

Anika nodded. She wanted to rush in, but she knew he was right. "Okay."

"Good. Get some rest. We'll move when the sun crosses its peak." He paused. "And, Anika—"

"Yeah?"

"Thank you."

He nodded, pulling his hat low, letting the silence settle. For a while, he just listened to the wind, and the memories that never quite left him.

7

By the time they reached the abandoned mine, the sun had climbed a third of its way across the sky. The drifter had let them leave earlier than he'd have liked, seeing how the girl's nerves were fraying. They'd waited out the worst of midday, but the heat still pressed in, and he knew he'd be dipping into his precious hydration tablets before long.

They stopped half a mile out, sheltered by a low outcropping of wind-scoured stone. From there, the mine sprawled below—a quarter mile across, a spiral of rings cut into the earth, vanishing into shadow. The drifter pulled his glass from his pack, extended it, and scanned the pit. No movement. No horses. The place looked dead.

"You sure this is where they took him?" he asked, still peering through the glass.

"Yes. I told you. I followed them here."

He grunted. "Could've stopped here, then moved on." He squinted, adjusting the lens. "I don't see any sign of—wait…" He twisted the glass, breath catching. "I see movement."

Two shapes emerged, winding up the rings. The drifter's gut knotted, hairs prickling on his arms. "What…?" he whispered.

"What is it!?" Anika's voice cracked, louder than she meant.

"Goblins…" he said, the word coming out low and uncertain. Then another figure lumbered into view behind them—massive, towering over the goblins, skin a deep, bruised green, armor bristling with spikes, a mace like a wrecking ball in its fist. No helmet, just a mane of black hair spilling down its back.

The drifter snapped the glass shut, already turning back to his horse.

"What?" Anika called, startled. "What is it?"

"Not worth it."

"What?" She hurried after him, confusion and fear in her voice. "I don't understand. What did you see? What's not worth it?"

"This job."

"Please," she begged, voice breaking. "I don't understand. You can't just leave."

He stopped, her desperation halting him. "Look. You know what I just saw down there?" He paused, voice flat. "Goblins. And a fucking orc."

"What...?" she whispered.

"An orc. I don't do orcs. Goblins, maybe, if it's a handful. But not orcs. That's how you die. And if your brother's down there with goblins and orcs... which makes no sense, by the way, because you never see them together..." He shook his head, brow furrowed. "Orcs conquer and kill. That's all they do. Only thing they tolerate is other orcs, and even then, only until they're strong enough to kill the next one up. And I just saw two goblins walking with one. I... I have no explanation for that." He looked away, jaw tight. "Nah. I'm out. Best of luck."

Anika stared at him, pleading. "Please," she whispered. "They'll kill him."

"And you think they won't do the same to us if we walk in there?" He shook his head. "No. My life may not be glamorous, but I ain't in a hurry to part with it."

She stood there, fists clenched, breath coming in ragged bursts. The air around her shimmered, heat rising from her skin. Then, with a cry, she slammed her palms down. "PLEASE!" she screamed as blue fire erupted from her hands, scorching the sand at her feet, glassing it in an instant.

The drifter froze, shielding his face from the sudden heat. When the flames faded, he lowered his arms. The girl stood trembling, tears streaking her cheeks, panic in her eyes.

"Please..." she whispered again, voice small.

He stared at her, wary now. "I thought so." His tone was stern, but there was something else in his eyes—reluctant respect, maybe, or fear.

She looked down at the molten glass, voice barely a breath. "My mother was powerful. Her mother too. All the women in my family. She taught me never to use it. Warned me what could happen." She swallowed. "Please. I just want my brother back. I can't do this alone. Even with my abilities. He's all I have. If I don't try... If you don't go with me... I have to save him."

The drifter watched her, weighing the odds. He knew, in that moment, if he didn't go, she'd walk into that mine alone. He'd have done the same, once, for someone he loved.

"If you go in there alone, you'll die. And your brother, if he's still alive, will end up dead too."

"Then I'll die. But at least I'll have tried."

He cursed under his breath, staring at the mine. "This armory is real, right? You're not bullshitting me about the map?"

"No," she said, voice flat. "It's real."

He shook his head, exhaling hard. "Goddamnit," he muttered. "Why the hell did I take this job..." He looked her in the eye. "Look. I don't know what we're gonna find down there, but if those two goblins and that orc are any sign..." He checked his pistol, sliding it back into its holster. "You stay behind me. If it goes bad, you light that place up, you hear me?"

"I..."

"You do it."

Anika nodded, though she felt the last of her strength draining away. She'd never conjured more than a flicker before, and that blast had left her hollow.

"We leave the horses here and go on foot. Easier to duck if we have to." He fixed her with a hard look. "We move quick and silent. Stay low. Don't move unless I say so. Got it?"

She nodded.

He grumbled, "This is the kind of shit that gets you killed…" and started down the slope toward the mine.

Anika followed, just behind, as they made their way into the spiral's shadow.

8

The drifter knelt behind a sun-warmed rock, Anika crouched close. He watched as two goblins, followed by a hulking orc, slipped out of the mine's shadow. The orc barked something guttural, and the goblins scurried, nearly tripping over themselves as they hurried north. The orc lumbered after, and the trio vanished into the wastes.

The drifter waited, counting heartbeats, then rose—only to drop back down, yanking Anika with him.

"What?" she whispered, breath tight.

"Horses," he murmured, eyes narrowing.

"Horses?" Anika risked a glance.

Three men rode up to the mine, dust trailing behind. They dismounted, exchanged a few words, and started down into the darkness.

The drifter pressed his back to the stone, jaw clenched. "What the wastes have you dragged me into?"

Anika's eyes were wide. "Those men—my brother could still be alive down there."

He shot her a look. "Did you not just see that?"

"See what?" she snapped, nerves fraying. "Reapers?"

He swallowed, voice low. "There's something wrong here. Goblins and orcs together… that's unheard of. But goblins, orcs, and humans, all in the same place?" He shook his head, gaze distant. "Orcs kill humans on sight. Goblins run from orcs. Humans… well, we'll do either. But never have the three worked together. Our kind barely tolerates fairies and halflings, let alone those two."

Anika's voice was small. "But what about Europa? They say elves and humans share cities there. Halflings, dwarves—"

"Maybe," he cut in. "But I guarantee you, there's no goblins or orcs living side by side with anyone. There's no civility in their blood. The horde would never allow it. Orc chieftains declared war on us a thousand years ago. They won't stop till the last of us is dust. Goblins can't even keep peace with their own kind, let alone anyone else. None of this makes sense…"

Anika hesitated. "Do you think it's connected to the disappearances?"

He frowned. "What disappearances?"

"People have been vanishing from sector twelve. Blister Springs, Bilgewater, Old Port. Haven't you heard? You're a drifter."

He gave her a look. "Oh, I'm sorry, should I be checking the notice boards every time I pass through town?"

She shrugged. "I'm just saying. It's been happening a lot."

He glanced back at the mine's entrance, then scanned the horizon. "At this point… anything's possible." He paused, then nodded. "Let's go."

They moved quickly, Anika's eyes darting, the drifter's hand never far from his pistol. In minutes, they reached the edge of the mine. From above, the spiral path wound down seven rings to a flat, rust-stained floor littered with ancient equipment. The mine had been abandoned for a century, left to the ghosts and the dust.

The drifter peered down. "Once we start, there's no going back up. We could get boxed in from above or below. If that happens, we fight our way out. And if things go bad… you run."

Anika nodded, silent.

He drew his pistol, checked the cylinder. "Let's go."

They descended, circling down and down, pace just shy of a run. The drifter's mind churned—three races, centuries of blood and hate, now working together in the dark. He couldn't make sense of it. As they neared the bottom, he steeled himself for whatever waited in the shadows below.

9

It took nearly an hour to reach the bottom of the mine. Around and around, circle after circle, not a word shared as they spiraled deeper into the earth. The drifter was alert—hyperalert. Every sound set his nerves on edge, every flicker of movement drew his gaze. He kept watch on the darkened entrance behind them and the thin ribbon of road curling out of sight above. The sun beat down from the lip of the mine, half the ringed path draped in shadow. Hot, then hotter, then hotter still. By the time they reached the bottom, the drifter's eyes were wide and unblinking, his focus absolute.

As they approached the open mouth of a shaft, he held out his hand, signaling Anika to stop.

She slowed, moving up beside him.

Just ahead, a tunnel yawned into the side of the wall. The last of the sunlight exposed a dozen feet of rough stone before the darkness swallowed everything beyond. The drifter cast one last look up the spiraling rings, then turned to Anika. "You ready?"

She nodded, slow and uncertain, watching as he returned the gesture and stepped into the grasping dark. Part of her wanted to run—run all the way back up to the surface, back to the farm, back to a world that made sense. She wanted to curl up somewhere safe and hide from all of it. But she knew, deep down, that if she turned and fled now, she'd never forgive herself. That kind of pain, she'd never outrun. So, with a single breath, she pressed forward, following just behind the drifter.

The shaft ran twenty yards before opening into a larger chamber. The smell of earth pressed in around them, the air unusually cool. It was the deepest she'd ever been underground, and for a moment she wondered if it wouldn't make more sense for people to live down here—no sun-sickness, no thirst. But then again, no sun, no crops, no escape if trouble came.

"Which way?" she asked, her voice barely a whisper.

The drifter was already studying the room, hand out, gesturing between two tunnels that led deeper in. Both were wider than the one they'd entered, their walls braced with old beams and rusted struts. Piles of ancient mining equipment sat in one corner, and a battered wooden desk was scattered with hand tools. On opposite sides of the table, the two tunnels gaped, black and silent.

She stood, eyes flicking from one to the other. She had no idea.

"I'd probably guess this one," the drifter said after a moment, his voice low. "Take a look here."

Anika followed his gesture.

"See all the tracks? Lot of recent foot traffic down this one. The other, not so much. If I had to pick, this'd be the one." He realized, as he spoke, that some part of him was going out of his way to show her, to teach her. He wrestled with that notion as Anika studied the markings, her gaze shifting between the two paths.

She nodded. The drifter knew far more about these things than she ever would. To her, both tunnels looked the same. But the longer she looked, the more differences she noticed. "I see them," she whispered.

They slipped into the tunnel, boots scuffing softly on packed earth. After a dozen paces, the drifter halted, hand raised. "Shh," he breathed, head cocked to listen. He let out a slow breath, cheeks puffing. "Get ready…"

Anika strained to hear, but the silence pressed in, thick and ringing. Then, faint—a metallic clank, rhythmic, growing louder. Footsteps. More than one.

"Back," the drifter whispered, urgency sharpening his voice. He waved her back, frantic.

Anika hurried into the open room, heart pounding. The drifter pointed. "There—under the desk. Now!"

She dove beneath the desk, curling against the wall. The drifter vanished back into the tunnel. Alone, panic clawed at her. She wanted to run, to bolt after him, but fear pinned her in place. The footsteps drew closer, echoing in the stone.

A slender goblin, armored in studded leather, slipped into view. Red and gold smeared its chest plate—clan colors. Its nose jutted long and sharp, fading from gray-green to forest at the tip. It hunched, a dagger glinting at its belt. Anika held her breath, trembling.

Another goblin entered. Then another. Five in all. The fourth paused, nose twitching, sniffing the air. Its black eyes locked on her hiding place. A slow, wicked smile crept across its face.

It drew its dagger, creeping closer, the others slinking behind. Just as it neared, a flicker of movement—Anika's eyes darted up. The drifter stepped back into the room.

A deafening crack split the air. The goblin nearest him pitched forward, skull bursting, deep purple blood splattering the floor.

The others shrieked, spinning to face the threat. Three more shots rang out—three more goblins dropped.

The last two screamed, charging with daggers raised. The drifter moved the pistol between them, calm and cold, dropping each with a single shot.

Anika sat frozen, hands clamped over her ears, the ringing from the gunfire drowning out all else. The stench of gunpowder hung heavy.

The drifter knelt before her, hand outstretched, voice gentle. "Take it," he said softly.

Anika reached out, gripping his hand as he hauled her from beneath the desk. She noticed the roughness of his palm—hands that had known hard work, maybe once a farmer, before the wastes turned everyone into something else.

He said something, but the ringing in her ears drowned it out.

"What?" she called, her own voice echoing too loud in the close dark.

"They know we're here now," he repeated, sharper this time. "Let's move!"

He spun and took off down the tunnel, boots pounding, duster flaring behind him. Anika scrambled after, nearly jogging to keep up.

The air was thick with the stink of gunpowder and something sharper—ammonia, mildew, the coppery tang of goblin blood. She filed the scent away for later, trusting the drifter would know more if they made it out.

The tunnel seemed endless, darkness pressing in on all sides. All she could see was the drifter's back, moving fast, never hesitating. Then, ahead, a thin glow—an exit.

The drifter burst out first, pistol reloaded and ready. He'd swapped cylinders on the run. As he cleared the tunnel, a bullet screamed past, ricocheting off the stone by his head. He dove left, rolling as another shot rang out. He came up firing—two men across the room, one with clear goggles and a mohawk, the other shirtless, scars crisscrossing his chest.

The first bandit spun and dropped. Two more shots, and the second went down.

Anika barely dodged a bullet herself, tripping over her own feet and sprawling to the floor. Two slugs punched into the wall where her head had been a heartbeat before. She scrambled up, heart hammering, as the drifter reloaded with practiced speed.

"What in the hell have you gotten us into?" he growled, loading his pistol. It was starting to sound like a mantra. He glanced at her. "You okay? You weren't hit?"

"No," she managed, brushing dirt from her chest. "I tripped."

"Hmph." He almost smiled. "Gotta remember that one."

She stared at him, blank, still shaking. He turned toward the tunnel the bandits had come from. "I hope we're close," he muttered, moving forward.

He made it two steps before stopping dead.

From the darkness ahead, something massive emerged—a hulking shape, spiked pauldron scraping the tunnel ceiling, an axe as long as Anika was tall. A giant orc stepped into the light.

The drifter froze, gaze climbing the creature's bulk. Seven feet tall, four wide, crimson eyes burning. For a moment, he wondered how it had even fit through the tunnels. He realized, with a chill, that the gunfire had masked its approach. The ringing in his ears was still there, but now it was joined by the orc's low, rumbling growl.

"Oh, shit," he muttered, drawing his pistol and firing.

The orc moved with impossible speed, axe snapping up to block. Two bullets pinged off the blade, two more ricocheted off its shoulder armor. The last two shots—one grazed its hip, the other lodged in its thigh.

The orc roared—not in pain, but in pure rage. Blood barely started to flow before it charged.

The drifter dodged, rolling aside, swapping cylinders mid-motion. But as he came up, two massive hands closed around him. The orc had spun, snatching him out of the air. It lifted him, holding him inches from its face, and squeezed—crushing him with blinding fury as it screamed.

Foul-smelling saliva splattered across the drifter's face, the orc's grip crushing the air from his lungs. His ribs pressed inward, threatening to snap, and the world at the edges of his vision faded to white. The heat of the orc's breath was suffocating.

Anika stood frozen, paralyzed by awe and terror. She had never seen anything so massive, so violently alive. The orc moved with a brutal grace, its axe batting away bullets as if they were nothing. Even as one shot punched into its thigh, it didn't flinch. She watched, helpless, as the creature pivoted and scooped up her companion, squeezing until his face turned red. Two desperate shots rang out, the pistol firing uselessly at the ground. The orc roared again, a sound that rattled the stone.

The last of the light was fading. The drifter felt a rib crack—he wanted to scream, but there was no air left. All he could see was the orc's face, those deep crimson eyes boring into him. Then, suddenly, a blast of heat—blue-white fire—scorched past, and the orc's grip loosened.

He gasped for breath as the orc screamed, dropping him to the ground. Flames curled around the creature, melting flesh from bone, blistering its arm and face. Without thinking, the drifter raised his pistol and emptied the last four bullets into the side of the orc's head.

The massive body collapsed, snapping its own leg as it fell. The drifter staggered to his feet, breath coming in ragged, stabbing bursts. One rib was cracked, maybe more, but he was alive.

Anika stood just feet away, hands still raised, eyes wide and panicked. Her whole body trembled, as if a single breath might topple her. The drifter approached, swapping cylinders in his pistol.

"Are you okay?"

She didn't move, her gaze locked on the smoldering corpse.

He reached out, gently touching her shoulder. She flinched, jerking away with a small yelp.

"Whoa, whoa!" he said, stepping back, hands raised. "It's me... It's me."

Anika stood there, mind racing, the scene replaying over and over—the fear, the rage, the heat, the smell of burning flesh. Finally, recognition dawned. She saw the drifter, hands up, concern in his eyes. The weight of it all crashed down.

She folded in on herself, hugging her arms, and began to cry. The drifter watched, seeing the exhaustion etched on her face. He remembered his first kill, the way it hollowed him out. He moved closer, hands still up. "Hey," he whispered. "You saved my life." Another step. "If you hadn't done that, I'd be dead. And you too, most likely. You did nothing wrong." He stopped just short, gently resting his hands on her shoulders. "You saved me."

Anika shuddered, her tears slowing. She looked up, meeting his eyes—green, bright as emeralds in the gloom. She nodded, swallowing hard, and wiped her face. "Let's just find Jarek. Please. I just want to go home."

The drifter nodded, glancing back at the dead orc. "God, I hope there's no more of those," he muttered. "You ready?"

Anika nodded, sniffling, wiping her nose on her sleeve. She looked at her hands, as if seeing them for the first time.

"All right," the drifter said, drawing her attention. "Let's get moving."

Together, they pressed on, deeper into the tunnel from which the orc had come.

10

Time dragged, every step through the tunnel stretching into eternity as the damp claustrophobia pressed in. The walls seemed to close tighter with each breath, the air heavy and slick with moisture. Anika's nerves still thrummed from her last burst of magic, every muscle drawn taut, threatening to snap. The drifter moved ahead, steady as stone, but she caught the wince—his hand pressed to his side, breath coming shallow. The mine felt like it was shrinking, the darkness swallowing sound and hope alike.

They pressed on, the drifter pushing through the pain in his chest. After a few minutes, the tunnel curved, opening into a long, rectangular chamber. The drifter drew his pistol, glancing back at Anika before nodding her forward. She answered with a silent nod, heart pounding.

Inside, the room stretched a hundred feet, lit by the flicker of four electric torches—rare things, relics from before the world burned. The walls were lined with steel-barred cells, spaced two feet apart. Most were empty, shadows pooling in their corners. One stood open, barren but for a single bench. The drifter's lips moved, but only the sound of their breathing filled the space. "This is it."

He edged forward, eyes sweeping the room, noting another tunnel gated and locked, darkness yawning beyond. Together, they moved down the corridor, checking each cell. Then, two cells from the end, the drifter stopped.

A crumpled figure lay on the floor.

"Anika!" he hissed, voice sharp as a whip. "Here!"

Anika rushed forward, pulse roaring in her ears. The cell door was locked tight. "Jarek!" she cried, dropping to her knees. "Jarek, it's me! It's Ani."

The drifter scanned the room, eyes catching on a set of keys hanging near the entrance. He snatched them, pausing to listen for footsteps in the tunnels, then hurried back, unlocking the cell and tossing the lock aside.

Anika slipped inside, dropping beside her brother. She lifted his head, voice trembling. "Jarek, wake up. Please. I'm here. I brought help. We're here to get you out."

She searched his face for any sign of life, hope and fear warring in her chest. Behind her, the drifter kept watch, pistol ready, but his gaze lingered on the siblings—softened, just for a moment.

"Jarek, please," she whispered, willing him to open his eyes, to come back to her in the darkness.

It was clear her brother had taken a brutal beating. Jarek's face was swollen and purple, one eye puffed shut, the other barely open. Cuts and bruises marred his skin, and several fingers were bent at unnatural angles, broken at the knuckles. Anika's voice trembled. "Jarek, please..."

A weak cough rattled from the boy's chest.

"Drifter!" she called, hope flaring. "He's alive!"

"Ani...?" Jarek's voice was a rasp, his good eye struggling to focus.

"Yes! I'm here, Jarek. I'm here." She cradled his head, fighting back tears.

He tried to clear his throat, the sound wet and raw, the air thick with the scent of blood and old earth. "Ani."

"Don't talk. We're getting you out. I promise."

"Ani..." His voice was barely a whisper. "No..." He coughed again, pain wracking his body. "Ani. They know about Arcan... They—he has a key."

Anika froze, eyes wide. "What?"

"I'm sorry," Jarek whimpered, tears streaking his battered face. "I'm so sorry."

"It's okay, Jarek, it's okay. Shhh." She tried to soothe him, but his body shook with another sob, turning to a wet, rattling cough. "He's going to release the flame."

"Shh. It's okay. They can't, Jarek. They need two keys. And they'll never find Arcan without the map." She hesitated, voice trembling. "They don't have the map, do they?"

"No," he groaned. "The farm. I told them it was at the farm."

"Good." She swallowed, relief and dread mingling. "That's good."

"I'm sorry."

"It doesn't matter." She brushed his hair back, voice breaking. "How did they... Where did they find a key?"

Jarek struggled to breathe. "He. Had one."

"Wait—Jarek, what are you saying? How did he have one?"

He took two short, shuddering breaths. "Ani. I'm sorry. I tried."

"Jarek, it's okay." She turned, desperate. "Drifter, help me. We need to get him up."

"Ani. I told them about the key." His voice was barely audible.

Anika paused, pain flickering across her face. "It's okay. It doesn't matter."

"I had to. They wouldn't stop. It hurts. It hurts so much."

"It's okay. Where's the map, Jarek? Where did you hide it?"

"Belcor. Father's study. Ani, I'm sorry."

"It's okay. We're going to get you out of here." She turned, tears streaming down her cheeks. "Drifter. Help me."

The drifter started forward, but Jarek's head suddenly fell back, his body convulsing. Strange, wet sounds came from his chest. After a moment, his breath left him, and he went still, his head hanging limp in Anika's arms.

"Jarek? Jarek!?" Sobs wracked her body. "Jarek, wake up. Please. Wake up."

The drifter stood helpless as Anika's world collapsed, her body shaking as she rocked her brother's lifeless form.

"No," she sobbed. "No, no, no, no, no... Please don't leave me. Please. Wake up!"

He knelt beside her, voice gentle. "Hey. I'm sorry, but we have to go. We can't stay here."

Anika couldn't move, couldn't breathe.

"Look. There could be more coming."

As if summoned, footsteps thundered down the tunnel. "Anika, we need to leave. Now!" the drifter barked, stepping out of the cell just as two men burst into the room. He fired three shots, dropping them before they could raise their weapons.

"Anika!" he called, turning before the second body hit the ground. "We have to leave."

"What about my brother?" Her voice was hollow.

"I'm sorry. We have to leave him."

"I can't…"

"We don't have a choice. We can't carry him. There's gonna be more." He hesitated, knowing how deep the wound would cut. "Anika. He's gone."

Another pair of footsteps echoed closer. A moment later, two more men appeared. One fired, the bullet sparking off the wall beside the drifter's head.

"Anika, now!" he shouted, firing back.

"I'm so sorry, Jarek," Anika whispered, squeezing her brother one last time. "I'll come back for you. I promise."

"Anika…" The drifter fired again, dropping another attacker.

Anika pressed a kiss to her brother's forehead, then slowly set him down, stifling another sob. She nodded, barely able to stand.

The drifter reloaded, taking careful aim as another man appeared. In a heartbeat, a bullet found its mark, and the man crumpled, blood pooling on the stone.

Anika wiped her tears, nodded once more, and together they turned and fled into the tunnels, the echoes of gunfire and grief trailing behind them.

A voice slithered from the shadows. "Leaving so soon?"

The drifter spun, shoving Anika behind him, pistol snapping up. His eyes locked on a figure standing behind a heavy iron gate—nearly floor-length robes in the color of old blood, head shaved to a pale gleam, hands empty but for the weight of his presence. The man's lips curled into a small, knowing grin.

"I figured you'd be dragging the boy out with you," the stranger said, voice carrying a hint of mock surprise. His gaze slid past the drifter to Anika. "Oh. Looks like he didn't make it."

The drifter's finger tightened on the trigger. "Who the hell are you?"

The man's grin widened, a flicker of amusement in his eyes. "Me? I'm the prophet." He paused, letting the words settle like dust. "You come all this way, kill my followers, and don't even know my name?" His expression shifted, confusion giving way to something colder as his gaze found Anika. "I'm the one who's going to reset everything. The one with the key." He drew a slow breath, as if savoring the moment. "I'm the one who'll bring the flame."

Anika's voice was a hiss, sharp as broken glass. "You. You took my brother."

The prophet's reply was almost casual. "Of course. Couldn't release the flame without finding Arcan. Your brother was foolish enough to tell one of my people about a certain map—one that shows the old world's secrets." He shrugged. "You understand. I had to have it. It's the only way to restore the balance. Orcs, goblins, elves—they belong here. Humans had their time, and they squandered it. Now, with Arcan, I'll show them their place. Even if it means burning this world clean again." His smile grew thin, menacing. "We survived the last fire. I'm sure we'll survive the next."

Anika's lips trembled. "You..."

The drifter's patience snapped. "Enough." He squeezed the trigger.

The gunshot cracked through the corridor, smoke blooming in the air. But when it cleared, the prophet was gone—nothing left but darkness behind the bars.

"Where the hell did he go?" the drifter muttered, scanning the empty tunnel.

Anika stared after the vanished figure, her mind racing. He had a key, but not the map. If he found Arcan, if he found a second key... Her father's warning echoed in her skull. There was a reason the prophet hadn't found the map—her father had erased every trace.

"We have to go," she said, voice hard as flint.

The drifter turned, jaw set. "What was he talking about? What flame? What's Arcan? Who the hell was that?"

"Drifter. We have to go."

"We're not moving until you tell me what the hell you've dragged me into."

"I'll tell you. But we need to move. If he gets that map before we do—" She pointed at the empty space where the prophet had stood, urgency burning in her eyes.

He cursed under his breath. "Fine. But when we get topside, I want answers. The map, the keys, the flame—I want it all."

"You'll have it. But we have to go." Her voice broke, grief and fear warring in her eyes. "I just lost my brother. But if we don't beat him to that map, we lose everything."

He studied her for a long moment, then nodded. "Stay close." With one last look at the locked gate, he turned, stepping over the dead and leading her into the tunnel.

They moved fast, stopping only once—long enough for the drifter to put down three more goblins. The rest of the mine was empty, the silence pressing in. By the time they emerged, dusk had settled over the wastes, painting the sky in bruised purples and dying gold.

11

The drifter broke the silence as they crested the last ring, boots crunching over gravel, the sky above bruised with dusk.

"Reckon now's as good a time as any for that talk," he said, voice low.

Anika's gaze drifted over the wastes, the wind tugging at her hair. "My grandfather found a place. Pre-world. Still had power humming in its veins, even buried under half a desert. For three cycles, my family's been scrapping it. When he died, he left the key to my father."

The drifter listened, eyes following a lizard darting beneath a rock, the world holding its breath.

"There's more tech in there than I could ever name. Computers, terminals—messages left by the ancients. They talked about the Merge, about the war, about raining fire down to cleanse the earth. My parents spent years in that place. Then my father found a map, hidden deep in the machines. It showed four other facilities, each with its own purpose. Belcor, where we've been working, is an archive—every book, every scrap of knowledge from before the world burned. Deltron's a weapons vault. Thousands of guns, ammo, things we can't even imagine. Pharma holds the secrets to every medicine, and Cultiva's a seed bank—every plant, every crop, waiting to be brought back. And then there's Arcan." She paused, watching a lone hawk circle overhead. "Arcan's where they released the fire. Where more is kept."

The drifter's brow furrowed. "What fire?"

"The fire they unleashed a thousand years ago, after the Merge. It was meant to wipe out everything that came from Corithia—elves, goblins, orcs, fae. But it nearly took the world with it." She let the silence stretch, the weight of it settling between them. "If that prophet—whatever he is—finds Arcan and gets inside, all it takes is two keys. He could burn the world clean. Nothing would survive."

A dry chuckle escaped the drifter. "Oh, shit…"

"Yeah," she echoed, voice flat. "Oh, shit." She stopped, waiting for him to meet her eyes. "But we can stop him. He needs two things: the map, which my brother hid, and a second key. As long as I'm alive, he'll never get it. There's a third key, too—one my brother and I were going to use to destroy Arcan for good. That's why we needed an escort. Not for the guns. To make sure no one could ever repeat the ancients' mistake."

The drifter squinted at her. "You know where that second key is?"

She drew a slow breath, a hint of a smirk on her lips. "I might."

He shook his head. "If you do, you need to destroy it. Burn it, bury it, whatever it takes. Without that key, he's got nothing."

She shook her head. "With the third key, we can make sure no one ever does it again. It's an override—kills the terminal for good."

He stared, not quite understanding. "A what to do what?"

She smiled, tired. "Easier to show you."

He looked away, jaw tight. "Look. I got you to your brother. My job's done. I'll follow you as far as Deltron, but after that, I'm taking what I can carry and I'm gone."

Anika's face twisted with grief and anger. "I just lost my brother. My only family. And you—after hearing all this, after knowing what's at stake—you're just going to walk away?"

He hesitated, shame burning in his cheeks. "I just wanted to do the job and be done."

She stared at him, anger giving way to sorrow. "And I just wanted my brother back..."

The drifter stood silent, the wind tugging at his coat. He felt the weight of her words settle in his gut, heavy and cold. The orcs, the goblins, the prophet—suddenly it all made sense. The mine, the tunnels, the gathering storm. If the prophet got what he wanted, there'd be nothing left for anyone.

Slowly, he nodded, voice barely above a whisper. "Okay." He looked up, meeting her gaze. "Your brother... he called you Ani."

She nodded, a small sob threatening to break free. "Yeah."

"I like it."

She managed a faint smile, sadness etched deep in her eyes.

"How far to Belcor?"

"Two days."

He nodded. "Then we'd best get moving."

Anika smiled, her face softening. There was a terrible sadness resting inside of her, but she would have time to grieve later. For now, she had to avenge her brother, and the only way to do that, was to reach that facility before the other. She would beat him there, and she would find a way to stop the flame from being released. She had her father's key, and the third. The only thing she didn't know, was the location of the facility, of Arcan. First, she would find the map. Then she would find the prophet and she would kill him.

12

The moon hung impossibly large overhead, swollen and watchful, while the milky way stretched from one end of the wastes to the other. Stars glittered in their millions, a blanket of suspended snowflakes, indifferent to the world below. At their feet, a small fire flickered, its pale glow feeble against the vastness of the night.

Anika watched as a single ember broke free, spiraling upward, crackling into the darkness before vanishing. They'd stopped for the night, though she'd argued against it. She still worried the prophet's followers might be out there, hunting them with packs of orcs and goblins. But the drifter had insisted—a fire was the only thing that kept the desert hounds, snakes, and worse things at bay. So, she sat, knees drawn up, the drifter just opposite, his face half-lit by the flames.

He broke the silence first. "You said you studied the world before the great fires. What was it like? Before the Merge?"

Anika pulled her gaze from the fire, letting out a slow breath. "It was different." She paused, searching for words. "They had technology you wouldn't believe. Cities with millions of people. The lights were so bright, you couldn't see the stars. The ruins we see now—like Parmithia up north—those were just a fraction. The world was covered in them. Not ruins, but living, breathing societies, bigger than anything left now."

The drifter scoffed, shaking his head. "Hard to believe. All those people…"

"Yeah…" Her voice softened. "Did you know, they could talk to anyone, anywhere in the world? Not letters—devices that let you speak to someone across the world, even see them, like they were right there. If we had one, I could call someone in Europa, and we'd see their face." She paused, a smile flickering through the dust. "Oh, I can't wait to show you the holovids."

"Hollow, what?"

"Holovids!" she replied excitedly. "Like, pictures, but instead of one still image, they are recordings, with movement and sound. You can literally watch the ancients talking."

"Really?"

"Yeah!" She shrugged. "Most of it is about the war, and other places in the world. A lot of it is about Corithia and the merge. But still. You can *actually* see them, the ancients."

"How do they look?"

"They look just like you and me. They dress a bit funny, and they all have a heavy accent, but… They're us. or our ancestors." She paused. "You want to see one? A city?"

"Uh. Yeah. Sure, I guess. Why not."

Anika reached over, pulling her bag to her and opened the flap. She rummaged for a moment before pulling out a small rectangular piece of paper. "My mom brought me this the day my grandfather showed them Belcor." She reached out, handing the photograph to the drifter. "They look so happy."

The drifter held up the postcard. On the front stood a younger couple. They were standing in front of a massive red bridge, spanning a large body of water. There was a small island off to the side with a large stone structure, and in big, curved writing across the top, it read, *Greetings from San Francisco.* He stared, taking in the city and the structures in the background, the clear blue of the water. But his eyes kept getting pulled back to the smiles on their faces. No one smiled like that anymore. No one had anything to smile about. He sighed, handing the card back.

"San Francisco," she said, looking at the photo for a moment before sliding it back into her bag. It must have been a beautiful city full of shops and saloons. I bet it was like one big party all day long with endless food and pure, clean water. I bet *everyone* smiled like that, all the time."

The drifter scoffed lightly.

"What?"

55

"Nobody smiles like that all the time."

"Well, I bet they did."

He smirked, a small smile slipping past as he shook his head.

"What else was there?" he asked, the photo piquing his curiosity a touch further.

"They had machines that could fly."

"Really? Flying machines huh?"

"Yeah. People would climb inside, and the machine would take them wherever they wanted to go, anywhere in the world."

"Anywhere in the world?"

"Yes." She paused. "Are you mocking me?"

"No," he chuckled.

"Because it really seems like it."

He shook his head. "I just. I haven't exactly had a lot of conversations the past few years. I'm a little rusty. Apologies"

"You don't need to apologize."

"I lost my wife."

The air between them stilled.

"Ten years ago, her family and her were taking supplies from Aberdyne to Paradise Wells. Their caravan got come up on by reapers. The men were killed on the spot, but the women…" The drifter's voice trailed off, rough and low. He took a long breath, exhaling as if it might carry some of the weight away. "I found my wife, my beautiful Coralin, two weeks later. Her and the other women. They'd…" He stopped, wiping at his nose, eyes fixed on the fire. "I tried. I tried to move on, to get past it. I went back to Aberdyne, tried to continue with the trade. But every single day there was a reminder of what I'd lost. So, I left. Left the farm, left everything. Packed up my horse and headed east. I went looking for the men who'd done it."

He fell silent, gaze lost in the flames, the firelight flickering across the hard lines of his face.

Anika watched him, the fire dancing in his eyes. "Did you find them?" she asked, voice barely above a whisper.

His brow furrowed, jaw tight. After a long moment, he nodded. "I did."

Another silence stretched between them, heavy as the night.

"I thought it'd help me feel better. But it didn't." He cleared his throat, rubbing his hand across the scruff on his chin. "They were gone. She was gone. I just... I figured maybe I was better off alone. It hurts less that way, I think."

Anika let her gaze fall to the fire, her own thoughts drifting to her family—her mother, her father, her brother Jarek. He didn't deserve what happened. None of them did. But she didn't have thoughts of revenge. There would be no hunting down her brother's killers, no justice. She would honor him by making sure the prophet failed, that the flame would never be released. And if she ever got the chance, she'd tell the prophet he failed because of her brother.

The drifter's voice pulled her back. "Look," he said, softer now. "I think I'm gonna get some rest. It's been a long day." He paused, a rare gentleness in his eyes. "You probably should too."

She nodded, seeing him in a new light. She'd always assumed drifters became what they were for greed, to live outside the codes. She'd never thought they might be just like everyone else—a wife, a family, a farm. She felt a tinge of embarrassment for having assumed otherwise.

"Anika," he added.

"Yeah?"

"Don't worry," he said, voice low. "We'll get that map, and we'll stop that bastard."

She nodded. "Drifter."

He looked over. "Yeah?"

"Call me Ani." She hesitated, a small smile flickering. "That's what my family did."

He smiled, lowering himself back to the ground. "Good night, Ani."

"Good night, Drifter."

The silence stretched between them, the fire's glow painting shifting shadows across the sand. After a while, the drifter spoke, his voice low, as if the night itself might overhear. "If your folks had a key to the weapons facility… why didn't they go there and collect them? Why not use them to protect themselves? Couldn't they have sold off the guns and bought your way out of the wastes?"

Ani lay quiet, thinking. "I heard my parents talk about it once," she said at last. "My dad thought it was a good idea—just that. Sell the guns, leave the wastes behind. But my mother… she didn't see it that way. She thought letting those pre-world weapons out of Deltron would cause too much harm. She didn't want to be responsible for the death and violence it would bring. She knew those guns would end up in the wrong hands, and a lot of people would die because of it. That's why."

The drifter looked up at the blanket of stars, their cold light scattered across the endless sky. "Your mother sounds like she was a good person. That's rare in the wastes."

Ani smiled, her mother's face flickering in her mind. "She was."

She lay back, staring up at the endless stars, listening to the soft crackle of the burning cactus. Her thoughts drifted to the farm, to the thrill she'd felt when her parents returned from their hauls, the excitement in their voices when they spoke of the first facility, and the hope that maybe, one day, they'd leave the wastes for the old Californias, or even Europa. She remembered her brother, chasing fairies through the dusk, laughing as they darted away from his stick, the sound echoing across the dry fields. Exhaustion pulled at her, and as tears pricked the corners of her eyes, she let herself drift, the stars blurring overhead. Two breaths later, she was asleep.

13

Ani woke to the sound of movement—soft, careful, like someone trying not to disturb the hush of dawn. The drifter was already up, rolling his small pillow and tucking it into his side bag. Beyond him, the horizon was just beginning to glow, thin bands of yellow and orange pushing back against the deep cobalt of the receding night.

"Morning, sleepyhead," he said, a faint smile tugging at his lips as he rummaged in his pouch.

Ani groaned, stretching against the ache in her hips from another night on the hard ground.

"Here," he said, tossing something small her way.

It tumbled between her hands and landed in the dust. "Sorry 'bout that," he said, not quite hiding his amusement.

She picked it up, brushing the dirt off. It was a piece of dried meat—tough, dark, and unfamiliar.

"Ox rump. It'll help get your energy back."

"Ox rump?" she scowled, eyeing it with suspicion.

"If you don't want it," he shrugged, "I'll take it back. Just trying to help."

She hesitated, then took a tentative bite. The flavor surprised her—salty, rich, with a hint of something wild. "This is actually good."

"Of course it is," he replied, a touch of pride in his voice. "Cured it myself. Perfectly salted, with a bit of desert sage."

"Huh…" She took a larger bite, chewing as she pushed herself upright.

"So how long you reckon it'll take us to get to Belcor?" he asked, glancing at the brightening sky.

She chewed a moment, thinking. "We should be there by afternoon."

"And if we don't stop for midday?"

Her chewing slowed, suspicion flickering in her eyes. "Midday…"

He nodded. "If we ride fast, you reckon we could be there before the sun's at its worst?"

"I think so," she said, struggling to her feet.

"Alright. Then let's get a move on."

She watched as the drifter climbed up onto his horse, moving with the easy confidence of someone who'd spent a lifetime in the saddle. "Drifter," she called, pausing as she gathered her things.

He turned, waiting.

"I never asked your name."

He looked at her for a long moment, as if weighing whether to answer. It had been a long time since anyone had asked that question. "It's Fenix," he said at last, the name sounding strange in the morning air. "Fenix Walker."

Ani considered it, then smiled. "I like it."

A small grin tugged at his cheeks. "Come on. Let's go."

She made her way to her horse and climbed up. By the time she'd turned her mount, Fenix was already moving, his horse at a steady trot. Ani nudged her own to catch up, the two of them riding out beneath the waking sky.

14

The pair rode through the morning, the sun cresting well above the horizon. Ani had seen the sunrise more times than she could count, but today felt different. She let her horse find its own path, trailing just behind Fenix. Each ray of sunlight stretched out across the wastes, settling over the arid land like a blessing and a warning. The sky shifted from soft blue to gold, then to a harsh, blinding white. Shadows grew long and strange, the fifty-foot cacti reaching out like the fingers of old gods. There was a rare, quiet peace to it all—the last of the night's coolness giving way to the weighted heat that would soon press down until the moon returned.

When the sun finally burned away the morning's gentle glow, Ani looked ahead to the drifter. Fenix Walker. She liked the name. It fit him—gruff, solitary, a drifter with a haunted past. Like a figure torn from one of her father's pre-world stories. She was glad to have him along. She knew she'd have been killed if she'd gone to the mine alone. Or worse—captured, locked in a cell with her brother, left to die as he had been. Even with all the magic in the world flowing through her, it would have done no good. She would have frozen up. Thinking back, she was surprised she'd managed to conjure fire at all. But it hadn't been her mind that acted—it was her body, pure instinct. The memory of the orc crushing her companion still haunted her. She wondered if she'd ever truly be in control.

Ahead, the drifter slowed, letting her ride up beside him. "You sure you're ready for this?"

"For what?"

"Everything." He paused, listening to the steady clop of his horse's hooves. "You know what we're up against. You've seen it." He scoffed, shaking his head. "I still can't wrap my head around it. How the hell did that crazy bastard get goblins, orcs, and us working together...?"

"Hate," Ani said, her voice low.

Fenix rolled the word around in his mind, his gaze drifting toward the rising sun. It made sense.

"What's the one thing they have in common?" he asked.

"They're mean sons of bitches?" he offered, half a smile tugging at his lips.

She shook her head slowly. "They'd all be better off with the rest of us gone."

He smirked. "Guess I hadn't thought of it that way."

"It doesn't take much to get a crowd riled up," Ani said, remembering stories she'd read on the old terminals. "You just need enough folks who feel the same way, and one spark."

"Yeah. Suppose so," he replied, and together they rode on, the wastes stretching out before them, silent and endless.

Fenix had seen it more than once himself. He'd watched how a single rumor could ignite a mob, how folks crawled out of the woodwork, rallying behind their hate like it was a birthright. He remembered the elven couple—how they'd been dragged into town, beaten near to death, then strung up on the gallows. The rope had been a mercy after what the crowd had done. He could still hear the shouts, see the twisted faces, the violence that seemed to come so easy. And afterward, when a shopkeeper finally admitted he'd only started the talk because he was jealous—the elves' shop had been doing better, cutting into his business. Fenix scoffed to himself. Every person who'd been part of it went on as if nothing had happened. Maybe they carried guilt, maybe not. But none showed it. The rest of the elves—two dozen or so—left a week later, heading north into the tundra, carrying the tradition of hate with them.

He rode in silence for a while, letting the memory settle like dust. Out here, it was always the same. Folks stuck to their own. Familiarity, safety—maybe that's all anyone ever really wanted. Wasn't much different in the wastes, and he doubted it ever would be.

After a time, he shook off the weight of it and glanced over at Ani. "So, tell me more about this map," he said, voice low, as the sun climbed higher and the wastes stretched on.

"My dad drew it," Ani said, her voice quiet as the horses picked their way through the dust. She took a long breath, letting it out slow. "You remember I told you my family's been scrappers for as long as I can remember?" She paused, searching for the right words. "Well, my grandparents were the first to find one of the old facilities. They found Cultiva. I don't know how they learned about it, or how they managed to get inside, but they did. What they found in there... it changed everything for us. They used what they learned to build the farm my parents raised us on. Most of the food that grows in the wastes now, most of the farms—those seeds, those methods, they came from what my grandparents brought back."

She glanced at Fenix, her brow furrowing. "But they also found something else. The locations of other facilities. The ancients built more than one—each with its own purpose. Cultiva was for growing things, but there were others. Places for medicine, for weapons, for knowledge. My grandparents kept that secret as long as they could. But word got out. Before they could bring Cultiva fully back to life— before they could get it online, as the ancients called it—reapers and scavengers found it. They stripped it bare. Every seed, every piece of equipment, gone. By the time they were done, there was nothing left but an empty shell in the ground."

She fell silent for a moment, the memory of loss flickering across her face. "That's when my grandfather decided to keep the only key sacred. He hid it, made sure no one else could get in. Sometimes I wonder if more keys weren't found back then. But if they had been, I figure all the guns from Deltron would've been scattered across the wastes by now. Still... it's hard to know."

Fenix rode in silence, listening as Ani spoke.

"So, my grandparents destroyed their map. They didn't talk about it. They didn't go searching for the other facilities. They took what they'd managed to find and used it to build a new life. They built the farm, started growing old world plants as best they could, using whatever technology and ideas they'd scavenged from the facility. They learned how to filter water so it could be reused—didn't need to haul it from Corith or Paradise Wells. Built sheds to keep the temperature steady, figured out how to manipulate light. The tech they gathered helped keep our family and a lot of others alive." She lowered her gaze to the rust-colored earth. "It's a pity," she went on. "That technology could have helped everyone in the wastes, but it was lost—torn apart and sold for scrap credits. My grandparents didn't believe in charging for something that could help the betterment of the world."

A few feet off the trail, the half-buried skeleton of a long-dead horse jutted from the copper-toned earth, jaw twisted open in a silent scream. Ani stared at it as they passed, her gaze drawn to the empty sockets staring back.

"It's almost as if folks don't want the wastes to get better."

"There's a lot of folks who don't," Fenix replied. "A lot of folks prefer it like this. They take pride in knowing they can survive out here, where normal folk would turn tail and run after their first midday." He shook his head, a wry smile flickering. "The wastes have been like this for a thousand years. They'll be just like this a thousand years from now, I reckon."

"It's sad," Ani said, pulling her gaze from the skeletal remains.

"It's the wastes…" the drifter replied, voice low.

She sighed, looking across at him. "What about you?"

"What about me?"

"Are you ready? For what's coming?"

He shrugged, a dry scoff escaping. "I figure I ain't got much of a choice at this point. You're right. I can take my payment and hightail it, or I can see this through to the end. If that prophet fella succeeds… well, I doubt I'll have anywhere to spend the credits I make from this job." He paused, the lines of his face deepening. "Am I ready? No. Can't rightly say that I am. But I'll do what I always do."

Ani rode in silence, waiting for him to continue. When she realized he'd left the thought hanging, she pried, "And what's that?"

He glanced at her, a tired smile flickering. "What I always do? Make the best of it and try to survive."

"Hmph," she smirked. "I guess that's all anyone can do."

The pair fell back to silence, each lost in their own thoughts. Overhead, the sun crept closer to midday. They each made their preparations, pulling sun-goggles and ponchos from their side bags. It was barely enough to keep the sun from cooking them and scorching their eyes, but for emergencies, it did the trick.

Ani could feel the sun beating down on her. The heat became almost unbearable at times, the sweltering air searing as it filled her lungs. At midday, the temperature could easily creep up into the mid one-forties. By the time midday had passed, she'd used three of her hydration tablets. Ahead, the drifter rode hunched over on his horse, head hung low, bobbing lightly in the saddle. Ani wondered if he hadn't fallen asleep, but she was so beaten down by the blaze overhead that she didn't have the energy to call out. So, she rode in silence, lowering her hat further and taking short, sharp breaths to avoid scorching her throat.

15

The next two hours dragged by, the heat battering the two travelers with relentless fury. By the time the sun had climbed past two o'clock, Ani and Fenix were both fighting the dizzying nausea of sun-sickness. Out here, everyone knew the signs—first the headache, then the shakes, the mouth gone dry no matter how much water you drank. Too much exposure, and your mind and body would start to break down. Memory loss, convulsions, organs shutting down one by one. Everyone in the wastes had seen it, or would. The final days were always the same: a body curled up, shaking, skin drawn tight as parchment, the cries echoing through the night.

Ani had seen it once herself, back in Blister Springs. A man brought into the clinic, arms hooked up to lines, fingers curled at impossible angles. His body shook with every breath, a thin, skeletal frame draped in sun-beaten leather. His lungs rattled, two dust-shriveled bags cracking with each gasp. And that stare—vacant, pleading—haunted her still. It was an image she knew she'd carry for the rest of her days.

She pushed the memory aside as an arid breeze stung her cheeks. Taking a shallow breath, Ani lifted her gaze, scanning the wastes. "We head south from here," she called out to Fenix, who had gotten a bit ahead.

He slowed, turning his horse around. Where they stood, the remnants of an ancient road cut through the dust—spotted pieces of pavement snaking south, splashes of long-faded yellow lines leading away into the hills.

"It's about an hour, following the old trail," Ani said.

Fenix looked out at the broken path, the way it twisted through the low hills. "Hold up a sec," he said, eyes narrowing as he studied the land ahead.

Ani watched the drifter drop down from his saddle and stride toward one of the towering cacti, its arms twisted skyward like the bones of some ancient beast. He rummaged in his battered side bag, pulling free the odd little device he'd shown her once before—a scavenger's relic, all dull metal and clever springs. He pressed it to the cactus and thumbed a button. There was a faint click, and the cylinder extended, needles glinting in the harsh light. For a few minutes, he let the machine do its work, drawing what little moisture the desert would give. When he pulled it free and retracted the needles, he turned back, holding the canister out to her.

"Here," he said, voice flat as the wastes. "Have some."

Ani hesitated, eyeing the canister. "Uh, I think I'm good."

"It's water," he said, not moving. "You need it. We both do." He stepped closer, the device still outstretched. "Hydration tablets'll keep you alive, but they don't quench a thirst. Your mouth's just as dry as mine."

Reluctantly, she reached out and took it. "How do I use it?"

"You see that ring near the tip? Give it a twist."

She did as told. The metal clicked, the top popping open. She glanced at Fenix, who gave her a nod. "Go on," he said. "It ain't gonna kill ya…"

She smirked, lifted the canister, and took a cautious sip. The water was clear and warm, but it slid over her tongue and down her throat like a blessing. She took another, longer drink, feeling the dryness in her mouth and chest fade, replaced by something like life.

"Go on. Finish it," Fenix said, watching as she tried to hand the rest back. "There's plenty more in that cactus."

Ani nodded, draining the last of it, the taste of dust and heat finally washed away. For a moment, the wastes felt almost bearable. Almost.

Ani tipped the last of the water into her mouth, savoring it, letting it slosh around before swallowing. She handed the canister back, and Fenix returned to the cactus, refilling the device and draining it in one long pull. He filled it again, stowed it in his side bag, and dusted off his hands. "Alright," he said, heading for his horse. "Let's get a move on."

Ani nodded, swinging up into the saddle and nudging her horse down the old road. Behind her, Fenix paused, pulling his battered eyeglass from his bag. He swept the horizon, scanning for dust trails, any sign they were being followed. Satisfied the wastes were empty but for the two of them, he tucked the glass away and caught up.

The path wound through a scatter of low hills, broken patches of ancient asphalt and concrete snaking between them—ghosts of the world before. They passed a field of sun-bleached skeletons, cattle by the look of them. Not many of those left now. Real beef was a luxury, water too scarce to keep herds alive. These days, lizard farms supplied most of the meat in the wastes, lizard sticks the staple. It cost, but it saved the time and risk of hunting, skinning, and deboning. Out here, energy was better spent surviving.

They chatted lightly as they rode, voices low, the land swallowing their words. Fenix kept his pistol resting across the saddle horn, eyes flicking to every rise and shadow. He didn't like being boxed in by so many high spots. Ani, though, seemed at ease—she'd made this trek before. The reapers and scavengers had long since given up trying to break into the old facility. Without a key, nothing in the wastes could get through six feet of tungsten and concrete. The ancients had built their bunkers to outlast the end of the world, and so far, they had. Even buried under a mountain of dust and time, they still stood, silent and impenetrable.

16

A little over an hour later, the last of the hills fell away behind them, and the wastes opened up—flat and endless, save for a single mound rising from the earth ahead. Ani pointed, her voice tight with anticipation. "That's it," she said. "We're here."

Fenix felt a shiver crawl up his spine, the kind that came before a storm. He glanced back at the hills, then out across the emptiness, as if weighing the distance to every possible threat.

They rode on, the horses' hooves muffled by dust and broken stone, until a wide excavation came into view—a pit a hundred yards across, dug deep into the earth. At its heart, the beginnings of a structure emerged, massive and alien against the barren land. Fenix had seen the ruins of Parmithia, their bones shattered by quakes and time, but this—this was something else. The facility stood intact, its lines unbroken, as if the world's ending had simply passed it by.

They dismounted at the edge, and Ani was already leading her horse down the sloping path. "We should bring them inside," she said, glancing back. "It'd be a long walk back if someone happened across them."

"Yeah," Fenix replied, still staring at the structure. "Good thinking."

He followed her down, boots crunching on gravel and sunbaked clay. The path led straight to a massive, rounded doorway—fifteen feet across, sunk into the steel face of the building. There was no visible door, just a circular depression, the metal scorched and pitted from a hundred failed attempts to break through. Scratches, blast marks, and the scattered remains of scavenger gear littered the approach, mute testimony to the years of desperation and futility.

Fenix let the enormity of the place settle in his bones. Only the topmost part had been unearthed, but even that stood thirty-five feet tall and stretched fifty yards across. He could feel the heat radiating from the metal, the sun's fury soaked up and thrown back at him. For a moment, he just stood there, letting the silence and the weight of the old world press down, while Ani led her horse toward what must have once been the main entrance.

Ani walked up to the door, stopping and letting the horse's reins drop to the ground. Just to the left of the massive doorway was a smaller indentation. It appeared to be empty, like something had been set inside and taken long ago. "You ready?"

Fenix pulled his eyes away from the structure, watching as his companion reached into her shirt, pulling a small necklace out. There was a small rectangular item attached to it. It was metallic and caught the light for a moment as she held it up to the indentation. Then he watched in amazement as the metal lit up, a series of lights that seemed to appear out of nowhere hovered in front. Then a single light flashed green, and he heard a loud *thunk* come from the massive doorway. Moments later a cloud of dust began to fall downwards as the circular door began to move. The massive door began to roll sideways, disappearing into the wall. Fenix could see that it was shaped like an enormous gear and rolled along a single track. Debris and small stones popped under its impossible weight; the detritus that had gathered since its last opening being pulverized as it continued to groan sideways. As it rolled, he could see that it was solid metal and was nearly eight feet thick. He'd never seen anything like it. As the door locked into place the interior of the facility lit up, the flickering lights growing brighter until the inside was as bright as daylight. "Holy shit." The words fell out of his open mouth.

Ani turned and smiled. "Just wait till you see what's inside."

Fenix watched as she turned and led her horse in. He took a moment to compose himself. Then, he followed.

When they were inside, Ani walked over to a small device next to the door and held her key against it. With a loud *clank* the door shook and began closing.

"What if we can't get that back open?" Fenix asked, a flicker of claustrophobia tightening his jaw as he eyed the massive door.

Ani shrugged, a wry smile tugging at her lips. "Well, then I guess we'll be trapped in here forever, and it won't matter if the prophet finds the second key."

"Oh, that's real comforting..." Fenix muttered, glancing back at the thick slab of metal.

"Are you scared?" she teased.

"No!" he shot back, a little too quick. "I just... I like to know my exits, that's all."

"Oh," she replied, her tone dry. "Your exits..."

He glowered at her, shifting his weight. "Look, I ain't ever been in nothing like this before, okay? It's just... gonna take me a minute to adjust, that's all."

"Oh, I see. Just an adjustment period, that's all."

"Girl..."

She grinned, letting the tension break. "Okay, I'll stop." She paused, letting her gaze sweep the vast, dustless corridor. "So, this is it. Welcome to Belcor Facility. This is where all the knowledge of the ancients was kept. Everything for thousands of years before the Merge is here."

Fenix looked around, still uneasy. "That's great and all. Where are these weapons you told me about?"

Ani's face fell, just a little. "The weapons are in Deltron. That's a different facility."

Fenix let out a long, heavy sigh. "So. There's no weapons here?"

"No," she said, her voice gentle but firm. "Like I said. Each one of the facilities had its own purpose. This one was for the preservation of knowledge. The facility that holds the weapons, that's Deltron. It's on the other side of Parmithia." She hesitated, then added, "We're here to get the map, so we can find our way to Arcan—and destroy it."

He nodded, resigned. "Okay. So, once we have this map, what then?"

Ani shook her head. "I don't know. I just know we had to get to the map first. My brother threw them off, but once they get to the farm, it won't take them long to figure out the map isn't there. My parents left all kinds of information about this facility at the farm. When they realize the map's not there, this'll be the next place they look. And if what Jarek said is true, then they have a key they can use to get in... We need to get the map and be on our way before they do."

Fenix brought a hand up, wiping firmly from his moustache to the scruff on his chin, the gesture slow and thoughtful. "Alright then. So, where's the map?"

Ani hesitated, a flicker of something unreadable passing across her face. "There's something I want to show you first."

Fenix stared at her, jaw tight. Part of him was angry, part disappointed. He'd been looking forward to gearing up for the coming fight, letting the weight of steel and ammunition settle his nerves. But hope—hope was a dangerous thing in the wastes. He'd learned that lesson a decade ago, and he was embarrassed to feel even a trace of it now, gnawing at the edges of his resolve.

"Follow me," Ani said, already turning, her boots whispering over the dustless floor as she led the way deeper into the facility.

Fenix watched her go, then sighed and fell in behind.

17

Fenix moved through the corridor in silence, awe flickering across his face as they ventured deeper into the heart of the facility. The walls were impossibly smooth, the kind of finish no one bothered with anymore, and the overhead lights glowed in perfect rows, untouched by time. A thin layer of dust coated everything, but aside from that—and a few cobwebs in the corners—there was nothing to suggest the place had been abandoned for a thousand years.

As they walked, Fenix peered through glass panels into room after room. Strange machines blinked and hummed, screens flickered with symbols and images he couldn't begin to decipher. Desks were still cluttered with books and faded photographs, as if their owners had only just stepped out. One picture caught his eye—a family, smiling in front of a mountain lake, the kind of happiness that felt like it belonged to another world entirely.

"Where did everyone go?" he asked, voice low.

Ani's reply was quiet, almost reverent. "My parents cleared out the bodies when they first came here. They're buried a short distance from here. Said it only felt right." She turned a corner, boots echoing in the empty hall. "My father's study is down here."

They walked on, the silence broken only by the soft scuff of their steps. Fenix read the names on the doors as they passed—people long dead, their legacies reduced to plaques and dust. Hallways branched off, each labeled in faded lettering: Philosophy & Culture, Social Sciences, Arts, Science & Medicine. Each corridor stretched on, lined with doors, hundreds of rooms in all. The scale of it was staggering—a monument to a world that had tried, once, to save itself.

"In here," Ani said, holding her card against a small reader beside the door. A green light flickered, and she pushed the door open, revealing the name: Dr. Michaels.

Fenix stepped inside. The room was cluttered with the detritus of a life spent in study—dozens of books and stacks of paper piled high on a broad desk, a wall of shelves crammed with spines, floor to ceiling. Against the far wall, a small desk held a computer terminal and a flat device, its surface dulled by dust and time.

"Now," Ani said, snapping his attention back to her, "we just need to figure out where my brother would have hidden it."

"What's it look like?" Fenix asked, eyes scanning the room.

"It's a piece of paper, about this big," she said, holding her hands apart to show the size. "Might be folded and tucked into one of these books." She let out a heavy breath. "We'll probably have to go through them one by one."

Fenix grimaced. "That's gonna take forever." He paused, thinking. "Did your brother have a favorite?"

"A favorite?"

"Yeah," he said, nodding toward the shelves. "Favorite book?"

Ani stood there, searching her memory. She had her own favorites—Peter Pan, Gulliver's Travels, The Dragon and the George. But her brother... he'd always been drawn to philosophy and the arts. They'd spent countless days in these archives, reading while their parents catalogued finds. Her gaze drifted along the spines, then stopped on a deep red book among the browns. She reached up and pulled it free. "Dante's Inferno," she read aloud, flipping the cover and rifling through the pages. "He talked about this one a lot."

Fenix watched as Ani flipped through the pages, eventually holding the book upside down and giving it a shake. Nothing. She sighed, setting it aside.

"Any others?" he asked.

"I really don't know."

He nodded, resigned. "Alright. Let's get to looking."

They started at opposite ends of the shelves, each grabbing a book, sprawling it open, shaking it, hoping for something to fall free. Book after book, shelf after shelf. The next hour crawled by, Ani occasionally talking about one of the titles she'd picked up.

"How many of these have you read?" Fenix asked at one point.

Ani smiled, a little wistful. "Not as many as I wish I had."

They went back to their search, another hour creeping past, when Fenix pulled a thick volume—Foods from the Americas—from the shelf. He opened the front cover and noticed a gap between the pages. As he thumbed through, a folded piece of paper slipped out and landed at his feet.

"Ani," he called, pulling her attention from a book she'd stopped to read. "I think we might have something."

Ani closed her book and slid it back onto the shelf. Fenix bent down, picked up the paper, and unfolded it.

"That's it!" she said, excitement breaking through her fatigue. "That's the map." She reached for the book it had been hidden in, reading the title softly. A big, toothy grin broke across her face, and she chuckled. "Of course. Of course it was…"

"Your brother. He like these kinds of books?"

The smile faded, lingering only at the corners of her mouth. "Yeah. He did." She thumbed through the pages. "He was fascinated by ancient foods. He'd go on and on about the ingredients, how things must have tasted, and that if he'd lived back then, he would've been a famous chef."

Fenix raised an eyebrow. "What's a chef? Something with food, I presume?"

"Yeah. They were like cooks, but better. They created all kinds of amazing foods—famous foods like hamburgers, pizza, hot dogs."

"Ech," Fenix replied. "I mean, I've had to eat dog a couple times out on a job, when there was nothing else and I ran low on supplies, but I wouldn't go saying it was amazing…"

Ani grinned. "Well, you never know. They could've had the most amazing tasting dogs you've ever had."

He shook his head. "Yeah. Think I'd still pass on that one."

"Let me see that," she said, carefully taking the map from him.

Ani held the map out in front of her, studying it. She'd seen it many times before, but never really taken the time to memorize it. It had always been her parents', and until now, she hadn't had much reason to. "Okay," she said, eyes tracing the lines. "I think the quickest way to get to Deltron would be by caravan."

"Caravan!?" Fenix replied, startled, as if the word itself was a threat or a promise.

"Yeah," she replied, her tone flat as the wastes. "Unless you'd rather ride across the desert for three weeks on horseback." She paused, glancing at the map. "The caravan stops in Aberdyne. From there, we can take it to Serenity, and after that, we just have to make our way through Parmithia."

"Oh," he replied, voice thick with sarcasm. "That's all? Just Parmithia. No big deal." He shook his head, a dry chuckle escaping. "Almost forgot that's one of the most dangerous stretches in the wastes."

"You want your weapons, we have to get to Deltron. There's no other way except straight through the ruins. If we go by horse, it'll take us nearly three weeks. The caravan could have us there in one. Three days from Aberdyne to Serenity, and from the look of the map, two more to Deltron."

"Girl," he growled, "stop talking to me like it's my first week out here. You're not telling me anything I don't already know. Or did you forget I've been drifting these wastes for thirty years?"

"I'm sorry," she said, voice small. "I just... I'm just trying to help."

He took a breath, letting it out slow, calming himself. "And you have. You got us this far, didn't you?"

She nodded. "Yeah. I guess."

"I'm not arguing. It's just... taking the caravan puts us out in the open. And we have to go through Paradise Wells and Brimhall. If that prophet bastard's got people watching, they'll be waiting in one of those towns. I'm just saying—it puts us at risk."

"Time's more important," she replied, her voice softer now. "We're not the only ones looking for the other facilities."

76

"I get it," Fenix said, his tone lowering to match hers. "But we're the only ones with the map. We need to keep it that way." He paused, watching her expression shift in the firelight. "End of the day, you hired me. Until I get paid, I'm still working for you. So, if you think the caravan's the better way, that's what we'll do." He hesitated, then added, "But I do think we should stay here for the night and regroup. We've been riding hard under the sun, haven't had a real rest since we started. We've got walls around us, and a roof. Might as well take advantage of it while we can."

"Yeah. But they've got a key too. All they have to do is walk up and open the door."

"Where was your farm again?" Fenix asked, voice low.

"Outside of Blister Springs. Three days' ride."

He nodded, calculating. "Well, there you go. If they went to your farm first, that puts them three days the wrong direction, and another three to backtrack here." He paused, letting the thought settle. "I reckon we're safe enough for the night. I don't know about you, but I'd like to get at least one night's sleep without having to keep one eye open." He let the words hang, heavy with the kind of weariness only the wastes could bring. "Who knows when we'll get the next chance…"

Ani nodded, the tension in her shoulders easing. "Okay. You're right. We'll stay the night and leave first thing in the morning."

"How about after midday?" Fenix suggested, a tired grin flickering. "Could use to not ride through another one of those if we don't have to."

She hated it—wanted to shove the map in her bag and leave that moment—but he was right. Riding through midday was hell, and she had no desire to do it again soon. "Yeah. Me neither."

"Why don't you grab a book and take a load off?" he offered.

"I have a better idea," she replied, a small grin returning. "Follow me." She set the book aside and turned, boots whispering over the tile as she headed down the hall. "Come on. Trust me."

Fenix shook his head, but followed, curiosity getting the better of him.

They made their way down the corridor, turning left at the sign marked Science & Medicine. The halls were silent, the air cool and still. Ani stopped at a door labeled Dr. Xu, a plaque above reading Records and Preservation. She swiped her card and stepped inside, Fenix trailing behind.

The room was a world apart from the cluttered archives—neat, almost serene. A small bookshelf held a handful of books and bound manuscripts, a desk sat against the wall, and a comfortable couch and two chairs flanked a low table. Nature portraits hung on the walls: waterfalls in lush woods, a sunset over a white-sand beach, palm-roofed huts painted in impossible colors.

"You should see this," Ani said, moving to the desk and tapping a button on the keyboard.

Fenix stepped up beside her, the faint hum of the old machine filling the quiet as the screen flickered to life.

"Pull one of those chairs over," she said, using a small plastic device to move a tiny symbol across the screen.

"Okay," he said hesitantly. "Guess we're gonna be here for minute."

He walked over, grabbing one of the chairs and sliding it over. "How is everything preserved so well?" he asked. "A thousand years. It's been a thousand years, and yet, there's barely dust on anything. The cloth on this chair feels... new." He pressed down on the padding. "Everything looks like it's never been touched."

"They call it climate control." She paused as he took a seat and scooched the chair closer. "The facility is powered by something called *fission*. I don't pretend to know anything about how it works, or what it is, but it means that as long as this facility exists, it will have electricity. That's why everything is so perfectly preserved."

"Then what happened to the people?"

"Who knows?" she replied. "Ran out of food maybe? Sickness? Could have been anything." She paused. "We don't know how long they were down here before they died. Could have been hundreds of years. The people my grandparents found could have been the great, great, great, great grandchildren of the people that first lived here."

Fenix exhaled sharply, taking it all in.

"You ready?" Ani asked, her finger hovering over the small object.

"Ready for what?" he asked, his eyebrows closing in on each other.

She smiled, pressing her finger down with a click. A moment later the flat device beside the computer sprang to life, illuminating. A breath later a woman in a long white lab coat standing a foot tall and bathed in light blue light stood before them.

Fenix startled, nearly falling back in his chair.

Ani snorted, laughter she tried to hold back following the sound. "It's okay, Fenix," she said as he tried to compose himself. "It's just a picture." She waited, allowing himself to situate. "Remember I said there were things like pictures, but with movement and sound. This is one of them. They call it a *holo-vid*." She smiled. "You want to know what happened? Before all this?" She reached out and clicked the button again. This time the image sprang to life and the older woman began to speak.

The woman in the blue-white light smiled, her voice echoing with a warmth that felt impossibly distant. "Hello. I'm Dr. Ling Xu. Welcome to the Belcor Facility. I'd like to give you a brief introduction to this place and what we do here, and touch briefly on the other facilities scattered across the southwest—and the roles they serve.

"As I said, this is the Belcor Facility. Our sole purpose is the preservation of the world's history. In these archives, we've scanned and catalogued every manuscript, every book, every scrap of parchment and written history from every culture we could find. This

79

is the most comprehensive and complete compendium of human history ever created. We take pride in the vast catalogue of works contained within these walls, storing it so that one day, our distant descendants can access this knowledge—and maybe add to it themselves."

She paused, her smile lingering, eyes shining with a hope that felt almost alien in the wastes.

"Belcor is one of five facilities. You now know that this place is dedicated to the preservation of history and knowledge. But what about the others? Let me tell you a bit about them. To the northwest, there's the Cultiva Facility. Cultiva houses roughly two hundred of the world's brightest agriculturalists, biologists, horticulturalists, botanists, and phytologists. It has the most advanced climate controls ever built, and has surpassed even Svalbard Global as the largest seed bank in the world. In an end-case scenario, Cultiva could, theoretically, be used to reseed the entire planet. To our west, we have the Pharma Facility. As the name suggests, Pharma holds copies of every patented medication and their chemical makeups. With the information stored there, we could recreate every drug ever released by any pharmaceutical company—everything from aspirin to chemotherapy, right at your fingertips. Pharma is a bit smaller, housing about a hundred of the brightest chemists and pharmacists from around the globe, ready to begin reproducing vital medications at the press of a button. To the north of Pharma, just outside the city of Albuquerque, stands the Deltron Facility. Deltron is our military stronghold. Within those walls is the history of every war and conflict ever documented, with weaponry and relics from every era. There's a comprehensive database of every battle ever fought, as well as schematics for every patented weapon ever created. Deltron is by far the largest facility, set to house three hundred of the greatest tacticians and military minds in the world. Through a joint venture with NATO, each of the allied countries has sent their best to create the greatest military the world has ever known. And finally, there's Arcan. The

Arcan Facility is the northernmost of them all. This is our nuclear defense facility—our last stand, as some of us have come to call it. Housed in Arcan are three hundred of the world's most powerful nuclear warheads ever manufactured. This facility is capable of launching worldwide at the press of a switch. Well, two switches. There's a failsafe, of course, to keep any accidental launches from happening." She chuckled softly, the sound strange in the hush of the archive. "We all hope that Arcan stays dormant for as long as these facilities exist. These places are for a possible 'what if' scenario."

She let the words hang, her smile gentle, almost wistful. "This is just a brief description to help you understand the incredible steps we at Americorp have taken to ensure we are the greatest protector of humanity's past, present, and future. Again, I am Dr. Ling Xu, and on behalf of all of us here at Americorp, thank you, and have a wonderful day."

"Wow," Fenix breathed, still amazed by the ghostly technology—watching one of the ancients speak, her voice echoing out of the blue-lit past.

"There's more," Ani said, her fingers deft on the controls. Fenix watched as she flipped through the icons, settling on another. She clicked, and the woman in the white duster appeared again, but this time the light in her eyes was gone, her voice stripped of hope.

"If you're watching this, then the worst of case scenarios has happened. As of zero eight hundred hours, August twenty-first, two thousand twenty-seven, the Americorp facilities were placed into active status. This includes the Arcan facility, in its full capacity..." The woman paused, the smile from before vanished. Her hair was unkempt, dark circles under her eyes. "What have we done...?" She wiped at her eyes, voice trembling. "Everything we know is gone; the world above burned. We've lost contact with the other facilities and, through algorithmic projections, we assume that nearly seventy percent of the world's population has effectively been eliminated."

Ani glanced at Fenix, who sat silent, transfixed by the flickering image.

"I'd like to think we did the right thing. The wars, the fighting... it showed no sign of lessening, and the creatures..." She trailed off, voice breaking. "For now, we're safe, those of us in the facilities. We have enough supplies to last the next three generations. That's the estimated time it will take for the fallout to decay and for us to be able to return to the surface. Everything is gone, and none of us will ever see daylight again. Not our children, nor theirs. What did we allow ourselves to do...? God help us."

The woman on the holo-vid turned and walked away, leaving only a flickering blue light atop the small flat device.

Ani reached out and closed the file.

"We did this to ourselves?" Fenix said, the sour realization sinking in. "But why? Why would we destroy seventy percent of the life on our planet? It don't make sense."

"Because of the merge," Ani replied quietly, turning to him. "The ancients did something that merged two realms—two dimensions—together. That's when the attacks began. Orcs and goblins, the elves... Somehow, the merge brought them here, to this planet."

Fenix frowned. "What is a realm, or di—"

"Dimension?" Ani finished for him.

"Yeah, that."

Ani shook her head, brushing a stray lock of hair behind her ear. "I'm not really sure. It's kind of like... there's this world, but there's also another world just like it, only different. They exist at the same time, but in different places. The places they exist are called realms, or dimensions. Their scientists did something—something that brought them together, that merged our realm with another. Corithia. When that happened, part of their realm was left here, like a residue. It wasn't long after that merge that orcs and goblins appeared. Elves, halflings, fairies. They all came soon after. Magic became stronger.

Witches began using their powers for destruction. Our world changed. That's why it was called the merge."

Fenix stared at her, disbelief flickering in his eyes. He'd heard stories—whispers in taverns, half-drunken tales told around dying fires. He'd never put much stock in them, never really thought it true, never cared.

"There's more," Ani added, her voice low. "A lot more."

Fenix took a deep breath, glancing at the flickering blue light of the holo-vid once more. Then he turned to Ani, his voice rough. "Show me."

Ani nodded, flicking through files and loading holo-vid after holo-vid. Time slipped away unnoticed as Fenix caught up on hundreds of years of forgotten knowledge. History, the industrial era, the great depression, world wars, the merge. File after file, he soaked in as much as he could. He learned about the scientists building the supercollider, smashing atoms together. He learned of the unforeseen fallout and the devastation left from the merge. Millions disappeared, replaced by what they called Corithians—elves, goblins, orcs and halflings, fairies, dwarves, and all manner of small creature. Goblins and orcs fought savagely for territory in those first years. Millions of humans died or were enslaved. Elves and halflings struggled to live alongside humanity, only to be persecuted and killed, or imprisoned. There were rebellions and riots worldwide as Corithians fought to make their place in the new world they'd been dropped into. But in the end, humans did what they knew best. They destroyed it all. They spent fifty years building the facilities, gathering their resources for what they knew was coming. And once they'd gathered the best and brightest, and the facilities were operating at peak capacity, they loaded them in and sealed the doors. Then they pushed the button and rained down fire from above, hoping to eradicate every last remnant left from Corithia.

But what they didn't anticipate was that Corithians didn't react to radiation the same way humans did. It only served to enhance their abilities. Goblins grew smarter, learning to build enclaves. Orcs grew not only in size, but in intelligence and violence. Their horde became a nearly unstoppable force. The elves scattered to different corners of the earth, building new cities. Humans—those who survived—hid underground, in caves and far-gone places where the radiation didn't reach. They too adapted, returning again to an age of scavenging and surviving. For a thousand years, each society struggled to gain its foothold on earth.

Fenix sat in a padded chair, a book about the roman era held loosely in one hand. He'd fallen asleep reading, a headache pounding from trying to absorb too much at once. Ani slept across the room, curled up on a large couch. She'd fallen asleep hours before, Fenix opting instead to stay up and keep flipping through holo-vids. Both had stayed up well into the next day, and by the time they finally awoke, the following night had arrived. So, they decided to stay one more night, and leave the following afternoon.

18

"Drifter."
"Drifter."

The word drifted through the haze of sleep, rough as sand in the wind. Fenix blinked awake to find Ani standing over him, her silhouette framed by the pale, dust-choked light filtering through the cracked window. Her hand lingered on his shoulder.

"Hey," she said, voice low. She hesitated, as if weighing the moment, then let her hand fall away. "You oughta see this."

Fenix rubbed the grit from his eyes, the ache of old wounds and restless nights settling in his bones. "What time is it?" His voice was hoarse, barely more than a growl.

"Midday," Ani replied, stepping back into the gloom.

He sat up slow, breath heavy in his chest. "What's going on?"

"It's better if I show you."

He nodded, pushing himself to his feet. Ani was already moving, boots whispering over the warped floorboards as she slipped into the hallway. Fenix followed, the silence between them thick as the heat outside.

They wound through the belly of the old facility, corridors branching like veins. Three turns later, Ani stopped at a door marked Research & Development. She glanced back, eyes sharp beneath the brim of her battered hat, then swiped her card. The lock clicked, and the door swung open.

Inside, the room was stripped bare—just a battered desk, a shelf heavy with dust, and a monitor that glowed faintly in the gloom. No comfort, no color. Just the cold bones of the old world.

Ani moved to the desk, fingers dancing over the controls. The screen flickered to life, casting blue light across her face. She scrolled through files, her jaw set. When she found what she was looking for, she turned to Fenix.

"After the Merge, folks started changing," she said, voice barely above a whisper. "Some got abilities. Magic." She looked down, the weight of memory pressing on her. "It scared people. Led to what my mother called the witch-hunts. They tracked down people like me, like my mother and her mother before. The things they did…" Her words trailed off, breath shuddering in her chest. Then she clicked the screen.

A video flickered to life. On it, a young girl with reddish-blonde hair sat shackled in a bare white room, hands bound to metal rings on a cold steel desk. Tear tracks stained her cheeks, her eyes fixed on the table—haunted, hollow.

A voice crackled from unseen speakers, clinical and cold. *"Test subject Three One Five Six. Could you please clearly state your name for us?"*

The girl looked up, fear and defiance warring in her eyes. "Marie Clemens."

"Thank you, Marie. And could you please tell us how old you are?"

"I'm seventeen."

"Thank you."

"Why am I here?" The girl's voice trembled, pleading. "I didn't do anything."

"When did you first start to show symptoms?"

"I don't know what you're talking about. Please, just let me go home."

"When did you first start to show symptoms?" The voice was relentless, inhuman.

Marie's gaze dropped. Another tear slipped down her cheek, lost in the silence of the wastes.

"Three One Five Six, I will ask you again. When did you first begin to show symptoms?"

The girl stayed silent, her head bowed. The silence stretched, heavy as the heat outside. Then, slowly, her gaze lifted. "Last year."

"And what are your abilities?"

"My what?" Her voice was barely a whisper.

"Your abilities. What are they?"

"I… I don't know." She hesitated, voice trembling. "Cold."

"Show us," the voice commanded, flat and merciless.

"No," she whimpered.

"I said show us, Three One Five Six."

Her eyes snapped up, fear hardening into anger. "NO!" she shouted, her face flushed with defiance.

"I'm not going to ask again. I said, show us."

"No," she spat, voice raw. "Never."

A pause. The room filled with a silence that felt like the edge of a storm. Then, a crackle of electricity arced between the restraints. The girl screamed, her body rigid as the current tore through her. For half a minute, the only sound was her agony. Then the power cut, and she slumped, limp and shuddering, a thin strand of drool slipping from her mouth.

The voice returned, cold as ever. *"Three One Five Six. Show us your abilities."*

She sat, breathing ragged, hair hiding her face. Hatred simmered in the air.

"Three One Five Six—"

Her head snapped up, eyes burning. The metal desk beneath her hands began to frost, ice spreading in jagged veins. A scream ripped from her, primal and wild. Shards of ice exploded across the table, the metal groaning under the force. Frost crept up the walls, crawling over the camera lens. With a wrench, she shattered the restraints and rose, breath steaming in the frozen air.

The door burst open. A soldier stormed in, rifle raised. He fired. The shots echoed, red blooming across her chest as she twisted, stumbling. More shots, relentless. She fell, the room falling silent but for the soldier's heavy breathing.

"Status?" the voice behind the camera asked, flat and unfeeling.

The soldier made his way to where the girl lay, blood pooling outwards on the cold floor. He nudged her body with the barrel of his rifle, then knelt to check for a pulse. After a moment, he turned to the camera and shook his head. His breath hovered in the air, a thin cloud in the sterile chill.

"Trial two hundred fifty-six incomplete. Subject, Marie Clemens, number three one five six. Status: deceased." The voice on the intercom paused, flat and unfeeling. *"Sterilize the room and prepare for next trial."*

Ani reached out and clicked the monitor, the screen going dark with a hollow snap. She turned to Fenix, her eyes shadowed with grief. "There are hundreds of these. Just like this." Her voice was thick with sorrow. "They killed thousands of us. Hunted us down—anyone with magic, anyone different. They dragged us to places like this. Tested, interrogated, tortured, and in the end, killed. So many died. Why? Just because we were different. Because they were afraid."

Fenix sat in silence, reading the pain etched across Ani's face.

"When I told you I hate being called witch… that's why. That's what they did to people like me. Men, women, children. Always the same. Locked in a room, forced to perform, and then—eventually— killed."

"I'm sorry," Fenix said softly, his voice barely more than a whisper.

Ani shook her head, her gaze distant. "Humanity destroyed itself. All because they were afraid of what they didn't understand."

Fenix let out a bitter scoff. "Guess not much has changed in a thousand years."

"We can't let that happen again," Ani said, her voice trembling with resolve.

"We can't change how the world thinks," Fenix replied. "You can't just erase that kind of hatred. It doesn't go away."

Ani looked up, a flicker of hope in her eyes. "But look at Europa— "

Fenix cut her off gently. "You ever been to Europa?"

Ani shook her head. "No."

"Exactly. And neither have I. Could be nothing but fairytales—elves and humans, halflings and dwarves, all living side by side." Fenix scoffed, the sound dry as the dust outside. "Sounds like a damned bedtime story."

Ani fixed him with a look, a squint of challenge in her eyes. "And until a week ago, if I'd told you orcs, goblins, and humans could work together—led by a man calling himself the prophet—you'd have said the same thing."

Fenix opened his mouth, but the words caught in his throat. She was right, and he knew it.

"Maybe things aren't like that in the wastes," Ani went on, her voice steady, "but that doesn't mean it can't be different somewhere else. There's no reason it can't."

Fenix nodded, a flicker of regret in his eyes. "I'm sorry for what they did to your kind. It wasn't right." He hesitated, then pressed on. "So, you think we can find another one of those keys in one of the other facilities? You really believe we can stop that maniac before he rains fire on what's left of the world?"

Ani nodded, her gaze unwavering. "I do." She paused, searching his face. "If we can get to Deltron, we'll find the second key. And maybe—just maybe—we'll have enough firepower to stand a chance in the fight that's coming."

Fenix let out a low breath. "And you think we can do this alone? No help?"

Ani's eyes dropped to the floor. "I don't have the credits to hire another drifter."

He gave a short, humorless laugh. "Yeah. I suppose that's a problem. Not sure anyone would take the job, truth be told. Hell, if I'd known what I was getting into, I'd have told you—politely or not—to have yourself a nice day."

"But you're still here."

"I got less to lose than most," he replied, voice softer now. "And I guess it's a little late to turn back."

"We need to get to Deltron."

Fenix managed a crooked smile, a spark of something lighter in his tone. "Well, we got a few hours till we can make for Aberdyne. You got anything a little less grim to show me?"

Ani's lips curled in a faint smile as she turned back to the terminal. For the next few hours, they sifted through the ghosts of the old world—commercials, nature reels, music from a time before the wastes. Fenix watched, uneasy, as faces smiled from a world that had never known thirst or hunger. It all seemed easier, brighter, but he knew better. Every society had its shadows. None of the videos showed the ones left behind.

By the time they were ready to leave, Fenix felt the weight of two thousand years of history—hope and ruin, light and darkness—settle on his shoulders. For better, and for worse.

19

The pair left the facility behind, winding through the broken hills toward Paradise Wells. Four days on the trail, the first two spent pushing their horses hard—riding from dawn until the sun's fury forced them to ground, then pressing on well into the night. By the end of the third day, the animals were spent, ribs showing beneath dust-caked hides. Fenix called a halt as the last light bled from the sky.

"We can stop up there a ways," he said, nodding toward a patch of ground where the sun had just slipped below the horizon, painting the clouds in bruised pink and orange.

Ani trailed just behind, her gaze snagged on something jutting from the earth. "Drifter?" she called, her voice tight.

Fenix turned, following her line of sight. A short distance ahead, an overturned wagon sprawled in the dust, a dead horse still tangled in the traces. Instinctively, his hand went to his pistol, thumb flicking the strap loose as he eased it from the holster.

They rode closer, slowing as the scene unfolded. It was a merchant's cart, one wheel split clean through—must've been running hard to flip like that. Fenix's gut twisted. They'd been fleeing something.

"Reapers?" he muttered, scanning the horizon.

"No," Fenix said, voice low, eyes darting over the empty land. He brought his horse to a stop, nodding toward a pair of bodies sprawled twenty feet from the wreck. "Look."

A man and a woman, face down in the dirt, a handful of arrows jutting from their backs. The dust around them was already drying to rust.

"They were killed trying to escape." He swept the horizon again, every muscle tense. "Goblins…"

Ani's head snapped toward him, eyes wide. "Goblins!?"

He nodded grimly. "The arrows. Those are goblin."

She stared at the scene, the silence between them heavy as the coming night. "But—"

"Reapers would have taken them and their horse alive. Their wagon would've been stripped bare. Look—everything's still here. Doesn't look like they took anything." Fenix drew a slow breath, eyes scanning the horizon, then dropped his gaze to the ground. "Tracks head off that way, back toward the mine. If I had to guess, these folks were just in the wrong place at the wrong time." He paused, following the faint lines in the dust. "Best we don't linger. We should keep moving."

Ani looked back at the dead couple. The blood hadn't dried yet—still glossy, dark, clinging to the dirt. It would be hours before the desert finished its work.

Ahead, Fenix nudged his horse forward. "We should put some distance between us and that wagon before we bed down. No sense getting caught up in someone else's trouble."

Ani nodded, casting one last glance at the arrows jutting from the wagon before urging her horse after him.

A few minutes later, as the sky deepened into twilight, she broke the silence. "Is this how it's gonna be now?"

Fenix rode on, the hush stretching between them. "It's starting to look that way."

They rode in silence, the world around them sinking into darkness. After a while, Fenix spoke again, voice low. "I've been trying to find a reason to get out of the wastes for a long time. Maybe this is it. Orcs and goblins moving in... might be as good a reason as any to head west, or north to the tundra." He managed a crooked smile. "Not sure how well I'd get along with the elves, though. Or if they'd even have me. Who knows what the politics are up there?"

"I think the west would be nice," Ani said quietly. "I always wanted to see the ocean."

"Even though it's dead?"

"Yeah," she replied. "I've seen so many pictures. I know you can't go in it, but just to see it. Just to sit at the edge and listen to the waves crash in."

Fenix nodded. "I've heard there's more opportunity out west. Big communities. Calexico, maybe. I'll take rain over another orc any day."

"Yeah," Ani said, her voice fading at the memory of the hulking shape that had nearly killed Fenix. "Me too."

They rode on, letting the silence settle. As the last light bled from the sky, they stopped and made camp—no fire, just the cold comfort of the stars overhead. They lay back on the hard earth, letting the desert's hush lull them to sleep, the world around them vast, empty, and indifferent.

20

It was just before midday when the pair stopped again. An abandoned well off the side of the road caught Fenix's eye—a lonely relic leaning beside the sun-bleached bones of a farmhouse, half-collapsed and surrendered to the dust. The well itself was a squat ring of brick, a single bucket tied to a fraying rope. Fenix tugged his reins, guiding his horse toward the ruin. "Come on," he called, voice low and wary. "Let's check it out."

Ani followed, trailing just behind as Fenix swung down from his saddle and approached the well. The air shimmered with heat, pressing in on them from all sides. Fenix drew his pistol, scanning the empty yard and the sagging house before holstering it again, satisfied nothing waited in ambush.

Most wells out here were dry, but it never hurt to check. Sometimes, if you were lucky, groundwater still seeped up from deep below—enough to keep a traveler alive. Fenix had heard stories of a well between Corith and Heirako that still held water, a rare blessing in the wastes.

He stepped up, lifted the bucket, and peered down into the darkness. "Alright," he muttered, "let's see what we got." He let the bucket drop, rope hissing through his hands as it tumbled down the shaft. For a moment, there was only silence—then a sudden, familiar buzzing rose up from the dark.

A swarm of fairies burst from the well, wings glinting in the harsh sunlight. Fenix flinched back, cursing as six of the tiny creatures shot into the air, hovering above the well and glaring down at him with beady, inhuman eyes.

"Ah, shit!" he spat, scowling up at them. "Fucking fairies."

The fairies chittered and spat back, unleashing a string of curses—half language, half insect noise—before darting away, trailing dust and resentment.

"Gods, I hate those things," Fenix growled, grabbing the rope and starting to haul the bucket back up.

Ani chuckled from behind. "Wow."

Fenix shot her a look. "We all got something. Some folks can't stand snakes, some don't take kindly to dogs. Me? I can't stand fairies." He shuddered. "Ech. They just creep me the hell out."

Ani grinned. "Okay, jeez."

He shook off the feeling and turned back to the well, pulling the bucket up hand over hand. When it finally reached the top, he saw it was bone dry. With a grunt, he drew his knife and cut the rope, letting the bucket tumble back into the darkness.

"Why'd you do that?" Ani asked, surprised.

"Saving someone else the time we just wasted figuring out it's dry," Fenix replied.

The small gesture drew a smirk from Ani. Everyone had their quirks, she supposed. But in that moment, she appreciated the thought—how he'd taken the time to spare some future traveler a little disappointment. It was a strange, quiet thing, but it spoke volumes for his character. The smirk went unseen by Fenix, as did the soft smile that followed.

"I reckon we could wait out midday here."

"Yeah," Fenix replied, glancing up at the sky for any more of those flying aberrations. "That's a good idea."

A short while later, they'd hung their shades from the splintered rafters of the ruined farmhouse, settling in the thin patch of shade. Each had a container of water, drawn from a saguaro they'd tapped earlier that morning.

Ani set the last piece of lizard stick in her lap, her gaze distant. "I've been thinking," she said. "When the Merge happened, and all those creatures from Corithia were phased here... I wonder how many of us were left there. Do you think what happened here, also happened wherever it is that all the other creatures came from?"

"Safe to assume," Fenix replied, stretching his legs out in the dust. "Wouldn't think orcs or goblins would be any friendlier there than here. Elves... well, elves are elves. Usually stick to their own."

Ani nodded, chewing on the thought. "I wonder what else came here?"

"What do you mean?" Fenix asked, curiosity flickering in his eyes.

"Well, what other creatures merged here that we don't even know about?" She paused, her voice growing more animated. "Like us. We only know what's in the wastes. But there could be all kinds of things in other parts of the world. We used to have elves down here, till they all moved north. And nightstalkers—we didn't even know about them until a hundred years ago. They'd been here since the Merge." She shook her head, marveling. "That's what I'm talking about. How much stuff was left here from the Merge?"

Fenix gave a slight smirk. "Well, that's... that's definitely something to think about."

Ani smiled, the wonder in her voice softening the edge of the day. "I just find it so fascinating. The world was the same for thousands, millions of years, and then bam, in the time it takes a person to blink, everything is different. You go from humans being the only intelligent creatures on the planet, to a whole handful. It must have been the biggest shock."

"Yeah," Fenix replied. "Must have been a bigger shock to the others when we started huntin' em down and killin' em." The words hung in the air.

Ani fell silent, the weight of history settling between them.

After a moment, Fenix shifted, glancing at his horse. "And I don't know what you're talking about. Dirtweed's as intelligent as they come."

"Dirtweed?" Ani asked, brow furrowing.

"Yeah. Dirtweed. My horse."

"Your horse's name is Dirtweed?"

"Yeah," he replied, matter-of-fact. "What's yours?"

Ani hesitated, then shrugged. "Um. Just... horse, I guess."

"You're telling me your horse ain't got no name?" Fenix turned, half incredulous, half amused.

She smirked, a little embarrassed. "No. Just... horse."

"Wow," Fenix said, turning to Ani's mount, standing a few feet away. "I'm really sorry to hear that, horse, I truly am."

Ani rolled her eyes. "Why would you name your horse?"

Fenix looked at her as if she'd just told him the sky was green. "Why would you not? It's a living creature, just like you and me. Eats, sleeps, breathes. Carries our sorry asses from one place to the other." He paused, a faint smile tugging at his lips. "I've had conversations with Dirtweed I could never have with anyone else."

Ani gave him a look, dry as the desert. "Horses can't talk..."

"And that's the beauty of it," Fenix replied, pulling his hat down and leaning back against a beam, making it clear he was settling in for a nap.

Ani scoffed, arms crossed, watching the drifter for a moment before huffing. "Fine," she muttered. "I'll name my stupid horse."

Fenix let out a single chuckle, eyes already closed beneath the brim of his hat. "Go ahead and wake me when the sun's passed," he finished.

"Unbelievable," Ani grumbled, popping the last piece of lizard stick into her mouth.

She sat there, chewing, mind wandering as she tried to think up names for her horse. But to her, it had always just been a horse—something to ride, to feed, to pat on the neck now and then. She'd never understood how someone could have a different kind of connection with an animal. To her, they were just that. Animals.

She sat in quiet contemplation for the next hour, the silence of the wastes pressing in, before finally settling back and deciding on a short nap herself. When she woke, the sun had dropped to three o'clock. She stretched, then extended her leg, tapping her foot against Fenix's boot.

He grumbled, startled awake a split-second later. "Oh," he mumbled, blinking. "Slept a little longer than I'd have wanted to. Guess we better get a move on."

The pair rose, untying their sunshades and folding them into their bags. They untethered the horses and climbed back up, riding the next few hours in companionable silence. They stopped only briefly outside Paradise Wells to discuss their plan, then readied themselves and rode in, the dust of the wastes trailing behind.

21

Paradise Wells was a small town, home to about three thousand souls. The tallest building—a terra cotta-spackled, three-story structure—stood out against the low skyline, serving as saloon, inn, and the Silver Stallion Brothel all in one. The rest of the settlement sprawled in a patchwork of rough-hewn buildings, narrow streets, and sun-faded boardwalks that ran the length of the main strip. The colors of the earth bled into the wood, and dust swirled in the wind, carrying the scent of heat and old timber. A scorpion darted beneath Ani's horse, narrowly avoiding a heavy hoof as they made their way in.

The main road cut straight through town, an artery leading them toward the heart of Paradise Wells. They passed a handful of shops and squat, single-story homes. Ani's eyes lingered on a book-and-potions shop, making a mental note to return if time allowed.

"Reckon we could stay here for the night," Fenix said, pulling his gaze from a halfling in battered goblin armor, who was browsing the weapons rack outside a small shop. "I could use a drink and a bed."

Ani nodded, silent, checking off her mental note as they continued. "Inn's just up ahead," Fenix added, nudging his horse forward.

They passed townsfolk moving along the boardwalk, dust swirling around their boots. The air was thick with the smell of dirt and sun-bleached wood, and the faint aroma of freshly skewered lizard stick made Ani's stomach grumble.

"You been here before?" Fenix asked, glancing over.

"Once or twice," Ani replied, her voice distant. For a moment, the memory of her father's duster and the sound of his laughter drifted through her mind. "Long time ago."

"Long time ago," Fenix chuckled. "You're what, fifteen?"

Ani's face stiffened. "Nineteen," she snapped.

"Oh," Fenix smiled, raising his hands in mock surrender. "'Scuse me."

"And age doesn't mean anything in the wastes," Ani muttered. "Everyone ages quicker in the sun."

Fenix smirked. "You ain't wrong there."

He slowed Dirtweed to a stop, climbing down and leading his horse to the hitching post in front of the Silver Stallion. Ani followed suit, sliding off her own horse.

"Is it safe?" she asked, eyeing the saloon's battered doors.

"Safe as anywhere, I suppose," Fenix replied, looping the reins around the post.

Ani did the same, then turned and followed Fenix inside, leaving the dust and the dying light behind.

As Ani stepped inside, the heavy scent of stale alcohol and sweat hit her like a wall. The saloon was dim, lit only by a handful of oil sconces that cast a flickering yellow glow across the battered floorboards. Four large tables filled the center of the room, each one claimed by its own weary, dust-caked group. At the far end, a long bar ran beneath a brass rail, tended by a grizzled man in a dirty button-down and a stained apron. Above the shelves of bottles, a massive taxidermied orc head glared down, its bottom tusks jutting out like sun-bleached spikes.

"Beer and a rye," Fenix called as he strode to the bar. "And let me get two waters."

Ani's gaze lingered on the orc's tusks before she turned to watch the bartender, who eyed them with a wariness born of long years in the wastes.

"You want 'em cold?" the man asked.

"Cold?" Fenix echoed, cautious. "That an option?"

"Is here," the bartender replied, a flicker of something sly in his eyes.

"No shit," Fenix said, a stunned smile breaking through his usual reserve. "And how ain't you been drug out into the street and strung up?"

The man just smiled, filling two glasses with beer from the tap. He set them on the counter, then placed a broad, calloused hand around each glass. Ani watched as a thin layer of frost crept across the surface, the beer inside crystalizing ever so slightly.

"Would you kill the only man in Paradise Wells who could serve you a cold beer?" the bartender asked.

For the first time in a long while, a genuine smile cracked across Fenix's lips. "Won't tell a soul."

The bartender pulled his hands back and leaned down to grab two glasses of water, chilling them in the same manner before setting them on the bar. He leaned in, voice low. "Your girl may not get the same treatment, though."

"Duly noted," Fenix replied, lifting the mug and taking a long sip. He let out a small sigh, savoring the cold. "Thank you, for both."

The bartender nodded, glancing at Ani, who stared back, puzzled.

"How did he know?" she asked a moment later, voice low, still trying to puzzle out how the man could tell she was a witch.

Fenix took another sip, setting the mug down. "Oh, my god. That is exactly how this should be served. God damn…" He glanced over at her. "I just always figured you all could smell each other out, like some weird, magical sensation whenever you get close. Least that's what I was told by one of your kind a few years back." He paused, considering. "You didn't… feel anything when you got near him?"

Ani shook her head. "No."

Fenix gave a half-smirk. "Well, guess you got something to work on. Now go on and enjoy your water 'fore it gets warm."

Ani sighed, a low, tired sound, and reached for the glass. The chill bit at her fingers. "Oh. Wow. That is cold."

Fenix arched a brow, approving, and took another slow sip from his mug. A moment later, Ani set her glass down, empty.

"OH! OW!" she yelped, hands flying to her temples. "What the hell?"

Fenix laughed, the sound rough and genuine, glancing to the barkeep, who grinned back. "Oh damn. You ain't never had anything cold like that?"

"Ah!" Ani winced as the pain faded. "No. What was that?"

"That's head-freeze," the barkeep replied, wiping a glass with a rag that had seen better days. "Happens if you drink it too fast."

"You should warn people," Ani shot back, a crooked smirk on her lips.

"Warn people?" The barkeep looked genuinely shocked, glancing at Fenix. "That'd suck all the fun right out of it."

Fenix caught himself smiling, the expression breaking into a rare laugh. He reached for the shot of rye, poured it down, letting it burn before swallowing. "You the man to talk to about a room for the night?"

The barkeep's smile lingered. "Yup. That'd be me. Just a room, or you looking for some entertainment as well?"

"Maybe later," Fenix replied, voice dry. "Just the room for now."

"Whelp, be three silvers, four if'n you want two beds."

Fenix glanced at Ani, who nearly snarled in response before digging out four silvers and sliding them across the bar.

The barkeep scooped up the coins, dropped them in his pocket, and made his way to a battered cabinet at the end of the bar. He fished out a single key and slid it across the counter to Ani. "Room twelve, second floor." He leaned in, voice dropping. "Remember what I said. I get a pass here. Not so likely you would. This ain't Corith. There's a mighty strong dislike of our kind in these parts, if you catch my drift."

Ani searched his eyes for the tell-tale flicker, then nodded, voice steady. "Thank you." She reached for the key. "I do have a question."

"Shoot," the man replied.

"Has there been any goblin attacks near here recently, or... orcs?"

"Where'd you say you were coming from again?"

"Blister Springs."

The man smiled, slow and knowing. "You ever leave Blister Springs?"

Ani's brow furrowed. "Of course."

The smile grew. "Then you should know how dumb of question that is."

Fenix smiled quietly beside her.

Ani's gaze drifted to a sword hanging on the wall, just to the right of the orc's head. "It's elven, isn't it?"

Fenix nodded. "Yep."

"Have you ever met an elf?"

Fenix let out a heavy sigh. "Yeah. A long time ago."

"So, you've been to the north?"

"I had a few jobs that took me in that direction. There's a pretty big trade city a few weeks' ride from here. Not as big as Corith, but it's at the edge of the northernmost of the wastes. You see all manner of folks there."

"Even elves?"

"Sure. Even elves."

"And everyone gets along?"

Fenix shook his head, a dry smile flickering beneath the brim of his hat. "Tolerate, maybe. That's about as good as it gets. Trade's the only thing that keeps folks civil up there. Elves keep to their own, dwarves do the same, halflings stick together. You'll see all kinds in the northern cities, but don't mistake proximity for peace. Old grudges run deep. Nobody forgets what happened after the Merge. Not really."

Ani's gaze lingered on the sword, then drifted back to the room. "Still, it must be something to see. All those people, all those stories, in one place."

Fenix shrugged. "Maybe one day you'll see it for yourself. Just don't expect any fairytales."

Ani shook her head. "No."

Fenix gave a half-smirk. "Well, guess you got something to work on. Now go on and enjoy your water 'fore it gets warm."

Ani sighed, a low, tired sound, and reached for the glass. The chill bit at her fingers. "Oh. Wow. That is cold."

Fenix arched a brow, approving, and took another slow sip from his mug. A moment later, Ani set her glass down, empty.

"OH! OW!" she yelped, hands flying to her temples. "What the hell?"

Fenix laughed, the sound rough and genuine, glancing to the barkeep, who grinned back. "Oh damn. You ain't never had anything cold like that?"

"Ah!" Ani winced as the pain faded. "No. What was that?"

"That's head-freeze," the barkeep replied, wiping a glass with a rag that had seen better days. "Happens if you drink it too fast."

"You should warn people," Ani shot back, a crooked smirk on her lips.

"Warn people?" The barkeep looked genuinely shocked, glancing at Fenix. "That'd suck all the fun right out of it."

Fenix caught himself smiling, the expression breaking into a rare laugh. He reached for the shot of rye, poured it down, letting it burn before swallowing. "You the man to talk to about a room for the night?"

The barkeep's smile lingered. "Yup. That'd be me. Just a room, or you looking for some entertainment as well?"

"Maybe later," Fenix replied, voice dry. "Just the room for now."

"Whelp, be three silvers, four if'n you want two beds."

Fenix glanced at Ani, who nearly snarled in response before digging out four silvers and sliding them across the bar.

The barkeep scooped up the coins, dropped them in his pocket, and made his way to a battered cabinet at the end of the bar. He fished out a single key and slid it across the counter to Ani. "Room twelve, second floor." He leaned in, voice dropping. "Remember what I said. I get a pass here. Not so likely you would. This ain't Corith. There's a mighty strong dislike of our kind in these parts, if you catch my drift."

Ani searched his eyes for the tell-tale flicker, then nodded, voice steady. "Thank you." She reached for the key. "I do have a question."

"Shoot," the man replied.

"Has there been any goblin attacks near here recently, or... orcs?"

"Where'd you say you were coming from again?"

"Blister Springs."

The man smiled, slow and knowing. "You ever leave Blister Springs?"

Ani's brow furrowed. "Of course."

The smile grew. "Then you should know how dumb of question that is."

Fenix smiled quietly beside her.

Ani's gaze drifted to a sword hanging on the wall, just to the right of the orc's head. "It's elven, isn't it?"

Fenix nodded. "Yep."

"Have you ever met an elf?"

Fenix let out a heavy sigh. "Yeah. A long time ago."

"So, you've been to the north?"

"I had a few jobs that took me in that direction. There's a pretty big trade city a few weeks' ride from here. Not as big as Corith, but it's at the edge of the northernmost of the wastes. You see all manner of folks there."

"Even elves?"

"Sure. Even elves."

"And everyone gets along?"

Fenix shook his head, a dry smile flickering beneath the brim of his hat. "Tolerate, maybe. That's about as good as it gets. Trade's the only thing that keeps folks civil up there. Elves keep to their own, dwarves do the same, halflings stick together. You'll see all kinds in the northern cities, but don't mistake proximity for peace. Old grudges run deep. Nobody forgets what happened after the Merge. Not really."

Ani's gaze lingered on the sword, then drifted back to the room. "I'd love to meet an elf." Her gaze worked back to the ornate mithril blade. "I've only seen them in pictures. They look so... elegant."

"Some are, I suppose," Fenix said, taking another sip of his quickly warming beer. "Most I met were pretty plain. Regular folk like you and me, just a bit more in the ear."

Ani gave a small, thoughtful nod. "Oh."

"I'm sure back wherever it was they came from, before winding up here, they were something else. I've heard tales—giant cities built in monstrous trees, spires carved into mountains. Even seen a few paintings of what's supposed to be their homes. Impressive, to say the least."

"I'd love to see that," Ani murmured.

Fenix gave a dry chuckle. "Yeah, well. Out here, we got goblins, orcs, and the damned fairies."

"Oh, they're not so bad."

He shot her a look. "Which ones?"

"The fairies."

Fenix shook his head, a shudder running through him. "You keep telling yourself that."

Ani pressed on, changing the subject without missing a beat. "I was thinking. If we circled Paradise Crater, we could probably cut at least two days off our ride to Aberdyne. Skip Brimhall, cut a straight line from here."

A look of disapproval warped Fenix's features. "That's a terrible idea."

"Why?"

"Why?" He scoffed. "You ever been to Paradise Crater?"

Ani shook her head. "Well. No."

"There you go." He shook his head again, drawing a slow breath. "Wouldn't shave two days off, not the way you think. Back country's slower than the road, and it's a half-day just to circle the crater. If we get caught out in the open, who knows what's calling that place home.

I've heard stories—nasty things living around there. With all the orc and goblin activity lately, I don't think it's wise to put ourselves so far from any settlement. Plus, some of the old nightcrawler tunnels run beneath Paradise Crater. Nobody's heard anything from them in years, but I'd hate to be the one to find out they're still down there..."

Ani nodded, considering. "Didn't they all get hunted down?"

Fenix scoffed again. "If you believe the stories, sure. But they had centuries to dig those tunnels. You think we wiped them all out, just like that? Some of them must've tunneled out. I'd say it's just a matter of time before their numbers are back and the attacks start again. That's just my two coppers."

Ani folded her arms, a small pout settling on her lips.

"Look, girl. An extra day ain't gonna kill us. Passing that close to the crater, that far out? That just might." Fenix tipped his glass, savoring another sip. "Man... Cold beer." His tongue clicked against his cheek. "Who'd have thought?"

Ani rolled her eyes. "You can stay here and enjoy your cold beer. I'm heading upstairs to get some rest. Maybe even try to wash some of this trail dust off." She turned to the barkeep. "Scuse me?"

The man looked up from polishing a glass.

"Is there a washtub in the room?"

He smiled, a flicker of recognition in his eyes. "There is. Want me to have it filled for you?"

"Please."

"Normally that'd be three coppers, but it's not often I see my folk around here, so for you, on the house." He paused, eyeing her a moment. "Need me to heat it, or is that something you can take care of?"

Ani studied him, catching the subtle glint that passed between them. "I think I can handle it."

"All right then. It'll be filled by the time you get upstairs." He turned, moving to a row of brass handles behind the bar, each one engraved with a room number. He pulled the one marked twelve.

Ani watched in mild amusement, then called out, "Can I ask you a question?"

The man turned, lifting an eyebrow.

"How could you tell?"

He smiled, slow and knowing. "How could I tell what? That you and I are alike?"

"Yeah," she replied.

He studied her for a moment, weighing something behind his eyes. "You mutant, or natural?"

Ani blinked, puzzled.

"Natural," Fenix answered for her, not looking up from his glass. "And still green."

"Ah," the man behind the bar said, his expression turning serious as he leaned in, voice dropping to a hush. "You ought to practice. Spend as much time as you can honing those abilities. Use 'em. Your life might depend on it one day, and you don't want to get caught unable to protect yourself. There's been a lot of us going missing lately. There's a group out there—don't rightly know their name, but they're hunting our kind." His gaze narrowed, the warning clear. "Practice. Every day. And to answer your question—you know that feeling you get when you're about to cast, that little tingle in your fingertips?"

Ani nodded. "Yeah. I think so. I feel it in my fingertips."

The man smiled, nodding. "That's it. You focus on that. Keep that feeling in your fingertips at all times, you'll be just fine."

Ani lifted her right hand, flexing her fingers ever so slightly, feeling for that spark.

"Don't let your guard down. Ever."

Ani nodded, lowering her hand. "Thank you."

The man gave a knowing smirk, then turned back to his glasses and the slow rhythm of the bar.

Ani turned to Fenix. "I'm going to head up. I wanna soak for a bit."

Fenix smirked, giving her a nod and motioning to the barkeep for another as Ani turned and made her way upstairs, the weight of the warning lingering in the air behind her.

The last three days weighed heavy on Ani's chest as she climbed the narrow stairs, the barkeep's warning still echoing in her mind. The grief of her brother's death, the attacks, the relentless pressure of stopping the prophet—all of it pressed down on her, squeezing her heart until it ached. She hadn't had time to mourn, or even to catch her breath. From the moment she'd stepped into that saloon outside Blister Springs, it had been one unbroken storm, and now, all she wanted was to let the warmth of a bath soak some of the sorrow from her bones.

She moved down the dim hallway, stopping at the door marked twelve in tarnished brass. The key turned with a soft click, the lock disengaging beneath her fingers. She swung the door open, the overhead electric light flickering to life, flaring bright for a heartbeat before settling into a dull glow.

The room was small—two beds pressed close together, just enough space to step between. A battered tub sat in the corner, and two large windows, curtains drawn, let in a sliver of the dying day. The walls were bare wood, the floor uncarpeted, no decorations or candles to soften the edges. For three silvers a night, in a place that mostly rented rooms by the hour for reasons other than sleep, it was exactly what she'd expected.

Ani closed the door behind her, locking it and setting the key on the small table by the entrance. She crossed to the bed nearest the wall—if trouble came in the night, Fenix would be better suited to deal with it than she was. She dropped her pack onto the mattress and sat to pull off her boots, her gaze drifting to the tub. It was already filled, just shy of the rim, the water looking clean enough.

She pushed her boots aside and shrugged off her vest, laying it next to her before pulling her shirt over her head. The air brushed against her skin, raising goosebumps. It had been days since her last bath, and she wrinkled her nose at the scent of sweat and dust clinging to her. For a moment, she just sat there, letting the silence and the promise of warm water settle around her like a balm.

Ani stood for a long moment at the edge of the tub, the last of her clothes pooled at her feet, the air cool against her skin. The water's surface trembled, her reflection warped and ghostly in the dim light. For a heartbeat, she saw her mother's eyes staring back—her own nose, her father's smile, but the rest was her mother, clear as day. The ache of memory pressed in, sharp and sudden, and she felt a shiver of grief crawl up her spine, raising goosebumps along her arms.

A tear slipped free, then another, until she was sinking to the floor, knees drawn to her chest, the cold wood biting into her bare skin. The sobs came in waves, silent at first, then wracking her body as she folded in on herself. She wept for her brother—his last, desperate gaze as he died in her arms. For her mother, fading slow and thin from sun-sickness. For her father, the worried smile he wore the day he left, promising to return, and the door that never opened for him again. She wept for the endless days spent scouring the wastes with Jarek, searching for hope that never came. The grief was a storm, and she let it break over her, let it hollow her out until there was nothing left but the ache and the salt of her tears.

When the storm finally passed, Ani lay there, spent and trembling, her head throbbing with the onset of a headache. She pushed herself upright, wiping her face with the back of her hand, and turned to the tub. Her reflection stared back, eyes red and swollen, mouth set in a hard line. She reached out, breaking the surface with her palm, watching the ripples scatter her image.

She held her hands above the water, feeling the warmth gather in her fingertips, the old familiar tingle of magic building until faint flames licked at her skin. She let the fire flow, sending heat down into the tub until heavy steam curled up, fogging the air. Only then did she step in, bracing herself as the heat bit at her legs. It was hotter than she'd meant, but she eased herself down, gripping the edge until her body adjusted.

Soon she was lying back, submerged to her neck in the steaming water, letting the warmth seep into her bones. She closed her eyes, letting the silence and the heat cradle her, hoping—just for a little while—it might wash some of the sorrow away.

Ani jolted awake at the sound of knocking, the chill of the now-cold water clinging to her skin. She sat up, heart pounding, and took a steadying breath as another knock echoed through the small room.

"I need to go get another key?" came a muffled voice from the hallway.

"Give me a minute!" she called back, voice rough with sleep. She pulled the plug at the bottom of the tub and stood, water streaming from her as she grabbed a towel and wrapped it around her hair. Moving with the slow, heavy limbs of exhaustion, she crossed to the bed and dressed quickly, the weight of the day settling back onto her shoulders.

The door creaked open and Fenix stepped in, the scent of liquor and something faintly floral—lavender, maybe sage—trailing after him. "You fall asleep in there?" he asked, a tired smile on his lips.

"I needed it," Ani replied, stepping aside to let him in. "How long was I out?"

"Couple hours, I reckon."

She nodded, catching the warmth in his eyes and the fatigue in his posture. He looked like he'd been through his own kind of storm.

"If it's okay with you, I think I'm gonna turn in for the night," he said, voice softer than usual. "We should probably be up early tomorrow if we wanna make the best time."

Ani nodded again, closing and locking the door behind him. Fenix made his way to the nearest bed and sat heavily, pulling off his boots and setting his hat on the small table. He looked up at her, concern flickering across his face. "You all right, kiddo?"

She nodded, brow furrowing as she remembered her father's voice calling her the same. "Yeah."

"Okay," he replied, taking in the way she stood—knees turned in, shoulders hunched, worry etched across her brow. He sighed, the sound barely more than a whisper, and fell back onto the bed, making no effort to cover himself with the thin blanket. Within moments, he was asleep, snoring softly before Ani had even laid down herself.

22

The first light of dawn crept across the horizon as Ani and Fenix mounted up, the streets of Paradise Wells already stirring with the quiet bustle of shopkeepers opening their doors. Fenix drew in a long breath of the cool morning air, holding it for a moment before letting it out in a heavy sigh. "Gonna be a good day," he said, his tone somewhere between hope and habit, a soft scowl creasing his face.

"How long until we reach Brimhall?" Ani asked, glancing down the sunlit street.

"Well, that depends on how fast we travel, and how little we run up against on the way." Fenix paused, considering the road ahead. "We keep a good pace and the road's clear, only rest a couple hours at night. Should be there by tomorrow morning." He caught the flicker of concern on Ani's face and offered a reassuring nod. "Don't worry. We'll get there."

Ani nodded, swinging up onto her horse. As she settled into the saddle, she realized she'd never given the animal a name. "I was thinking Dusty," she said, running her hand along the horse's neck.

"Dusty?" Fenix echoed, a smirk tugging at his lips.

"Yeah," she replied, a small smile breaking through. "For a name."

Fenix chuckled. "Okay. Good as any, I suppose."

"We have Dirtweed and Dusty," Ani said, the faintest trace of warmth in her voice.

Fenix grinned, the sound of his laughter light in the morning air. "Well. That settles it. They're best friends now."

"Exactly," Ani replied, nudging Dusty forward to follow as Fenix led the way out of town.

The morning sun climbed fast, burning away the last of the night's cool as Ani and Fenix rode out, the horizon already shimmering with heat. By midmorning, the temperature had soared—ninety, then pushing a hundred. Sweat trickled down Fenix's back, soaking into his shirt beneath the duster. It was shaping up to be one of those days where the wastes felt like a living thing, pressing down on them with every mile.

They passed an abandoned outpost, two buzzards perched atop the sagging roof, watching with hungry patience as the riders moved by. Off to the side, a well sat dry and useless, a white X painted across its front—a warning to any desperate enough to hope for water.

The next mile was silent, the only sound the steady clop of hooves and the distant buzz of insects. The heat pressed down, relentless. Fenix lifted his hat, wiping sweat from his brow, then used it to shield his eyes as he scanned the horizon. Something flickered in the distance—a shimmer, like a mirage rising off the baked earth.

Ani caught up, falling in beside him. "What is it?"

Fenix kept his gaze fixed on the wavering trail of dust. "Drifter?"

"Maybe nothin'." He watched the pattern, eyes narrowing. "Could be something." His voice was low, cautious. "We'll know soon enough. They're headed in our direction."

"Travelers?" Ani asked, her tone uncertain.

"Maybe." Fenix's hands tightened on the reins. Whoever it was, they were moving fast—too fast for comfort. In the wastes, speed meant trouble. Either you were chasing, or you were running. And whoever was out there, they were coming straight for them.

Then, from the corner of his eye, a glint of light flashed from a ridge off to their right. Fenix's gut tightened. "Oh hell…"

No sooner had the words left Fenix's lips than the earth around them erupted—dirt and debris launching skyward as a series of hidden trapdoors sprang open. Like desert roaches, a dozen figures burst from the ground, clad in tattered dusters and makeshift breathing masks, faces lost behind layers of cloth and grime. Their howling screams cut through the morning heat.

Fenix yanked back on the reins, his horse rearing up, hooves pawing at the air as the ambush closed in. Ani froze, heart hammering, as Dusty danced sideways, nostrils flaring in panic.

114

In a blink, they were surrounded—twelve barrels leveled at them from every direction.

"Drifter!" Ani yelped, the word cracking out like a gunshot.

Fenix kept one hand tight on the reins, the other rising slowly, palm open. He didn't dare move for his gun.

None of the men moved, their weapons steady.

"Drifter?" Ani's voice trembled behind him.

"Don't do a thing," Fenix said, eyes never leaving the two men in front. "Do not reach for your gun."

One of the men's gazes drifted to Ani, lingering.

"We're just passing through," Fenix continued, his voice steady but low. "Girl's family passed a week back. We're just making our way to Brimhall. We ain't got much, but you're welcome to it."

"If we wanted your supplies, we'd take 'em off your corpses," the man in front growled, his voice muffled beneath the mask.

Fenix squinted through the sunlight, taking in the thick goggles— round, pitch black, hiding any hint of humanity.

"Give us the girl."

Ani felt a cold spike of fear stab through her gut, her knuckles whitening as she clutched the reins.

"Fenix..."

Fenix tensed, mind racing through every possible outcome. He swallowed, never breaking the other man's gaze. "Two gold."

"Fenix?" Ani's voice was wet with panic, scraping at his heart.

"I don't ask again," the masked man growled.

"And I could kill you and at least three more of you before you take me down," Fenix replied, voice flat. "Or—you give me two gold, and all of you get to leave with the girl."

"Fenix, what are you doing?" Ani's voice was barely a whisper.

"This is the only way we both leave alive," he said, eyes still locked on the leader, his peripheral vision tracking the men on either side. He could feel the heat building in Ani's palms behind him.

"Are we good?" Fenix asked, his hand inching ever-so-slightly closer to his pistol.

The next two breaths stretched into eternity, the desert holding its breath as he sold his companion to a waking nightmare.

Then, finally, the man nodded to a reaper behind them and reached into his duster.

The next moment, chaos erupted. Ani was yanked screaming from Dusty's back, her hands wrenched behind her and a rough sack pulled down over her head. Fenix sat frozen in the saddle, listening to her cries as the reaper in front reached into his duster, pulled out a small pouch, and tossed two silvers into the dirt between them. The man nodded to his crew and let out a shrill, ear-splitting scream before spurring his horse and tearing off into the wastes.

Behind him, another reaper slung Ani over the back of his horse, punching the sack hard enough to silence her. Her body went limp. In seconds, she was bound hand and foot, lashed tight, and the whole pack thundered away, dust trailing behind.

Fenix's hand clenched around the grip of his pistol, knuckles white, as he watched the riders vanish in a cloud of grit. When the last of them disappeared over the rise, he slid down from his horse, boots sinking into the hot dirt. He stared at the two pieces of silver glinting in the sand, then bent down, scooping them up and bouncing them in his palm. He looked to the horizon, the dust still hanging in the air, before dropping the coins into his pocket.

He paused, hand on Dirtweed's reins, looking the old horse in the eye. "I hope I know what I'm doing, buddy, or this is gonna be a real short trip for us…" Dirtweed lifted his head, snorting as if in answer.

Fenix spat into the dirt, voice low and bitter. "Fucking reapers…"

23

Fenix waited until the last of the dust faded on the horizon before reaching down to pat Dirtweed's neck. "All right, Dirtweed. You ready for what may very well be our last ride?" The old horse shifted beneath him, muscles tense and uncertain.

"Yeah," Fenix muttered, eyes fixed on the trail of dust rising up in the distance. "Let's go get her..."

He kicked his heels into Dirtweed's side and shouted, "HYAH!" The horse lunged forward, launching into a full gallop.

For the next three hours, Fenix rode as hard as he dared, pushing Dirtweed to the edge but careful not to break him. The sun climbed higher, the heat pressing down like a blacksmith's hammer. He knew where he was headed—a reaper camp rumored to squat on the edge of Paradise Crater. He'd heard stories, half-truths and tall tales, but out here, sometimes the stories were all you had to go on. This time, he hoped the stories were true.

As midday bled into the sky, Fenix slowed Dirtweed to a stop, both of them lathered in sweat. He climbed down, rummaged through his sack, and pulled out two containers of water. He drained one in a single pull, then poured the other into a foldout bowl for Dirtweed, letting the horse drink deep. When they'd finished, he popped two hydration tabs into his mouth and gave one to Dirtweed. Then he pulled up his cowl, covering his face against the furnace wind. "Sorry, buddy. This ain't gonna be fun for either of us..." He climbed back up and nudged Dirtweed into a trot.

For the next three hours, Fenix rode straight through the worst of the sun, breaking the first rule of survival in the wastes. The heat was merciless, baking him beneath his duster, sweat pouring down his back. Even with the sunshade draped over them, the air felt like fire in his lungs. The hydration tabs had long since sweated away, and he could feel the heat radiating up from Dirtweed's body. He knew the reapers would have stopped, waiting out midday in the shade. They were crazy, but not stupid. That was his only advantage.

He couldn't have stopped Ani from being taken. That was never an option. If he'd tried, they both would have ended up dead—or worse. He'd made a gamble, bartering his own life for hers, hoping to live long enough to get a single shot at getting her back. It was a risk greater than she could have known, and he knew the only reason he was still breathing was because the reaper in charge knew it would cost lives to take him down. He'd played a dangerous hand and come out alive. Now, he was risking it all again, riding through the blistering heat to beat the reapers to their camp and have enough time to set up his attack.

24

By the time Fenix reached the reaper camp, the sun had finally begun to dip, its glare easing just enough for him to fold away his sunshade. The heat still pressed down, but it was no longer the kind that threatened to kill. He could feel the warning signs of sun-sickness gnawing at him—skin dry as old parchment, a dizzy nausea swirling in his head, fever burning beneath his shirt. He knew he'd pay for this ride in the days to come, but it was nothing compared to what Ani would face if he failed.

The camp itself sprawled across a shallow basin, ringed by the broken skeletons of old mesquite and the rusted hulks of scavenged wagons. Twenty-odd structures, thrown together from scavenged sheet metal, warped planks, and sun-bleached tarps, formed a loose circle around a central yard. In the middle, a heavy iron cage squatted in the dust, its bars blackened and bent from years of use. The ground was churned to powder by boots and hooves, and the stench of sweat, blood, and old fire hung thick in the air. A makeshift corral stood at the edge of camp, a handful of gaunt horses shifting restlessly inside. Beyond that, a single rutted road snaked away toward the horizon.

Fenix slowed Dirtweed to a halt at the edge of the camp, climbing down and feeding the horse another hydration tab. He wrapped the reins around the saddle horn, then set to work—unloading every round of ammunition from his bag, checking his rifle and both pistols, making sure each was loaded and ready. He moved quickly, knowing he had only a short window before the reapers emerged from their midday hiding and the rest of the pack arrived.

He scanned the camp, counting the buildings, noting the lack of sentry posts or watchtowers. No one in their right mind would attack a reaper den head-on. "You, you are, you dumbass. That's who…" he muttered, eyeing the hatch leading down into the tallest building.

Fenix climbed the warped slats to the roof, rifle slung over his shoulder, and crawled to the edge. From up high, he could see the whole camp laid out beneath him: the tangled maze of alleys between shacks, the flicker of movement behind torn curtains, the glint of steel at the cage's edge. He laid out his ammo, double-checked his weapons, then pulled his hat low and let himself rest in the thin sliver of shade the roof offered. He drifted in and out of uneasy sleep, ears tuned to every sound, the taste of citrus from a dissolving hydration tab lingering on his tongue.

Hours passed. Then, a sound caught his ear—distant at first, then growing. He rolled to his stomach, peering over the edge. A half-mile out, a cloud of dust rose into the air. A horn sounded, a long, low blast that sent a ripple through the camp.

Fenix took a deep breath, steadying his nerves. He reached for his rifle, chambered a round, and settled in to wait. The time for rest was over. The reckoning was about to begin.

25

Ani came to in darkness, the world muffled and close. Shouts echoed through the haze, distant and distorted by the rough canvas sack cinched over her head. Each jolt of the horse beneath her sent a spike of pain through her gut, the rhythm of hooves pounding out a merciless tattoo. Her hands, bound tight to her ankles, had long since gone numb. Her arms tingled with pins and needles, her shoulders aching from the awkward angle. Every breath was a struggle, ribs throbbing as if something inside her had cracked. She had no sense of time, no idea how far she'd been carried into the wastes.

"Two gold and you get to leave with the girl."

The words circled in her mind, sharp as broken glass. Betrayal burned in her chest, hotter than the desert sun. For weeks, she'd trusted him—shared secrets, shared hope, shared the long, hard road. She'd thought they were partners. Now, the truth cut deeper than any blade: he'd traded her away for a handful of coins, just to save his own skin. Tears slipped down her cheeks, lost in the stifling dark, her sobs broken by the relentless bouncing of the horse.

Somewhere ahead, a chorus of howls rose up, wild and triumphant. The horse slowed, the air thick with the stink of sweat and fear. Riders screamed back and forth, voices blending into a savage chant.

"I bring a gift for Brona!"

The words sent a chill crawling up Ani's spine. She didn't need to know who Brona was to understand what it meant to be a "gift" in the wastes.

"Put her with the others. Brona can have first take when he returns." "You heard him. Put her with the others."

Rough hands untied her ankles, and she was hauled from the saddle, slung over a shoulder like a sack of grain. Blood rushed back into her feet in a storm of needle-pricks, each step from her captor jarring her battered body. She gasped as the man shifted his grip, squeezing the air from her lungs.

"Stop moving," a voice growled, low and mean.

A gate squealed open, metal scraping against metal, and then she was dropped—hard—onto packed earth. Pain flared in her arm and she cried out, only to be silenced by a boot to the ribs.

"Shut it!" the voice barked, and she curled in on herself, breath ragged.

A moment later, the sack was ripped from her head. Blinding light stabbed her eyes. She blinked, vision swimming, and made out the blurred shape of a youth in scavenger's patchwork—dirty, sunburned, a sneer twisting his mouth. He stared at her with a hunger that made her skin crawl, a snarl carved deep into his lips. Ani stared back, heart pounding, as the world of the wastes closed in around her.

"Please—" Ani's voice cracked, but the youth only kicked at the dirt, sending a spray of dust and pebbles against her legs. He spat, a wet, contemptuous sound, then turned away, hands already reaching for the heavy iron latch. The cage door clanged shut, the lock snapping home with a finality that echoed through the barren camp.

Ani watched him go, her vision slowly sharpening as the sun's glare pressed through the bars. The world outside was a patchwork of ruin—a handful of shacks cobbled together from scavenged wood and rusted metal, sun-bleached cloth flapping in the wind. She scanned the settlement, mind racing for any hope of escape, but the futility of it pressed in on her like the heat. The cage was welded iron, the gate secured with a thick brass lock. Around her, the ramshackle buildings offered no cover, and a half-dozen men lounged nearby, their eyes crawling over her with the same hunger as the youth's.

She forced herself to look away, but movement caught her eye. A flap on one of the shacks snapped open, and a hulking man stepped out, a curved blade glinting in his fist. Sunlight flashed crimson along the edge. "You!" he barked, his voice slicing through the camp. The tableful of men jerked to attention.

"Bring the new haul to the salt room."

The men grumbled, but two stood and trudged toward a nearby structure. Ani watched, heart pounding, as the big man stepped aside to let them pass. His gaze lingered on her, a black-toothed grin spreading across his face—a promise of cruelty. Then one of the men emerged, carrying something that twisted Ani's insides to ice: a torso, limbless and headless, pale flesh mottled and slack. The other followed, arms loaded with severed limbs, swinging them like firewood.

They vanished between the buildings, leaving Ani staring after them, horror and nausea roiling in her gut. The big man's grin widened, then he turned and disappeared inside.

Ani scooted back until the iron bars pressed into her spine. She drew her knees up, hugging them tight, chin buried between her arms. The world shrank to the cage, the heat, and the taste of fear in her mouth. "Why?" she whispered, voice trembling. "Why did you do this? Why?"

26

It wasn't long before the reaper cries echoed up to the rooftop where Fenix lay hidden. The raiding party had returned, their prize in tow.

Through the cracked, makeshift scope—little more than a battered pipe and two warped lenses lashed together with wire and melted cloth—Fenix watched the procession wind its way into camp. He scanned the line of horses until his gaze caught on the last one: Ani's limp form draped over the saddle like a sack of grain. He pulled his eye from the glass, letting his gaze drift to the splintered edge of the roof. He knew enough about reaper ways to understand what came next. In their world, hierarchy was everything. The warden—whoever held that bloody title—claimed first rights to every haul: supplies, coin, flesh. The position was never given, only taken, and always at a cost. In-clan skirmishes were constant, each challenger vying for dominance, the victor earning control and the spoils that came with it.

Fenix's jaw tightened. He knew what happened to those taken by reapers. Some of the larger clans ran what the wastes called "people farms"—the name as plain and grim as the reality. Men and women, penned and bred, harvested piece by piece for food, for pleasure, for sport. He'd heard stories of survivors, if you could call them that, living for months without limbs, their bodies slowly whittled away until there was nothing left to give. The tales about the women were worse—stories that made even the hardest drifters flinch.

He was lucky, and he knew it. Lucky he wasn't the one slung over a horse, or worse, scattered among the bags. He'd played a dangerous game, refusing to back down when the reapers came. If he'd shown weakness, he'd be dead already. The smart move would have been to take the silver and ride hard for the horizon, leaving the girl and the job behind. But Fenix had never been accused of being smart. Instinct and a stubborn sense of duty had kept him alive this long, and now, lying on the roof with the sun baking his back, he knew exactly why he was still here. If he wasn't, Ani's fate would be the kind that haunted even the worst nightmares.

He forced himself to look back through the scope. The reapers had reached the camp, dust trailing behind them. Another cloud rose up in the distance—more trouble on the way. "Shit," Fenix muttered, low and bitter. He'd have to wait, bide his time, and hope things didn't go south before he could act.

"I bring a gift for Brona!" one of the reapers howled, the words carrying on the hot wind.

Fenix watched the next few minutes unfold through the battered scope. He saw them drag Ani from the horse, saw her kicked down in the dirt, saw the cage door slammed and locked behind her. 'Good,' he thought grimly. If she was in the cage, it meant the warden wasn't in camp yet. That meant he had time—time to recover from the brutal ride, time to get his head straight. He fished the last hydration tab from his pocket and let it dissolve on his tongue, the bland citrus taste a small comfort as it worked its way into his blood. He needed to get his fever down, needed to keep the shakes at bay. If he lost control now, if the hallucinations started, he'd be no use to anyone. And out here, there was no room for mistakes—not the kind that ended with you muttering in a closet, waiting for death to find you.

27

The day dragged on, the sun beating down mercilessly through the iron bars of the cage. The reapers offered Ani no comfort—not a drop of water, not a scrap of shade. She tried digging into the packed earth beneath her, but after only a few inches, her fingers struck cold iron. Defeated, she stripped off her vest and draped it over her head and arms, curling up as best she could beneath the meager shield. The heat pressed in, relentless, and she could feel her skin blistering beneath the sun's fury. For hours, she lay there, half-dreaming, half-cooking, until exhaustion finally pulled her under.

A blaring horn jolted her awake. She shoved the vest aside and blinked into the harsh light, her mouth dry as bone.

"Brona returns!!"

The words echoed through the camp, and Ani's tongue scraped painfully against the roof of her mouth as she swallowed. Men poured from the shacks, each one pausing just long enough to let their gaze linger on her before hurrying on. She pulled her vest back on, wincing as the leather scraped her sunburned skin. The youth from earlier swaggered toward her, the same sickening sneer twisting his lips.

He stopped just outside the cage, eyes locked on hers. Ani stared back, clutching her vest closed.

A cracked smile split his face. "We're waiting…"

She felt a ripple of dread crawl up her arms, her skin prickling with pain.

"First Brona. Then everyone."

The hollowness inside her deepened as the boy's smile widened and his hand drifted to his belt, a twisted pleasure flickering in his eyes. Ani's stomach turned. She snatched up a small rock at her feet and hurled it at him. It clanged off the bars and landed in the dust. The boy only grinned wider, then turned at the sound of shouting and hurried away.

Ani slumped back against the bars, a hot tingle buzzing in her palms. She wanted to let the fire loose, to burn the whole camp to ash, but she knew it would do no good. Even if she managed to scorch the boy, she was still trapped—iron and brass holding her fast. She pressed her knees to her chest, chin buried between her arms, and tried to think of a plan, any plan. But the heat, the pain, and the hopelessness pressed in from all sides.

"God damn you, Fenix…" she whispered, her voice barely more than a breath, lost in the endless, sun-blasted silence.

28

The sun had finally dipped behind one of the shacks, casting a thin sliver of shade into the cage. Ani huddled in the narrow respite, her skin raw and burning, the sting of broken blisters running in hot rivulets down her back. Every movement sent a jolt of pain through her, but she forced herself to stay alert as the sound of excited voices drifted closer.

A group emerged from between the ramshackle buildings—a towering reaper in battered armor, chest-length dreadlocks swinging, leading a handful of others. The leader's gauntlets were studded with riveted blades, a heavy duster trailing behind, and a grisly collection of scalps hung from his belt. He stopped at the cage, staring through oversized goggles before pulling them away and lowering his mask. His face was a patchwork of scars and pockmarks, a jagged line running from his mouth up behind his scalp. His eyes lingered on Ani, cold and appraising, before he uttered two words that made her blood run cold.

"Open it."

Ani felt the heat building in her palms, the old urge to fight rising up, but she knew the odds. One of the men stepped forward, key in hand, and unlocked the cage. As the leader pulled the door open, the man with the key barely had time to step aside before his body jerked, a spray of blood and bone splattering the dirt—a gunshot echoing through the camp.

Chaos erupted. One by one, the reapers fell, bullets whistling through the air, dropping them before they could react. Ani stood frozen, watching in slow motion as the men scrambled for cover, confusion and panic breaking their ranks. Someone screamed, "ATTACK!" and the leader spun, drawing a massive pistol and crouching low, firing wildly as more bodies hit the ground.

Gunfire exploded around the cage, the air thick with smoke and the sharp tang of blood. Ani dropped to a crouch, arms over her head, instinctively shielding herself from the hail of bullets. For a moment, she forgot the fire in her hands, forgot escape—her only thought was to survive the storm raging around her.

29

Fenix had drifted in and out of uneasy sleep for hours, the heat and exhaustion gnawing at his mind. Another blast from the horn jolted him awake, and the words he'd been waiting for rang out across the camp: "Brona returns!"

Blinking grit from his eyes, Fenix pressed his face to the battered scope—little more than a pipe and two warped lenses lashed together with wire and melted cloth. He watched the returning riders, his gaze locking on the warden: a hulking brute clad in metal-bound leather, spikes and blades jutting from his armor, a mask torn from some apocalyptic nightmare. The horse beneath him looked small by comparison. Fenix watched as the warden dismounted, his presence shifting the mood of the camp. Even without hearing the words, Fenix could read the tension in the way the warden's gaze flicked toward the cage.

He kept the scope glued to the warden as the man stalked through the alleys, slipping in and out of shadow, until he emerged in the open space by the cage. Fenix didn't let the man's skull leave the center of his sights for a single breath.

The warden stopped short of the cage, unblinking, then stepped aside as another reaper moved forward and unlocked the door. This was the moment Fenix had been waiting for. He couldn't risk making his move too soon—if he dropped the reapers before the cage was open, Ani would be trapped, and the lock on his pistol wouldn't crack that kind of problem. He had to wait for the perfect instant.

As the man with the key stepped forward, Fenix did a quick headcount—twenty-three. He drew a slow, steady breath, exhaled, and squeezed the trigger. The first bullet flew, and the chaos began.

30

Ani watched as the reaper camp dissolved into chaos. Gunfire cracked through the dusk, each shot dropping another reaper in a spray of dust and blood. Panic swept the yard—men trampled one another, desperate to escape the invisible death cutting them down. In the first wild seconds, nearly a dozen fell before anyone even knew where the bullets were coming from. Then, at last, the survivors rallied, returning fire in a blind, furious volley.

A reaper near the cage jerked violently, half his neck erupting in a crimson mist. Ani stared, transfixed, as he collapsed, eyes bulging, mouth working uselessly at the air as blood bubbled from the gaping wound.

The warden, face twisted with rage, slammed the cage door shut. He started toward the tall, battered tower where the shots rang out—then hesitated, doubling back to snap the lock in place. Another reaper dropped, and then, for a heartbeat, the gunfire ceased. The camp held its breath, the silence sharp as a knife, before the shouts and screams surged back, drowning out the quiet.

"They're in the tower!" the warden bellowed, voice raw as he charged toward the source of the attack, boots pounding over the blood-soaked earth.

Atop the roof, Fenix set the rifle aside and drew both pistols, thumbing back the hammers with a practiced flick. He moved fast to the hatch, nerves tight as wire. Only half the reapers were down— enough left to make a bloodbath. One reaper was trouble; a dozen, wild-eyed and desperate, were a death sentence. "Don't fuck this up," he muttered, voice barely a breath, and hauled open the hatch.

Inside, darkness swallowed everything. The sun's glare still burned in his eyes, leaving him blind as he dropped into the black. He knew the reapers would have the advantage—goggles off, eyes already tuned to the gloom. He'd be stumbling for minutes before he could trust his sight, and in that time, he'd either be dead or close enough to taste it.

The stairway down was so steep it might as well have been a ladder. Fenix took the first steps steady, then guessed at the rest, boots scraping wood as he descended into the pitch.

By the time his feet hit the floor, the shouting below had reached a fever pitch. The first of the reapers burst in, boots pounding toward the stairs. Two more behind, less than a minute to spare.

He squeezed his eyes shut, forcing them to adjust. Thin blades of sunlight slipped through warped slats in the walls, just enough to paint the outlines of the room: a mound of clothing and shoes in one corner, scattered relics of the old world, a half-built hydration pump, coils of metal tubing. The pile of personal effects—hundreds of them—spoke of all the souls who'd never left this place. "Fucking reapers..." he growled.

His hands tightened on the pistols' grips. He pressed himself to the wall, just off the doorway. The first reaper barreled in, boots slamming the floor. Fenix leveled his pistol and fired, the shot echoing like thunder in the dark. The man pitched forward, a hole blown through his back. The next spun at the sound, just in time to catch a bullet under the eye—his skull bursting open as he crashed to the floor. Two more shots, quick and cold, punched through the third reaper's chest, a final round snapping his head sideways as he crumpled in the doorway.

More shouts erupted from below as Fenix rushed the doorway, pistols drawn, spinning into the next room with both barrels leveled. The thunder of gunfire echoed through the battered building, driving the reapers into a frenzy. Screams ricocheted off the walls as another six men charged in, boots pounding, eyes wild with panic and bloodlust.

Fenix fought his way downward, each shot measured. He moved through the charging group, pistols barking in the gloom—never wasting a bullet, every round finding its mark. Bodies dropped in his wake, the acrid tang of gunpowder mixing with the stench of fear and sweat. He paused only to reload, hands steady even as chaos raged around him, then pressed on, continuing his path through the storm of violence.

By the time Fenix reached the bottom, ten more reapers had fallen to his guns. He paused, letting his eyes adjust to the thin light bleeding through the open doorway. The shouting outside had faded, replaced by the nervous calls of survivors urging each other to go inside and see what had become of their kin. Hesitation hung thick in the air. Then the warden's voice boomed, echoing through the camp: "Fucking COWARDS!"

A gunshot cracked, followed by the heavy thud of a body hitting the ground. Fenix tensed. He knew the reapers would burn their own enclave to the ground just to kill him, and if he got caught inside, a fight with the warden would end with him at the mercy of those monstrous arm blades. He edged toward the door, pressing himself against the heated wood, and risked a glance through two warped slats.

The warden stood just beyond, the body of a reaper sprawled at his feet. Another man was backing away, hands raised, as the warden leveled a pistol and shot him down. Two more turned and fled between the buildings. Fenix checked his pistols—thirty rounds spent, only six left: four in one, two in the other. The rest of his cylinders were empty. "Ah, shit," he muttered, leaning out and firing two shots at the warden. A cry rang out, followed by three gunshots in return. Four bullets left.

Splinters exploded from the doorframe as two rounds slammed into the wood beside him. "You hide like a sand-rat!" the warden roared. "You hide in OUR walls!"

Fenix fired again, the bullet pinging harmlessly off the warden's metal armor. Laughter bellowed out. "You die like the rest! I'll peel the flesh from your bones while I cook you alive, meat!"

"Oh, fuck it," Fenix growled, spinning out of the doorway and charging full tilt at the hulking man. He leveled his pistol, firing the last two rounds as he closed the gap. One shot went wide, the other punched into the warden's side, just beneath the leather armor. The warden howled in rage as Fenix swung the pistol at his head.

But the warden moved with brutal speed, sidestepping and slashing out with a blade. Searing pain tore across Fenix's back, from shoulder to hip, flesh splitting wide. He staggered, back arching as agony ripped through him, and dropped to his knees, the world spinning in a haze of blood and dust.

A thunderous roar split the air behind Fenix, boots pounding heavy against the earth. He felt the ground tremble beneath him, the vibration crawling up through his bones. Blood ran hot down his back, soaking his shirt. The pounding feet closed in—almost on top of him—when he spun, raising his pistol in a single, desperate motion. He fired, sending his last bullet straight up through the warden's chin and out the back of the skull.

The reaper stopped, bladed arm poised to strike, anger twisting into confusion as death pulled the light from his eyes. A breath later, the massive brute pitched forward, crashing into the dirt with a final, heavy thud.

Fenix edged away, sliding backward in the dust. His gaze fell on the ruin of skull and brain pooling beneath the warden's head. He pulled himself up to a seated position, the pistol slipping from his hand to the ground beside him. For a moment, he just breathed—then movement caught his eye, and he braced himself for whatever fate the wastes had left for him.

Ani heard the gunfire slow, the echoes fading into a hush broken only by the drip of blood from the corpses scattered around her cage. For a long moment, she stayed huddled, heart pounding, until the silence pressed in. Gathering her courage, she rose and edged to the door. The reaper in charge had locked the cage, but in his panic, hadn't checked the clasp. Ani reached out, pulled down, and the lock fell open. She listened—shouting, then two sharp gunshots, then silence, then a single shot. Nothing.

A lone reaper burst into the clearing, eyes wild, but barely glanced at her as he sprinted past. Ani flinched, hands up, but he was gone in a heartbeat. She slipped from the cage, the door creaking as she pushed it open, and started toward the tall building at the camp's heart.

As she crept through the camp, the quiet pressed in, broken only by distant shouts and the stench of blood. Whoever had attacked the reapers was either more dangerous than they were—or maybe, just maybe, someone who could help her escape. She'd never heard of anything worse than the reapers, but in the wastes, there was always something.

A cry—raw, angry, and pained—cut through the stillness. Ani crept closer, edging to the corner of a battered shack. She peered around just in time to see the reaper leader swing his bladed arm in a vicious arc, cutting deep into the back of a bloodied figure. The man staggered, back arching in agony. The leader paused, hand pressed to a wound above his hip, then roared and charged, blade raised for the killing blow.

A gunshot split the air. The back of the leader's skull exploded in a spray of bone and hair, and the giant stiffened, then crashed to the dirt. Ani's gaze shifted from the corpse to the wounded man on the ground—and in that instant, she recognized Fenix, battered and bloodied, but alive.

She rushed to him, nearly stumbling as she dropped to his side. "How bad is it?"

Fenix winced, pain etched deep in his face. "It's bad…"

"Why?"

Fenix stared up at Ani, pain etched deep into the lines of his face. The question hung between them, raw and trembling.

"Why…? Why did you leave me? Why did you let them take me?" Ani's voice broke, her lip quivering as a single tear traced the grime on her cheek. "Why?"

He met her gaze, swallowing hard. "I… There was no other way that was going to play out." He paused, wincing as he tried to shift his weight, the agony across his back nearly blinding. "If I hadn't let them take you, or if either of us tried to fight it… they would have slaughtered us right there. We'd be nothing but meat in the dirt. I took a gamble." He winced again, breath catching. "I never would have let them hurt you. I swear it. I can't imagine what you thought, and more than you can know, I'm sorry. But if I hadn't…" A tear slipped from his eye, cutting a clean line through the dust. "I'm sorry. I'm sorry, Ani."

Ani searched his face, tracing the pain and regret in his eyes. Slowly, she nodded, another tear following the dirty trail down her cheek. "I thought—"

"No," Fenix interrupted, voice rough. "Never." Another tear fell, a soft sob breaking through. "Never." He reached out, grasping her hand, squeezing tight as if to anchor himself to the world.

Ani wrapped her other hand around his, holding on. "What do I do?"

Fenix groaned, shifting with effort. "My pack. Get my pack."

"Okay. Where?"

"My horse." He peeled his gaze away, nodding to his left. "There's medicine, a sewing kit." A cough wracked him, drawing another wince. "Go."

"What if more come?"

He shook his head, voice low but certain. "They're gone. The rest… scattered. They won't return."

Ani nodded, slowly letting go before rising and sprinting toward the horses.

Fenix watched her go, the pain across his back a white-hot brand. He could feel the lightheadedness from blood loss, the world threatening to tilt away. There was medicine in his pack—a numbing salve, a coagulant paste. He'd been cut bad before, a scar across his side to prove it. But this… If Ani hadn't found him, or if she'd chosen to run, he figured he had maybe an hour before he bled out in the dust. Just seemed to keep being his lucky day…

Ani tore through the maze of battered shacks and tents, the chaos of the reaper camp fading behind her as she sprinted for the edge of the wastes. Her breath came in ragged bursts, heart hammering in her chest. She scanned the horizon, desperate, until her eyes landed on a lone horse standing against the backdrop of scorched earth and dying light.

"Dirtweed!" she called, her voice cracking through the stillness. The horse lifted its head, ears flicking at the sound. Ani didn't slow— she ran full tilt, boots kicking up dust, the world narrowing to the distance between her and that familiar shape. Dirtweed, as if sensing her urgency, started forward at a lazy amble, closing the gap.

Moments later, Ani swung herself up into the saddle, hands trembling as she gathered the reins. Without a backward glance, she wheeled the horse around and kicked into a gallop, racing back toward the camp and the wounded drifter who needed her now more than ever.

Fenix was drifting at the edge of consciousness, the world around him a blur of pain and dust. Then, through the haze, he caught the distant thunder of hoofbeats—heavy, urgent, drawing closer. Instinct took over. He fumbled for his pistol, fingers wrapping around the worn grip, but as he raised it, memory crashed in: the cylinder was empty. No bullets left. The weight of the weapon suddenly felt immense, useless. With a bitter exhale, he let the pistol slip from his grasp, the cold steel thudding softly against the earth as he braced himself for whatever new nightmare was approaching.

Ani yanked back on Dirtweed's reins, bringing the weary horse to a halt in a swirl of dust. She swung down in one fluid motion, boots hitting the cracked earth. In a heartbeat, she had Fenix's battered side bag off the saddle and was digging through its contents, hands trembling. The air shimmered with heat and the coppery scent of blood.

"What am I looking for?" she called, voice tight, glancing over her shoulder. Fenix was slumped against a sun-bleached boulder, his breath ragged, eyelids fluttering. "Fenix!" she shouted, panic threading through her words.

He forced his eyes open, blinking against the glare. For a moment, he seemed lost—then memory returned, pain sharpening his features. "Small pouch. Leather," he rasped. "Numbing salve first. Little green vial, no label. Sewing kit—same pouch. Medicine's in a metal screw-top. That's after."

"Okay," Ani said, voice barely steady as she pulled the supplies free. Her hands shook as she laid them out on the dusty ground. She'd never stitched a wound before—never done more than clean a scrape or wrap a sprain. The thought of sewing flesh made her stomach twist. "But... I don't—"

Fenix shifted, turning his battered back toward her, jaw clenched against the pain. "Just sew," he growled, voice rough as the wastes. "Don't think. Just do it."

She looked down, getting her first view of the wound. Her stomach turned over. From between his shoulder blades to just above his hip was a large gash, puffed fat bulging from between the peeled back folds of flesh. In the space where the gash ran across his spine, she could see the white bone of his vertebrae. "Oh, fuck."

He swallowed hard, voice barely more than a rasp. "Just sew."

Ani tore her gaze from the wound, hands shaking as she pulled the top off the vial of salve. She hesitated, staring at the thick green liquid. "How do I put this on?" she asked, voice small.

Fenix didn't answer. His head lolled, eyes already slipping shut, breath shallow.

"God damnit, Fenix." Ani gritted her teeth, forcing herself to steady. She tilted the vial, letting the salve trickle into the gash. Fenix flinched, a shudder running through him as the liquid seeped into torn flesh. Then, slowly, the skin around the wound faded numb, the pain receding until only a dull pressure remained.

Ani fumbled with the needle and thread, her heart pounding. "I've never done this," she whispered, voice trembling. "I don't know what I'm doing…"

"Just sew. One side to the other. Pull it together tight." His words were little more than a breath.

Ani threaded the needle, hands slick with sweat. She leaned in, the world narrowing to torn skin and crimson. The needle hovered above his back. "I don't know if I can do this."

"You have to." He drew in two ragged breaths. "Or I die."

"God damnit…" Ani swallowed, forcing down the fear. She took a deep breath, then pressed the needle through his skin, pulling it out the other side. She looped the thread, drew the edges together, and repeated—again and again, until the wound was closed, the bleeding slowed to a trickle. Ten minutes passed in a haze of blood and grit.

"It's done," she said at last, voice hoarse.

"Medicine," Fenix croaked.

"Okay." Ani grabbed the metal container, unscrewed the lid, and shook four pills into her palm. She pressed them into his waiting hand, her own fingers stained with blood and dust.

Ani eyed the pills for a moment, then pressed them into Fenix's palm, watching as he clumsily brought them to his mouth and chewed them down. He lay there on his side, jaw working, eyes half-lidded. When he finished, he croaked, "Water."

Ani fetched the battered canteen from Dirtweed's saddle, unscrewed the top, and knelt beside him. She poured a careful stream into his mouth—he gulped the first three swallows, but choked on the fourth, sputtering. She pulled the canteen away and capped it, worry flickering across her face.

"I need sleep," Fenix muttered, voice thick with exhaustion. "The medicine takes time, and the salve's gonna wear off in an hour or so. We stay here tonight. I'm no good to travel."

Ani hesitated, glancing at the door and the shadows beyond. "You're sure nobody's coming back?"

"Yes," he replied, voice flat. "The warden's dead. They're all dead."

"I saw one of them escape."

"Clanless," Fenix said, struggling to sit up. "He'll try and join another. He's already dead." He paused, breath hitching. "We need to get inside. Help me up."

Ani slipped her arms under his, lifting and steadying him until he was upright. She stood, hands out, uncertain. "Are you sure?"

He nodded, glassy-eyed and pale.

"Okay." She gripped his hands and hauled him to his feet. Together, they staggered toward the nearest shelter.

Inside, the place was little more than a shack: three rough cots, a chamber pot reeking in the corner, and a table with a few stubby wax candles. Ani helped Fenix to the closest cot, guiding him down. He let gravity do the rest, collapsing sideways, unconscious before his head hit the cloth.

For the next three hours, Ani sat at the end of his cot, ears straining for any sound from outside—wind, hoofbeats, voices. Only silence answered. When she was sure the night was safe, she slipped out to gather the horses. Dirtweed was right where she'd left him, and it didn't take long to find Dusty penned with the others. She opened the corral gate, ushered a few of the horses out, then led Dusty and Dirtweed back to the shack and tied them outside.

When she was done, Ani returned inside and took the cot beside Fenix. She told herself she'd stay awake, keep watch. But the day's fear and exhaustion pressed her down, and within minutes, she was asleep as well.

32

Torchlight danced with shadows across the stone surface, the fading glow disappearing into the pitch of the cavern above. The roaring echoes moments prior had faded to a low rumble, hundreds of hushed whispers filling the air with a low growl. Standing on a small outcropping overlooking the massive cave room stood the Prophet, his steeled gaze washing over the excited crowd of goblins and orcs. Slowly his hands lowered, ushering the murmurs to settle into a frenzied silence.

"A thousand years ago," he bellowed, his words echoing off the distant walls, "the great fires purged the world of those who sought desperately to destroy it." He paused, his gaze narrowing as it searched his flock below. "Disease, famine, WAR!!!"

A violent eruption of howls and screams roared up from the crowd.

"With their great machines, humanity brought death and chaos. Fear ruled man!" He paused, allowing the room to settle once more. "It was then that the great Merging showed us that the world was not to be ruled by man alone, and would not end, by man, *alone*. It brought forth the great hordes!"

Again, a roar lifted up, screams ripping through the air.

"Orc, and Goblin. True magic!!!"

The prophet lifted his hands, whispering a silent incantation as flumes of blue flames rose from his outstretched palms.

"But what did the humans do? Did they welcome us? Did they learn our ways, or make any attempt to coalesce? No... They instead branded us monsters, *witches*. They burned and slaughtered our kind, hunting and exterminating us. Our clans, our people, the horde, were all but exterminated, crushed like insects and driven to the caverns below. The elves were granted lands, and given cities in which to prosper, dwarves given their mountains in exchange for their knowledge of the great forge. But *our* ancestors were hunted. The Great Cleanse…"

The room fell silent as the memories of the Cleanse fell between them.

"For a generation, our kind were slaughtered and driven further and further underground, fighting to survive. Famine, darkness, nightstalkers. And then the great fires cleansed the hatred and burned away the pestilence sewn by humanity."

A great roar filled the cavern.

"But once again, we find ourselves pushed back to the shadows, relegated to our tiny lands in the north. Once again, we feel the weight of humanities foot pressed against our neck. And it is but a matter of time before they find a way to cleanse us again."

Slowly the prophet reached into his cloak, producing a small item on a thin chain.

"NO LONGER!!!" he screamed, holding the small usb key up into the air.

Rage echoed out, orc and goblin cries resounding, a battle cry filled with a thousand years of hatred and animosity.

"With this! *We* will reignite the flames of old. *We* will rain fire down upon humanity and *we* will once again cleanse this world of the disease that rots it. We will take what is ours. And this time, *we* will hunt them to the ends of the earth, and feast on their bones until none remain to challenge us again!"

The chamber erupted once more, the walls shaking from the sound, particles of dust and debris raining down onto the crowd below.

"Now go! Spread across the wastes. Gather your clans, ignite the horde and slaughter any who stand in your way. Tell them a *new* Cleanse is upon us and that we will rain down fire and dance in the ashes of humanity!"

The roar in the cavern grew to a deafening pitch, dirt and debris continuing to fall as the sound of hundreds of turned to charge into the wastes above.

33

The sun had long since slipped beneath the horizon by the time Ani's eyes fluttered open. The world was painted in the bruised blue of twilight, shadows stretching long across the battered floor. Her throat was raw, lips cracked from hours spent parched and caged beneath the merciless sun. Every muscle ached, her skin still burning with the memory of heatstroke twisting through her veins.

She shifted, slow and stiff, and caught sight of Fenix sitting on the edge of his cot across the dim room. He was little more than a silhouette, shoulders hunched, the lamplight catching on the battered line of his jaw.

"We should get moving," he said, voice rough as gravel, gaze fixed somewhere far away.

"But...?" Ani's voice was a croak, confusion threading through her exhaustion.

Fenix leaned to the side, exposing his back to the faint glow. Ani blinked, puzzled, then pushed herself upright, wincing at the pull of her own wounds. In the half-light, she saw the long gash that had nearly killed him—now scabbed over, the angry red faded to a deep pink.

"How?" she breathed, disbelief and relief mingling.

"Elven medicine," Fenix grunted, reaching for his shirt.

"Elven?" Ani echoed, still trying to make sense of how he could even sit up, let alone move.

"Yeah," he replied, pulling the shirt over his head with only a slight wince. "Elven. Hard to come by, and worth more than gold out here. But you see the difference." A smirk flickered across his lips. "It's the line between dying and keeping on. Only thing is, that was the last of it—so let's make damn sure nothing like that happens again." He paused, clearing his throat, bracing himself to stand. "Hell, maybe when this is all over, you and I can head north and re-up on it."

Ani managed a sad smile, the ache of recent days still heavy in her chest. "I'd like that."

"Yeah," Fenix replied, rising slow, steadying himself. "So would I."

"You sure you're good to ride?" she asked, concern threading her words.

"Been worse," he said, voice dry.

Ani nodded, watching as Fenix stepped out into the night. Through the open flap, she glimpsed the ocean of stars spilling across the sky, the wastes silent and endless beyond. Companion, she thought—the word echoing in her mind. He was a drifter, paid muscle, a man who should have left her behind. But he hadn't. He'd risked his life for her, more than once, and not for coin. Maybe for something else. Maybe for reasons neither of them could name.

As she rose and followed him into the warm hush of night, Ani felt something stir deep inside—a feeling she hadn't known since childhood. For the first time in a long while, she felt protected.

They left the reaper enclave behind, riding through the darkness and into the next day, stopping only when the sun's fury forced them to ground. By the time they reached Brimhall, the sky was painted in purples and pinks, the first stars waking above the horizon.

34

Brimhall barely deserved the name of town. Other than the squat saloon with its six-room inn perched above, a general store, and a handful of weather-beaten homes, there wasn't much to speak of. Around the center, folks had thrown together ramshackle shacks—dozens of crude shelters that changed hands as often as the wind changed direction. Most who passed through were either bound for bigger places like Corith or Aberdyne, or else ended up dead and forgotten in the dust. Brimhall was a pit stop, nothing more. But for Ani, still raw from her time in the reaper cage, and Fenix, his back a patchwork of scabs, it was as close to comfort as the wastes ever offered.

Fenix slowed Dirtweed to a halt in front of the saloon, a battered sign above the door reading "Alton's Tavern," the letters burned deep into the planks. He groaned before he even swung his leg over the saddle, nearly pitching forward as he hit the ground. Only the reins kept him from eating dirt.

"God damnit," he muttered, wrapping the reins around the iron hitching post. He gave Dirtweed a grateful pat. "Sorry, buddy. Thanks for the catch."

Dirtweed snorted, tossing his head as if to say he'd done it a hundred times before.

Ani slid down from her own horse, tying him up beside Dirtweed. She followed Fenix inside, boots heavy on the warped boards.

Inside, the saloon was a world of shadows and flickering candlelight. Deep crimson walls soaked up what little glow the wrought iron chandelier offered, thick candles casting shifting halos across the black ceiling. Fenix half-stumbled to the bar, dragging out a stool and climbing up with a wince. Ani trailed after, taking in the room's other denizens: two dust-caked drifters hunched in the back corner, eyes sharp and suspicious; a dark-skinned halfling with a younger woman perched on his lap, her gaze raking Fenix as he passed, then flicking to Ani with a sneer. Ani ignored her, too tired for backwater games.

"Two spirits and a water," Fenix grumbled to the barkeep as he shuffled over.

"Oh," Ani said, voice hoarse. "Just water."

"Wasn't for you," Fenix replied, not looking away from the bar.

Ani raised her hand, catching the barkeep's attention. "One water, please."

The man nodded, pouring out the spirits and sliding the glasses across. Fenix downed the first shot before the barkeep's hand had even left the glass. He paused, letting the burn settle, then tossed back the second in a single, practiced motion.

When the barkeep returned, Fenix tapped his hand on the bar, signaling for another round. The man nodded, already reaching for the bottle.

Ani watched, concern flickering across her face. "Are you sure you should?" she asked quietly. "Being injured and all."

Fenix took a long, rattling breath, the sound wet in his chest. "That's exactly why I should," he replied, voice rough as gravel.

She lifted her brows, a faint, resigned smile tugging at her lips. "Okay…"

The barkeep returned a moment later, filling the glasses again with a practiced hand. Fenix reached for the next shot, but paused, glancing up. "You got anything to eat?"

"Gots lizard stick and carrot stew," the man replied, voice flat. "Gots hare too, but it'll cost you."

Fenix considered, silent for a moment, then nodded. "Just give me two of the sticks." He glanced at Ani. "Guessing you're hungry?"

"I could eat," she said, lifting her glass of water and taking a sip, the coolness a balm to her cracked lips.

"Go on and make it three then."

"Yep," the barkeep replied, turning to the small heating unit at the end of the bar.

Ani let her gaze wander, taking in the long strand of orc tusks strung above the bottle display, each one yellowed and cracked, a grim trophy from another age. "Interesting place," she murmured.

"Yeah," Fenix replied, his voice distant. "Interesting…"

The barkeep returned, setting two battered metal plates on the bar. "Ten silvers or twenty creds."

Fenix snorted, a dry laugh escaping him. "You still accept credits here?"

"Buys supplies, same as ore."

"How much for a room?"

"That'd bring it to fifteen or thirty."

Fenix nodded, glancing sidelong at Ani. "I'm gonna let you get this one, on account of my injury."

Ani smirked, shaking her head as she dug out the silver coins and slid them across the bar.

"Upstairs, third room on the right," the barkeep said, voice as flat as the wastes.

Fenix exhaled heavily, grabbing the fourth glass and tossing it back in one motion. Then he lifted his plate, struggling to his feet. "If you don't mind, I'm gonna go on and turn in. Let this rye and the salve on my back work their magic."

Ani nodded, watching as he made his way toward the stairs, boots dragging across the warped floorboards.

"Where ya'll coming from?" the barkeep called as Fenix reached the bottom of the stairs, but Fenix only grunted in reply, too tired for stories, and disappeared into the shadows above.

Ani turned back to the barkeep, her voice rough from the road. "Huh? Oh." She glanced down at the half-eaten lizard stick on her plate, searching for words. "Uh, Blister Springs."

The barkeep's lips curled into a knowing smirk. "Blister Springs, eh. That's a hell of a trip." He paused, eyes narrowing with curiosity. "Where ya'll headed?"

"We're headed to…" Ani caught herself, careful not to give too much away. "Serenity."

The man let out a single, sharp laugh. "Serenity? Ya'll sure making one hell of an outta the way loop to get there if you're coming from Blister Springs."

"We had some things needed doing," Ani replied, voice guarded. She hesitated, then added, "Say. You know if the old caravan is still running out of Aberdyne?"

The barkeep nodded, a sly glint in his eye. "I reckon it is. Ain't been there myself in a hot minute, but I hear folks talking about it."

Ani reached for her water, her hand trembling just a bit. "Have you heard how the road is between here and Aberdyne?"

The barkeep shrugged, wiping a glass with a rag that had seen better days. "Same as always, I reckon."

"There haven't been any… attacks, or anything like that?" Ani pressed, her tone cautious.

"No more than usual." The man's gaze sharpened, suspicion flickering in his eyes. "Why? Ya'll expecting some trouble?"

"No!" Ani snapped, a little too quick. "Just… you know. It's been a while since either of us has made the trip. I know there's been problems with the reapers coming out of the crater recently. Better safe than sorry, you know. Just thought I'd ask."

"Hmph." The barkeep studied her for a long moment, as if weighing her words. "It should be fine."

"Thanks," Ani muttered, lowering her gaze to the plate. She finished off the lizard stick, washed it down with the last of her water, and made her way upstairs to the third room on the right.

The room was small, just a single bed and a battered chair. Fenix was already sprawled atop the mattress, boots still on, eyes closed. As Ani closed the door behind her, his voice rasped out, dry and cracked.

"Sorry. I gotta take the bed."

"It's fine," Ani replied, eyeing the padded chair in the corner.

"There's room if'n you want," Fenix added, eyes still shut. "Saved you space."

Ani glanced at the narrow strip of mattress beside him, then at the chair. "I think I'll stick with the chair. Thanks though."

"Suit yourself," he mumbled, unmoving.

Ani dropped into the chair, only to be jabbed by three stubborn springs—one in her back, another in her leg, and a third right in the seat. "Ow!" she yelped, springing to her feet. Fenix didn't even stir.

She rubbed the sore spots, glared at the chair, then sighed and sat on the edge of the bed. Fenix lay still, eyes closed. Ani pulled off her boots and stretched out, careful not to take up too much space. She lay there, staring up at the cracked ceiling, her arm pressed against his.

"Tell me more about the old world," Fenix murmured, startling her. She'd thought he was already asleep.

"You saw the videos at Belcor," she replied softly.

"I know. Just…" He let the silence stretch for three long breaths. "It'll help me fall asleep."

Ani smiled, letting out a slow sigh. "Before the great fires, before the Merge and the Cleanse, the world was all connected. They had machines called airplanes—hundreds of folks would climb inside, and it'd fly through the sky like a giant bird, taking you anywhere you wanted. You could ride one all the way from Newvada to Europa."

Fenix let out a low, amused sound.

"They had devices like our radios, but everyone had one. You could talk to anyone, anywhere, just by pulling it from your pocket. And did you know, they even sent people to the moon?"

"Really," he sighed, sleep thick in his voice. "Are they still there?"

"Maybe," Ani replied, a wistful smile on her lips. "For all we know, there's a whole society living up there."

"Hm," he murmured, the sound trailing off as sleep claimed him.

Ani watched him for a moment, then let herself relax, folding her arms over her stomach. She closed her eyes, letting the day's exhaustion pull her under, the stories of the old world drifting through her mind like distant, half-remembered dreams.

35

The tavern was empty when Ani and Fenix made their way downstairs the next morning. The hush of early light filtered through the dusty windows, catching on the motes that drifted in the still air. The night's rest had done Fenix good, and the elven salve on his back had worked its quiet magic—by the time he'd woken, most of the scab had sloughed off, leaving only a thin pink line where the wound had been deepest.

"I can't believe how well that works," Ani said, boots thudding softly on the old wooden floor as they crossed to the door.

"Whelp," Fenix replied, rolling his shoulders and feeling the difference. "There's something to be said about the elves' knowledge of medicine."

Ani nodded, pushing open the door. "I suppose it only makes sense. They do live for thousands of years." Sunlight splashed across her face, making her squint. The heat pressed down, already heavy. "Imagine how many times they must get sick or injured…"

"Yeah," Fenix said, lowering the brim of his hat as he stepped out into the glare. "Don't reckon they get sick all that often, to be honest. If they've got salves that can mend a wound like mine in a couple days, I bet they've got something that'll kill a cold in an instant."

"Suppose so," Ani replied, reaching out to pat her horse's muzzle, the animal's ears flicking at her touch.

Fenix walked up to Dirtweed, patting the horse on the jaw. "You ready, boy?" The horse looked back at him with a blank, unimpressed stare.

"Yeah," Fenix added, a wry smile tugging at his lips. "Me neither…" He unwrapped the reins and climbed up. "Let's get ourselves to Aberdyne. Should be there by midday if we keep our paces."

Ani nodded, pulling her own hat brim down low. Together, they rode out of Brimhall and back onto the main road, the wastes stretching before them in endless, sun-bleached silence. As they rode, Ani's thoughts drifted to home—her brother, her father, her mother. She missed them all, but it was her mother's face that lingered in her mind's eye, smiling through the haze of memory as the morning sun beat down and the world ahead shimmered with heat.

They rode for hours beneath the relentless sun, the wastes stretching out in all directions, empty and shimmering. Conversation drifted easily between them, the kind of talk that only comes after shared hardship. Fenix, usually guarded, found himself opening up—telling Ani about Thornbrush, the hard-edged little town out west where he'd grown up, and about the ancient ruins of Vegas, where machines with broken lights and rusted bones still whispered of a world that had burned away. He spoke of the Mojave Dunes, a sea of shifting rock and sand that could swallow a caravan whole, and the jagged mountains that marked the edge of the world, beyond which lay the dead sea.

Ani shared her own stories—scavenging runs with her family, tales her grandfather had passed down of lost cities and buried secrets, of societies that lived only in the flickering holovids she'd watched in the old facilities. They laughed, swapping memories and half-truths, letting the miles slip by beneath their horses' hooves as the empty road wound toward Aberdyne.

After a time, a shape began to rise on the horizon, growing taller as they drew near—a solitary structure, stark against the sky.

"What is it?" Ani asked, shading her eyes as the tower loomed overhead.

Fenix's gaze swept the land, sharp and wary. He watched for the telltale signs of trouble—dust kicked up by riders, sand shifted by something more than wind. His drifter's instincts were on high alert, sharpened by too many close calls. "It's an old solar tower," he said, nodding toward the·battered farmhouse slumped beside it. "Collected energy from the sun, back when folks thought they could outsmart the wastes." He followed the tower's length upward, noting the rusted brackets and the single black panel dangling by a bolt. Most of the panels had long since fallen away, scavenged or shattered by storms. His eyes dropped back to the farmhouse, scanning the gaping hole in the wall for any sign of movement, any hint of an ambush. He'd been cautious before, but after the reapers, he was downright jumpy.

"I wonder who used to live here?" Ani mused as they drew closer.

Fenix shrugged, moving his duster aside to reveal the worn grip of his revolver. "They're long dead by now. Guessing the wastes got 'em."

The thought brought Ani little comfort. Out here, comfort was a memory, and security a luxury that faded a little more with every sunrise. She glanced up as a pair of crows watched from the tower's peak, one of them cawing, the sound sharp and hollow in the stillness.

"We uh… we should probably pick up the pace a bit," Fenix said, his gaze lingering on the birds before shifting to the sun's position in the sky. "We got another two hours before we get there, and at this pace, we're gonna be cutting it close."

"We could stay here if we need?" Ani asked, eyeing the battered farmhouse and the looming solar tower, its shadow stretching long across the wastes.

Fenix glanced at the sagging structure, the wind rattling loose tin and sun-bleached boards. "Let's just get there," he said, voice low. He tapped his foot against Dirtweed's flank, nudging the horse into a quick trot.

For the next three hours, they pressed on, the world shimmering with heat. The road was empty, save for the distant shimmer of dust devils and the occasional vulture circling overhead. By the time they reached the outskirts of Aberdyne, they'd covered nearly fifty miles. The sun was a white-hot brand overhead, and the air shimmered with the promise of midday's worst.

"You ever been to Aberdyne?" Fenix asked as they rode toward the city's edge.

Ani's eyes widened as she took in the massive fence—an improvised wall of scavenged metal, warped planks, and rusted roof panels, stretching for miles in either direction, encircling the city like a battered crown. "No," she said, her gaze drifting to the heavy gates and the two guards standing watch. "Not before now."

Fenix smirked. "Ain't as big as Corith, but it's got everything a man—or a girl in your case—could need. Weapon stores, tincture shops, food, clothes. Even a dwarven smith, if you got the coin. Knives, swords, crossbows, you name it. All dwarven made. Pricey as hell, but worth it. Ain't nobody makes a blade like the dwarves— maybe the elves, but don't let them catch you saying that. Might end up with one inside you."

As they approached, the guards shifted uneasily, rifles in hand. One stepped forward, voice sharp. "Hold! State your business!"

Fenix didn't miss a beat. "Oh, you know. We're on vacation. Figured we'd have ourselves a nice little tour of the wastes, maybe swing by old Aberdyne and see how the nightlife is."

The guards exchanged a look. One growled, "Fucking drifters," and raised his rifle a hair.

Fenix brought Dirtweed to a stop, hands open. "Calm your tits. Girl and I are just here to resupply—some food, ammo, maybe a drink if we're lucky. I'm escorting this little lady to meet her folks over in Serenity." He nodded toward Ani. "I know the rules. No fightin', no killin', no thievin'. You won't have any trouble from us. None started by us anyhow."

The guards shared another look, then the first lowered his rifle, relaxing just a touch. "All right. Go on. Just stick to the rules and we'll be all good."

"Yes sir, boss," Fenix replied, earning another irritated glare.

Ani spoke up, drawing their attention. "Is the caravan still running between here and Serenity?"

"Yes ma'am," the guard replied, his tone softening.

"Yes ma'am," Fenix echoed, a teasing lilt in his voice, earning another glare.

Fenix nudged Dirtweed forward, the horse falling into a slow trot as the guards called out for the gates to be opened. A moment later, the massive doors groaned inward, revealing the city of Aberdyne—sprawling, sunbaked, and alive with a sallow, restless energy.

Almost at once, the scents of food and forge swept over them—smoke, hot metal, and the mouthwatering aroma of fresh bread and slow-cooked meats. Ani felt her mouth water as the smells of roasting hare, lizard sticks, and the rare treat of wild horse or desert coyote drifted through the air, mingling with the sharper tang of spices and rubs. Hunger gnawed at her, and she realized just how long it had been since her last real meal.

The streets of Aberdyne were alive with noise and movement, a chaos contained by the city's patchwork walls. Horse hooves clopped on packed earth, wagon wheels creaked and groaned, and the steady clang of a blacksmith's hammer rang out above the din. Vendors shouted over one another, hawking everything from dried fruit to battered tools, their voices rising in a melee of sales pitches that tangled in the dusty air. Shopkeepers called out from crooked doorways, and the crowd surged and shifted, everyone jostling for space.

At the city's edge, the buildings were little more than shacks—single-story structures crammed together, every inch of space claimed and built upon, as if the city itself was trying to keep the wastes at bay. But as Ani and Fenix rode deeper, the city grew upward: two- and three-story buildings, a handful even reaching four or five, rising above the jumble like battered sentinels. Ani remembered the capital from her childhood—brick and mortar, glass and iron, ornate doors and archways. Aberdyne was different: reclaimed wood, rusted metal, patched roofs, and a haze of dust that never seemed to settle. It was a city built for survival, not for beauty, and the heat pressed down on everything, relentless.

They passed endless shops and stalls—food vendors, curiosity dealers, brothels, and inns. Saloons spilled laughter and music into the street, while clothiers and weapon shops displayed their wares behind grimy windows. Ani caught sight of a central bank, its sign faded but proud, and a mail service boasting delivery anywhere in the wastes within two weeks. It was a city that had learned to endure, and as they moved through the bustle, Ani felt both the weight of the place and the strange comfort of being surrounded by life, even in the heart of the wastes.

"Looking for a good time drifter?"

Ani pulled her gaze away from the courier shop and lifted it to a second story balcony where three scantily clad women stood at the railing, their breasts nearly exposed beneath the thin cloth that loosely covered them. One of them smiled down at her, winking. "I could take care of you too sweetheart." The woman licked her lips, moving her tongue slowly from one corner of her mouth to the other before biting her lower lip seductively.

Ani pulled her gaze away, glancing over to Fenix who was looking up at the women with a smile on his face.

"You know," Fenix said, the smile not fading as he pulled his gaze away and looked over to her. "I think I might just need to come back and say hello to those lovely ladies."

"Ugh," Ani snorted, her face wrinkling at the thought.

Fenix chuckled, the smile lingering for a bit longer. "Reminds me of Old Port," he said with a smirk, his gaze moving to a clothing shop they were passing. "The ladies there were *very* friendly and equally accommodating."

"Ugh!" Ani repeated, the sound louder and more pronounced.

Fenix smiled even bigger.

The pair continued on, riding through the city.

They had nearly reached the center, twenty minutes later, when a distant bell tolled. It echoed out, ringing three more times to signal midday.

The pair watched as people started making their way to whatever their destination was to be for the next few hours, until the heat dissipated. Fenix took notice of a saloon not too far away. "Just ahead," he called out, nudging his horse a touch quicker.

Ani followed suit, keeping up with him as they closed the distance to the saloon.

As they rode up, Fenix noticed that they had a covered shelter for horses. "That's nice," he smiled, reaching down to pat Dirtweed's neck. "You got a nice shade and everything."

They rode up to the open-air barn and Fenix saw that there was a large trough running from one end to the other, a few inches of water lining the bottom. "They even got a nice little watering trough for you." He chuckled. "Who-wee, looks like you're gonna be living lavish for the next few hours my boy."

Ani smiled, glancing over to see the actual happiness on his face as he spoke to his horse.

They rode into the shade, climbing down and hitching their horses to the long post that ran above the trough. Then, they turned and made their way to the entrance in front.

As Ani and Fenix stepped through the swinging doors, the world outside vanished behind them, replaced by a hush and a darkness so complete it took a moment for their eyes to adjust. The saloon's walls were painted a deep, blood-red, swirling with black filigree that caught the flicker of candlelight and made the shadows dance. The air was thick with the scent of old spirits, wax, and the faint tang of sea salt— remnants of the room's nautical bones. Overhead, beams carved to look like massive ropes stretched across the ceiling, and the hulls of old fishing boats hung like ghosts, their weathered wood gleaming in the low light. Glass bulbs wrapped in rope netting glowed softly above the bar, casting colored pools across the polished floor, worn smooth by decades of boots and spilled drink.

A dozen round tables filled the room, each ringed with high-backed stools. At the far end, a bar ran the length of the wall, its bow curved outward like the prow of a ship, shelves behind it lined with bottles—row after row of spirits, their labels faded and mysterious. The polished metal behind the bottles shone like a mirror, reflecting the candlelight and making the room seem twice as deep, twice as secret. Behind the bar stood a woman with a mane of fiery red hair, her eyes sharp and welcoming as she watched the newcomers take it all in.

Ani's voice was a whisper, full of awe. "This is amazing." She couldn't help but let her gaze wander, catching on every detail—the ropes, the ship parts, the colored glass, the sense of being somewhere both ancient and alive.

"Welcome to Aberdyne," Fenix said, his tone low and amused as he started toward the bar. "Keep your coin close," he added, not bothering to look back.

The woman behind the bar greeted them with a smile that was both warm and knowing. "Welcome to the Nautilus," she said as they took the last two seats at the bar. "Your first visit with us?"

Fenix simply nodded, his eyes still adjusting to the gloom, but Ani could feel the sense of arrival settle over them—a rare moment of comfort in the wastes, wrapped in the glow of candlelight and the promise of a cold drink.

"This place…" Ani's voice trailed off as she slid onto a battered barstool, the cracked leather sighing beneath her. She set her travel-worn satchel on the scarred counter, eyes wide as she took in the saloon's dim, lantern-lit sprawl. "It's… unreal."

The barkeep—a woman with sun-bleached hair and a smile sharp as a razor—leaned in, elbows on the bar. "Ain't it something?" she said, voice low and warm as whiskey. "You two here to drink, or just hiding from the sun's wrath?"

Fenix tipped his hat back, dust swirling from the brim. "Bit of both, I reckon," he drawled, glancing around at the nautical relics and the flicker of colored glass. "What's a thirsty soul find in a place like this?"

The barkeep's grin widened, never leaving her lips. "Depends how brave you are. I got fifteen kinds of rye, twelve grain spirits—six of 'em with a kick of flavor—four beers, one cold as the old world, and a cactus blend that'll knock the sand right outta your boots."

Fenix let out a low whistle, shooting Ani a crooked grin. "Hear that? We just stumbled into a spirit-lover's oasis."

"We do our best to drown the dust," the barkeep replied, playful as a coyote. "So, stranger, what'll it be?"

Fenix considered, eyes glinting. "I'd be a fool to pass up a cold beer in a place like this. And maybe one of those flavored spirits— something to remind me the world ain't all rust and ruin."

She rattled off the flavors, each one a relic of a world gone by: "Rhubarb, ginger, wild grain, strawberry, rose hips, desert flower."

Fenix's brows shot up. "Desert flower, then a mix of strawberry and ginger after, if you please."

"Coming right up," she said, then turned her gaze to Ani, who was still staring at the rows of bottles, half-dazed by choice and the cool gloom. "And for you, sweetheart?"

Ani blinked, caught off guard. "Uh... I... I guess—"

The barkeep's tone softened, seeing Ani's uncertainty. "Cactus blend's a favorite 'round here. Light, a little sweet, goes down easy. Even the drifters like it."

Ani nodded, grateful. "Yeah. That sounds good. Thank you."

"Of course, darling." The barkeep spun away, bottles clinking as she worked. Ani watched, mouthing a silent wow to Fenix, who just shook his head, grinning.

"Told you," he murmured. "Welcome to Aberdyne."

Ani turned on her stool, letting her gaze sweep the saloon's shadowy corners—the ship's wheel above the bar, the ropes strung like spiderwebs, the battered hulls of old boats hanging overhead. "This is wild," she whispered. "Never thought I'd see a place like this out in the wastes."

Fenix watched her, amused. "Didn't you say you'd been to the capital?"

She shook her head, eyes still roaming. "When I was five. My folks were scrappers—took me across the wastes before the orcs started raiding, before the goblins came this far south. Back then, it was just scavengers and reapers you had to worry about."

Fenix let out a low chuckle, shaking his head. "Oh, yeah," he replied sarcastically. "Just reapers. Nothing too bad."

"You know what I mean," Ani shot back, her voice edged with old dust and fatigue, watching as the barkeep measured out three different bottles—each label faded, glass clouded by years of sun and sand. The woman shook the mix hard, poured it into a battered glass, and a swirl of green shimmered beneath the flickering lanterns. "It was different back then."

Fenix watched the ritual, the ghost of a smile on his lips. "Maybe you remember it that way," he said, eyes following the slow spiral of color in the glass. "But I'll tell you, as a man who's drifted these wastes longer than he cares to admit, they've never been safe. And they sure as hell aren't getting any kinder."

The barkeep slid the frothy green drink in front of Ani, then set a clear spirit—garnished with a single desert flower—before Fenix. The beer she placed down last, beads of cold already gathering on the glass. "So, will y'all be running a tab, or is this a one-and-done? I heard you mention that strawberry-ginger blend, figured I'd ask."

Fenix glanced sidelong at Ani, a smirk tugging at his mouth. "I reckon we could start one up with you," he said, turning back to the barkeep. "We got a few hours to kill before we ride out again."

The woman's smile sharpened. "All right, then. If you wouldn't mind leaving me your pistol as collateral, I'll get you set up."

Fenix stiffened, drawing back a fraction. "My pistol?"

She shrugged, all business now. "You want a tab, I need something to hold. Folks come in, drink up half my stock, and vanish into the wastes. It's just how we keep things fair."

Fenix scoffed, his smirk fading into something harder. "Your protection? That pistol's the only thing protecting me." He turned to Ani. "Why don't you hand over that lizard popper you keep tucked in your jacket?"

"My what?" Ani blinked, caught off guard.

"Your sidearm."

Reluctantly, Ani reached into her coat and pulled out the small pistol, setting it on the counter. "My daddy gave me this gun, and I'll have you know, it works just fine."

Fenix grinned. "Oh, I'm sure it does. Every lizard and desert squirrel for miles trembles when you draw."

"Ass," Ani muttered, sliding the pistol across the bar. The barkeep took it, popped the cylinder open in one practiced motion, and dropped the cartridges into Ani's palm. "You keep those. Don't like loaded guns behind my bar. Policy."

Ani watched, puzzled, as the woman crossed to a small cabinet, hung the pistol on a dowel beside three others, and shut the door with a soft click. Then, without another word, she moved out from behind the bar, collecting empty glasses, leaving the two of them to the hush and the glow of the lanterns, the taste of old world spirits lingering in the air.

"So, what now?"

"Now?" Fenix leaned back, letting the lanternlight catch the swirl of gold in his glass. "Now we sit and enjoy our drinks." He lifted the desert flower spirit to his lips, took a cautious sip, and his eyes widened. "Holy hell. That is amazing. God damn."

Ani lifted her own glass, pausing to breathe in the scent—cactus sweetness, a whisper of something wild and floral beneath. She watched Fenix take a long pull from his beer, the frost clinging to the glass.

He grinned, leaning close. "The witch's beer was colder," he whispered, a glint of mischief in his eyes.

Ani couldn't help but smile, then took her own sip. The flavors washed over her tongue—sweet, strange, and bright as the desert after rain. For a moment, the world outside the saloon's thick walls faded away.

"So," Fenix said, setting his glass down with a satisfied sigh, "I reckon we can wait out the sun in here, then maybe take a walk. Check out the shops, grab a few things for the road. We ought to secure our spots on the caravan, too. Might as well spend the night here and ride out at first light."

Ani nodded, setting her glass down. The cool drink had taken the edge off her nerves.

"You've had a rough couple days," Fenix went on, his tone softening. "I figure you could use a real meal—something that doesn't come on a stick. Maybe even find a shop where you can get some new threads…"

Ani scowled, glancing down at her worn clothes. "My clothes are just fine, thank you very much."

Fenix chuckled, raising his glass in mock salute. "If you say so."

Ani watched him drink, then shrugged. "I guess… I have had these pants for a while. They're getting thin in the seat. Wasn't made for this much riding."

Fenix grinned. "Well, maybe you should do that more often."

Ani's smile faded as she did a quick tally of her coins. "I don't know. I… I don't have much saved up, and I'm not sure what I'm supposed to do after we… after we finish the job." She trailed off, worry flickering in her eyes.

Fenix heard the shift in her voice, recognized it from years of scraping by himself. He glanced at his own battered coin pouch, then reached for the cactus flower drink. "Look," he said quietly, "if you see something you like, I'll take care of it. Just add it to your tab."

Ani looked at him, surprised, then nodded, a small smile breaking through the worry. For a moment, the saloon felt like a safe haven—

just two souls, sharing a drink, waiting out the sun in the heart of the wastes.

"Oh, I couldn't do that."

Fenix shrugged, swirling the spirit in his glass. "Suit yourself. But if someone offered to put me in new threads, and mine were as sun-bleached and threadbare as yours... I'd jump at the chance, quick as a coyote on a jackrabbit."

Ani gave a reluctant nod.

He leaned in, lowering his voice. "Besides, gotta spend all this reaper coin somehow."

Ani's eyes narrowed. "Wait, what!? What reaper coin?"

Fenix grinned, hefting his battered bag so it thudded against the bar. "You didn't think I left that camp empty-handed, did you?" He chuckled, voice dropping to a conspiratorial whisper. "Yeah, we're about three hundred gold heavier in the purse."

"Wait!" Ani hissed, glancing around. "Are you serious?"

He nodded, scanning the room for eavesdroppers. "See, that's the thing. Reapers don't care much for coin or credits. They take what they need, make their own ammo, live off the land. Ore and credits? No use to 'em. Can't eat it, can't wear it, can't trade it in the wastes. But here..." He tapped the bag. "Here, it's worth something."

Ani scoffed, shaking her head. "Three hundred?"

"'Bout that, yeah." Fenix leaned back, a satisfied glint in his eye. "So, I figure we can afford to get you a new outfit. I could use a new mag-belt myself—the one I got's about to fall apart."

Ani hesitated, then shrugged. "Well. I guess if we have the coin, wouldn't hurt to take a look."

Fenix's grin widened. "For now, let's just try a couple more flavors of spirit. No sense rushing. We got time to kill."

Ani eyed her glass, a smile tugging at her lips. "I don't know. I think I'm already feeling this first one."

Fenix laughed, raising his glass. "Oh, it's all uphill from here."

Ani looked down at her drink, the green liquid catching the lanternlight. "It is yummy."

"Then drink up," Fenix said, settling in. "We got another two and a half hours to kill, and for once, nowhere else we gotta be."

36

By the time Fenix and Ani staggered out of the Nautilus, the world outside had shifted. Four hours had slipped away in the dim, lantern-lit haze of the bar, and now the sky burned with a deep orange, the last light of day bleeding across the battered rooftops. The main street of Aberdyne was alive with the restless shuffle of boots and the clatter of wagon wheels, dust swirling in the heat as the settlement's folk hurried to finish their business before nightfall.

They'd sampled nearly every spirit the Nautilus had to offer, and Ani, for her part, was feeling the weight of it. She'd never been much for drink—her father had always kept a clear head, and her mother only raised a glass on rare celebrations. The taste was foreign, the burn unfamiliar, and the liquor hit her harder than she'd expected. As she stumbled into the street, mouth dry and eyes stinging, a flicker of regret curled in her gut.

"Whoa, girl," Fenix said, catching her by the collar just as she drifted into the path of a passing horse. He pulled her back, steadying her before she could become another casualty of the wastes. "You barely had a couple glasses."

"I tried to tell you I don't drink," Ani muttered, pausing to blink at him, her gaze glassy in the dying light. "And I'm not drunk. I'm just… a little lightheaded."

Fenix chuckled, the sound rough as gravel. "Oh, a little lightheaded. Sure…"

"What?" she snapped, bristling at his tone.

He just grinned, shaking his head. "Nothing. Let's take a walk. Fresh air'll do you good."

"I'm not drunk," she insisted, stubborn as ever.

"And I'm the Silver Spur. Come on." He tipped his hat and started down the street, boots thudding against the sun-bleached boards.

Ani lingered for a moment, gathering her balance as the world spun gently beneath her feet. Then she followed, trailing after him past the flickering windows and the faded signs of Aberdyne's shops.

A few paces later, as they passed a fastener and hardware store, she glanced over. "What's a *Silver Spur*, anyway?" she asked, her voice still a little unsteady, but curiosity shining through the haze.

Fenix's smile was tinged with nostalgia. "Well, before your time, there used to be these little publications that drifted out of the west. My folks would save up for 'em—thin paper, cheap ink, but inside, there was always a strip, a picture story about a fella called the Silver Spur. Lone vigilante, rode the wastes on a pale horse, hunting down reapers and scavengers, bringing a bit of justice to a world that'd lost the meaning of the word." He let out a rough scoff, shaking his head. "Funny thing is, I think that strip's half the reason I ended up a drifter myself. Used to picture myself out there, riding through the dust, saving folks, rescuing pretty women from the jaws of the reaper clans. Seemed like a grand life, back when I was a kid—before I knew what the wastes really were. Dirt and sun, always hungry, always thirsty, and let me tell you, the bar for 'beautiful' out here is a hell of a lot lower than those old stories made it seem." He paused, a low burp rumbling up from his gut. "But yeah. The Silver Spur. He was something else. Always dressed in white, horse the color of ash, and he had this hat—wide-brimmed, covered in some kind of reflective stuff. Said he could ride straight through midday and never break a sweat. Man... he was cool."

Ani looked at him and smiled. "Well," she said through a burp of her own. "You did fight the reapers."

Fenix smiled at her, his grin warm. "I suppose I did, didn't I?" For a moment, he let himself drift—back to the old picture strips, back to the days when he'd imagined himself as the Silver Spur, lone hero of the wastes. But Ani had already lost interest, her attention caught by the shopfronts and the strange, battered wares of Aberdyne. He watched her for a heartbeat, a faint smile tugging at his lips—there was something about her youth, her curiosity, that made the world seem a little less worn.

He pulled his gaze away, and that's when he saw it: a massive, oversized pistol hanging above a shop entrance, the metal dulled by years of dust and sun. The sign above read, in faded paint, Bill's Armory.

"I found our first stop," Fenix said, tapping Ani on the shoulder before striding toward the shop.

Inside, the air was thick with the scent of iron, gun oil, and old powder. Racks lined the walls, crowded with weapons of every make—crude pistols cobbled from pipe and scrap, long rifles with battered stocks, a few relics from the world before the fires. Most were the kind of guns folks in the wastes carried: rough, functional, built to last through dust and desperation. Only a handful of smiths out west still had the blueprints and molds for the old war-style weapons—revolvers, bolt-action rifles, the kind Fenix wore at his hip. Those had cost him more than a few jobs' worth of credits, and more than a little blood. Even now, he could feel the weight of them, a reminder of just how hard-won survival could be in a world like this.

"Need some ammo," Fenix said, approaching the counter.

"What kind?" the man replied flatly.

Fenix reached into his pocket and pulled out a spent casing, setting it on the counter.

The man glanced down at it and then turned, making his way to one of the shelves. "How many?" he called out, not looking back.

"How much a box?"

"Three silver."

"Best make it four."

The man pulled four boxes of ammo from the shelf and turned, making his way back and setting it on the counter. "That be it?"

Fenix turned to Ani who had just strolled up. "Let me see that little fairy popper you have?"

"Little *what*...?"

"Your pistol," he replied, holding his hand out and curling his fingers up a few times.

She reluctantly pulled the gun out of her side bag, handing it to him.

Fenix took the small gun and unceremoniously set it on the counter. "You reckon we could trade this in for something with a little more stopping power?"

The man looked down at the small pistol on the counter. "I ain't seen one of those in a minute." He reached out, picking it up and hefting the small weight in his hand. "That is one small lizard plinker."

"Yeah. Figured it was time to upgrade."

The man smirked, setting the pistol back down. "What you plannin' on pointing it at?"

"Hopefully, nothing," Fenix replied, glancing at Ani.

"I think I got something," the man replied, turning around and making his way to a weapon rack behind him. He eyed it for a moment and then grabbed a medium sized pistol from it.

"Thirty caliber, eight round cylinder, bout a pound and a half in the hand." He set the pistol on the counter. "It'll stop a goblin in its tracks. Reaper too if'n they ain't armored up. If they are, just aim for the leg, it'll work just as well."

Fenix looked to Ani who was staring at the pistol as if was poised to bite. "Well. Go on, give it a heft."

Ani took a deep breath, exhaling heavily.

Fenix could smell the alcohol vapors wafting out.

She lifted the gun. It was much heavier than her other one, and the grip larger. It fit in her hand but felt massive in comparison. "It's big."

"Needs to be," Fenix replied. "If you're pointing a gun at someone, it needs to be able to do the job."

"What's wrong with that one?" she asked, looking at her small pistol on the counter.

Fenix sighed, not wishing to bring up the fresh trauma, but not knowing a better way of explaining. "It's the difference between ending up in a reaper cage and not…"

She looked up at him, the memories flashing past as her eyebrows furrowed downward. Slowly she nodded. "Okay."

Fenix gave a single nod in reply, turning to the man. "Better add three boxes for that one as well. And you wouldn't happen to have a mag-belt that would fit me, would you? Maybe one for the girl too?"

"I'm pretty sure I got something laying around," he said, turning to make his way to the ammo shelf. "Might as well keep ahold of the lizard gun, wouldn't be able to give you much for it anyways. No one around here's gonna want something that small. No offense, but it'll just sit on the shelf taking up space."

Fenix smirked with a light huff, reaching out and picking up the gun. "Well. Looks like you get to keep it after all."

Ani took the gun and placed it in her bag. Then she hefted the weight of her new pistol from hand to hand, pulling back the hammer and testing the action.

The man returned, setting three boxes of cartridges on the counter. "Let me take a look for the belts, I'll be right back."

Fenix watched as the man made his way towards the other side of the shop. "I think that one'll work just fine for you. I hope you don't have to use it, but I for one, feel a little more confident in you carrying that, versus the one in your bag."

"I like my little gun."

"I'm sure you do. But have you ever had to use it?"

"No…" she replied sheepishly.

"Well," he said with a scoff. "You're lucky you didn't, I can tell you that much."

The man returned, setting two belts on the counter.

Fenix picked up the larger belt, turning it over in his hands. Black leather, tough as old boot, ran the length, threaded with a strand of magnetic braiding that caught the lantern light in a dull glimmer. Small magnetic strips were sewn in at careful intervals—every two inches, a place to snap a loaded cylinder or shell. Between the magnets, the old-fashioned casing holders remained, a nod to the days when things were built to last. Near the buckle, a snap attachment waited, ready for another belt if the need ever arose.

He unbuckled his own, setting the frayed, sun-bleached strap on the counter. The extra two cylinders snapped to it came off with a practiced flick. He thumbed them open, loaded each with fresh rounds, and then slung the new belt around his waist. The buckle clicked home with a satisfying weight. Fenix slapped the cylinders to the magnets, pulled one off, let it snap back—testing the resistance, feeling the surety of it.

"That's better," he muttered, a rare note of satisfaction in his voice.

Ani reached out, holding the belt for a moment before wrapping it around her waist and buckling it closed.

"You got a couple extra cylinders for that 30 cal?"

"Sure do." The man reached under the counter and pulled an extra two out, setting them down.

"Go on and load those up," Fenix instructed her.

She removed the shells from the ammo boxes and filled the cylinders.

"Now go ahead and snap em to your belt."

She did, feeling the belt nearly yank the cylinders from her hand, snapping them into place, where they were in a position to be used quickly.

"Now all's you gotta do is flip the lever like this," Fenix said, showing her with his pistol. "That drops the cylinder." He caught it in his other hand. "Then you just press the pistol down like this, and *click*, the next one is loaded. That's all there is to it."

Ani repeated the process he just showed, but at about a third of the speed. It took about three times to get the cylinder lined up in order to lock into place. Then she pressed it sideways into the gun and locked it in. Her alcohol impaired movements did nothing to help.

"Just a little flick of the wrist," Fenix said, showing her by opening the cylinder and then closing it with a flick. "Bingo."

"Learning to be a drifter huh?" the man behind the counter asked.

Ani looked at him disapprovingly. "No."

"Oh," he said, leaning back. "My apologies." He paused. "Well. Six boxes, the 30 cal and two belts." He ran a quick calculation in his head. "That'll run you five gold, five silver."

Fenix reached into his bag, pulling the coin out and setting it on the counter. "Much obliged," he said, turning back to Ani who was still fumbling with the pistol. "You good?"

She nodded, looking up at him. "Think so."

"All right then. What do you say we go do something about that outfit?"

She nodded, a hint of a smile escaping.

The next two hours slipped by in a haze of lamplight and city bustle. Ani traded her worn trousers for a pair of sturdy denim, the kind meant to last through dust and hard riding. She swapped her blouse for a tougher button-down and picked out a lighter leather vest to throw over it—something that would breathe in the heat but still hold up against the wind. She treated herself to a handful of snacks and sweets, small comforts for the road ahead. Fenix, meanwhile, found a silver flask to replace the battered tin one he'd carried for a decade, and even splurged on a new vest, this one stitched with a rose motif across the lapels—a rare bit of color in a world gone rust and bone.

By the time they reached the caravan station, the sun had already slipped beneath the horizon. Oil lamps flickered to life, casting golden halos across the city's crooked streets and the shopfronts lining them. As they approached, Ani caught her first glimpse of the caravan: a hulking, armored train, four cars long, its engine plated in thick, riveted steel. The wheels were hidden behind long panels, giving the whole machine the illusion of floating above the tracks. The two cars behind the engine were dotted with small, reinforced windows, while the last car was sealed tight with solid plating—no windows, no hint of what lay inside. At the very front, a massive scoop jutted out, nearly as tall as the engine itself, ready to smash aside anything foolish enough to block its path.

"It's so much bigger than I thought…" Ani said as they walked up.

"Yep," Fenix replied. "By far the quickest way across the wastes." He admired the steel paneled engine for a moment.

"Wow," Ani said, still taking it in.

"Yep. The whole roof is covered in massive solar panels, so it doesn't need fuel or steam to run. The back car is mostly battery and cargo space. It's where the horses and luggage ride. We'll be in one of those two," he added, pointing to the two cars that had windows dotting the sides. "If you behave, I'll even let you have the window seat."

"*If I behave*," she replied sarcastically.

He smiled. "If. Now come on, let's go procure our travel arrangements."

"What?"

"Come on," he said, walking towards the entrance.

The interior of the station was stripped-down and utilitarian—bare wood floors and walls, the grain worn smooth by countless boots. A handful of faded caravan posters clung to the walls, their colors sun-bleached, showing smiling travelers with luggage in hand, faces from a world that no longer existed. Safety notices were tacked up beside a long, official statement releasing the company from any liability for injury, death, or loss. Dominating one wall was a poster of the armored engine itself, boasting every safety measure from the front-mounted scoop to the fold-out gatling guns and anti-mounting spikes. Above it all, a bold notice declared: The safest way across the wastes.

Fenix strode up to the ticket counter, where a short man in a battered visor greeted them with a practiced smile. "Good evening," the man said as they approached.

"Evenin'," Fenix replied, tipping his hat. "Need two tickets to Serenity."

"Ah. Serenity. Perfect. That'll be six silver. Caravan leaves first light tomorrow."

Fenix dug into his bag, the coins clinking as he slid them across the counter. The man scooped them up quick, dropping them into a battered lockbox. He pulled two tickets from a drawer and slid them across the scarred wood.

"Now, we do ask that you arrive promptly at sunrise. The train will depart regardless of your presence, and there will be no refunds for late arrival. And do keep ahold of your tickets—any lost tickets will mean buying a new one at full price." He pushed the tickets toward Fenix, his tone all business now. "Other than that, your travel time will be roughly fourteen hours, with a one-hour stop in Corith. We recommend you stay on the caravan at that point—luggage left on the train will be considered abandoned and will become property of the caravan company. This includes personal items up to and including horses and large luggage kept in the cargo car."

Fenix turned to Ani. "You catch all that?"

Ani nodded, a slight ping of headache starting to tickle behind her eyes. "Yep. Stay on the caravan."

"Stay on the caravan," Fenix replied, taking the tickets and putting them in his bag. "I'll keep ahold of these for us. Now what do you say we go get ourselves a room. I could use a nice bath and a bed."

Ani nodded, her eyebrows raising at the thought. "I agree. I think the cactus drink is starting to wear off."

Fenix smiled. "Headache starting to kick in?"

She nodded with a grunt.

"Well. I know a good cure for that."

"Really?" she asked, "What?"

174

A smile grew across his face. "More cactus drink."

"Ugh," she grunted, turning and making her way outside.

"Remember," the caravan worker reminded as they walked away. "Be here promptly at sunrise."

"Sunrise," Fenix called back without looking. "Got it."

The pair made their way back toward the saloon, weaving through the slow-moving current of townsfolk. Most of the settlers in the wastes looked cut from the same sun-bleached cloth—faces weathered and wrinkled by years beneath a merciless sky, clothes faded to the color of dust and bone, shoulders slouched from endless days in the saddle. There was a languid, almost defeated air about them, as if the heat itself had pressed the urgency out of their bones. Nobody hurried; maybe after so many years of conserving sweat and breath, the notion of hustle had simply dried up and blown away.

Ani watched the faces as they passed—men and women alike, eyes dulled by thirst and hunger, their expressions set in the same mask of resignation. Apathy was the common thread, woven through every glance and every step. Folks here had surrendered to the wastes, to the endless cycle of scavenging and barter, to the knowledge that for most, there would be no escape. The world had shrunk to the boundaries of survival, and for many, that was enough.

But the more Ani saw of the wastes, the more she felt the ache to leave. With her brother gone, her mother lost to the sun, and her father likely claimed by the same fate, there was nothing left for her here. The family farm was just a patch of scorched earth with a name marker—no crops, no well, nothing but memories that had soured into burdens. She longed for something beyond the dust and the heat, something she'd glimpsed in the flickering images of the old world, in stories of Europa before the fires, in tales of the green northern lands. There had to be more than this—something worth living for, something worth chasing.

As soon as she shut down Arcan and stopped the prophet from releasing the flame, she promised herself, she would turn her back on the wastes and never return. Ever.

The pair wandered on, boots scuffing the dust as they made their way through Aberdyne's streets. Twenty minutes slipped by, the city shifting from the last blush of sunset to the deepening blue of night. Then, a sudden brightness caught their eyes—a three-story building rising above the rest, crowned by a massive electric coil. Blue and white arcs of lightning danced from one side to the other, illuminating the sign that swung overhead: The Rusted Spark Inn.

"Looks like we found our bed," Fenix said.

Ani looked up, watching the electricity crackle against the indigo sky, the last corals and pinks of dusk pressed low on the horizon as the first stars blinked awake overhead.

Inside, Ani barely noticed the décor, the weight of drink and exhaustion settling over her as she trailed Fenix to the counter. He requested two rooms, and when Ani asked why, he just shrugged, "Might like some company other than yours tonight." She smirked, took her key, and trudged upstairs.

The moment she hit the bed, sleep claimed her. Sometime in the night, Ani woke, the room dim and quiet. She drifted to the window, watching a handful of late-night wanderers shuffle beneath the electric glow. Then she returned to bed, undressing for the first time in what felt like ages, letting the cool sheet brush her skin. She pulled her battered book from her bag, found her place, and read by the faint light spilling in from the open window, the hush of the wastes settling around her like a blanket.

37

Dust billowed in thick, choking clouds beneath the moon's cold gaze, the silver light painting the wastes in ghostly hues. The night was unnaturally still, as if the world itself was holding its breath, waiting for the storm that crept ever closer to the tiny settlement. A ragged cluster of houses huddled around a single, ancient well—six families within, their doors barred, children curled beneath threadbare blankets, all blissfully ignorant of the nightmare racing toward them through the darkness.

Three miles out, the ground trembled beneath the thunder of boots and hooves. A dozen orcs surged forward, their massive silhouettes black against the moonlit sand, axes gleaming with the promise of slaughter. Behind them, a clan of goblins—twenty strong—scrambled in their wake, eyes wild with anticipation, blades and pikes clattering in their hands. The air was thick with the stench of sweat, old blood, and something fouler still: the raw, animal hunger of predators on the hunt.

Armor flapped and rattled, metal plates and scavenged trophies clinking in a discordant symphony. Orcs bellowed guttural war cries, the sound rolling across the wastes like thunder, while the goblins hissed and chittered, their voices sharp and eager. Fury burned in their eyes, hatred twisting their faces into masks of violence. The taste of flesh lingered on their tongues, the memory of their last kill driving them faster, harder, toward the sleeping settlement.

Inside, the families dreamed on, unaware that death was already at their doorstep. Shadows flickered across the windows as the horde drew near, the moonlight catching on blades and broken teeth. The orcs' breath steamed in the chill air, their hands tightening on axe handles, knuckles white with anticipation. Goblins darted between them, licking their lips, eyes darting from house to house, already imagining the screams, the blood, the feast to come.

As the horde crested the final rise, the settlement lay exposed before them—fragile, defenseless, utterly doomed. The orcs broke into a run, boots pounding the earth, axes raised high. The goblins fanned out, circling the houses, their laughter shrill and inhuman. The first door splintered beneath a blow, and with it, the last fragile barrier between the families and the horrors that had come for them.

In that moment, the wastes were alive with terror. Screams tore through the night, mingling with the triumphant howls of the invaders. Blood splattered the dust, and the moon watched, cold and indifferent, as all the horrors of the wastes were unleashed in their full, merciless glory.

38

Ani awoke the next morning, lifting the book off her chest and setting it aside before stretching. A breath later there was a knock at the door.

"Time to go."

She drew in a long, shaky breath, holding it for a moment before letting it out in a slow, resigned sigh. "Out in five," she called, her voice roughened by sleep and the lingering ache of last night's excess. The urge to collapse back into the thin mattress was strong. Her eyelids hung heavy, her limbs weighted with exhaustion—but she forced herself upright, planting her feet on the warped floorboards and sitting at the edge of the bed. Her stomach churned, a sour reminder of the spirits she'd tried to keep pace with, and a loud, hollow gurgle echoed through the small room. She pressed a hand to her abdomen, grimacing. The taste of old liquor still clung to her tongue, and she knew she'd be carrying the consequences until she could find a decent meal and choke down another hydration tab. At least she'd had the sense to buy a dozen of them the day before—one small mercy she'd learned to grant herself after years in the wastes. She rarely drank, but she'd learned the cost well enough.

She stood, swaying for a moment as the blood rushed to her head. Her gaze drifted downward, taking in her own reflection in the cracked mirror propped against the wall. Was she attractive? Did men find her pretty? She'd always assumed so—there were far fewer women than men in the wastes, and she'd seen the way some of the brothel girls drew attention, even those whose beauty was worn thin by sun and hardship. Some of them, she thought, were truly beautiful, in a way that seemed untouchable, almost otherworldly. Others, not so much. Where did she fit in? Was she beautiful, or just another face battered by dust and sun? The question lingered, heavy and unwelcome, as she traced the lines of her jaw, the freckles across her nose, the faded bruise on her cheekbone. She sighed, pushing the thoughts away—there was no time for vanity, not here, not now.

She bent to gather her clothes, each movement slow and deliberate. The room was cold, the air tinged with the scent of sweat and old wood. She dressed in silence, pulling on her trousers, buttoning her shirt, sliding her arms into the vest that still smelled faintly of leather and smoke. She laced her boots, fingers trembling just a little, and slung her battered pack over her shoulder. For a moment, she stood in the hush, listening to the distant sounds of the inn—the muffled voices, the creak of footsteps on the stairs, the wind rattling the windowpane. Then, with a final glance at her reflection, she squared her shoulders and stepped toward the door.

"Morning sunshine," Fenix said as she opened the door to find him standing there.

"Morning," she replied flatly.

"Wow," he smiled. "Someone still feeling last night?"

"I don't want to talk about it," she said, walking past. "I'm sure *you* enjoyed last night."

Fenix smirked. "Not as much as Lily I'd wager."

"Pig," she scoffed, making her way to the stairs.

"What?" He remarked, following after. "I'm a grown man. Grown men have needs too."

"Whatever," she snapped, making her way down.

He stopped, watching her make her way down the stairs with a puzzled look on his face. "Hmph," he grunted, starting after.

They unhitched their horses and climbed up, riding them the short distance to the caravan station. The sun hadn't peaked yet, the soft pre-glow just beginning to illuminate the horizon as they rode up. There were a handful of other folks already gathered on the platform.

They climbed down from their horses, passing them off to a caravan worker who led the two horses towards the luggage car in the back.

"Lily, huh?" Ani remarked, giving him a judgmental look.

"You know, if I didn't know any better, I'd say that was jealousy I hear in your voice."

"Ha!" she barked. "Jealousy..."

He stood there, staring at her for a moment. "If you gots something to say, let's go on and get it out. No sense riding all the way to Serenity with this hanging over us."

"It's gross. Having relations with women you don't even know. You don't even know their name and you get into bed with them?"

"Well, that's kind of the point Ani," he replied defensively. "It ain't exactly like there's a lot of other options out here?" He paused. "You do know I was married at one point, right? I told you that. So, it ain't like I'm some, sex crazed maniac. I just miss having some, *womanly* companionship every now and then."

Ani scoffed, staring at him in mild disgust.

"Look. I miss my wife. I miss her every day, more than you could ever imagine. And to be honest, I would never want to replace her. I don't think I could. And my not remarrying or getting involved in a serious relationship... That is how I choose to honor her memory. But spending an evening with some paid company. That is purely physical. And I'm sure as you get a little older you might gain a little stronger understanding of what I'm talking about. There ain't nothing wrong with paying for a service that's offered. Least none as I'm concerned."

Ani's expression shifted. "You still miss her? Your wife?"

Fenix scoffed, his face softening. "Every day. Every, single day."

"I'm sorry."

"Yeah. Me too."

"The caravan to Serenity is now boarding."

Ani held Fenix's gaze, feeling the loss in his eyes.

The man at the door to the second caravan car continued calling out. "Have your tickets in hand please, all large bags need to be placed in the luggage car to the rear. Only bring what you can fit on the seat with you.

"Shall we?" Fenix asked, reaching out and placing his hands on her shoulders.

Ani nodded.

"All right," he said, patting her twice before putting his hand on her back and shoving her lightly towards the car.

Ani stepped up into the belly of the caravan car, boots echoing on the cold metal floor. Rows of battered seats lined either side of the narrow aisle, their cushions patched and faded by years of sun and dust. Overhead, luggage racks ran the length of the car, shadows flickering beneath the recessed lights that buzzed and hummed with a tired, electric glow.

She moved halfway down, weaving past a handful of silent travelers, and settled into a seat by the window. With a practiced motion, she slung her bag onto the rack above, then slid down, letting the weight of the journey settle into her bones. Outside, the world was still—a city wall looming in the half-light, the wastes beyond painted in the bruised colors of dawn. Fenix set his own bag beside hers and dropped into the seat across the aisle, the two of them sharing a quiet, companionable silence.

For twenty minutes, they waited, the hush broken only by the distant clatter of boots and the low murmur of voices. Then the caravan operator's voice rang out. "Final boarding!" A breath later the heavy door clanged shut behind him, sealing them in with a metallic finality. He rattled off the safety notices, his words echoing off steel and glass, before vanishing through the armored door that separated their car from the engine. The bolt slid home with a deep, resonant ka-thunk.

A few minutes later, the engine rumbled to life, the vibration running up through the soles of their boots. Outside, a section of the city wall groaned and slid aside, and the caravan lurched forward, steel wheels grinding against the rails as they slipped out and back into the wastes.

By the time the sun crested the horizon they were rolling across the wastes, traveling ten times faster than on horseback and roaring towards their destination.

Outside the caravan's thick glass, the world was a graveyard of color and silence. A desolate swath of land stretched undisturbed to every horizon—a vast, endless sea of rust and ochre, where mesas and buttes rose like the bones of ancient titans, their shadows long and sharp beneath a sky so blue it seemed to pierce the earth itself. The land rolled by in slow, hypnotic waves, each mile a reminder of how empty the world had become.

Ani sat with her face nearly pressed to the window, breath fogging the glass. She watched the landscape slip past, her eyes tracing the jagged silhouettes of stone and the distant shimmer of heat. She'd seen pictures on the Belcor terminals—images of this same land before the great war, before the fires, when rivers still ran and green things grew. Now, nothing but dust and memory remained.

As she stared out into the vacant wastes, her gaze drifted upward to the endless blue above. There hadn't been a cloud in the sky since the fires, since the Merge. The Merge had changed everything—ripped two worlds together and left scars that would never heal. The wars that followed, the death that swept across the land… all of it had left the world hollow, a place where hope was as rare as rain.

Ani wondered what it must have been like before—before the silence, before the sky turned hard and empty. She pressed her palm to the glass, feeling the cold seep into her skin, and let herself imagine a world that no longer existed.

"It looks prettier from in here, don't it?"

Ani pulled her vacant gaze from the window. "Huh?"

Fenix was looking past her, his eyes following the landscape outside. "Said it looks a lot prettier from in here, don't it?"

Ani nodded, her gaze moving back to the window, the prior thoughts slowly fading. "Yeah. I guess so." It was a full day's trip from Aberdyne to Serenity by caravan, a week's travel by horse. With everything that had already happened, the short caravan ride seemed an almost inconsequential respite, a single breath when drowning. "Think we'll get to see the capital?"

"Reckon it's gonna be hard to miss, seeing as we'll be going right through the middle." Fenix paused, watching a lone bird circle above a small forest of cactus.

"I wish he was here," Ani said softly a moment later.

Fenix pulled his gaze from the circling raptor.

"I miss him something fierce."

He could see the sadness drawing heavy on her face.

Her chest lifted twice, shuddered breaths hitching within. A single tear made its way down her cheek, followed by another.

Fenix lifted his hand with the intention of resting it on her shoulder for some form of comfort, feeling suddenly misguided and allowed it to rest back in his lap. "I think you did more than any normal sister would."

A moment went by in silence, the low rumble of the caravan wheels grinding the tracks below working up.

"It wasn't enough."

"But you tried. You can't let that rest on you. You can't take that fault. I know this may sound harsh to hear, but that boy got himself into that predicament. He shoulda known better. The wastes ain't forgiving, and neither are the folk who inhabit it." This time he did reach up, his hand resting on the soft warmth of her shoulder. "You look at me."

Ani peeled her gaze from the window, turning to face the drifter.

"You did everything anyone could have done—more than most, truth be told. You were smart about it. You knew if you'd gone charging in, half-cocked, no matter what kind of power you've got in those hands..." Fenix's gaze dropped to her fingers, callused and trembling, before meeting her eyes again. "You'd have ended up dead, same as the rest. You made the right calls, even when your brother didn't. You kept your head when it counted." He paused, the lines in his face deepening, voice rough as the wastes. "You know what I'd give to have said goodbye to my Cora? Just one more word, one more moment. But you—you got that. I know it hurts. I know it's tearing you up inside, and nothing I say will make it easier. But you did everything you could. I'd wager you saved that boy more times than he ever knew." He let out a long, heavy sigh, the silence between them thick with dust and memory. "You did right by him. That's all anyone can ask out here."

Ani slowly nodded, the times she had saved Jarek from injury, or getting lost, or bit by a desert viper flashing past.

"You carry his death with you, cause that's what we do, but you shed that blame, and you do it right here, right now, cause that ain't on you. We focus on what needs to get done, and if you're lucky, you may just find a bit of revenge tied up in it as well." He paused, lifting his other arm to her shoulder and turning her slightly towards him. "We're gonna get that son of a bitch. We're gonna keep him from releasing that flame, and we're gonna put him in the ground. And we're gonna take as many of those god-damned goblins and orcs as we can with him. You hear me?"

Ani swallowed hard, her face scrunching slightly as she nodded. The ache of losing her brother still churned inside her, but the sharpness of it dulled, just a fraction. Fenix was right—they couldn't let grief swallow them, not now. Stopping the Prophet was all that mattered. If they failed, it wouldn't just be her loss to mourn, but thousands—tens of thousands—across the wastes and beyond. The first flames had already erased nearly seventy percent of humanity, and with them, uncounted Corithian lives: elves, goblins, halflings, dwarves, humans, orcs—all swept away in fire and fallout. It had taken a thousand years for the world to claw its way back from that abyss, and now, the burden of keeping it from happening again rested on her shoulders—and the drifter's beside her.

She would have her time to grieve, but not yet—not until the Prophet was stopped, not until the wastes were saved, if there was anything left worth saving at all. Or she'd die trying, and in the end, it wouldn't matter. But Fenix was right about one thing: as much as she loved and missed her brother, she'd warned him to keep the map secret, to trust no one. He hadn't listened. He'd gone out alone, testing the patience of the wastes one time too many, and this time, she hadn't been there to shield him. Now, she had to be stronger than her sorrow. The fate of the world depended on it.

"Now, I think you should try your best to get some shut eye. Might do you some good. We're both gonna need to be well rested for what's to come." He studied her for a moment. "I'm guessing you still got that liquor sloshing in your gut too. Might help to take advantage of the ride and try and sleep that off."

Fenix pulled his hands back, his face softening. In that moment he saw her age peer through, a flicker of youthful innocence shining dimly for a single breath.

Ani sniffled, dragging her sleeve across her cheeks to wipe away the salt-tracks of grief. She nodded, swallowing hard, then turned her gaze to the window, letting the silence settle between them. For the next hour, she sat in quiet contemplation, her mind circling every possible scenario, every what-if and regret, every small change that might have saved her brother. But none of that mattered now. The drifter was right. The only thing that mattered was stopping the Prophet. If she got to feel the warm caress of revenge, if she could claim retribution for her brother, she would savor it when the time came. But for now, she had to keep herself together, had to hold the pieces of her heart tight and not let her brother's loss—or the horrors still unfolding—tear her apart.

Ani continued to watch the world outside drifting by. It was only a short time later that she shifted her weight and allowed her head to rest against the warm glass and sleep to pull her away.

39

Ani awoke with a start, the tapping against her foot ripping her from the not-so pleasant dream she was living. Her eyes snapped to Fenix who smiled and nodded towards the window.

As she turned her gaze a voice crackled across a single speaker in the car. *"Folks we'll be arriving at the capital in just a few minutes. Be sure to take all your personal belongings with you if this is your stop. If you're continuing on to Serenity, please stay on the caravan, we'll be leaving shortly."*

A moment later, the outskirts of the sprawling city began to emerge. Corith—capital of the wastes for five centuries—rose from the dust like a promise and a warning. The city had been born around the largest underground water source ever found in these lands, and in the early days, thousands had flocked to its promise of survival. Within a hundred years, the population had swelled to nearly a hundred thousand, and when a scrapper stumbled into a pre-war mineshaft, the Silver-Cor mine was born, drawing even more souls to the city's edge. Now, nearly half a million called Corith home. It was the only place in the wastes where humans and Corithians—elves, dwarves, halflings, and others—lived side by side, though the mingling was uneasy and rare. Most stuck to their own kind, and the few elven or dwarven wares that made it to the markets fetched a premium. The city's patchwork sprawl was a testament to survival and uneasy alliances, its skyline a jagged blend of old-world ruins and new-world desperation.

As the caravan drew closer, the true scale of Corith revealed itself: a sprawl of sun-bleached towers, rusted metal, and adobe walls, all clustered around the shimmering heart of the city's well. The city pulsed with life and tension, a crossroads where hope and hardship met beneath the endless, glaring sky.

"It's so much bigger than I remember."

Fenix smiled. "Yep. It's got pretty much anything a person could want, and quite a few things they don't. Hard to believe this started as a tiny settlement around a spring."

"Really?"

Fenix leaned back. "You're telling me, that with all that knowledge you have about the pre-world, that you don't even know how the capital of the wastes was formed?"

"I prefer older history."

"History is history girl. It's all old."

"You know what I mean."

Fenix shook his head with a smirk, pulling his gaze away from the window.

"Well?"

"Well, what?" he replied flatly.

"You're dying to tell me."

"Dying to tell you what?"

"Oh, don't play coy with me. Go on. Tell me about how our great capital was founded."

Fenix scowled at her.

"Go on then."

He took a deep breath, exhaling with a grunt. "Couple families found a spring, city got built. The end."

"Wow," she remarked. "You sure you weren't a teacher before you became a drifter?"

"Smart ass…"

"Better than a dumbass…"

Fenix smirked. He was happy to see that she seemed to be feeling better. He knew how long it took for wounds like hers to heal. He still felt his and it had been years, decades…

Outside, the city seemed to close in around them, the caravan slowing as it wound its way toward the heart of Corith. Ani pressed her face to the window, eyes wide with a mix of awe and apprehension as the city unfolded before her. Thousands of people moved through the streets in a restless current—traders, drifters, families, and scavengers, all weaving between battered wagons and the flicker of oil lamps. The tracks led straight into the city's core, where four- and five-story buildings rose up, their silhouettes a patchwork of twisted iron, sun-bleached steel, and crumbling adobe. The architecture was a strange, beautiful collision of the old world and the new, a testament to survival and stubborn hope.

Ani had never seen so many souls gathered in one place. The sheer press of humanity—humans and Corithians alike—sent a thrill through her, but it was quickly chased by a ripple of anxiety. The city was alive, pulsing with noise and movement, and for a moment, she felt impossibly small. "There's so many people," she whispered, her voice barely audible above the low rumble of the caravan and the distant clamor of city life.

"Yep," Fenix replied. "Welcome to Corith."

"How many times have you been here?" she asked, turning to him.

"A handful." He paused. "Tend to stay out of the larger settlements. Makes me a little... claustrophobic."

"I can see that," she replied, turning her gaze back to the window, watching as a group of scrappers pushed a large cart overflowing with salvage down the main street.

The caravan slowed even further, creeping into the capital's station. Then with a loud groan it jerked to a stop. The doors to the engine car opened a few moments later and the driver stepped into the passenger car. "For those of you getting off, make sure you have your effects. You leave it, it becomes property of the Caravan Company." He paused, allowing his words to settle in. "For the rest of you continuing on to Serenity, you can stay seated, or get up and move around a bit, but don't go too far, caravan'll be boarding in one hour, and if you ain't on when we leave, well. We ain't coming back for you."

Fenix caught the attempt of humor in the man's words and watched as most of the other folks began gathering their belongings and making their way to the now open door. "You wanna go have a quick look around?"

"Do we have time?"

"I reckon we got a short bit." He reached out, tapping her leg with the back of his hand. "Come on. Let's go see the capital."

Ani smiled, nearly jumping up after Fenix who had already started towards the door.

Fenix knew the capital well. He'd been there a handful of times over the past few years. Most of the jobs he had taken as of recent had been escort jobs. Take this person or people from here to there. Most of those jobs had either started in or ended in the capital. Most folks had better sense than to go out to the smaller outskirts settlements unless they had good reason to. "I think I know a spot you might like," he said, nudging her with his elbow as he walked past. "Come on."

"Better not be a saloon," Ani replied flatly, moving to catch up. "I ain't trying to feel like that again for quite a while, if ever again."

"Ain't a saloon," Fenix replied, mumbling, *"though it wouldn't hurt,"* to himself.

The pair stepped out of the station and onto the main road, where the city's pulse beat strongest. The avenue was broad—wide enough for the iron-bellied caravan to roll straight down the center, with room to spare for wagons and riders weaving along its flanks. Ani paused, boots planted on the sun-bleached boards, her gaze drawn down the length of the street. On either side, buildings pressed close, their facades a patchwork of adobe, rusted metal, and scavenged glass, all leaning in as if conspiring together. Far ahead, the road seemed to narrow to a vanishing point, where the city's bones converged in the haze.

"Watch it!"

Ani felt a hand reach around her arm and pull her backwards. She was about to lash out when a horse drawn carriage rumbled quickly past.

"Best pay attention," Fenix remarked, letting go of her arm. "This ain't Bilgewater or Blister Springs. You step out into the street like that you're liable to get run over."

Ani exhaled sharply, feeling a prickle of embarrassment.

"Just… There's a lot going on, that's all I'm saying."

Ani nodded with a sigh.

"Come on," he said, turning and starting down the wood planked edge of the street.

Ani trailed behind, her boots echoing on the tightly pressed cobblestones that ran the length of the main street. The sound of horse hooves and wagon wheels clattered and rang between the tall, patchwork buildings—adobe and scavenged metal rising higher than she remembered from her childhood, some reaching three stories or more. She found herself craning her neck, staring up at open windows where faded laundry and battered blankets fluttered in the faint breeze, catching the last of the evening's light.

Shops lined both sides of the avenue, their signs hand-painted or scavenged from the ruins, each one promising something different—tools, dried goods, old-world relics, charms, and tinctures. For as far as Ani could see, the city stretched on, every storefront a testament to survival and adaptation, every doorway a glimpse into a different trade or dream. The sheer variety was dizzying, a far cry from the lonely, sun-bleached outposts she'd grown up around. Here, in the heart of Corith, the world felt impossibly vast and alive.

"Just up ahead," Fenix said, pulling her attention away from a store called Terra's Imports.

As she walked past, she saw a large sign in the back of the shop that read *Direct from Europa.*

"They have things from Europa in there!" she said excitedly, reaching out and tugging on Fenix's sleeve.

Fenix looked back at her, and she immediately pulled her hand away, feeling the soft ping of embarrassment at having acted like a child.

"If we have time we can stop and have a look on the way back, but I there's something I want to show you first."

Ani nodded, following after.

It was only a few minutes later when Fenix stopped in front of a building that had a sign hanging off that read *Drifter Post 112*.

"Here we are."

Ani stopped, looking up at the sign confused. "Drifter Post?"

Fenix smiled. "Come on. Let me show you."

Fenix turned and made his way inside.

Ani stepped through the battered doorway and paused, letting her eyes adjust to the dim, dust-choked light. The room beyond was wide and hollow, the air thick with the scent of old paper and sweat. At the far end, a single office sat behind cracked glass, its door hanging slightly ajar. Scattered across the warped floorboards were a handful of benches and mismatched chairs, each gathered around scarred tables pitted by years of hard use.

Along one wall, a massive board dominated the space—a patchwork of faded photographs and curling wanted posters tacked up in uneven rows. Across the top, painted in stark, ghostly white, was a single word: BOUNTIES. Faces stared out from the board, some marked with crude Xs, others curling at the edges, their eyes long since forgotten by the living.

Opposite, another wall was divided by hand-painted signs: LOCAL JOBS and ESCORT. Beneath each heading, scraps of parchment and torn notes fluttered in the faint breeze, offering work to any soul desperate—or reckless—enough to take it. The whole place hummed with the quiet tension of the wastes, a crossroads for drifters, scavengers, and those with nowhere else to go.

"This is where you come for work if you're a drifter by trade."

"Wait," she replied, confused. "So, drifters are an actual *thing*?

"What do you mean a *thing*?"

"I just. I kind of always thought drifters were, I don't know, people that went from town to town looking for work."

Fenix laughed. "Some do. But this is where the real work comes from. Escort jobs, transport, muscle. You just come here and browse the boards." He paused, his gaze moving across the walls. "Bounties are where the real credits are, but that's for fellas with a lot less to lose than me."

"You never went for bounties?"

Fenix smiled. "For a bit. After Cora… I was angry, just, angry at everything, at the world." He paused. "Yeah, I hit the bounty board pretty hard. The bottle too." He shook his head, clicking his tongue. "Not a good combination…"

"So, what were you doing in Blister Springs?"

"At the saloon?"

"Yeah."

"Drinking," he replied flatly.

Ani stared at him unamused.

"You asked."

"You know what I mean. Why were you in Blister Springs."

Fenix smirked, glancing at the job boards. "I was taking a break. I'd just finished up a transport job, some paperwork from some rich fella out of Heirako. I was just taking a rest."

"Timing."

He scoffed. "Timing indeed… Come on," he smiled. "I won't bore you with my profession any longer. We can go have a look at that shop you were eyeing."

Ani smiled, following him outside. "It doesn't bore me," she said a few moments later.

"Ain't gotta be polite."

"It doesn't. I had no idea it was, like, an actual profession." She paused. "I guess what I'm trying to say, is that it's way more organized than I thought. I just. I don't know. Had it pictured differently."

"It's a real profession. Just like scrapping and smithing. People gotta get from point a to point b, and most wanna get there alive, so…"

The pair drifted through the city's last traces of civilization, Ani lingering in the import shop, her fingers trailing over relics from a world that felt more myth than memory. Fenix eventually pulled her away, and soon enough, they were swallowed once more by the endless brown hush of the wastes.

Ani sat quietly, unwrapping a handful of sweets she'd bartered for—small treasures she let dissolve on her tongue, one by one. Fenix nursed a battered bottle of whiskey, the glass catching stray beams of sunlight that slipped through the caravan's windows. Outside, midday pressed down like a blacksmith's hammer, and thin metal panels— punched with a thousand tiny holes—slid down over the glass, muting the sun's fury but not the world's emptiness. Through the perforated steel, the wastes blurred past: a shifting tapestry of rust, bone, and dust.

For five long hours, the only sounds were the low hum of the engine and the soft rustle of pages as Ani lost herself in her book. Fenix, lulled by the rhythm of the rails and the slow burn of whiskey, drifted into a heavy, dreamless sleep. Inside the caravan, time stretched thin, and the world outside faded to a distant, sun-bleached memory.

40

A short distance outside Serenity, the train began to lurch—first a gentle tug at the gut, then a sudden, jarring pull that sent Ani pitching forward in her seat. Across the aisle, Fenix stirred awake, pushing his hat brim back and squinting through the dusty window.

The train's momentum bled away, the world outside slowing to a crawl. Beneath their feet, the screech of steel wheels rose up, a banshee wail echoing through the carriage and rattling the glass.

"What's happening?" Ani asked, a prickle of fear edging its way into her voice.

"Not sure," Fenix replied flatly, a thin squint moving to his eyes. "I wouldn't worry much though. This thing's got more armor than, well. Pretty much anything you can imagine. Not to mention the rotating guns up top." He paused. "Have to be a fool, or suicidal to come at the caravan."

The train had jolted to a halt, and outside the windows stretched nothing but a vast, vacant desert—an endless expanse stripped of color and life, as if the world itself had been scoured clean. Ani scanned the horizon, searching for any sign of movement, even going so far as to lean over Fenix's seat for a better look through the front window. But there was nothing—only the shimmering emptiness of the wastes.

Then, without warning, thick steel shutters slammed down over the windows, plunging the carriage into a sudden, metallic twilight. The daylight vanished in an instant, and Ani flinched back into her seat, heart pounding, as the world outside was sealed away behind cold, unyielding metal.

"Fenix?"

Fenix stayed silent, his eyes still locked to the blocked window, his ears perking up.

'There it is,' Fenix thought, just as the muffled rattle of gunfire erupted from above—the twin gatling guns mounted on the train's roof spitting out a storm of lead, nearly five hundred rounds in a few short, furious seconds. The sound was distant but unmistakable, a mechanical growl that vibrated through the steel bones of the carriage. Then, as suddenly as it began, the guns fell silent, and the car was left in a heavy, expectant hush.

Ani sat frozen, counting three slow breaths in the tense quiet. Before she could find her voice, the thick shutters over the windows rattled upward, letting in the harsh, washed-out daylight once more. The train gave a gentle tug, then began to roll forward, regaining its momentum as if nothing at all had happened.

"Must not have been much," Fenix added matter-of-factly. "Probably just some stray reapers. Mounted guns likely made short work of that."

A few moments later, the true reason for the stop slid into view, and Ani felt the skin tighten along her arms. Just beyond the tracks, a stone's throw from the train, the first of the greenish-grey corpses rolled into sight—goblins, half a dozen of them, sprawled in the dust. Their bodies were twisted and still, fresh blood pooling into the thirsty earth beneath.

"Huh…" Fenix grunted, the sound falling out in an almost amused sort of apathy.

Just beyond the sprawled goblin corpses, the land bore the scars of fresh violence. The remains of a farmhouse smoldered in the heat—main house, barn, and windmill reduced to blackened ribs and ashen cinders, their skeletal frames jutting from the dust like the bones of some long-dead beast. Smoke curled lazily from the ruins, the last breath of a life burned away.

As the caravan rattled forward, the rest of the scene slid into view. Ani's stomach clenched as she caught sight of the bodies—men, women, children—strewn in the dirt beside the ruined house, their forms twisted in the final throes of terror. A goblin pike jutted from the back of one woman, its tattered tassel fluttering in the furnace wind, a grim banner marking the massacre.

Ani stared, frozen in bewildered horror, as the wastes rolled past the window and the grisly tableau was swallowed once more by the endless, indifferent desert. "It's getting worse," she whispered, her voice thin and trembling, searching Fenix's face for any sign of comfort.

Fenix drew in a slow, stale breath and let it out, his gaze drifting back to the window, to the emptiness beyond—where the only answer was silence and the long, unbroken road ahead.

41

The caravan rolled into Serenity later that afternoon, the iron beast hissing to a halt beneath a sky bleached bone-white by the relentless sun. Serenity was a smaller settlement—larger than the dust-bitten outposts of Blister Springs or Brimhall, but still dwarfed by Aberdyne's sprawl. Here, homes hunched close to the ground, built around the hollowed husks of old-world ruins. Crumbled brick and rusted iron, all that remained of a city that had once stretched to the horizon, now stood as silent witnesses to the passage of centuries.

Faded ruins ringed the town, their outlines half-swallowed by drifting sand. It was clear Serenity had once been a metropolis, a place of promise and plenty, but the wastes had done what they did best—stripped it bare, erased its memory from all but the most stubborn history books. Now, only the bones of the old world lingered, and the living clung to what shelter they could find amid the wreckage.

"You know," Fenix said as the caravan rolled to a stop, the brakes hissing beneath in a loud gust of steam. "Mostly all of the munitions in the wastes comes from Serenity." He paused, waiting for the uninterested reply from his companion he knew was coming.

"Really?" Ani replied, a small interest actually piquing.

"Yep," Fenix continued. "Largest bullet foundry in the wastes right here. Not a lot of those, and kind of funny if you think about it." He paused, giving a breath to the moment. "The name; Serenity. Kinda the opposite if you think about it."

"Ironic," Ani suggested.

"Yeah," he returned flatly.

The caravan driver appeared in the car and once more repeated his sermon slash warning, before opening the door and stepping out. One by one the remaining patrons filtered out into the daylight.

"I think it's best we spend the night here," Fenix said as Ani stepped down to the platform. "Best we get our bearings 'fore we head out. We'll get a fresh start in the morning."

Ani nodded, replying silently as her eyes moved across the small settlement sprawling lightly before her.

Rusted iron and battered signs from the old world hung crooked above the doorways, each one scavenged from some distant ruin and dragged here across the wastes—some even bearing the intricate marks of dwarven or elven craft, faded but unmistakable. The buildings themselves slouched beneath the weight of centuries, patched with whatever scrap could be found, their bones a patchwork of brick, iron, and hope.

A trio of guards sauntered down the main street, sidearms swinging loose from cracked leather belts, their tarnished chest armor catching the sun in dull, fractured glints. They moved with the slow confidence of men who'd survived too many summers, eyes half-lidded against the glare. Ani paused, feeling the heat press down on her like a blacksmith's hammer. For a moment, she thought Serenity might be hotter than anywhere else in the wastes—but she pushed the thought aside. Out here, the sun was always merciless. It was only the memory of the caravan's cool, filtered air that made the world outside feel so unforgiving.

"Let's go get us a room before they fill up," Fenix said, tapping her arm and moving towards the luggage car.

A short time later the pair were making their way down the main street of the town, their horses in tow just behind. Fenix had slung his pack over his horse's saddle, freeing himself of the weight for just the moment. Ani walked beside him, her horse not bearing anything other than the saddle.

"You know," Fenix said, eyeing a building that had a pair of scissors burned into the wood on its front. "It's been a long time since I've been anywhere near Parmithia.

"I've heard stories," Ani replied, thinking about the trek they would have to make through the old ruins in order to reach the Deltron facility.

"Stories don't compare," Fenix replied sullenly. "The ruins are a special kind of bad."

"I read that the ruins used to be a great city, bigger even than Corith. It had towering buildings as tall as the sky and spread for as far as the eye could see, like the one in my picture."

Fenix took the next few steps in silence. "Well, it ain't like that now. Nothing but crumbled buildings and long forgotten corpses." He paused, his last visit to the ruins dripping vile in his mind's eye. "You'll see…"

A short time later they arrived at an inn that aptly carried the same name as the settlement. They made their way in and procured a room and two glasses, one beer and the other plain water. Then they retreated to the back of the brightly lit room to a small, uninhabited table.

There were a handful of patrons, mostly the folks that had accompanied them on the caravan. They were keeping amongst themselves, isolated like everything in the wastes was. Lonely and alone.

Fenix and Ani were amongst themselves in conversation.

"Let me see the map again," Fenix requested, but not before his eyes had scanned every person nearby in a flash.

Ani reached into her pack, fetching the folded piece of paper and setting it on the table, herself taking a cautious glance of the room.

"You know," Fenix continued a moment later, leaning in as the volume of his words dropped down. "The thing I can't help but wonder. What is it that the orcs know that we don't? We haven't seen a single one. Sure. The goblins we saw dead back there, but not a single orc." His words trailed off as his thoughts took up the empty space. Then he sighed, a small sniffle escaping. "Just doesn't add up." He paused, his finger tapping the table at the base of his beer glass.

Ani met his gaze, holding it for a moment. Fenix swore he saw a thin flicker behind it. "None of it does," she replied flatly, lifting her glass and finishing it in two gulps. "I think I'm gonna turn in. It's been a long day."

Fenix smirked with a nod. "Not far behind you."

He watched as the girl rose from the table and slipped quietly down the dim hallway toward the rooms. Not so long ago, she'd been just a girl—naïve, untested, a scrapper in name only. The wastes had a way of burning the softness out of people, and lately, he'd seen the change in her. She wore her bravado like a battered duster, hiding the raw ache beneath, and where he might have found such posturing irritating in another, with her he saw only courage. Out here, most folks broke or turned mean. But she'd held herself together, kept her head when others would have lost it. There was a strength in that girl— a stubborn, quiet grit that he found himself admiring more with every mile they traveled. She was becoming something formidable, and he knew it. One day, she'd be a force the wastes would reckon with.

He lifted his glass, draining the last of the warm liquor in a single swallow, and set it down with a heavy sigh. She hadn't even begun to tap into the magic that simmered beneath her skin. "Oof," he muttered, the thought sending a shiver down his spine. Then he pushed back from the table and started down the hall, toward the room where his young companion lay, lost in her book and the quiet stillness of the coming night.

42

Ani was tightening the straps of her saddle the next morning when a piece of paper settled against her leg. She noticed Fenix stepping towards his horse as she bent down to pick it up, a splash of color catching her eye. As she lifted the page the expression on her face shifted, a subtle gesture that Fenix caught. The page had a crude picture of a woman tied to a burning stake, the orange and red flames rising upwards, a look of grimace across their face. The words, *never forget, never forgive*, were typed in large letters at the bottom.

Fenix took a step forward, the consoling words forming on his tongue when Ani crumbled the page in her hand and held it out, a flare of smoke puffing as the page ignited into flames. His consolation quickly shifted to warning. "Easy with that," he growled, his gaze working back and forth to see if any passersby had seen.

Ani turned her gaze to him, opening her hand and allowing the ashes to catch in the breeze. Then she spat at the ground and climbed atop her horse, turning it, and starting down the street.

"Oh hell," he sighed, patting Dirtweed on the neck. Then he climbed up and started after.

It was a half a day's ride, not including the three-hour stop for midday before they reached the outskirts of the ruins. Neither had spoken about the flyer, or the brazen use of magic out in the open. The words had disappeared behind hours of quiet contemplation, each lost in their own thoughts as they crossed the arid desert.

Fenix was the one to finally break the silence, his gaze looking at the twisted remnants of a once great society. "It used to be one of the biggest cities in the world," he said, his sudden words causing Ani's hands to tense on the reins in her hands. "Querque."

"Curr-key?" Ani responded phonetically.

"Yeah," Fenix replied, gazing at the twisted rubble that jutted upwards on the horizon like a broken smile full of fractured teeth. "We named it Parmithia, but before the war, the flames. It was called

Querque." He paused, looking over at her. "I know a bit about history myself too kiddo."

"Wow," she replied, her words sounding less enthusiastic than they felt coming out. "I'm surprised."

Fenix rode the next few paces, the silence once again beginning to build. "I'm sorry people are like that," he said, deciding to breach the matter of earlier. "You'd think with all the troubles we already have, orcs, goblins, the wastes. You'd figure we'd be able to put aside old superstition and hatred."

"It's fine," she replied bitterly.

"It's not," he said, slowing Dirtweed. "And it shouldn't be. You were right to burn it."

Ani slowed, turning to face him. Her gaze fell to the dirt below for a moment before lifting back to meet his. "Thanks."

He smiled, the gesture soft and forgiving. Then he let his eyes move to the distant ruins. "I've been thinking. We should probably skirt the ruins, circle round versus going straight on. There ain't nothing good hiding in there, just clans and scavengers, and I think we've *both* had our fill of reapers."

"That'll add over a day to our travel," Ani argued, not wanting to lose a moment of time.

"Yeah," Fenix remarked. "But it'll increase our chances of actually making there alive by tenfold." He paused, watching her formulate her reply. "Look," he continued. "I'm fully equipped and capable of taking on a small clan myself. Hell. You could even throw in a handful of orcs or scavengers, and I'd likely still come out on top, as you've seen." The last three words were slowed to emphasize the weight. "But even I can't take on the horde. And it ain't just a few scavengers in there. I've heard tales of what lay within those ruins. No. I'd rather not end up in one of their people farms…"

"People farms?"

"Exactly what it sounds like."

Ani shifted her gaze to the ruins. She'd spent a single afternoon in a reaper encampment, and from what Fenix had later described, that was more like a tiny outpost. The larger enclaves housed hundreds, and if the tales went uncorrected, their main-stay diet was tanned and bipedal.

"I think we can stand to lose an afternoon. I'd rather not end up with a stick going in one end and out the other."

Ani took a deep breath, the hot air filling her lungs. Then she nodded, not pulling her gaze from the twisted remains of the ancient city.

The pair pressed on, giving the ancient ruins a wide berth. The shattered bones of the old city loomed in the distance—jagged silhouettes against the scorched sky, haunted by the ghosts of a world long dead. Fenix knew, sooner or later, they'd have to brave those broken streets to reach the facility marked on their map. But that was a problem for another day. For now, they kept to the open, steering clear of whatever shadows or survivors might still linger in the wastes, letting the silence and the endless dust swallow their passing.

43

"—it went all the way back to Newvada. Everything was submerged."

Ani spent the better part of an hour recounting to Fenix, with a storyteller's zeal and his half-amused patience, the legend of the great flood—a calamity that swept the world a century after the great fires. She spoke of how the seas had risen in a single, furious year, the arctic ice melting as if the sun itself had grown vengeful. Oceans climbed a hundred meters, swallowing everything between what had once been Texas and Florida, drowning whole nations beneath salt and silence. Brazil, Australia, the northern reaches of Europe—all vanished beneath the waves. Islands became memories, their names lost to the tides.

For two centuries, the world belonged to the water. The ocean's grip was unyielding, holding fast until the poles began to freeze again, and the currents slowly pulled the ice back north and south. Only then did the waters recede, leaving behind a world forever changed.

"All those dry lakebeds," she continued. "All from the flood. The cliffs near Bilgewater, the same. Old Port got its name because for two hundred years, it *was* a port."

"That must have been something to see," Fenix replied, his gaze working across the space between them and the ruins that had grown closer. "Must have made things a might easier though. Least they didn't need to dig a well...."

"Uh. Salt water. Can't drink it."

Fenix threw his head back and let out a booming laugh, the sound echoing across the empty wastes. "A desert surrounded by water you can't drink," he said, shaking his head in disbelief. "Ain't that just the way of things out here? Nothing's ever easy in the wastes." His laughter faded, replaced by a wry grin. "Suppose it could be worse, though. Up north, they say folks have to deal with frost trolls and wolves. I'll take the heat and the dust over that any day."

Ani nodded. "There is that."

They rode the next few paces in silence, their minds conjuring images to match the words.

"So, if your map's correct, we should reach the facility by sunup if we don't stop. "You reckon anybody's found their way inside?"

"I hope not," Ani replied, sharing her agreement to keep trudging through. "Only way in or out is with a key. All the facilities we have found so far are underground, and the walls are too thick to penetrate. You'd spend your whole life pounding away at them and never even make a dent. Old steel." She paused, her tone shifting. "I just hope that the orcs haven't beat us to it."

"You reckon they could beat their way in?"

"No. But if the prophet had a key…"

"And if we get there and they've managed to get inside?"

She looked over at him, no humor in her tone as she spoke. "That's why you're here."

He smirked, his brow furrowing together. "That's why *I'm* here," he scoffed. "Well, good to know."

He shook his head, casting a wary glance toward the distant ruins as the sun began its slow descent, painting the sky in bruised shades of orange and rust. They didn't stop. Midday's rest was behind them, and with the facility so close, neither expected to find sleep anyway. Better to push through and reach their destination before first light. Fenix figured daylight was an advantage—riding up with the sun at their backs, not creeping through the dark where every shadow could hide an ambush. If orcs—or anything worse—had already made it inside, at least they'd have time to see what they were up against, maybe even hatch a plan before the bullets and arrows started flying. He just hoped it wouldn't come to that. He'd faced his share of trouble in the wastes, but a horde, or even a handful of orcs, was another matter entirely. Still, they pressed on, the dark at their backs, the unknown ahead, and the hope that daylight might tip the odds in their favor.

44

The pair rode on through the night, the sky bleeding from orange to bruised purple, and finally into a deep, starless black. It was the kind of moonless night that seemed to freeze time, where the world shrank to the sound of hooves and the hush of their own breathing. Somewhere out in the darkness, the ruins brooded—silent, ancient, and full of secrets best left undisturbed. Fenix and Ani kept to the edge, close enough to sense any trouble, but far enough to slip away if the shadows started to move. By the time the first pale hints of dawn touched the horizon and the outline of the facility emerged from the gloom, Fenix found himself wondering if they'd find anything at all waiting for them in that haunted place.

"Are you sure?" he said, his words just above a whisper, hovering just above the sound of their horses' hooves against the dirt.

"It shouldn't be far," Ani said, squinting down at the map in her hand. "It should be right here…"

Fenix took a deep breath, exhaling the warm air out quietly to avoid her hearing the anxious sigh. Then a flicker of light caught his eye. He leaned forward, pressing into the darkness. "You see that?"

Ani looked up. All she was blackness looking back, the stars above spread out like a blanket of fractured diamonds. She was about to reply when something slowly approached from the black wall before them.

A few meters ahead was the twisted remains of a long since rusted fence. A few posts sticking up from the dirt and a section of twisted wire sticking out could be seen. As they drew closer, they could make out the ancient fence line.

Fenix slowed his horse to a stop. "Got about an hour before the sun starts to come up. I reckon we should wait it out. No sense catching one of horses' legs in a bundle of wire or landing in a deadfall." He paused. "This is it? On the map?"

Ani nodded unseen in the dark. "This is it."

Fenix studied the darkness, straining against the pitch. The desert was silent, not even a breath of breeze was audible in the dark.

Beside him, Ani sat silently, watching her companion staring into the void. Then he glanced over at her and nodded.

They slipped from their saddles, boots crunching in the dust. Fenix unrolled his battered bedroll and spread it across the cracked earth, a small island of comfort in the endless wastes. They sat together in the hush before dawn, voices low as they traded stories—Ani spinning tales of the old world and the secrets buried in forgotten bunkers, Fenix sharing fragments of his own past: the ache of lost love, the hard lessons learned under a merciless sun.

The hour passed in a blink, the darkness slowly thinning to a bruised blue along the horizon. Before sleep could claim them, the first hints of morning pressed against the sky. They watched in silence as the sun began its slow climb, painting the world in pale orange and gold. Without another word, they packed up, mounted their horses, and rode on—shadows stretching long behind them as they made for the facility, the day just beginning to bleed into the wastes.

45

It didn't take long for them to reach the edge—if you could call it that—of the old facility. Before them yawned a scar in the earth, an excavation site dug and redrawn by desperate hands over generations. A steep slope, loose with dust and broken stone, led down a hundred yards to where the structure crouched beneath the surface, half-buried and defiant.

In the pale morning light, Fenix could make out the entrance: a tunnel-shaped maw cut into the concrete and steel, leading a dozen feet into shadow. The walls bore the scars of centuries—deep gouges, blackened scorch marks, the stubborn signatures of wastelanders who'd tried and failed to break through. But all those efforts, all that violence, had left little more than scratches on the surface. The real defenses ran deeper: twelve feet of plasticrete and tungsten, a fortress built by a world that had vanished a thousand years ago. Whatever machines or tools might have cracked it open were long lost to the dust. Out here, all that remained were stone-age methods and the ghosts of better days.

"That's a good sign," Fenix remarked, looking down at the rectangular structure. "What do you say we get a closer look?"

Ani nodded, waiting for Fenix to nudge his horse forward before following.

Down and down they rode, the world narrowing to a winding path carved through dust and broken stone. Twenty minutes slipped by before they reached the bottom of the excavation, and there, the sheer scale of the place left them speechless. The structure loomed—two hundred feet of battered concrete and steel, stretching a thousand feet across the pit like the bones of some ancient beast. The walls bore the scars of centuries: broken tools, rusted crowbars, and the blackened remains of failed charges littered the base, mute testimony to generations of desperate souls who'd tried—and failed—to break through. All those attempts had left little more than scratches on the surface, the real defenses buried deep beneath layers of plasticrete and tungsten, relics of a world that had vanished long before either of them was born.

Fenix sat atop his horse, eyes wide, unable to take in the whole of it at once. Then his gaze drifted to a tunnel-like opening, a gaping maw fifteen feet high and just as wide, leading back into shadow where dirt and sand had drifted up against a massive circular door. He reckoned it would take hours to clear the way, but before he could say as much, Ani was already dropping from her saddle, boots hitting the earth as she strode toward the entrance, determination burning in her step.

"Be careful!" Fenix called out, his mind a whirl with images of all manner of traps that could lay in wait.

Ani continued, as if deaf to his warning.

Ani slipped into the cool shadow of the tunnel, her boots scuffing softly on ancient concrete. With practiced fingers, she reached beneath the grime-stained collar of her shirt and drew out the cord that hung around her neck. The key—a relic from a world that had burned—dangled in her grip, catching the faint morning light as she approached the massive door.

Just like Belcor, she thought, hope and dread tangling in her chest. Her eyes swept the battered surface, searching for any sign of a lock. To most, the wall would have looked unbroken, save for a shallow, two-inch indentation—nothing more than a blemish in the concrete. But to Ani, it was everything.

She stepped towards the recess and held out the key. She took a deep breath and exhaled slowly. "Please work…" she pleaded silently to the concrete. Then she lifted the key to the recess and pressed it in. Nothing.

She stood there, Fenix watching silently from behind. She felt the weight of the world come crashing down, her heart sinking into her stomach as only silence responded. "No," she whimpered before pulling the key back to try again.

Then a single beep was heard from within the wall, faint, almost unnoticeable. To Ani, however, it was as loud as a gunshot. She exhaled a lungful of breath heavily with a sharp sigh. Then the panel illuminated in a dull blue and a loud grinding sound rang out. Behind her, Fenix tensed, his hand shooting towards his pistol.

Ani stepped back, dust sifting down from the stone above as the ancient mechanism shuddered to life. With a grinding groan, the massive entrance began to pull away, the earth around it collapsing inward as the door edged back, inch by inch. Then, with a thunderous clank that sent a tremor through the ground beneath her boots, the door rolled aside—like some colossal gear, vanishing into the wall and revealing the darkness beyond.

"Fenix!" she called, turning to him, her face alight with a rare, unguarded excitement, the kind that cut through the dust and dread of the wastes.

Fenix eased his grasp on the handle of his pistol. With a heavy exhale, he climbed down from his horse and started forward.

Ani waited, not wishing to, but just in case, for her companion to approach. Then, when the door had finished grinding into the wall and had come to a stop, she carefully made her way over the threshold and into the main entrance.

She had made it about ten feet in when lights overhead slowly flickered to life. She felt the cool relief of knowing the facility still had power, that its reactor was still operational after all this time. *'These facilities truly were a marvel,'* she thought as she let her gaze move around the room, a smile spread across her lips.

Fenix made his way in, Dirtweed needing a bit of coaxing to cross the threshold.

"To think," Ani said proudly, with a profound wonder in her voice. "We're the first people in a thousand years to step foot in here."

Fenix looked around the massive room, the smell of dust and age rising up as the arid breeze from outside met the climate-controlled air within. "Smells like it," he remarked, silently enjoying the coolness that brushed over his face.

The main entrance was a large room, a hall to be more precise. It was barren save for a security checkpoint area which consisted of a large desk, two metal detectors and a running line of stanchions. Beyond that were two large doors that led further in and two doors on opposite sides, elevators leading downward to the five floors below.

Ani started forward, lifting the stanchion cords and making her way underneath in a straight line towards the back doors. Then she stopped in her tracks and turned, making her way back to the doorway. There was a sign that read, *Door Control,* and was slightly raised, the panel marked. She lifted her key up, pulling it away. The door cried out again and slowly began to move back into place.

"I'd be lying if I said watching that door close didn't make me a might nervous," Fenix remarked, staring as the massive portal rolled shut.

"It's fine," Ani remarked non-chalantly.

Fenix grumbled, watching his companion turn, her arms moving out to her sides, palms up. "Let's explore."

"Let's explore, she says," he replied flatly, his gaze moving back to the massive doorway that was edging itself closed.

The pair made their way in, past the security booth. Fenix nearly had a heart attack as a blaring siren sounded when he walked through the metal detector. It took Ani nearly a full two minutes to stop laughing. Fenix had never started.

"Oh, you should have seen your face," Ani laughed, her smile nearly splitting her cheeks as they made their way down the main corridor leading further in.

As they moved deeper into the facility, the overhead lights flickered to life one by one, each glow triggered by their passing— cold, electric ghosts in the gloom. They drifted past faded signs: Administration, Clerk, Janitorial—remnants of a world that once ran on order and routine.

Soon, they entered a smaller chamber, far more intimate than the cavernous entry hall. Rows of battered benches lined the walls, with scarred little tables scattered between, the kind of place where lost souls might have once waited for judgment or mercy. The air was thick with the hush of abandonment.

Fenix paused, his gaze drawn to a gallery of old photographs— faces staring out from another age, their eyes full of hope or warning. In the corner, three tattered flags hung from rusted poles: one red, white, and blue; another a sun-bleached yellow, blue, and red; the last a faded blue stamped with a white star. Beneath them, the word "Americorp" lingered in peeling paint.

"Check it out," Ani called out, pulling his attention from the three pieces of cloth.

Fenix turned to see Ani standing at a large panel that was hanging on the wall. There was a map of the facility displayed, with descriptions of the different sections beside it. As he approached, he watched Ani reach out and touch the screen. To his surprise it moved when her fingers brushed it.

"What...?" he remarked as he stepped up.

"It responds to touch," she smiled, flicking the image to the side and displaying the different floors. Barracks, Mess, Research and Development, Administration, Armory. Each floor had its own designation. "Bam," she said, reaching out and pointing at the bottom floor. "That's why we're here."

He leaned closer. "Armory?"

She smiled, looking back at him. "Armory."

Fenix cast a last glance at the glowing display as Ani turned and strode down the corridor. Making sure she wasn't watching, he reached out and brushed his fingers across the glassy surface. To his surprise, the image slid beneath his touch—alive, somehow, with a ghostly light. He jerked his hand back, startled, as if he'd touched a hot stove. For a moment, he stared at the screen, suspicion and wonder warring in his eyes, before glancing down the hall to be sure Ani hadn't noticed.

They moved on, choosing the stairs over the elevator—not out of any fear of tight spaces, but because neither of them truly understood what an elevator was, or why a storage room would need doors that opened by themselves. Fenix found himself quietly unsettled by the strangeness of it all—the doors that moved without a hand, the surfaces that responded to a touch. He felt the weight of his own ignorance, but masked it with a practiced indifference, unwilling to let on just how out of place he felt in the bones of the old world.

The pair continued down the stairs, past the Administration floor and Research and Development, past the Mess and finally the Barracks. As they were descending the final turn to the bottom floor Fenix asked, his words echoing loudly in the twisting corridor, "Where do you think everyone is?"

"Dead," Ani replied flatly, her response causing him to ponder if that was how he sounded when he responded to questions like that with such indifference.

They reached the bottom of the stairwell, and Ani pressed the door open. A long corridor stretched before them, lined with doors that vanished into the unlit dark. The air was thick with the hush of abandonment. Along the walls, faded paintings and memorial plaques caught the flicker of their passing—occasional portraits of grim-faced officers in tarnished military dress, names etched into wood and brass: Jack Harvey, Lisette Galindo, Randy Morrison. Fenix found himself wondering who these people had been, what it meant to have a room in a place like this, to have your name endure when the world outside had turned to dust.

They moved on, the lights overhead stuttering to life one by one, chasing away the shadows as they passed. When the last bulb flared, Ani felt a shiver of anticipation run up her spine. At the end of the corridor, a set of heavy double doors waited—bigger than the rest, marked by a small, dust-choked panel. She stepped up, pressed her key to the reader.

A flash of red. An automated voice echoed through the gloom: "Authorized clearance required."

Fenix pulled his pistol in a flash and spun, looking in every direction at once.

"It's automated," Ani replied flatly.

"What?"

"It's not real. Just a recording."

Fenix relaxed, though just slightly.

She turned back to the panel, perplexed. Then she tried again.

"Authorized clearance required."

"No..."

"What does it mean?" Fenix asked, staring back at the panel as if it was poised to attack, his pistol still hanging in his hand.

"No..."

His brow lifted.

"This key doesn't work."

"Wait," he replied, his grip tightening on his pistol. "What?"

"Just. Give me a minute, okay? Let me think."

"Try it again."

"It isn't gonna work."

"Just try–"

"It won't work!" she snapped, immediately feeling bad for responding as she did. But she pushed the feeling away and continued to think. "Look. There had to be someone in here with access, the right key. We just have to find them. We find the person with *authorized clearance*; we find the key. We find the key; you get your guns."

Fenix sighed heavily, holstering his pistol. "The fascination with the damned keys. Jesus. Couldn't they just have one?"

Ani ignored the comment, glancing again at the large steel doors. Then she made a sound that resembled a deep sigh morphing to a low growl. "Let's start in the barracks. We'll work our way up."

"Lovely," Fenix replied, shaking his head as she made her way past.

"Maybe we should check these rooms?"

"Yeah," Ani replied bitterly. She was mad, and it wasn't his fault, but there was no one else to direct her irritation towards, so he got to deal with it. Besides, she had put up with him in the beginning, so it was only fair he got to take it for once.

"Lead on scrappy," he remarked as she started towards the first door.

She ignored the comment.

For what felt like hours, the pair moved from office to office, rifling through drawers and scattering yellowed papers across battered desks. Each room was a tomb of dust and silence, the air heavy with the ghosts of those who'd once called this place their post. Sixteen rooms, and not a single sign of what they were after. The deeper they searched, the more the facility seemed to sprawl—its endless corridors and locked doors swallowing time and hope alike. At this pace, Fenix reckoned, they'd be searching for a month—time they didn't have. Out there in the wastes, the prophet could be closing in on another facility, or even this one. The walls pressed in, the building growing larger and larger with every fruitless search, the weight of urgency settling over them like the desert heat.

46

"How are we even supposed to know who had *authorized clearance*? Not exactly like we can ask anyone. Shit."

Ani glanced at Fenix who was lifting a stack of papers off of a desk and rifling through them. They had finished on the Armory floor and had worked their way through the barracks, mess hall, lavatories and gym. They had discovered where a good portion of the facilities residents had ended up when they entered an area labeled *Commons Area*. Dozens of corpses decorated the hall, a mass of decorated skeletons all reporting for duty. Judging from how the dead were displayed, it appeared that many of them had simply decided to take their own lives, a collage of empty plastic and glass bottles littered the floor, prescription drugs and alcohol, an age old get out of life free card played by two dozen soldiers all at once. The barracks had held its own collection of the dead, some tucked neatly in bed, some curled up with one another, spooning in an eternal embrace. The first few had settled uneasily with Ani, but after the fourth, the fifth, the thirtieth. Now she looked at the skeletons in the same brash disregard as she did the furniture they rested on.

"Everyone here was a soldier," Ani replied, pulling her gaze from a skeleton sagging in a couch a short distance away. "There was a hierarchy, just like the reapers, or the scavengers. We just have to find the one with, I don't know, the most stuff on their outfit; the most *decorations*." The last word fell out more phrased as a sentence than a suggestion.

"Great," Fenix chirped, reaching out and pulling at the bars on the jacket of a chair-bound skeleton. "How about you? You important?"

"Really?" Ani barked.

Fenix looked up to see her staring at him disapprovingly.

He sighed heavily. "Sorry."

"Let's try the next floor."

The next floor was the second floor, Administration. There was an additional sign that read *Officer's Quarters, War Room, Debriefing Room* and *Records*.

They made their way up the stairs and into the corridor. The hallway mirrored the others, doors marked with names, intersecting hallways that led further in. They stared with the first of the doors, Records.

By the time they reached Officer's Quarters Fenix had begun to feel the pang of hunger. His stomach grumbled beneath his shirt, and he could taste the dry sourness of his gut. "How much longer we gonna keep looking? I could use a bite."

"Till we find it," Ani replied flatly.

Fenix shook his head, moving towards the first door in the officer's quarters hallway. He stopped, reading the plaque on the door. "Eastwood," he read out loud to himself before reaching out and opening the door.

As the door opened, he saw what appeared to be a small bedroom with a living space attached. Off to the side was a toilet room. A desk was at the opposite side of the room. His eyes moved to the shape atop the bed, a skeleton wearing nothing with an empty bottle at its side. *'Naked and drunk,'* he thought silently to himself. *'Not a bad way to go...'*

He made his way in, the door across the hallway sounding open as Ani made her way into that one.

He rummaged through the room, checking the drawers and cupboards, the desk and the pockets of the dead man's clothes. By the time he emerged Ani was already starting towards the next room. He wanted to tell her he was losing hope and beginning to think it was going to be hopeless, but how would that help? It wouldn't, so he kept the thought to himself and decided to follow her into the next room.

He glanced at the name next to the door of the room. Louis Hondo. He smirked, making his way in. "Alright Hondo," he quipped. "Let's see what you got."

Ani paused just inside the threshold, boots scuffing the dust. She'd seen death in every room of this forsaken place, but something about this one made her breath catch. The skeleton in the chair faced the door, as if waiting for a visitor who never came. Its skull lolled back at an unnatural angle, the top blown clean away—a silent testament to a final, desperate act. One arm dangled uselessly, bone snapped and hanging by a thread, but the other still gripped a rusted pistol, fingers locked tight even in death.

A dark stain trailed up the wall behind, ending in a grisly spray around a ragged hole in the ceiling. Ani's gaze lingered on the splatter, then drifted back down to the remains. The skeleton was draped in the tattered remnants of a uniform, chest heavy with rows of tarnished bars and medals—proof that this had once been someone important, a leader maybe, or a survivor who'd carried too much for too long.

On the desk beside the corpse, an empty bottle of liquor lay on its side, a stained glass catching the last of the weak light. A nearly finished cigar rested in an ornate ashtray, its end long since gone cold. There was a strange device, too—something small and rectangular, with a dead black screen and buttons she didn't recognize. Ani stared at it, knowing only the bottle and the glass, and wondered what stories the dead kept locked behind their silent teeth.

"This looks promising," Fenix said from behind her, startling her. "Could be our guy."

"Or girl," Ani replied matter-of-factly as she liked to do. Then she started forward.

Fenix made his way to the desk, picking up the bottle and sniffing the top. It smelled of old air and dust. There was no dust in the climate-controlled facility, especially with the filtration system still in operation and no movement to kick anything up in the last thousand years. As he set the bottle down, he found himself wondering again how long it had taken for the folks inside to either go crazy or to starve to death. Had they gone quietly, or sobbing and begging for life?

Ani grasped the back of the chair, pulling it free from the desk. The decorated corpse slouched to the side, nearly falling from the chair. Then she gingerly patted the dead man, or woman's pocket. Nothing. She reached out, pulling the desk drawer open. Inside were some scattered papers, another pistol, a package of cigars, and a single plastic card with a light blue cord attached. She felt her stomach tickle inside and reached out, pulling the card out and turning it over in her hand.

A man's face stared back, older, grey hair and no smile, eyes that flickered dully with life. General Louis Hondo it read in a plain font beside the picture. Beneath, read the words that pushed the air from her lungs. *Level 4 clearance.*

She looked up, the look on her face stopping Fenix mid-lift. He had the snubbed end of the cigar that had been resting in the ashtray and was bringing it to his nose. "What?"

She smiled, holding the card out so he could read it.

"Well, hot damn," he replied, dropping the cigar butt on the floor. "Thank you, Mr. Hondo."

Ani lowered the card, tapping it against her palm, the smile of relief growing. "Let's go see these guns…"

47

Ani and Fenix stood frozen, mouths agape, eyes wide and unblinking, as if time itself had slowed to let them take in the impossible. Before them, stretching from floor to ceiling and wall to wall, was an arsenal beyond reckoning—a graveyard's worth of firepower, preserved in the dust and silence of the old world. Rows of shelves groaned beneath the weight of thousands of weapons: rifles and shotguns, pistols and revolvers, crates of magazines and grenades, claymores and landmines, and guns so massive a horse would have buckled beneath their heft.

Ammunition was stacked in neat, endless rows, the dull brass and steel catching the flicker of their lantern. There were weapons here that belonged in legend—tools of war from a time when the world still dreamed of victory. The sheer scale of it left them dumbfounded, a cathedral of death and iron, a hall where the ghosts of a thousand battles waited in silence for the next hand to claim them.

For a long moment, neither spoke. They simply stood, two survivors in the wastes, dwarfed by the legacy of destruction that sprawled before them—a testament to the world that was, and the violence that had survived it.

"Fuck me…" Fenix whispered, his face turning to meet Ani's.

She stood speechless, rooted to the spot by awe and uncertainty. Ani had never seen anything like this—her knowledge of guns was next to nothing. Other than the battered little pistol her father had pressed into her palm—the "lizard gun," as the drifter liked to call it—she'd never even hefted another firearm until Fenix had bought her one. She couldn't tell a revolver from a rifle, or a shotgun from a machine gun. The difference between them, the way they worked, the purpose of each—these were mysteries, as foreign as the old world itself.

Now, surrounded by this impossible arsenal, Ani felt utterly overwhelmed. The sheer number and variety of weapons left her reeling: pistols and rifles, shotguns and monstrous guns that looked as if they'd need a horse to haul them. She'd grown up thinking there were only two kinds of guns—the kind you held in your hand, and the kind you braced against your shoulder. But this... this was an entire universe of death and iron, a legacy of violence from a world that had burned itself away.

Fenix, however, knew a little more. "This, changes *everything*," he grinned, starting forward.

Over the next two hours, Fenix all but forgot his hunger, swept up in the feverish excitement of discovery. He hefted nearly every weapon in the room, moving from rack to rack with the wide-eyed wonder of a scrapper stumbling on an untouched oasis. Pistols, rifles, long-range shooters—he handled them all, weighing their balance, testing the action, and making mental notes as he went. With Ani's help at the old-world terminal, he flipped through schematics, learning calibers and brands, short-range, long-range, sniper. He peered through scopes, tried on battered straps and belts, and began to set aside his favorites, assembling a personal arsenal from the ghosts of a lost age. For a while, he was a child again, nearly skipping between the shelves, lost in the endless possibilities of firepower and fate.

Ani had grown bored nearly twenty minutes in. She had hefted the weight of a few guns, holding them with apprehension before setting them down. She was fine with the one she had. But to be honest, she still preferred the feel of her *lizard gun*. It fit her hand better. She did, however, find a rather nice knife with a scabbard that attached nicely to her belt. And it had a working compass on the top. That, she liked.

"Man," Fenix chuckled. "Those orcs wanna war? Let's give em one."

Ani looked up blankly, sliding the knife into its sheath. "I'm starting to get hungry."

At those words, his stomach cried out.

He stopped, setting a heavy rifle back onto the rack. "Yeah. I suppose they're not going anywhere." He paused. "Really wish I could try em out. I'd love to pop off a few shots with each just to see how they feel."

"And I'd really like to get some food in my stomach," Ani replied, her eyebrows lifting.

"All right," he replied, starting towards her. "Let's take a break."

The pair made their way back to the first floor. It was the only floor that didn't have any dead on it. Though they were pretty much desensitized at this point, neither of them had the urge, or desire for that matter, to eat with a corpse. Besides, they both wanted to check on their horses.

They sat together in the dim hush of the facility, chewing strips of lizard jerky and letting the salt and spice linger on their tongues. Ani savored a hydration tab, the tangy fizz dissolving the dust in her mouth. There was running water here—hot showers waiting behind steel doors—but old habits died hard. Neither trusted the pipes, not when the memory of poisoned wells and tainted streams haunted every settlement in the wastes. Safer to stick with what they knew, even if it meant the comfort of a real drink was just out of reach.

As they ate, their voices were low, drifting between plans and worries. With two working keys, they finally had a shot at reaching the Arcan facility—if they could find it before the prophet did. If they managed to get inside, maybe, just maybe, they could disable the weapon that had haunted the world for a thousand years. But the path ahead was uncertain, and the prophet was out there somewhere, moving fast, maybe with a second key in hand. Ani tried not to dwell on that possibility. They'd already crossed half the wastes to get to Deltron, risking everything on a hope and a handful of secrets. Now, every mile mattered. If the prophet reached Arcan first... she didn't want to imagine what would come next.

"That's even assuming he knows how to get inside the place," Fenix remarked, reaching down to scratch a mosquito bite at his ankle. "You really think anyone now would know what the key looks like, or how to use it? You know because of your old man, and he because of his. Hell. Even just to know where to hold it against the wall to get the door open…"

"We can't assume he's ignorant," Ani replied, the light citrus tingle of the hydration tab still lingering. "We don't know how much Jarek told him." She paused. "And remember what he said. He was already going in and out of Belcor when we weren't there. We have to assume he knows the other facilities will be the same…"

He growled. "Yeah. Suppose you're right."

"Assume the best, prepare for the worst."

"I like that," Fenix replied with a smirk.

"It was my granddad."

"Smart man."

"I'd like to think so." A thin flicker of a smile tickled her lips.

"All I know," Fenix continued, shifting topic. "With the arsenal sitting down there, we'll win any war we go into. Orcs, reapers, scavengers, hell. Strap a few of those big ones to Dirtweed over there, I'll ride straight into a horde."

"Let's hope they work…"

"Now why'd you gotta go and say that for?" Fenix barked, smirking at her disapprovingly. "Now I'm gonna be second guessing when I'm pulling back on the trigger."

She shrugged. "Just being rational."

"Well, don't, okay." He stared at her from under a furrowed brow for a moment. "Ugh…"

"I'm sure you could take em into one of the hallways and test em out."

He smirked again, shrugging his shoulders. "Guess it couldn't hurt." He paused. "Gonna be loud as all hell though."

"Put some wet cloth in your ears."

"Wet cloth…?"

She looked at him like he had asked the world's dumbest question. "You've never put wet cloth in your ears?"

He stared at her like she had just made the world's dumbest comment. "Now why would someone go and put wet cloth in their ears?"

She shook her head. "Never mind."

"You are a weird one," he remarked, staring at her for a moment longer.

The two lingered in quiet conversation for a while longer, the weight of exhaustion finally settling over them. Eventually, Fenix's restless energy got the better of him—he excused himself, boots echoing down the concrete corridor as he disappeared toward the armory below, unable to resist the siren call of so much old-world firepower.

Ani, meanwhile, wandered deeper into the facility's records wing. The air here was cooler, thick with the scent of dust and ancient paper. She found a battered terminal tucked away in a corner, its screen flickering with the pale blue glow of a world long gone. Sinking into the cracked leather chair, she let herself burrow into the archives, fingers dancing over the keys as she lost herself in the digital ghosts of the past.

For the first time in weeks, Ani allowed herself to relax. The journey across the wastes had left her raw and hollow, nerves frayed by too many sleepless nights and the constant threat of violence. But here, surrounded by steel walls and the promise of a hot shower and a real bed, she felt the tension begin to slip away. With the armory stocked and the doors sealed tight, she no longer felt the need to sleep with one eye open and a hand on her pistol. For a fleeting moment, the world outside—the dust, the sun, the endless hunger—felt very far away.

48

Fenix made his way back down the corridor towards the armory. He could feel the pricklings of excitement sparking beneath his shirt, thin ripples flaring out. The muscles in his arms flexed and he brought his hands together in a solid clap, rubbing them together briskly as he approached the door.

Once inside, that electricity dispersed, replaced by a calmer, more serene emotion. It was one he hadn't felt in many cycles. Accomplishment.

Fenix's gaze drifted slowly along the shelves and racks, the air thick with the ancient tang of steel, dust, and old machine oil. He moved with a kind of reverence, boots echoing on the concrete as he approached a battered counter where a neat row of dark green canvas duffel bags waited, untouched by time. For a moment, he just stood there, a thin, crooked smile tugging at the corner of his mouth. Then, with a quiet chuckle, he reached out and grabbed two of the bags, slinging them over his shoulder. He turned back to the arsenal— thousands of weapons glinting in the dim light, a dragon's hoard of firepower and death. The smile widened as he imagined the weight his horse would soon be carrying. "Sorry, buddy," he muttered, already picturing the old beast's long-suffering glare.

Fenix made his way through the room, pulling gun after gun off the racks. He hefted their weight, pulling levers and flipping switches as he dry-fired them while checking their action. He didn't know what any of the guns were, but that didn't matter. He knew what they did, and that the bigger the ammunition they took, the bigger the boom they would make. That was enough. The minutia of time spent on the terminal was enough to know how to load, reload and fire.

Nearly two hours slipped by before Fenix was satisfied with his haul. He'd found a pair of battered shoulder holsters and slid two gleaming, old-world service revolvers into them—silver catching the dim light like relics from a forgotten age. An ankle holster now held a compact semi-automatic, and on the counter beside him, one duffel bag brimmed with automatic rifles and shotguns, while the other was stuffed to bursting with ammunition—heavy enough to make any horse think twice. He'd even scrounged up a side bag, filling it with whatever else might tip the odds: hand grenades, stun grenades, a shock baton, and a scatter of caltrops. By the end, he was a walking arsenal, every inch of him bristling with the ghosts of wars long past.

He slung the side bag over his shoulder, then hefted the first duffel, shifting its weight until it settled against his back. The second bag—ammunition, dense and unyielding—he tested with a grunt before throwing it over the other shoulder. The ammo weighed more than the guns themselves, but he figured that was just the way of things: less empty space, more trouble.

At the threshold, Fenix paused, casting one last look over the rows of pre-war weapons, his gaze lingering on the silent promise of violence and survival. Grim determination settled in his bones, but another thought crept in—selfish, but impossible to ignore. With just one of these bags, he could buy his way out of the wastes for good. Credits enough to vanish, maybe even start over somewhere green. Or, with a wagon and a couple of sturdy horses, he could run the wastes himself, become a legend or a ghost, depending on how the wind blew.

Fenix lingered in the doorway, staring back at the armory—a dragon's hoard of old-world steel and violence—before a furrow creased his brow. He shook his head, as if to scatter the thoughts that had begun to coil in the back of his mind. Those were the thoughts of a drifter, the man he'd been for too many years. But that wasn't who he wanted to be anymore. Not after everything that had happened. Not after Ani.

His time with the girl upstairs had changed something deep inside him, reminded him of the man he'd once been—before the wastes had taken his wife, before the world had stripped him down to nothing but grit and regret. Fate, it seemed, had offered him a second chance, and he knew if he wanted to help Ani, help the people scraping by in the wastes, he'd have to let go of the old habits that had kept him alive but left him hollow. He had to remember who he was.

As he trudged back up the corridor, the weight of the duffel biting into his shoulder, memories flickered through his mind: the small patch of green he'd once called a farm, the warmth of his wife's laughter, the way her eyes crinkled when she smiled. He'd been a good man, once. She'd been the best part of him. But she was gone, and he'd been broken. Broken could be mended, though. And as he climbed the stairs, he realized this was his chance to do just that.

He passed the open door to Ani's room. She was sprawled atop the bed, a towel twisted around her hair, a book cradled in her hands. She looked up, catching his eye with a glint of mild amusement, her gaze flicking between him and the two heavy bags slung over his shoulders.

A small chuckle escaped her lips as she allowed the book to lower to her lap. "You really need all of that...?"

Fenix smiled, shrugging under the weight. "Probably not," he replied, the smile not fading. "But couldn't hurt." He shifted his shoulder under the strap. "I reckon we could sell some of em. Probably get a good amount of credits too. Wouldn't hurt."

She smirked in agreement.

"I'm guessing," he continued, the smile growing slightly wider. "That judging by the uh, *comfort* of your attire, that we'll be bedding down here for the night?"

A smile flickered at Ani's lips.

"Whelp," Fenix said, turning his gaze into the hallway. "Then I guess I got some time to kill." He looked back across the room at her, tipping his head slightly. "Madam." Then he turned and started towards another of the rooms.

49

Ani had just woken up from a nap when she heard the first of the gunshots. She shoved the book from where it had fallen atop her lap, and leapt to her feet, scrambling to dress as quickly as she could. The repeated firing sounded out. It sounded like a war had started.

She yanked her boots on, grabbed her pistol and darted into the hallway. She walked quickly, following the sounds of the rapports, her heart pounding in her chest. They had found them. They had managed to find a way in, and now her companion was doing everything he could to fight them off. He needed her help.

Ani moved as quickly as she could, not running in fear of turning a corner and running full force into the bladed end of an orc's axe, or a goblin pike. A dull heat worked its way up her fingers into her arm. She had been practicing keeping that warmth a constant, and realized how much faster it was to bring it to life.

A few moments later she emerged from the bottom of a stairwell that led to the mess hall and kitchen.

Ani froze, a cold anger flashing through her.

Standing twenty feet away, two twists of wet cloth sticking out of his ears, was Fenix. He had a display of guns laid out across one of the stainless-steel prep tables and was firing one of the rifles into a stack of rice bags across the room.

Ani exhaled slowly, waiting for the moment he stopped pulling back on the trigger. Then she shouted, "Fenix!"

Fenix turned, his brow lifting. "Hey, girl," he replied, lowering the weapon.

She stood there, her head shaking.

"You okay?" he asked, a thin look of concern working across his features.

"You gave me a freaking heart attack," Ani replied. "I thought they had gotten in and we were under attack. I thought they were killing you."

He stared at her for a moment, puzzled. "Huh?"

She grunted, making her way the twenty paces to where he stood. Then she reached up and pulled one of the pieces of cloth from his ear. "What are you doing?"

He looked at her like she had just asked why he tied his boots before walking. "I gotta see how they work. Don't I?" He continued to eye her. "These guns aren't gonna do us much good if'n I don't know how to use em…"

"You scared the hell out of me," she snapped.

"I would have told you, but I didn't want to wake you."

She shot him an irritated look. "And shooting off a bunch of guns wasn't gonna do just that?"

He smirked. "Well. Guess I hadn't put enough thought into that…"

"I'm heading back upstairs," Ani said, her face softening as relief continued to fill her. "I suppose you're hungry?"

Fenix smirked again. "I could go for a bite. I'll rustle us something up when I finish up here. Why don't you go get ready and I'll wrap things up. I think I'm good with all these," he finished, gesturing with a nod towards the display of weapons.

She turned and started back upstairs with a shake of her head.

It was a short time later that the pair were sitting in the small commons area, a heated plate of MRE sitting before them.

Fenix shoveled a forkful of what was supposed to taste like a salisbury steak into his mouth. He had no idea what salisbury steak was, but by the taste, he didn't imagine it was the most popular pre-world food. "It's still strange to me," he said, swallowing the bite, "how well everything's been preserved down here." He scoffed lightly. "Kind of creepy if you want my opinion."

Ani looked across to him. "Climate control," she repeated. "It keeps things like moisture from building up. These facilities were designed to function for thousands of years. All the maintenance is automated. They could run for the next five thousand years without anyone in them."

Fenix scoffed; his fork poised above what remained of the small pile on his plate. "Well, you'd think that if they were smart enough to build things like this, that they'd have been smart enough to not let the great fires happen in the first place. They might not have *needed* these facilities then."

"I don't think they anticipated the merge," Ani replied, setting her fork down. She'd had her fill of the steak paste.

"Well," Fenix smirked. "Then maybe they shouldn't have been messing with things they didn't understand."

"Well, that's what science *is*. Science is about meddling with things we don't understand, experimenting and testing, so that we can have a better understanding. That's the only way we can get better. You have to study and experiment to create a reaction, to create better technology, medicine, cures. Without science, humanity will never grow."

"Yeah," Fenix replied. "Well. The great fires. That's all I'm saying. Cause that was one *hell* of a reaction."

"Can you imagine what it must have been like before?" Ani said, moving the topic. She smiled. Just imagine. The cities, the flying machines, going anywhere in the world you wanted in a matter of hours. The freedom." She pondered the thought for a moment. "Ugh. Just having clean water, any time you wanted, or to be able to go to the store and have as much food as you could carry."

"Must not have been that great," Fenix replied. "They built these facilities for a reason. And there were still wars."

"They didn't build the facilities until *after* the merge."

Fenix chuckled. "Could you imagine *that*?" He shook his head. "Just imagine lying down to bed one night, and then you wake up to a fairy buzzing around your room, knocking everything over and cursing and spittin'. Then you open your window and see the orcish horde, or a goblin war party making their way past, trophies on their belts. Or hell. Even just seeing an elf for the first time." He shook his head. "That right there, *that* must have been one *hell* of a shock. No wonder they scrambled to put these things together."

"It took fifty years to complete the facilities," Ani reminded. "That was fifty years of having to learn to live alongside the new races. And that was with goblin raiding parties fighting for clan territory, and the orcs slaughtering everything in their path. Then the witches... I can't imagine how terrifying that must have been for them."

"Terrifying enough to create the fire."

"They already had the bombs," Ani said, her tone softening. "I think they just wanted to try and save as many people as they could, before they used them. They'd used them on themselves prior..."

The pair went quiet with the thought, Fenix setting down his fork on the plate as the last of his appetite drifted away. "Well," he said, sitting back. "This has been an enlightening conversation, but I think it's about time we get on our way. You about ready?"

Ani nodded.

"Well. Then let's go find us this Arcan facility."

Ani and Fenix gathered the last of their things in silence, the weight of the armory and the ghosts of the old world pressing in around them. Packs slung and weapons secured, they made their way back through the echoing corridors to where their horses waited at the entrance. With a final glance at the cool, shadowed safety of the underground, they triggered the massive vault door, waiting as it groaned and rolled aside, sunlight spilling in like a flood.

The moment they stepped out, the wastes greeted them with a vengeance. After two days in the climate-controlled hush of the facility, the sun's fury felt almost personal—an old enemy waiting to settle a score. Heat slammed down from above, the air shimmering and raw, dust swirling in the wind. It was just past midday, and the world outside was a white-hot anvil.

For a moment, they lingered in the doorway, letting the last breath of cool air slip past their shoulders. Then, with no choice but forward, they stepped out into the blaze, squinting against the glare as they started their long ride back toward Serenity, the wastes stretching endless and merciless before them.

50

The sun battered down from above, the dust rising from beneath. The culmination of heat, dirt and blaring light oppressed the two lone travelers as they crossed the arid land. Fenix's horse was moving slower, bogged down by a weight it was by no means built to endure. Muscles strained beneath the skin on its legs, and frequent *snorts* informed Fenix just how unhappy Dirtweed was about the attached luggage.

"How to reckon we're gonna find your Arcan facility?" The heat worn words fluttered through the scorching air, delivered through parched lips and a desert dry throat. "It ain't listed on your map. And it don't bother you none that it's the only facility that's not?"

Ani rode with her head hung low, the brim of her hat doing everything to block the blindingly bright light above. "There has to be something I missed," she replied dryly.

"There weren't any of those terminals like we seen back in Belcor either."

"No," she replied. "There was one, but it was only for facility maintenance." She pondered that thought for another moment. "I don't think the people that were living there cared much for knowledge of the pre-world. I think Deltron was mainly for weapon's storage."

"Yeah," Fenix replied. "I kinda got that."

"Maybe we should go back to the Belcor facility."

"Are you out of your mind, girl?" Fenix remarked, his gaze lifting up. "I'm sorry sweetheart, but I ain't about to go retracing our steps all the way back to the beginning. That would take us weeks, and it don't appear as we have that kind of time. Not with that damned prophet hunting the wastes at the same time as us. It'd just be a wild lizard chase."

"Then what do we do…?"

Fenix pulled back on his reins, slowing his horse. He lifted his hat brim and wiped the sweat away, gazing up at the painful blue above.

"Ah, shit." He lowered his hat brim and looked at the girl who had slowed to a stop beside him. "I'm probably gonna regret this, and you're probably gonna hate the idea." He paused, thinking about it over and over for a moment. "Yeah. I already regret it…"

Ani stared at him, slightly confused, but waiting.

"There's one person that just might be able to help." He exhaled sharply, feeling the heat draw in with his next breath. "He's a scrapper. Or *was*. Now, he's just a bitter old man who buys and sells pre-world artifacts." A smirk danced across his face. "But in his prime… He was uh, he was one of the ones that helped get the caravans running again. He was the man who got em powered up."

Ani's eyes lit up. "Then what are we waiting for!? Let's go!"

"Now, hold on," Fenix added, his brow lifting slightly. "Not only do we gotta make it back to Serenity in one piece, which may prove to be slightly difficult as it's quite likely that we were followed here. It's lucky we didn't open that door to an entire goblin horde and a thousand scavengers just waiting. But we also have to get to Heirako, and from there… Outpost." He paused, letting the thought set in. When he realized that Ani didn't know what that truly entailed, he elaborated. "If we can make it back to Serenity—"

"When," Ani interrupted.

He sighed. "When," he corrected, "we get back to Serenity, we'll have to take the caravan back. But it don't go the whole way. The caravan'll get us as far as Heirako, but not the old man in Outpost. And let me just tell you, the road between Heirako and Outpost…" He scoffed. "You thought getting between Brimhall and Bilgewater was bad. The road between Heirako and Outpost makes that look like a springtime stroll through an oasis."

"You have your guns," Ani replied flatly.

"Oh," Fenix chuckled. "Yeah. That'll help. A little." He stared at her. "Look. I'm talking scavengers, reapers, probably goblins and orcs by now. All manner of groups that want nothing more than to separate us from our belongings, and our lives, walk that stretch of road. Outpost ain't somewhere you go unless you have to."

"But you're a drifter," Ani said, looking sternly at him. "You've been there before. I am most confident that you will be able to get us there again."

He smiled. "Like I said. I'm full and well capable of handling a small group of reapers, but we're not looking at no small group. We're talking dozens. That stretch of road's gotten *real* bad these past few cycles, and it's only getting worse, what with the goblins and orcs moving south…" He took a deep breath and exhaled through puffed cheeks, before reaching down and pulling his canteen up. He unscrewed it, let it hover just before his lips for a moment, before pulling a large swig, screwing the cap back on and sliding it back into place. "It's been a long while since I've been there. There's a reason why…"

"You're scared?" Ani remarked, pausing for his response.

He shook his head, letting his tongue soak up the moisture. "A lot of pre-world tech goes through Outpost. Folks know that. That's why people generally don't travel there unless they're part of a well-armed group. Now I'm not saying it can't be done, I'm just saying we have to be careful is all. Even *with* these guns. You need to understand. These guns'll make us just as much a target as they stand to protect us."

"But we have them."

"Damnit girl," he responded, slightly irritated. "Would you stop being so bull-headed for one minute. I'm not saying we ain't going. It *was* my idea. "I'm just saying that I'm one guy, not an army."

"They're gonna kill everything," Ani replied, her face tightening. "If they get into that facility, then it won't matter if you're just one person, or we do have an army, because we'll all be dead. They'll release the flame again, they'll blow up their bombs, and everything we know will be dead. There won't *be* anything to worry about then."

"Don't lecture me on what's at stake," Fenix snapped back, knowing the girl was likely just hot, thirsty and irritable. "I already agreed to this. I am *not* trying to back out. I'm just preparing you for what could possibly be waiting for us. Got that?"

She nodded.

He shook his head, turning to look out across the wastes. "Yeah," he mumbled to himself. "I regret it…"

Fenix nudged his horse forward, the old beast snorting as dust curled up around its hooves. The sun hung heavy and merciless overhead, painting the wastes in a haze of white and rust. Behind him, Ani tapped her heels to her own mount, falling in line, the rhythm of their journey as familiar as the ache in her bones.

She let her thoughts drift, replaying the words Fenix had spoken—words heavy with worry and the weight of all they'd seen. She'd known from the start that this path would be hard, that the odds were stacked against them. But there was no turning back now. It was all or nothing. She would either die trying to save what was left of the world, or die because she'd given up. After losing Jarek, the sharp edge of grief had dulled everything else. Stopping the prophet was all that mattered. What came after—if there was an after—she hadn't let herself imagine. Maybe she'd head north, maybe west to Europa, or just keep riding until the wastes ran out.

For now, her world had narrowed to the trail ahead, the heat shimmering off the horizon, and the memory of her brother's laughter—Jarek chasing lizards through the dust, sunlight tangled in his hair. She blinked away the sting in her eyes, forcing herself to focus on the road, on the next town, on the promise of Outpost—a place her father had spoken of in stories, where scavenged tech could buy a new beginning. But all that would have to wait. First, they had to survive the wastes, and whatever waited for them beneath the blazing sky.

Fenix rode ahead, silent as the grave, his silhouette wavering in the heat that shimmered off the wastes. Every so often, he'd glance at the horizon, jaw set, mind working through every grim possibility. He was searching for a plan—any plan—that might keep them alive through the stretch of hell between Heirako and Outpost. It was a road he'd avoided for years, a scar across the land where too many had vanished, swallowed by sand, steel, or something worse. Now he was headed back, not as a lone drifter with nothing to lose, but with the girl riding in his shadow—a responsibility heavier than any gun or bag of ammunition.

That was what gnawed at him most. The weapons they carried would draw every hungry eye in the wastes, but it was Ani's presence that truly unsettled him. Out here, a lone drifter might slip by unseen, but a pair—especially with a girl in tow—was a beacon for every desperate soul, every cutthroat and monster lurking in the dust. Fenix knew the odds, and he knew the wastes didn't care about hope or good intentions. He just hoped, when the time came, he'd be enough to keep them both from ending up as bones in the sand.

51

The following afternoon the pair rode back into Serenity. They'd circled the ruins once more, opting for the safer route, despite their self-imposed time constraints. The words *people farms* had run through Anika's head more than once since hearing it that first time.

"We can see if they have a caravan leaving tonight," Fenix said as they approached the edge of the town. "No need to stay here any longer than we have to."

Ani nodded. "I agree."

With that, the pair made their way straight to the caravan station.

As Fenix dropped down from his horse a few hours later, he took a moment to look around. He'd noticed the town was much less lively than when they had arrived those few days prior. Something tugged at him, but he filed it away in dumb suspicions and turned to make his way into the caravan office.

The man behind the counter inside looked up with a sleepy surprise. "Welcome, folks," he said as Fenix approached the counter. Behind, Ani had just stepped in.

"Two to Heirako," Fenix said as he approached the counter.

Ani let her gaze once more work across the old, pre-world images on the wall.

The man behind the counter shuffled over to a ticket machine. "That'll be eight silver," he called out as he grabbed a pencil and began to write on two of the tickets. "There're no refunds, and the caravan don't wait, so be here at first light."

"You don't have anything leaving tonight, do you? We're uh, kinda in a hurry."

The man paused, turning to Fenix. "Sunrise and sundown," the man replied. "But the sundown caravan's pretty full up. Probably best to grab a room and wait till mornin'."

"We don't mind being cozy," Fenix replied. "As long as there's room for the horses."

The man nodded.

"I was noticing when we arrived that it seems a bit *calmer* than normal. That have anything to do with the caravan being full up?"

The man finished writing on the tickets and returned, setting them on the counter. He sniffled, his brow furrowing slightly. "Report came yesterday. Goblin war party. Pretty large one at that. Apparently, it's headed this direction. Orcs too." The man pondered that thought for a moment. "Lot a folks just packed up and left." He shook his head slightly. "Don't make no sense to me. Never heard of goblins and orcs working together. Hell. Little bastards can't even work amongst themselves without fighting. It's strange, that one."

Fenix glanced over to Ani, who was admiring an old painting of the caravan in its heyday. "Whelp. We'll see you at sundown."

The man nodded with a smirk, turning to make his way back to his chair.

Fenix took up the tickets and turned, making his way over to the girl. "Go ahead and keep ahold of these," he said, handing her the tickets.

Ani took them and deposited them into her small side bag.

"We leave at sundown," Fenix said, letting his gaze drift to the front door. "I'd say that gives us just about enough time to grab a drink and a couple sticks before we head out. How's that sound?"

Ani nodded. "Good actually. I'm still trying to get the taste of that packaged food off my tongue."

Fenix smiled, reaching out to tap her on the arm. "Well, I think I got just the cure for that."

"Two pours of rye, two pints of cold if you got it and two lizard sticks."

Fenix turned, looking around the saloon as the barkeep turned to make his way to the shelf behind. There were two other pairs inside, staggered out between the small cluster of tables. "I figure it's a good two-and-a-half-day ride to Corith. Then we transfer to Heirako, and we should be there in a day and a half. That's with no delays or track issues."

Behind him, the barkeep set the two glasses of rye and two cold beers on the counter. "That'll be four silvers."

Fenix turned back, reaching into his pouch and procuring the payment, which he set on the bar casually. Then he slid two of the glasses towards Ani and lifted the small glass of rye in toast. "Here's to no issues."

Ani smiled, lifting the glass and *clinking* it against his.

The pair downed the rye, Fenix savoring the flavor, Ani wincing as it burned down.

The glasses thudded dully against the counter nearly in unison as they sat them down. Then the swing doors of the saloon opened up and four men stepped in, their eyes scanning the inside before immediately locking to Ani.

Beside her, Fenix stiffened. He'd seen that look, and in that moment, he knew *nothing* good was about to happen.

The four men stepped in from the dusk, dusters faded and wide-brimmed hats pulled low, shadows hiding their eyes. Each coat was trimmed with a thick strap of black leather, arcane symbols stitched in red along the hem—marks that caught the lantern light and seemed to flicker with their own uneasy magic.

"That's the one," muttered the tallest, boots scraping the warped floor as he started forward.

Ani felt the shift in the room, the way the air thickened. She turned, catching the men's approach, and saw Fenix's hand drift toward his pistol, slow and deliberate.

The lead man stopped just six feet away, boots planted wide. "Your kind's been outlawed for over six hundred years," he said, voice flat as the wastes.

Ani stared, confusion flickering across her face.

"We saw what you did," spat the shorter one, his nose sharp as a knife, lips drawn thin. "Witch."

"I don't—" Ani started, but the lead man cut her off with a growl.

"Oh, don't you try and bullshit us. We saw you with our own eyes. You used magic to burn that flyer last week, right here in this town. All four of us saw you."

Fenix's gaze moved between the men, calm but cold. "You sure you don't have her confused with someone else? Plenty of women pass through these parts." He let the words hang, then added, "And I've been in the wastes a long time. Never heard of any outlaw ban on magic."

"No. She's the one." The man's eyes narrowed, fixing on Fenix. "You were there too. And if we say there's a ban, then there's a ban."

Fenix's eyes narrowed as he measured the man across from him, his gaze flicking between the others—watching for the twitch of a finger, the shift of a coat, the telltale sign of a hand drifting too close to a pistol. "Look, fella," he said, voice low and steady, "we're on the next caravan out. No need for this to get ugly. We'll finish our drinks, and you'll never see us again. You can go back to singing tra-la-la around the campfire."

The man in front sneered, his fingers inching toward his holster. "I reckon you're a witch too," he spat, eyes narrowing.

Fenix drew a slow breath, his own hand hovering near his sidearm. "My friend here—she really doesn't like that word," he said, voice cold as iron. "And to be honest, it's starting to sour on me too. So how about you and your friends let us finish our drinks, and then you fuck right off." He knew it was wasted breath—knew the moment was coming, and there was no talking their way out.

The man's sneer twisted, his hand twitching for his pistol.

In a blur, Fenix cleared leather, a bullet splitting the space between the man's eyes. Before the others could even draw, five more shots cracked through the hush, echoing off the battered walls. The four men crumpled to the floor, the sharp tang of gunpowder and blood curling through the air.

Fenix spun, pistol leveled at the barkeep, who threw up his hands in a hurry. "I ain't no part of this!" the man barked, voice shaking.

Fenix let out a breath, lowering his weapon. "Sorry 'bout the mess." He grabbed his beer, downed it in four gulps, and nodded at the lizard sticks roasting by the fire. "We'll take those to go, if it's all the same."

The barkeep nodded, hands still trembling, and wrapped the sticks in paper before setting them on the counter.

Fenix reached into his pouch and pulled two more silvers out, dropping them on the counter. "That's for the mess," he said, his gaze moving to a stunned Ani. Then he touched her softly on the arm. "We should probably get going. I doubt these are the only hunters. Their friends probably aren't far behind."

Ani nodded, swallowing heavily as she stared at the four dead men on the floor, blood pooling out in a halo around them. Then she rose from the stool and started towards the door, stepping as widely past the corpses as she could.

A short time later they were watching as the caravan driver led their horses towards the cargo car. Fenix eyed the street, waiting for more men to arrive. Ani stood silently; a stunned look still worn across her worried face. Her mind replayed the blood slowly pooling outward, the dry wood soaking it up thirstily.

"I'm really sorry about those men," Fenix said as the caravan driver made his way past, opening the passenger car door for the line of folks waiting to board.

Ani shook her head. "Don't be." She locked her gaze on his. "I'm glad you did that."

"Oh," Fenix replied softly, expecting a lot of replies from her, but definitely not that one.

A scowl twisted Ani's face, the old fire inside her stoked to a blaze since the moment she'd first seen that flyer. Part of her had almost wanted the ones behind it to find her, to stand face to face with those who'd printed and spread their poison. For days, the thought had smoldered at the edge of her mind—a small ember, waiting for a gust of wind.

When the men strode into the saloon, it wasn't fear that gripped her—it was fear of herself. The moment they spoke, she felt the heat building beneath her skin, flames licking up her arms, hungry for release. She wanted to watch them burn, to see their flesh melt from bone. There were few times in her life she'd felt such pure, unbridled hatred: the day her father vanished, the day her mother died, the day Jarek was taken. This was one of them.

She hated, with every ounce of her being, that even after all the suffering and struggle in the wastes, people still clung to ancient superstitions—still hunted and killed their own for being different. Folks like her, born with magic in their blood, were marked for death for no reason but fear. She'd never heard of a witch gone rogue, never heard of one causing harm. Most spent their lives hiding, always looking over their shoulder, because of men like these. Worse than goblins, worse than orcs—at least those monsters didn't pretend to be anything else.

For a fleeting moment, Ani wondered what would happen if witches started hunting back. "They deserved worse than that," she whispered, her voice low and final, the words sealing her thoughts like a grave.

"All aboard!" the driver shouted, stepping back so that the folks could board.

Fenix nodded, taking a deep breath and exhaling slowly as he glanced back to the main street one last time. Then he tapped Ani on the shoulder and turned to step onto the caravan.

For a day and a half, the pair rode in the cool, armored belly of the caravan, each taking turns at the window, watching the wastes slip by in a slow, endless procession. Nights brought a blanket of stars, cold and sharp above the desert. Morning bled in with streaks of coral and gold, giving way to the blistering white of midday. When the sun was at its fiercest, steel shutters slid down, sealing them in a dim hush until the heat relented and the world outside softened back to ochre and shadow.

By the time dawn broke again, the caravan rattled into Corith—a city rising from the dust, alive with the promise of water and trade. They made their transfer in the half-light, and the cycle began anew: day giving way to night, the landscape shifting but always the same— dust, ruin, and the long, slow crawl of survival. Another day and a half passed in that rhythm, until at last the city of Heirako appeared on the horizon.

52

Ani stepped down from the caravan into the pale light of dawn, the sun just cresting the horizon—a molten coin already promising another day of relentless heat. The air tasted of dust and distant stone, and the city beyond the platform was alive with a restless energy. People moved with purpose, their faces drawn and wary, boots scuffing the cracked earth as they hurried through narrow streets. There was no shortage of souls here; the road just beyond the staging yard was a river of bodies, all flowing toward destinations unknown. What struck Ani next was the city itself. Buildings made from sunbaked clay and brick pressed close together, their flat terra cotta roofs splashed with bold strokes of color—azure blue, sunset orange, the yellow of brittle wildflowers. The architecture felt ancient, as if the city had grown up from the desert itself, shaped by wind and time. Red-rocked mountains loomed in the distance, their jagged silhouettes standing sentinel over the city's edge, while sage and cactus clung to the hillsides, stubborn bursts of green against the coral dust.

A single road cut through the gap between the peaks, leading away from the city and into the unknown. Ani's gaze lingered there, a shiver of nerves fluttering in her chest. That was the road to Outpost—the place her father had spoken of in stories, the place where fortunes and fates were traded in equal measure. She drew a slow breath, feeling the weight of the journey ahead, and let the city's strange, vibrant beauty settle over her like a second skin.

"We should hit the saloon," Fenix said, handing her the reins of her horse as he stepped up with them. "We can try and find a group headed to outpost and see if we can tag along." He looked upwards. "Still early. We move now we might find ourselves in luck."

Ani pulled her gaze away from the street beyond, taking Dusty's reins. "Come on, boy," she said, urging the horse forward as she followed after Fenix.

The pair wound their way through the city's heart, boots echoing on terracotta paving that ran the length of the main drag. Storefronts rose tall above the dust, their facades patched with old-world brick and sun-bleached wood, some leaning precariously as if bracing against the desert wind. Electric streetlamps jutted from ornate iron poles every fifty yards, their glass globes webbed with cables that snaked overhead, humming faintly with borrowed power.

They passed a mercantile, its window crowded with every manner of hardware—rusted tools, battered lanterns, coils of wire, and above it all, the massive skull of some long-dead beast, horns curling like the arms of a devil. The bone was bleached white by a thousand suns, a silent warning or a promise, depending on who you asked.

Next door, a different kind of relic: a storefront marked by a giant tooth, carved from wood and painted a ghostly white. "Larry Dobbs, Dentist and Barber" was scrawled in careful script across the molar, swinging gently in the morning breeze. The sign creaked, a strange comfort in a world where even smiles had to be patched and sharpened to survive.

"You see those mountains up there?" Fenix asked, pulling Ani's attention from the single leather and brass chair in the middle of the dental barber's shop. "That's the road to Outpost."

Ani nodded.

"It's a day and half's ride, if'n we're lucky enough to find a fast-traveling group. Two if they're pulling wagons." Fenix eyed a horse drawn cart passing by, and the two halflings that sat grizzled and sunbeaten atop.

"You're sure there's no other way?" Ani asked in trepidation.

"No other way getting there, or no other way than to go there?"

She pondered the difference for a moment before responding. "Both, I guess."

He shook his head, sighing away from her. "We can't chance a trip back to Belcor. I guarantee the man we're going to see will know the location of your facility. For the right price he could lead you to the chest of Cortez."

"Chest of Cortez?"

Fenix smiled, a fluttering of old treasure-laden stories and tales drifting past. "It's an old treasure, said to be hidden somewhere here in the wastes. An entire wagon that was buried with a chest full of gold and jewels. Said to be worth a million credits or more."

Ani turned, her brow furrowing deeply.

"It's horseshit," Fenix smiled grimly. "No more real than fresh water or peaceful orcs." He scoffed at the thought.

"Oh," Ani replied flatly, her amusement pulled away on a hot tuft of breeze.

"That's our saloon," Fenix said, gesturing towards a large, grandly facaded building a short distance away.

Ani stared at the massive, rusted metal boot spur that hung on the front of the building, watching as it slowly spun. Painted beneath in bright orange letters read, *The Rusted Spur*.

They tied their horses to the rail out front, the animals shifting restlessly in the heat. Fenix moved with practiced care, unfastening three battered duffel bags—two slung over his shoulders, the third, heavier than the rest, hoisted in one hand. Together, they pushed through the swinging doors and into the saloon's chaos.

Inside, the air was thick with the stink of rye, sweat, and something sourer—beer, vomit, and what Ani suspected might be the faint tang of urine. The place was alive with noise: three men in the corner sawed away at battered stringed instruments, their tune barely rising above the rumble of drunken voices. Conversation rolled through the room in a single, slurred current, punctuated by the clatter of mugs and the occasional bark of laughter.

Fenix led the way toward the bar, boots thudding on warped floorboards. Ani trailed behind, trying to take it all in—the flicker of lantern light on dusty glass, the battered faces hunched over their drinks, the sense of danger and possibility that seemed to hang in the air.

A bottle skittered across the floor, coming to rest against a man's chair. Ani followed its path, only to find the man's scowl fixed on her. She dipped her head, murmured a silent apology, and slipped past. In the corner, the music's tempo lifted, and three women—barely dressed in lace bras and chap-cut panties—danced wild and unashamed to the rhythm. Ani watched with a mix of sour amusement and disbelief, then tore her gaze away and hurried to catch up with Fenix at the bar.

"What'll it be?" the large, bearded man behind the bar asked, eyeing them both.

"Looking for transport to Outpost," Fenix replied, turning for a moment to scan the room, his eyes drifting to the three women dancing and lingering there for a moment.

"Over there," the bartender nodded, towards two men who were seated within arm's reach of the women. "They're headed up today."

Fenix nodded, pulling his gaze way from the women, a brunette with her hair pulled back to be precise. "Well, then let me get two waters and two beers."

The man nodded.

"Water filtered?" Fenix added, eying the man suspiciously.

"Charcoal and sand," the man replied, turning to grab four handled glasses from beneath the bar.

Fenix smirked in approval, then turned to Ani who had returned her gaze to the dancing women. "You see those two fellas over by the musicians?"

Ani nodded, not getting a particularly good vibe from them.

"Barkeep says they're headed to Outpost today. They let us group up with them, could be our ticket." He glanced at the two water glasses the bartender set down, eyeing them instinctually for debris. Satisfied that the glasses were clean and clear, and that the water *was* actually purified, he continued. "We'll grab our drinks and go say hello."

The bartender set the two beers on the counter. "Four silver," the man said, the low timbre of his voice rolling across the bar top.

Ani reached into her bag, pulling the silver pieces out and setting them on the bar top.

The pair made their way over to where the men were seated, Fenix narrowly avoiding a wild kick to his side as he passed the girls, taking only as long as it took to send a smile in the direction of the brunette.

"Bartender made mention that you fellas were headed up to Outpost today," Fenix shouted above the music. "I was wondering if we might put in with ya'll for the trip."

The men at the table shot each other a glance, taking only a fraction of a second to eye the bags Fenix was bogged down with, a gesture that didn't go unnoticed by him.

"What's business you got in outpost?"

"None that concerns you," Fenix replied, his tone curt but not impolite. In that moment, he realized he needed these men more than they needed him, so he let the edge soften and added, "Girl lost her father. I'm hoping Royce might have some information that could help her get reunited." He didn't usually hand out names, but he knew the type sitting across from him—hard-eyed, dust-worn, the kind who'd been to Outpost more than once. Dropping Royce's name, the most notorious information broker in the wastes, was a signal: he and the girl weren't easy marks, not just another pair of greenhorns to be fleeced. If these men had any sense, they'd recognize the name and think twice before trying anything foolish.

The men exchanged another glance that spoke conversations only understood by them. "Fair enough," one of the men replied. "We leave in thirty. Meet us at the caravan station and be ready to ride." The man paused, eying Ani. "That girl there ain't gonna hold us back?"

Fenix smiled. "Nah. She can hold her own."

The man nodded, lifting his nearly empty glass and draining the remainder in a single gulp. "Well," he said, setting the mug down. "Go on. We'll see you in thirty."

Fenix tipped his hat and turned, eying the brunette once more as he passed close enough for the electricity coming off of him to arc her attention towards him. He smiled, a wink flashing across one of his eyes. The girl smiled politely and kept dancing.

"Can we trust them?" Ani asked a moment later as they were making their way towards the entrance.

"Not at all," Fenix replied flatly. "But we're not exactly in the position to be picky. And to be honest, most the folks making their way to Outpost won't be any better. Let's just take what we got and keep the eyes in the back of your head open."

"Eyes in the back of your head...?" Ani asked as Fenix pushed the saloon doors open and stepped out into the blinding light.

"A colloquialism," he replied. "Just means stay alert. Be ready for anything."

"Oh."

Fenix removed two of the duffel bags, tying them to Dirtweed's saddle. "Sorry buddy," he said. "But you're a little better equipped for this than me." The lightest of the three, he slung over his shoulder.

The horse snorted as if in response. Then he untied the reins and climbed up.

A short while later, Ani and Fenix sat beneath the wide shadow of the caravan station's awning, the heat of the day held at bay for a moment. They'd stocked up—another bag of hydration tabs, a satchel of lizard jerky—and now waited, the silence between them filled with the distant clatter of hooves and the low hum of the city.

It wasn't long before the two men arrived, riding up on horses so thin and wiry they looked like they'd been carved from the bones of the desert itself. Fenix recognized the breed—old stock, the kind that had survived since the fires. These horses were all ribs and sinew, short-haired and wild-eyed, built for endurance, not comfort. They could go weeks without water, longer than any man, and were prized by reapers and drifters alike. But they were useless for hauling, barely able to carry a rider and a side bag, let alone a wagon. They were creatures made for the wastes, and for surviving the long, empty stretches where most would die. Fenix took note, but kept his thoughts to himself.

"Ya'll ready?" the man he had spoken to in the saloon asked as they rode up.

"We're good," Fenix replied, watching as the man eyed the duffels again. Then he turned and shot a very particular glance at Ani, hoping that she picked up on the subtleties behind it. A thin flash of concern confirmed that she had.

"Then let's get a move on. Gonna be midday soon and we ain't trying to get caught out in the open."

Fenix nodded, shooting one last silent glance to Ani as he turned and directed his horse after the others.

53

Morning bled into midday, and midday slipped quietly into night. The four of them pressed on, winding their way up and over the spine of a small mountain, the trail twisting through broken stone and wind-scoured earth. When they crested the far side, the world opened up before them—a landscape carved by time and fire, painted in the deep reds and ochres of a dying sun.

Towering monuments of stone rose from the desert floor, their shapes like the bones of ancient titans—spires and bluffs standing in silent congregation, a petrified forest of coral and rust. Arches swept across the horizon, casting long shadows that stretched into the coming dusk. Far off, a plateau loomed, its flat crown catching the last light, a silent promise at the edge of the world. Ani stared, breath caught in her throat, knowing she'd never seen anything like it—nor would she ever forget it.

"That's Outpost," Fenix said, leaning towards Ani, still watching as the men rode to themselves a hundred yards ahead.

The group had just made their way from the base of the mountain and were traveling along a thin trail roughly ten feet wide that led through a small canyon area. Twenty-foot walls rose up on both sides, the thick sand beneath muffling their horses' hooves as they clopped through the dirt. Then the trail dipped down and the Outpost plateau disappeared from view.

Ani edged her horse closer to Fenix. "I don't trust them," she said, eyeing the men ahead. "They've been acting shifty all morning. It's like they're... I don't know. Planning something?"

Fenix nodded. Then he glanced at her, a thin smile tugging at the edges of his lips. "Good girl."

She looked at him puzzled. "What?"

The smile grew as he reached down and unsnapped the safety strap from his pistol and leaned to the side in order to loosen the drawstring on one of the duffels. "You're paying attention. That's good. That'll keep you alive out here."

"They're gonna rob us, aren't they?"

Fenix scoffed, shaking his head. "They're sure gonna try."

Ani felt a cold shiver crawl up her spine. The canyon pressed in on all sides, the walls rising like ancient, painted tombstones—striped in ochre, rust, and sun-bleached gold. It would be so easy for trouble to find them here, boxed in with nowhere to run. The air was thick, stifling, dust swirling in lazy eddies with every faint breeze. She watched the two men ahead as they rounded a bend, one glancing back with a look that set her nerves on edge.

Out of the corner of her eye, she caught movement—Fenix, silent and grim, was drawing a rifle from the duffel, barrel-first, his eyes never leaving the trail ahead. Ani's heart hammered. She forced herself to look forward, and for a moment, despite the danger, she was struck by the beauty of the place. The canyon walls were a tapestry of color—broad bands of red and orange, yellow and pale brown, sweeping and curling like the memory of a long-dead river. For a heartbeat, it was almost easy to forget the threat that lurked in every shadow, the fear that gnawed at her bones. Almost.

They rode in silence for the next few minutes, coming up on the curve the men had disappeared behind. Then, as they rounded the tight bend, Fenix slowed to a stop.

Ani pulled her horse to a stop beside him.

Fifty yards ahead, the two men had stopped. Their horses were turned to face them and one of them held a rifle leveled in their direction. "I'm guessing by that rifle, you saw this coming," the man next to the one with the rifle called out. "I'm also guessing that story about the girl and her daddy was bullshit."

A warm breeze danced between them. Overhead a hawk circled, scanning the ground beneath for its early morning meal.

"You wanna know what I think?" the man asked loudly. "I think you got tech in those two bags, and I think my partner and I here, are gonna be taking those bags and trading them in for a whole shitload of credits." His gaze crackled across the air between them. That's what I think."

Fenix stared at the men. "That's a good plan you got there," Fenix yelled back. "Right location," he added, looking around at the canyon walls. "Single guy and a young girl." He nodded with a smirk. "Just one problem with your plan though."

"Oh yeah?" the man called back. "I don't see a problem," the man added, whistling loudly, the single, shrill pitch echoing off the canyon walls.

A moment later Fenix caught movement. One rider on each side of the canyon edged into view on both sides. Without even having to look, he knew at least two more had ridden into view behind them.

"Only problem I see is yours," the man shouted, a smile working across his face. "Now, we'll be taking those bags, *and* the girl. You. You can either ride out, or you can die." The man's words were delivered flatly, matter of factly with no hint of choice.

'I don't think I'm gonna give you these bags, or the girl... ' Fenix's next words drifted as a silent thought as he jerked the automatic rifle up and yanked back on the trigger.

A thunderous burst of gunfire shattered the canyon's hush—Fenix's rifle barking twenty rounds in the time it took the ambushers ahead to realize they'd been outdrawn. Bullets tore through the two men at the front, ripping them from their saddles and pitching them into the dust, bodies tumbling in a tangle of limbs and leather.

From the canyon walls, more gunfire erupted. Fenix jerked the rifle up, sighting along the ridge. He squeezed off a short burst—one of the men above toppled sideways, rolling from his horse and vanishing over the edge. Fenix pivoted, sending another shot after a shadow ducking behind a boulder.

A bullet screamed past his ear, the whistle sharp and close. He spun to see Ani hunched low in her saddle, hands clamped over her head, face buried in her horse's mane.

Three more men charged, guns blazing. Fenix braced the rifle against his shoulder, firing in tight, controlled bursts. The first rider pitched backward, foot caught in the stirrup as his horse bolted, dragging him in a cloud of dust and hooves. Another burst dropped the second man, and the third—Fenix's shot all but erased the top of his skull in a red mist.

The surviving horses thundered past, one kicking wildly at the dying man tangled beneath it. Fenix leaned aside as they barreled by, then turned, scanning the ridges for movement—listening for hoofbeats, whispered orders, the telltale click of a hammer being drawn back. But there was nothing—only the hot wind sighing through the canyon.

He lowered the rifle, breath ragged, and turned to Ani. "You all right?"

She nodded, swallowing heavily and letting her gaze drift between the men on the ground. "Why does it have to be like this?"

Fenix thought about it, the seconds it took to formulate an answer he had asked himself a thousand times before falling out. "It's just how it is," he said blankly. "Hunger, thirst, heat. This is what the wastes does."

"Is it like this beyond?"

Fenix pulled his gaze from the blood-soaked dirt pooling around the two dead men who had just minutes prior, led them into ambush. "Better," he replied.

Ani sat in silence, her gaze fixed on the two bodies sprawled in the dust. Some part of her had known, from the moment they'd left the city's edge, that it would come to this. The feeling had crept in slow, like the first tickle of sickness at the back of your throat—a warning you try to ignore, hoping it's nothing. She'd tried to convince herself she was just being paranoid, that maybe she was wrong about people, that the world hadn't grown as mean as she feared.

But now, staring at the aftermath, she felt the last of that hope slip away. Jarek had known it—he'd said as much, more than once. Her parents had known it too, especially her mother. The only reason they'd stayed so long in the wastes was because her father had sunk every last coin and dream into the farm, and leaving simply wasn't an option. She remembered the whispered arguments behind closed doors, the frustration that clung to her parents like dust, the way the wastes held them fast. Belcor was supposed to be their way out, a promise of something better. Deltron, too, if her mother hadn't put her foot down.

"We get through this," Fenix said, letting his gaze drift to the sky over the cliffsides. "There's nothing keeping you here."

She stayed silent. She'd been forcing herself not to think about it. "No. Not anymore."

Fenix took a deep breath, sighing heavily. "More of 'em are likely to come looking for these ones," he said, his brow furrowing deeply at the thought. "We should probably put as much distance between us and them as possible before that happens," he added, gesturing with a nod to the dead men.

Ani stayed silent, still staring at the men lying splayed on the ground.

Fenix nudged his horse forward, clicking his tongue twice. '*At least the birds would eat well today,*' he thought as they rode past.

54

The pair had put miles between them and the canyon by the time the sun dropped below the horizon. They had stopped under the shade of a large, natural stone archway to wait out midday, and had set out the moment the sun was again bearable. They traveled the next six hours without stopping, riding until the moon was well overhead.

Now, they sat tucked into a small outcropping, a hundred-foot wall backing them. A small fire burned, the outcropping keeping its dim glow contained to the area just around them. Fenix had reloaded and returned the rifle to the bag and had another, smaller version sitting close by.

"I've never seen a gun fire like that," Ani said, breaking a silence that had hung between them for long enough for the fire to shift, a burnt log falling to the side, embers taking flight.

"They had better weapons," Fenix replied, his gaze watching the flickering reds and oranges at the base of the flames. "One good thing about the pre-world I suppose." He held that thought. "Those guns might just give us a fighting chance."

"They should have disappeared with the fire. All of them."

Fenix shook his head softly.

"You take away the guns, men will use knives. Take those, they'll beat each other to death with sticks. It isn't the weapons doing the killing. They're just tools. I've seen men kill each other with their bare hands, drown each other in horse troughs." He scoffed at the thought. "It's man. Man is the abomination. We're territorial, and jealous. We covet and take what we don't need. All of us. Violence is in our blood. Has been since before the fires, was long before that, and will be long after we're gone. There is no cure for the condition of man. At least with orcs, and goblins, there's no deceit. They know exactly what they are, and they wear it on their chest. We like to hide that, conceal it behind smiles and handshakes. We take those feelings and shove 'em deep. But in the end, we're no different than them. Maybe worse, cause at least they won't help you find the knife you lost in order to cut your throat with it."

Ani soaked in his words. She hated that she had seen far too many times that had proven true. And one thing she did know, a thought that had been festering in her since that morning, was that there *was* nothing left for her in the wastes, and that the moment they were done, if she somehow managed to stay alive, and survive the prophet, the orcs and goblin war parties, and the fire. She was leaving the wastes and would never return.

Ani swallowed dryly. Then she looked across the flames and studied the sadness on her companion's face. "I'm... I'm gonna try and get some sleep," she said, lowering her gaze.

Fenix exhaled slowly, with a soft nod. "Go on. I'll stay up. Keep an eye out. You get some rest."

Ani nodded, scooting back and laying down. She lay there, her gaze wandering among the stars, her mind awash with the day's events, and the events that had led them to that moment. She thought of her brother, her mom and dad, the farm. She thought about her grandpa who would come visit infrequently, and the mercantile owner who would sell them grain seeds and water purification tabs. She thought about her life before all this and how different not only that was, but how different *she* was. It felt like she had aged incredibly in the past month, her time deeper in the wastes, the death, all of it adding years, decades to her. She lay there realizing that she didn't even think the same way anymore. Any semblance of little girl that had been left, any immaturities, had been seared away by the blistering sun and endless death that followed in its wake.

Fenix watched the fire until the embers lost their flicker to the thin layer of ash. He kept a careful watch until the sun was just beginning to tease its presence on the distant horizon. Then he lay down and allowed himself a light two hours of sleep.

55

By the time Fenix and Ani reached Outpost, dusk had already begun to swallow the horizon, painting the sky in bruised purples and dying gold. The city's electric lights flickered to life at the edge of the wastes, humming with a soft, unnatural warmth—a rare luxury in a world gone to dust. Streetlamps, strung like sentinels on either side of the battered gate, cast long shadows across the cracked earth. The gate itself—a massive iron door, split down the middle and left yawning open—stood as both a warning and a welcome.

Above the main drag, tangled strands of arc lamps crisscrossed the street, weaving a web of pale yellow light that shimmered like a spider's silk against the gathering dark. The whole street glowed beneath their watchful gaze, the soft radiance pushing back the night and turning the heart of Outpost into an island of fragile hope amid the endless, haunted wastes.

As the pair made their way in, Ani felt mesmerized by the sights. She had never seen so much lighting before. Storefronts and shops were brightly lit in a dazzling array of colors. The brightness of the city seemed to push back the sky above, and as the twilight grew, the night stars were held at bay.

"I've never seen *anything* like this," Ani said, her eyes trying to soak everything in at once.

Fenix let his gaze wander for a moment. "Outpost was one of the first settlements to get electricity back up," he replied, his gaze wandering to a strand of lights surrounding a saloon sign that seemed to be chasing one another. "There's an old wind turbine just beyond, at the bottom of the canyon that backs the town. One of their engineers got it up and running a couple hundred cycles ago. City built itself around it." He watched as a pair of scavengers exited the saloon, eyeing first him, then Ani, for a longer than comfortable moment. "You know that all the bulbs not scavenged, come from here?"

Ani shook her head.

"Yep. Outpost is known for three things," he elaborated. "Information and scrap trade, Anonymity, and their lights. They have a shop here that makes most of the bulbs you see in all the other towns. Aberdyne, Brimhall, hell. Even the lights on the caravan. They all come from here."

"Anonymity?" Ani quizzed, the word catching her attention.

Fenix smiled. "Outpost is the perfect place to disappear for a while if you need. With the kind of folks who regular this town, ain't no one collecting bounties, or turning on folks here. In a city of criminals, silence is a golden currency. That and information. And Royce controls that."

"Royce?"

"Yeah. He and I go *way* back." He thought about that for a moment. *'Too far back'* he thought silently.

In the early days of drifting, Fenix had been a regular at Outpost—a city where secrets traded hands as easily as bullets, and the right word in the right ear could buy you a future or get you killed. He'd come seeking rumors of bounties, escort work, and the kind of jobs you'd never find tacked to the sun-bleached boards in places like Bilgewater or Blister Springs. Outpost was where the real work happened, and it was there that Fenix first crossed paths with Royce.

Royce wasn't his real name—nobody in Outpost used the one they were born with. The name came from a relic of the old world: a pre-flame car, unearthed from some forgotten bunker. Royce had liked the sound of it, so he'd claimed it for his own. Fenix, on the other hand, was one of the few who kept his given name, though most folks figured it was made up anyway. He never bothered to correct them. He wasn't looking to make a name for himself, just to survive.

Royce had taken Fenix under his wing, teaching him the art of survival in a world that had little use for sentiment. "You've chosen one of the hardest professions in the wastes," Royce had told him, voice rough as gravel. "You aren't a drifter, you're a survivalist." Fenix had carried those words with him, even as the years and the miles piled up. He hadn't thought of Royce in a long while, and for a moment, he felt a pang of guilt. But he doubted the old bastard had spent much time thinking about him, either. Their relationship had always been more business than friendship—mutual benefit, not trust. There'd been a time, though, when Fenix almost considered Royce a friend, if only he could shake the suspicion that, for the right price, Royce would sell him out for a vault location or a loaded bunker.

Fenix pulled himself from his thoughts, looking across at a large trading post.

Scraptech loomed at the city's edge, the largest building in Outpost—a monument to scavenged ambition and the stubborn will to survive. Royce had named it himself, the word glowing in elegant tube lighting above the entrance, casting a pale, electric shimmer across the dust. On either side of the sign, two massive gears spun in slow, mechanical rhythm, their teeth interlocked—a promise that something in this world still worked, even if nothing else did. Above it all, a squat electric coil spat tiny blue sparks into the dusk, flickering like captured lightning atop a five-story sprawl of steel and glass.

The building stretched nearly a hundred yards in both directions, dwarfing everything around it. To Ani, it was a wonder—bigger than anything she'd ever seen outside the faded images on the terminals in the old-world facilities. In a land where most structures sagged and crumbled, Scraptech stood defiant, humming with the energy of a world that refused to die.

"It's been cycles since I've stepped foot in that place," Fenix said, his words low and almost lamented. Then he sighed heavily. "All right," he said, glancing over to Ani. "Let's go see the old man."

56

Two guards flanked the entrance to Scraptech, their hulking frames casting long shadows in the electric glow. As Fenix and Ani approached, the guards watched with the silent, heavy patience of men used to trouble, but made no move to stop them. Fenix offered a polite nod—met with nothing but stony indifference. Ani's gaze lingered on the necklace of orc tusks hanging from the neck of the guard on the right, a silent warning to any who might test their luck.

Inside, the world shifted. Instead of the battered, sun-bleached streets outside, they found themselves in a cavernous hall lined with shops—a miniature city under a single roof. The main aisle stretched a hundred yards in either direction, with another cross street fifty yards ahead, forming a grid of commerce and scavenged ambition. It was a street in every sense, but one sheltered from the wastes, humming with the low thrum of generators and the buzz of neon.

"Come on," Fenix said, tapping Ani's arm and heading straight for the back of the building.

As they passed, Ani's eyes darted from stall to stall. At first, it seemed no different from the markets outside—vendors hawking salvaged goods, battered tools, and threadbare clothing. But here, the wares were different. The first booth that caught her eye was a sprawling display of pre-world weaponry: racks of bolt-action rifles and heavy revolvers, knives with the old world's insignia stamped into their blades. The vendor, dressed in a faded military uniform adorned with tarnished medals, called out in a voice roughened by years in the dust. "Munitions! Guns from before the flame. All calibers at the ready."

Ani grazed the selection lightly before another stream of dialogue was slung in her direction.

"Browse our ancient artifacts," a well-groomed halfling said, his voice slightly higher pitched than normal, for a halfling that was. "We have mystical devices, loaded with pre-world sounds. Music, banter,

263

sounds of the world." She eyed some of the halfling's wares, eyeing the small rectangular devices that he had on display. "Take one, young miss," he called out, holding a light blue piece of equipment with a small screen on it, out to her. "Listen for an entire day. Then just bring it back and I can recharge it for a small fee. Enjoy the sounds of the world before the flame!"

She continued on, eyeing the contraptions that were attached to the devices by a small cable, two leather cups attached to a bent piece of plastic. She had seen people wearing these devices in some of the vids in Belcor.

She passed another shop selling what they had scrawled across the sign above the stand, as *farmasuiticals*. An assortment of plastic and glass vials, containing all manner of pills and concoctions stood lined up at the ready. Small tags hung across the front. Headache, toothache, sun-sickness, dimensha and fatigue were some of the ones she quickly scanned.

Ani followed Fenix, realizing that the shops that surrounded them were all based around the pre-world. There was even a bookstand that she made a mental note to return to before they left.

A few minutes later Fenix came to a stop at the foot of a large staircase leading upward. At the base was a metal gate, and beside it, two men who could have been the brothers, or cousins of the men at the front of the building.

"Here to see Royce," Fenix said as Ani stepped up beside him.

"On what business?" The smaller of the two behemoths asked.

"Just tell him it's Fenix Walker," he replied flatly.

The guard stood motionless, eyes narrowed in silent appraisal as Fenix and Ani approached. After a tense moment, he turned and strode to a battered device mounted on the wall near the stairwell—a relic from the old world, its surface worn smooth by years of use. He lifted the receiver to his ear, muttered something too low for either of them to catch, then hung it back in place with a soft click. Without a word, he returned to his post, nodding to his partner.

"They're good," he grumbled. The other guard pressed a button set into the wall, and with a heavy, mechanical clunk, the gate unlocked, the sound echoing through the entryway like a promise and a warning.

Fenix reached out, pressing it open and stepping through. Ani followed.

The pair made their way up the stairs, turning and repeating the process four more times. By the time they reached the top floor, Ani could feel the gentle burn in her calves.

Another large sentry met them at the top of the stairs, holding his hand out as they approached. Fenix slowed to a stop, watching as the man eyed them both.

"Come on," the man growled a moment later, glancing behind them before turning to open the large, ornately carved door behind him.

Fenix shot a smirk to Ani and followed after.

A moment later, Fenix stepped into Royce's domain—a room as familiar as the taste of dust on the wind. The far wall was nothing but glass, a single pane stretching ten feet high and fifty wide, framing the endless wastes beyond like a painting that refused to fade. He'd spent countless hours on the balcony just outside, watching the world burn gold and red beneath the setting sun, waiting for Royce to finish whatever shady dealings kept the old man busy, and wondering how many choices—good and bad—had led him back to this very spot.

The living space sprawled wide and open, scattered with plush furnishings scavenged from bunkers and forgotten vaults across the wastes. Every piece told a story: a battered armchair with elven filigree, a dwarven table carved with runes, a rug woven in the old world before the flame. Against the far wall stood a towering bookshelf, its wood dark and intricately carved—a prize from an elven city far to the north. Fenix remembered the day it arrived, the scavenger crew sweating and cursing as they hauled it in, and Royce pretending not to care, though his eyes never left it for a second.

Fenix drifted toward the glass, drawn by the view he'd never quite grown used to. Ani followed, her eyes wide as she took in the trove of relics and oddities—magical trinkets, ancient weapons, artifacts from a dozen lost ages. She'd never seen a room so vast, so meticulously kept, not outside the sealed halls of the old facilities. Here, dwarven axes hung beside pre-world sabers, and the air itself seemed to hum with the memory of magic and violence.

But it was the view that stole her breath. From the balcony, a thousand feet above the canyon floor, the world stretched out in a tapestry of rust and shadow, all the way to the edge of the wastes. Ani stood transfixed, the horizon burning with the last light of day, and for a moment, she forgot the dust, the danger, and the ache of the road behind them. Fenix glanced over, catching the wonder on her face, and a rare, quiet smile tugged at his lips.

"Royce says that on a clear day, it's possible to see all the way to the forbidden zone."

Ani didn't pull her gaze away, fearful that if she did, the dream would end, and the vision would be gone when she looked back. "Have you been there?"

"Where?" Fenix asked, his gaze locked to the horizon.

"The forbidden zone."

He shook his head. "Nah. Ain't nothing left there," he said, his brow furrowing at the few stories he had heard of men wandering too close in search of hidden staches and bunkers. "It's a dead zone. Nothing goes in, nothing comes out. Some have tried, but they say that even getting close to it brings on a sickness that never goes away. I may be dumb, but I'm not suicidal."

There was a gentle creak of metal hinges on wood as the large door opened behind them.

"You know," a voice bellowed. "When they told me that Fenix Walker had returned, I just couldn't believe it. Had to come see for myself."

Fenix turned, a smile growing across his lips. "Hey, old man," he said, the smile edging wider.

"Well, I'll be damned," the well-dressed man across from his said, a smile nearly splitting his face.

Fenix made his way towards the older man, the other mirroring the action. When they met in the middle, each brought their hands out, clasping each other on the shoulders. "God damn," Royce chuckled, pulling Fenix into a tight hug.

The two embraced for a long moment before Royce pulled back and allowed his gaze to drift past Fenix. "And who is the lovely young lady?" he asked, moving his gaze back to Fenix and giving him a coy look.

"Nothing like that," Fenix replied. "Just a client."

Something about that stung Anika, just the slightest, but more than it should have.

"The girl here needs to find something," Fenix continued, pausing for a breath. "*We* need to find something. I figured what better place to go for just that need."

Royce smirked with a slow nod. "If you find it somewhere else, let me know."

Fenix smiled.

Ani watched the exchange, sensing a strange current beneath the surface. The two men—Fenix and Royce—moved with the easy familiarity of old partners, yet they couldn't have looked more different. Fenix was all sharp edges and sun-bleached grit, a lean drifter wrapped in a battered duster, the hem frayed into tatters, his wide-brimmed hat faded nearly white by years beneath the merciless sky. Dust clung to him like a second skin, and the lines on his face spoke of long days and longer nights in the wastes.

Royce, on the other hand, looked every inch the gentleman—a word Ani found herself choosing deliberately, because it fit him in a way it never could Fenix. He was at least her father's age, maybe older, with a neatly trimmed beard that came to a fine point, merging seamlessly with a mustache groomed to perfection. His steel-grey eyes sparkled with a mischievous glint, and deep crow's feet radiated from their corners, hinting at a lifetime of laughter and trouble. He wore a tailored suit, the kind Ani had only seen in faded pre-world photographs: pale blue, crisp and pressed, with a dove-grey shirt beneath. His boots gleamed, polished to a mirror shine, and as he stepped closer, Ani caught the faintest trace of something sweet and wild—desert sage, perhaps, or some rare cologne scavenged from a forgotten vault. His hair, silver and neatly parted, was combed with care, and a faint flush colored his cheeks—whether from the warmth of reunion or the lingering effects of good liquor, Ani couldn't say.

She took all this in as the man spoke, his voice smooth and confident, confirming with a single word that he was exactly as he appeared: a relic of another age, thriving in the ruins of this one.

"Let's have a drink," Royce said, his smile flashing to Ani. "I have a bottle I've been waiting for the right occasion to crack open, and I can't think of a better one than this." He smiled, clasping Fenix on the shoulder once more. "God damn. Fenix fucking Walker..."

Royce turned and started towards a bar area at the opposite end of the room.

Fenix shot a smile to Ani and turned to follow after. "Well. You heard the man. Come on."

Ani felt a warmth between them, a kindship. It was an odd feeling from what she had grown accustomed to with Fenix over the past weeks. She liked it.

Royce made his way to a cabinet near the bar and opened one of the cupboards. He reached in, fishing out a clear bottle with dark brown liquid inside. Then he turned and flashed another smile to Fenix. "Kholtz Rye," he said, lifting his eyebrows. "Pre-world, before the flame."

"No shit," Fenix breathed in amazement.

"And before you ask. Don't ask."

Fenix stared at the bottle. "Whooo." He exhaled, his eyebrows high on his forehead. "That's gotta be worth—"

"More than most have," Royce finished, using a small blade to cut the purple wax seal. "Like I said. Don't ask."

Fenix and Ani watched as the man delicately removed the wax atop it and then used a strange, thin, double pronged tool to pull the cork free.

Royce lifted the bottle, wafting it under his nose. "Oh, my God." Then he turned, pulling three glasses down from the cupboard and setting them on the counter. He poured each glass half full and turned, handing one each to Fenix and Ani. Then he turned and lifted his.

Ani brought the glass to her nose, smelling the liquid inside.

"Give it a little swirl," Royce said, demonstrating with his glass.

Ani repeated the motion and then brought it back to her nose. She smelled cedar, sage, and sugar. There was something else there too, something sweet, like sugar but thicker.

Fenix lifted his glass to his lips and let the smallest portion dance across his tongue. "Ho-ly shit," he exclaimed softly, pulling the glass back and staring at it as if the beverage had just pulled out a hat and cane and had done a little ditty and dance. "God damn indeed."

Royce took a sip, slightly larger than the one Fenix had. "This is worth every credit I paid for it," he said in stunned amazement.

Ani thought it was good. She didn't get the *blown away* sensation the men apparently had, but she wasn't as adept at drinking as they were. It was good though. It hurt less than the liquor Fenix had served her prior, that was for sure.

"Come," Royce said, nodding towards the balcony. "Let's go enjoy the view. Catch up. It's been far too long. And I demand pleasantries before we go and sour this reunion with business."

Fenix smiled, nodding and following after.

"You always did enjoy this view," Royce said, closing the space to the balcony door.

The three stood on the balcony, looking out over the desert wasteland. They chatted and swapped stories. Fenix shared his cycles in the wastes, jobs he'd pulled, scary predicaments and escort missions. The minutes crept by, turning into an hour, then another. Royce told him about the changes in Outpost and the occasional odd characters that had passed through, and curious items he had come across and scavenged locations.

They stood chatting as another two hours stacked up, their glasses refilling twice over that time. By the time they settled in for business, they were all warm with a rye glow.

"All right," Royce said, emptying his third glass and setting it on the railing. "Let's hear it. I can practically see you just dying to ask me."

Fenix nodded. "Actually. I think the girl here's better equipped to ask what needs asking."

Ani played his words over in her head. She had a good glow on and tried piecing his sentence together in three different ways.

"Well," Royce said, apparently sobering up nearly instantly. "Let's hear what you are in such a bad need to find, that you would not only risk teaming up with this God forsaken heathen but come to this God forsaken outpost at the ass end of the wastes."

Ani glanced at Fenix for a moment before setting her glass down. There was still nearly a half inch left. "I'm. We're looking for a facility. It's called Arcan. It's pre-world—" She could see by the color leaving the man's face that he recognized the name. "You've heard of it…" The last sentence was delivered as a statement more than a question.

Royce swallowed hard, his hand flinching instinctively towards the empty glass, then pulling back at the twitch. "It would seem these pre-world facilities are quite popular as of recent."

Ani studied the man, though the rye in her added an extra layer of warm fuzz to each of her thoughts.

"Belcor," the man began. "Cultiva, Pharma. Deltron. And Arcan." He paused, now studying Ani. "And what interest do you have in *that* particular facility?"

The answer was a long one, one that Royce gladly sat through as Ani recounted the events with her brother, and her and Fenix's travels across the wastes, the orcs and goblins and reapers. All of this after a nod from Fenix, indicating it was okay to share. She told him of her father and the facilities, of her time in Belcor and their entering into Deltron. She finished up with the prophet and his desire to turn the world to ash.

The entire time, their host listened intently, and when she finished, taking that extra moment to emphasize that there was no more to tell, he replied simply with a "Hmph."

Ani stared at him as if he had spoken in some strange foreign tongue. "Hmph?" She struggled to understand. "After all that, all you have to say is *hmph*?"

Royce stared at her for a moment. "No. I have a lot more to say than that. Just digesting is all." Then he studied her a moment longer. "And therein lay the caveat…" A flicker danced across his eyes as he looked — no, stared at Ani.

Ani stared back, feeling the slightest discomfort in the man's gaze. Then it came, the question she could see forming.

"What was your father's name, girl?"

She studied the man staring at her, not liking the creeping feeling that was filling the air between them. "Caeleb," she said after a moment, her gaze flicking to Fenix. "Caeleb Summersong."

The man's gaze narrowed, and he drew in a breath that filled his lungs to capacity. Then he released the air, slowly, the thin hint of a smile edging back the corners of his mouth. "There it is," he said flatly, a squint tugging at the edges of his gaze, like he had discovered some great secret.

"What?" Ani asked uncomfortably. "There *what* is?"

The smile on Royce's face grew, a small single chuckle escaping. "There's an old saying. Don't hold much weight here in the wastes, what, with nothing but cactus, weeds and a couple grains being able to grow." He pondered the thought for a moment. "Saying goes, fruit doesn't fall far from the tree."

She stared at him, not knowing how, but even more confused now than she had been just moments prior.

The smile grew. "I know him," he said, the smile not fading. "Ain't seen him in quite a few cycles, but I know your daddy. Pretty well actually."

Ani's face dropped. "You knew my father…?"

Now Royce's face dropped. "*Knew*?"

The pair stared at each other; a flash of conversation shared in the silent breath.

"My father went missing some months back." Her gaze dropped to the floor, her brow furrowing deeply. "I don't…"

Royce nodded in understanding. "I saw your father last, maybe, two cycles ago. He said he'd come across something big, something that would *change* everything. He was finally gonna be able to get his family out of the wastes." Royce smiled, a quick lift of an eyebrow accompanying it. "He didn't say much about it. Smart man your father. Then he started bringing me things that piqued my interest to say the least." He sighed heavily. "The last time I saw your father, he showed up here with a cart full of pre-world artifacts in pristine condition. I'm not talking found in a bunker well-preserved condition, I'm talking, fresh off the line condition."

Ani listened in fixated concentration.

"That was when he told me about the facilities. He told me all about your grandfather, and his finding of the first. Belcor, I believe it's called."

Ani's jaw nearly dropped to the floor.

"See, your father and I—like Fenix here and I—go way back." Royce's gaze lingered on Ani, his voice low and rough as gravel. "So, when he told me he thought the scavengers were onto his find, I did something I don't often do: I took an interest." He paused, the lamplight catching on the deep lines of his face. "There aren't many folks in this world I'd go out of my way for, and even fewer I'd risk my own hide for. Your friend Fenix here, that's one. Your father was another."

Royce gnawed at his lower lip, clearing his throat before taking a slow sip from his glass. "Your father left me a map. Said he'd found it inside the one he'd been scrapping—old world, pre-flame. This map had the locations of four more of these facilities. Told me to keep it safe. Said it was his family's future." Royce scoffed, shaking his head as if still surprised by his own actions. "Like I said, I'm not exactly the type to look out for the wellbeing of others. Didn't get where I am by sticking my neck out. But Caeleb and I go way back, so... I did right by him."

Ani stared for a moment. "I don't know where my father is." There was a tone behind her words, the hint of an insinuation threaded through them.

Royce shook his head. "I don't know. I'm sorry. I really am." He took a deep breath, sighing. "He's a good man. Not a lot of those in the wastes. Did me some favors, made me a *lot* of credits. And he didn't have to."

Ani's gaze lowered to the floor, her head nodding softly.

"I suppose you're gonna ask for the map next?" Royce concluded.

Ani lifted her gaze.

"I have it." Royce's words hung in the air, edged with a hesitation that didn't suit a man of his reputation. "But I'll be straight with you. When your father vanished these past two cycles, I figured he'd finally scraped together enough to get his family out of the wastes. So, what started as a favor... well, it turned into more of a commodity." Royce's gaze dropped, the lamplight catching on the deep lines of his face. "Not long after, men started coming around, asking about maps to these secret facilities." He shrugged, a bitter smile tugging at his lips.

"I figured, what good's information if you can't make credits off it? Out here, everything's got a price—even the past."

Ani's gaze tightened. "You sold it...? You sold my father's map!?"

"Hold on," Royce said quickly. "I sold them *a* map," he replied, strongly emphasizing the single letter.

Ani held his gaze tightly. She could feel the heat rising in her fingertips.

"They offered me a pretty credit for that map." A smile returned to his face. "Every scrapper and scavenger in the wastes knows about those facilities, or at least knows of one." He paused. "Your father is the only man I know to ever find a way *into* one. So, I didn't exactly see the harm in selling information that was readily available with enough time and searching."

"They have a key," Ani whispered, turning to Fenix. "He has a key."

Fenix's face tightened. Then he turned his attention to Royce. "We're gonna need that map, Royce."

"What am I missing here?"

"That prophet this girl here just told you about. The crazy bastard who wants to release the flame again. That son of a bitch has one of the keys. So, you just sold the one other person in the wastes who can get inside those facilities, a map to the facility that holds the flame."

Royce's face grew grim. "Oh. Shit."

Fenix scoffed. "Shit indeed Royce. God damnit..."

Royce set his glass down, standing and making his way quickly away.

Ani stared at Fenix; her face pulled in on itself in worry.

"We get the map," Fenix began. "We take the guns, and we go to this Arcan facility. Then we do things my way, and we stop that son of a bitch from blowing us all to hell. You got that?"

Ani swallowed hard, her brow dropping further down. Slowly she nodded. The warm glow from the previous drink was now fully dissipated.

A moment later the door opened up and Royce stepped in, a plastic covered page in his hand.

"Here," Royce said, walking up with the page held out. "Take it."

Ani reached out, taking the large sheet in her hand, her gaze locking to it.

"It belongs to you," Royce finished, his gaze lifting to meet Fenix's.

Ani stared down at the map, her fingers tracing the faded lines and hand-drawn topography, each mark etched in her father's careful script. Every settlement, every facility name, carried a weight of sorrow—ghosts of a world lost and the ache of memories she still hadn't learned to bury. It had been so long since she'd seen her father's handwriting, and now it cut through her like a blade, stirring up pain and longing in equal measure.

But as she studied the map, the ache faded into something sharper—a question. Her gaze settled on a small, semi-circular symbol near the top, a single word scrawled beside it: Arcan? The question mark lingered, uncertain, as if her father himself hadn't known what secrets lay there. Ani's eyes darted between the other symbols, searching for answers. Then another caught her attention—Pharma? Again, the question mark.

Fenix watched her study the map and saw the change in her expression. "What?" he asked, seeing the confusion. "What is it?"

Ani swallowed, lifting her gaze to him. "He didn't know," she said, the panic fading. "Father knew where Belcor was, Deltron and Cultiva. He had never gone to Pharma or Arcan. He didn't know which as which…"

"The map didn't list the facilities by name?" Royce asked.

"The facilities were numbered," Ani replied. "One through five. There was a list of facilities on the terminal in Belcor, their functions and purpose, but not location. My father knew the location of three, because he had gone to those. He never got the chance to get to the final two." Her gaze moved to Fenix. "We may have time. If they get it wrong, if we get to Arcan first…"

"Royce," Fenix said, tilting his head slightly. "It's been far too long."

Royce nodded, a thin smile flashing out in silent understanding. "Don't be a stranger."

Fenix nodded in reply, stepping forward to share a tight embrace. "Thank you,"

Royce smiled. "Don't thank me. Thank that girl's father. He was the one that was smart enough to leave that with me."

Fenix smiled. "Be seeing you."

Royce nodded, turning his attention to Ani. "You're just like him," he said, a gentle smile on his lips. "It's in the eyes."

Ani smiled ruefully. "Thank you."

Royce nodded. "Well, go on. Go stop that bald bastard from killing us all. God knows the wastes isn't doing it quick enough…"

Fenix hoisted the two duffels, slinging one over his shoulder. Then he nodded to Ani who turned and started her way towards the door.

"If I don't see you again," Fenix began.

"You will," Royce interrupted. "Just come back and tell me how you did it." He smiled sincerely. "And bring me back a few of those," he added, nodding to the bag on his shoulder.

Fenix smiled with a nod. "You got it old man."

"Go on. Before I start getting sentimental."

Fenix nodded, taking one last look at his old friend and mentor. Then he turned and started after Ani who was already at the top of the stairs.

"I need to go back home," Ani said as he walked up.

"Home?" he asked, confused. "That's in Blister Springs. That's the complete opposite direction as we need to be going."

"I know," she snapped. "I have to. I have to visit my mother's grave."

Fenix stared at her as if she had suddenly bellowed in an orcish war cry. Overhead a fairy fluttered past, a thin vapor of shimmering dust falling after it. He didn't bother swatting it away.

"We have to," Ani said, punctuating the conversation.

Fenix took a deep breath, exhaling sharply as he adjusted the bag on his shoulder. "All right," he said. "Then we have to."

Ani nodded softly, then turned and started her way down the stairs, the weight of realization settling over her like desert dusk. The moment Fenix's old friend had pressed the map into her hands and she'd seen those question marks, it all clicked into place. Her mind drifted back to a conversation with her father, cycles ago, and to the flickering vids she'd watched in the silent halls of Belcor. Every facility needed a key—without one, the walls were as unyielding as the wastes themselves. They had a key. The prophet had a key. But neither was the key they truly needed. Theirs were keys for entry, not for what mattered most. It was her father's handwriting that gave it away, the careful script and the uncertainty in those question marks. Suddenly, she knew exactly where the real key was hidden.

They made their way back through the cavernous building, the echo of their boots lost among the relics and the hush of secrets too heavy to name. Outside, their horses waited in the deepening twilight. They spoke little of Blister Springs—Ani sidestepping the truth of why she needed to return, Fenix giving up on pressing her for answers. Together, they rode out onto the open road, the wastes stretching before them, two days' hard travel to Heirako. They stopped only for a few hours' rest at midday, sleeping beneath the thin shade, then pressed on through the night. A day and a half later, they sat side by side in the rattling belly of a caravan car, the rails humming beneath them, their destination: Blister Springs.

57

It took four days for Ani and Fenix to reach Blister Springs, the caravan rattling across the wastes beneath a sky bleached bone-white by the relentless sun. By the time they stepped down onto the cracked platform, a nervous anticipation hung in the air—so thick it was almost hard to breathe. Ani knew what was at stake: two keys were needed to reignite the flame, to unleash the old world's weapons. Every mile of the journey, she'd watched the horizon, half-expecting to see a flash of light, a mushroom cloud blooming in the distance. But the only thing that greeted them was the blinding glare of the sun and the endless, tarnished red and brown of the wastes.

The ride from the caravan station to the Summersong homestead was a half-day's trek beneath the merciless sky. By the time they arrived, midday was pressing down with all its fury, the heat shimmering off the land in waves. Ani led their horses to the white-roofed barn that stood a little ways from her small, battered home. She and Fenix made their way back across the yard, the scalding heat pressing on their backs, every step a reminder of just how unforgiving the wastes could be.

"That was a little closer than I like," Fenix said, shutting the door quickly behind him and squinting into the darkness of the room.

A moment later a dim light illuminated the interior, a single electric lamp coming to life in the middle of the ceiling.

Fenix paused in the doorway, taking in what was left of Ani's home. It looked as if a storm had torn through, leaving chaos in its wake. The floor was strewn with pre-world artifacts—broken relics, battered books, and scraps of memory scattered like bones. Against one wall, an empty bookshelf leaned at an odd angle, its contents gutted and pages torn, fluttering in the faint breeze that slipped through a cracked window. Furniture lay toppled and broken: a chair smashed to splinters near the kitchen, every cupboard yanked open and ransacked, the floor beneath littered with shattered plates and glass.

The place felt hollow, stripped of comfort and history, the last traces of family life buried beneath dust and ruin.

Ani stared, a tear working in her eye. "My mom hated it," Ani said, watching Fenix's gaze work across the dust-blank spaces on the walls. "But dad insisted it was only right that they carry on traditions. He said it was a reminder that times had once been better and meant that they could again."

"I'm sorry Ani."

Ani let her gaze work across the home. "It's fine," she replied flatly. "I somehow knew it would look like this."

"Not sure if *better* is the word I would use," Fenix remarked, pulling his gaze from the clutter as thoughts of war, and the flame, and the chaos that had led up to the flame worked past.

Ani made her way to the tilted bookshelf, picking up a large leatherbound book that lay on the floor beneath, and turned to make her way to the dining room table. "Look," she said, setting the heavy book down with a *thud*.

Fenix set the gun bags down and made his way over, pulling out a chair and taking a seat.

"Coffee?" Ani asked.

"We can clean this up if you'd like."

Ani glanced around the room. "Doesn't matter. I'm not sure I'll ever be coming back."

"Well," he replied. "If you don't have anything stronger, then coffee will do just fine."

"Father didn't drink," Ani replied flatly.

Fenix smirked and cracked open the battered front flap of the book. The first thing that greeted him was a photograph—large, glossy, impossibly bright. A city from the world before: a long avenue stretching to the horizon, a thousand lights burning through the dusk, blue sky fading down to a blanket of coral and orange. Storefront signs blazed in neon, not unlike the ones strung up in Outpost, but here they were everywhere—red and green lights strung across the street in careful intervals, yellow and white lines painted on the road, and tall, pom-pom crowned trees lining the boulevard like sentinels from a forgotten age.

He turned the page. Now, an endless beach unfurled—white sand and turquoise ocean, a single boat bobbing at the end of a rope. In the shallows, a handful of people laughed and splashed, their skin bare and sun-kissed, the world around them untouched by dust or fear. Fenix scoffed quietly to himself. Like to see them try that now, he thought, and let the page fall back into the past where it belonged.

Ani set the water kettle on the small electric range and returned to the table. "The pre-world was beautiful," she said, a strong sense of admiration in her tone. "For all their faults, the cities they built were amazing. Their technology, their, culture." She took a deep breath and sighed heavily, looking across to the book she had spent days of her life staring into.

Fenix turned the page, looking down at an ancient advertisement for something called *Delta Airlines*. There was a picture of a nicely dressed woman in a short skirt with a red cap on her head, and a sprawling cityscape behind her, all backdropped by the endless blue of the ocean. *Your destination awaits* was written in bold script across the bottom. Fenix closed the book, sliding it away from him. "Why do you torture yourself with things like this?" He eyed her, watching the change in her expression. "Things aren't like that anymore," he said, gesturing to the book with a nod. "Happy faces, ocean frolics and grandly lit cities that spread to the horizon." He sighed dejectedly. "They destroyed that. They destroyed everything. Their quest to wipe out the Corithian's. It will never be like that again. And I don't see why you keep holding on to that."

"Because we don't know," she replied. "Have you ever been to Europa, or to the far north? Have you ever been beyond the wastes?"

Fenix sighed. "I wasn't born in the wastes," he said. "Remember? And I can tell you that, though it might not be scorching heat and desert, things aren't much better anywhere else. It's still just folks trying to survive."

"But it could be," Ani added. "It could be."

Fenix held his reply. "Why don't we try and get some rest," he said. We can't go out till the sun drops down anyways. Might as well take advantage of the time we have." He paused. "Did they get what you came here for?"

Ani shook her head. "No. Once the sun drops, I will. But I need to do this alone."

Fenix's brow furrowed slightly at the thought. "You sure?"

Ani nodded. "Yes."

"Okay." He inhaled sharply, tapping his hands on the table. "Then if it's alright with you, I'm gonna go lay down on that couch over there and get me some shut eye."

Ani nodded, reaching out to pull the scrapbook towards her.

"Save me some coffee," he added, making his way to the couch.

Ani spent a long while drifting through the familiar pages of the scrapbook, letting her fingers trace the faded images and brittle corners. She admired the world that had come before—their cities, their cars, their flying machines. For all their faults, those people had built wonders. She knew the world was vast, impossibly so, and she clung to the hope that somewhere, beyond the wastes, something like that old world still survived. The elves in the north, the halfling cities to the west, Europa and lands beyond—surely, somewhere, there was a place that resembled the pictures in her book. There had to be.

Time slipped by, the hours stretching thin. Eventually, Ani dozed off in her chair, arms folded across the scrapbook, forehead resting atop its battered cover. She'd thought coming home would bring comfort, but the house felt hollow, stripped of warmth and memory. The place that once sheltered her now sat ravaged, a stark reminder of all she'd lost and all she still had to do. As sleep pulled her under, the ache of emptiness pressed in, and her last waking thoughts were of family—ghosts flickering in the ruins of home.

58

Ani awoke a short time later, her gaze drifting to the window. She could see by the brightness outside that midday had passed. She pushed out from the table and stood, making her way over the cluttered memories to the front door. She glanced back to where Fenix lay, snoring on the couch. Then she made her way out.

The midday heat still clung tightly in the air, the oppressive weight of it clawing against her skin. She pulled her sleeves down and made her way around to the back of her house, where she took up a shovel and started to where a tall artifact sculpture stood.

When she reached the obelisk shaped structure she stopped, setting the blade of the shovel against the earth, and let her gaze drift to the name scrawled cross a small plaque. *Desimay Summersong.* "Hey mom," Ani said, a tightness building in her chest.

Back in the battered house, Fenix drifted awake, eyelids fluttering as the pale light filtered through a crack in the boarded window. For a long moment, he stared up at the ceiling, listening to the hush that filled the empty rooms. A flicker of worry crept in—Ani was gone—but then he remembered her quiet words the night before: there was something she needed to do alone.

He stretched, joints popping, and let out a low yawn. The scent of old coffee lingered in the air, a small comfort in the ruins. Fenix pushed himself upright on the couch, boots scraping the warped floorboards, and shuffled to the stove. He poured a cup, the chipped mug warming his hands, and turned to take in the wreckage of the home. The place looked as if a dust storm had torn through—pre-world relics scattered across the floor, books gutted and tossed, furniture splintered and overturned. He tried to picture what it must have been like before the prophet's men had ransacked it: warm, lived-in, maybe even happy. The thought stung, a reminder of his own lost home, and he let out a slow breath, shaking his head to clear it.

He settled at the table, pulling the battered scrapbook close. For a while, he lost himself in its pages—old photographs, faded advertisements, fragments of a world that had burned away. Eventually, he wandered to the bookshelf, thumbing through the scattered volumes until one caught his eye: a thick book with the image of a ruined city on the cover, a lone figure strung up on a cross above a muddy street. Fenix smirked, reading the title, then flipped it over to scan the back. With a shrug, he returned to the couch, coffee in hand, and cracked open the first page, letting the ghosts of the old world keep him company as the wastes pressed in outside.

The hours slipped by in the quiet house. Fenix sunk deep into the story of the dead rising and a giant of a warrior carving a bloody path across a cursed land. The world outside faded to silence, the only sound the occasional creak of the wind against the warped boards. Then, the front door groaned open and Ani stepped in, closing it quietly behind her.

Fenix closed the book, not quite marking his place, and watched her for a moment. Dust clung thick to her clothes, and a darker stain of earth climbed up her boots and trousers—evidence enough she'd been digging, though she offered no explanation and he didn't ask. Secrets were a kind of currency in the wastes, and he'd learned not to spend them lightly.

He lifted the book in his hand, a wry smirk tugging at his lips. "Interesting selection," he said, the words carrying a note of approval and a hint of shared understanding. In the hush of the ruined home, it was as close to comfort as either of them could manage.

She smiled, taking her hat off and slapping it against her leg, releasing a cloud of dust that swirled and danced in the light. "Dad loved his books," she replied, setting the hat down and making her way to the stove. "He said it was like a window into the past. All you had to do was open the cover and peer in."

She filled a cup with the now room temperature coffee and turned to her companion, the smile growing. "That's a good one," she said, gesturing to the book in his hand with a nod. "I really like the Danielle character."

He smirked, taking one last glance at the cover before closing it fully and setting it on the couch beside him. "You have everything you need?" he asked.

She took a sip from her cup and nodded. "I hope so."

"Whelp," he said, slapping his knees as he rose. "Then I don't see much sense in lingering here. I say we go to check out those two facilities."

Ani nodded. "Pharma is closest. It's not too far past Brimhall. We should probably go there first."

"Pretty much what I was thinking." He paused. "The other once takes us right past the Tunnels of Gol, and I don't know about you, but I'm not too in a hurry to head right into old orc territory."

She shook her head.

"Well," he finished. "Grab whatever else you think you might need, and let's get back out there."

Ani finished her coffee in silence, the last dregs swirling in the chipped cup before she set it down on the counter. For a moment, she let her gaze wander the hollowed-out room—empty walls, scattered relics, the battered remains of a life torn apart. Her eyes lingered on the doorways: one leading to her parents' old room, another to the space she'd once shared with her brother. The ache of memory pressed in, heavy and raw, until she finally turned away, fingertips brushing the worn cover of the family scrapbook as she passed.

Outside, the world was all dust and heat. Fenix and Ani moved to the stable, saddling up their tired horses, securing the battered duffels before climbing into the saddles. As they rode out, Ani cast one last look over her shoulder at the house she'd grown up in. Something deep inside told her it would be the last time she'd ever see it. All she carried away were memories—most of them painful, some she hoped would soften with time. But for now, even the good ones stung.

They rode on, dust trailing behind, the house shrinking into the shimmering haze of the wastes. By the time they reached Blister Springs, they barely spoke, each lost in their own thoughts. They bought two tickets for the next caravan to Brimhall—a day and a half's journey—and settled into the rattling car. Ani stared out the window, watching the endless red and brown of the wastes slip by, while Fenix buried himself in the pages of a battered book, the silence between them as heavy as the road ahead.

59

A great cloud of dust billowed up, the thunder of boots and hooves grinding to a halt. The air was thick with snorts, guttural growls, and the hungry whine of beasts barely held in check. At the head of the horde—orc warbands and goblin clans tangled together in uneasy alliance—stood the prophet, his silhouette stark against the dying light. His eyes were fixed on the massive structure rising from the scarred earth, a relic of the old world, half-exhumed from the red clay wastes.

He drew a long, scorching breath, the desert heat burning in his lungs. The facility loomed before him, crude and rectangular, its armored door nearly free of the earth's grip. The prophet's gaze narrowed as he studied the entrance, then strode forward, the horde behind him shifting with anxious anticipation.

He crossed the open ground alone, mind racing with visions of what waited inside. Everything he'd schemed, everything he'd killed for, lay just beyond that vault. Now, with the key in hand, he was close enough to taste it—close enough that even the heat couldn't dry the hunger from his mouth.

At the threshold, the prophet paused in the shadow of the great door. He traced its outline, then found the small, recessed panel—ancient, but still waiting. He drew the key from beneath his robe, feeling the tremor in his hand as he turned it over, the weight of hundreds of eyes and a thousand whispered hopes pressing in behind him. The orc commanders and goblin chieftains jostled for position, their followers restless, the air alive with the threat of violence.

He pressed the key to the panel. For a heartbeat, the world held its breath. A single green light flickered, then vanished. A heavy clunk echoed, followed by a screech of metal as the vault door, unmoved for a thousand years, tore free of dust and debris and began to roll aside.

Behind him, the horde erupted—goblins and orcs howling in triumph, the sound rolling across the wastes like thunder. The human mercenaries at the prophet's side exchanged thin, hungry smiles.

The prophet turned to his followers, voice rising above the chaos. "Within these ancient walls lie the keys to our salvation! Here, we will unleash the flame and scour these lands of the unworthy. The wastes, and every land beyond, will be ours!"

The roar grew wild, feverish.

"A new fire will rain from the sky—a fire lit by us!"

The horde screamed, weapons clashing, armor ringing in violent approval.

"And all but our kind will die."

With that, the prophet turned, eyes burning, and stepped into the darkness of the facility, leaving the howling horde behind as the vault swallowed him whole.

60

"Tell me about Royce."

Fenix pulled his gaze from the dirt trail they had been following for the past few hours.

"Royce," he replied with a sigh. "Royce and I go back. Way back."

"I gathered that already," Ani replied. "How do you know each other?"

Fenix rode the next few paces in silence. It had been nearly three hours since they had left Brimhall and in that time, they had only shared a handful of sentences. It seemed like the closer they got to their end goal, the less they spoke. Likely, he thought, she was just as wrapped up in her own worrying thoughts as he was. "You remember I told you my uncle tried to attack me, and I ended up killing him?"

Ani nodded, looking across to him.

He reached up and wiped the sweat dripping from beneath his hat band with his arm. "Well. I ended up in the only place I figured I wouldn't be found." He rode the next few paces, bobbing in silent remembrance. "Here." He shook his head, turning his head to gaze across the wastes with a scoff. "I had no credits, no skills. I didn't know anyone out here. Ended up pulling odd jobs in Aberdyne for as long as I could. That was about until I wore out my welcome." He glanced over at the girl. "I wasn't exactly as well-mannered and reserved as I am now."

"Wow," Ani replied flatly. "I don't wanna imagine."

Fenix let out a low chuckle. "That's how I ended up in Outpost, truth be told. I'd heard stories about drifters—met a few, back when I was scrubbing shitters and mopping floors at the Nautilus. Never thought much of that life, but when you run out of options in the wastes, well... necessity don't always make for rainbows and puppies." He paused, watching a fat lizard scurry across a red-hued rock, half-tempted to draw his pistol and make a meal of it. Instead, he just watched as it froze, blinked at them, then darted beneath a fallen cactus. "Royce had just started up Scraptech back then. Wasn't anything like it is now—just a big shack on the edge of Outpost, surrounded by a dozen other vendors hawking pre-world junk. When I rolled in, some locals pointed me his way, said he was always looking for scrappers or scavengers to fetch him relics from the old world. See, Royce figured there'd be a resurgence of technology someday, and he wanted to be at the front of it. So, he paid folks to bring him anything pre-flame they could dig up. Paid better than most, too. Quantity over quality, he used to say. Funny thing is, now he's got so much, he can afford to demand quality."

Ani rode silently, listening to her companion's tale.

"It just so happened that right around the time I arrived, there was a family that needed escort out of the wastes. They were headed north. Supposed to be meeting up with a caravan that was headed into elven territory. Needed an armed escort to get them through the goblin lands. My dumbass jumped on the job."

"Wait," Ani barked, her eyes big as she turned to him. "You've been to the elven lands!?"

He chuckled. "No. The goblin lands, yes. Elven. I didn't go past the border."

"What was it like?"

"Do you wanna hear about Royce, or the goblins?"

Ani wrinkled her nose in a smirk, and for the briefest of moments, Fenix saw the little girl that was still hiding somewhere deep inside her.

"Not much different than this," he replied, satisfying her itch. "Just a little greener." He continued. "Needless to say, I dropped the folks off and made my way back almost without incident."

"Almost?"

"Yeah," Fenix said, voice rough as boot leather. "Scouting party—nothing I couldn't handle back then. I was a riley son of a bitch, full of piss and vinegar." A crooked smile flickered across his face, the memory warming him against the chill of the wastes. "Royce was plenty pleased I pulled off a job everyone else figured was suicide. After that, he started sending me on the tough runs—the kind nobody else wanted. In return, he taught me the ways of the wastes. I made him credits; he made me into what I am."

Fenix's gaze drifted to the horizon, the last light of day catching in his eyes. "I worked for Royce, damn near his right hand, for the better part of fifteen cycles. Then I met Cora. After that, the dangerous jobs lost their shine, and Royce's investment in me had run its course. So, I walked away—chose a new life with my wife. Royce kept building Scraptech into the beast it is now, and I left the old world behind."

"Did you keep in contact?"

Fenix smiled again. "I made it a point to stop by every now and again. To check in on the old man. But we didn't go writing letters to each other or nothing like that."

"Oh," Ani replied. "Is it as dangerous as they say? The goblin lands?"

Fenix nodded. "You gotta have your head on a swivel. See. That's the thing about goblins. One or two, they'll run, no questions asked. Ten or twenty. They might think about it, but if you drop one or two, they'll scatter. You find yourself in the middle of a clan thought, that's a whole other story... You get a hundred of those little bastards bearing down on you. Their numbers will far exceed their courage. And once they get that bloodlust flowing..." He sighed. "Twice. Twice I ended up in the goblin lands. Not again..."

"You've never been curious about the elves?"

Fenix chuckled. "No. They stick to their parts in the north, we stick to the south. See, the problem is, that elves live a *real* long time. I'm talking like, there are elves still alive that survived the flame.

"That was a thousand cycles ago," Ani replied skeptically.

"And they live far longer than that. And what that means is that that grudge they carry, the one from when humans decided to take it upon themselves to cleanse this world of their kind. That grudge is still fresh…"

"Oh," Ani replied flatly.

"Yeah. See, our great-grandfathers and theirs have long since turned to dust—so for us, it's just a story, a memory faded by sun and time. But the elves? They remember. They've still got brothers and sisters, wives and kin who were hunted down and slaughtered in the cycles before the flame. While our kind were digging bunkers and building fortresses, theirs were being hunted—elves, halflings, orcs, goblins… witches too. They haven't forgotten, and they sure as hell haven't forgiven. So, keep that in mind before you go riding north, thinking you'll find a warm welcome."

"But what about Europa?"

"What about it?"

"They say that they have cities there where humans and elves, and halflings, all live side by side."

Fenix stared at her for a moment. "Again, have you ever been there?"

She looked at him for a moment. "Well. No. Of course not."

He smiled. "Then it's nothing more than a story."

Ani fell silent, allowing the hot breeze to fill the space between them. She had to believe there was something more than the world that surrounded her. There *had* to be.

61

Boots rang out on the cold, polished concrete as the prophet stormed through the bowels of the ancient facility. Behind him, the rest of his horde waited at the threshold, left to gnash their teeth in the dark while only his most fanatical guards trailed after, silent and wary.

He passed through the cavernous entry, the air thick with the ghosts of a world long dead. Security detectors shrieked as he strode between their cracked plastic columns, but he didn't even flinch. The checkpoint desk, abandoned and dust-choked, bore a faded sign: CONTROL ROOM. The word sent a feverish thrill through him. Control. That was what he'd come for—what he'd killed for.

He stalked through a gauntlet of silent checkpoints, each one yielding to the key he clutched like a relic. At last, he stood before a heavy steel door, CONTROL ROOM stamped in tarnished silver above. He paused, breath ragged, eyes wild with anticipation, then stabbed the access key at the panel. A green light flickered, and the door rumbled open, grinding aside with the weight of centuries.

Inside, the room was a relic of lost power—a sweeping command console curved along the back wall, a dozen dead-eyed monitors staring down from above. Three chairs waited before the console, and behind them, a row of theater seats overlooked the deck, as if expecting an audience for the end of the world.

As the prophet entered, the overhead lights flared to life, bathing the room in a cold, electric glow. The console blinked awake, a sea of colored lights flickering across its surface. On the monitors, the Americorp logo flashed—five white stars trailing red, white, and blue, a memory of a nation burned away.

He descended the steps, a thin, manic smile twisting his lips. "It has all come to this," he hissed, voice trembling with a fever that bordered on delirium. His guards halted at the doorway, shadows against the sterile light.

He gripped the key, recalling the expensive photographs he'd bought from a crooked artifact dealer in Outpost—images of this very console. He knew enough to be dangerous. Two small plastic boxes, spaced a dozen feet apart, drew his attention. He lunged at the first, thrusting the key at it. A dim green light flared; the cover clicked open. He jammed the key inside. The light glowed green. He repeated the process at the second box—again, green. But nothing happened. He tried again, and again, each time more frantic, more desperate, but the system remained silent. One key was not enough.

A guttural, animal scream tore from his throat. "NO! NO! NO!" He slammed his fists against the leather edge of the console, the sound echoing through the empty room. He pounded again and again, until his knuckles split and blood smeared the ancient leather. "You will open for me! You will burn for me!" he shrieked, voice cracking, eyes wild with hate and hunger.

Two guards rushed in, startled by the violence. The prophet stood hunched over the console, breath ragged, eyes burning with a madness that seemed to flicker in the electric light.

"Prophet?" one ventured, voice trembling.

He spun, eyes blazing. "Do you wish me to gather the horde?" the guard asked, uncertain.

"No!" the prophet spat, voice raw and broken. "I must ready the flame!" His gaze dropped, then snapped up again, fever-bright. "Send a rider. Tell them to prepare. Tell them to stay below. Once the ashes of the flame settle, they will have a blood frenzy the likes of which this world has never seen." He leaned in, voice dropping to a hiss. "I want them to tear across the wastes, a flood of death. Destroy and devour everything in their path. Let the world choke on its own ruin!"

He paused, trembling, then fixed the guard with a stare that could have curdled blood. "But first, bring me the girl. The boy's sister. I need her here. With me. Now!"

"Yes, prophet," the guard stammered, backing away.

"Bring me the girl!" the prophet howled, voice echoing down the sterile corridors.

The guards vanished, two more taking their place at the door, eyes averted from the prophet's madness.

Alone now, the prophet staggered to one of the console's chairs, collapsing into the perfectly preserved leather. He rocked back and forth, hands trembling, blood smearing the armrests. His gaze drifted to the glowing logo above, and he began to mutter, words tumbling out in a fevered litany. His fingers danced across the keyboard, waking the monitors, as the hum of ancient machinery filled the room.

62

It was dark by the time Fenix and Ani reached the facility. They could just make out the outline against the ebony backdrop.

"I was just getting comfortable out here," Fenix said as he nudged his horse to a trot.

As they approached the facility's massive doorway, Fenix's eyes swept the ground, noting the thick crust of windblown dust and the way debris had drifted up against the entrance. No tracks, no sign of life—just the silence of the wastes pressing in on all sides. "I don't think anyone's been here in a very long time," he muttered, casting a wary glance over his shoulder. Only the empty desert stared back, endless and indifferent. "Could be a good thing…"

Ani stepped up to the battered panel and held out her key. The light flickered—a sickly, uncertain green—before the lock gave a tired click. The door shuddered, then began to grind sideways, scraping over centuries of sand. Inside, the lights sputtered to life, most of them dying again just as quickly, leaving only a handful to cast their pale glow into the gloom. One bulb, stubborn and steady, held on.

Halfway open, the door groaned, something deep within the wall protesting with a metallic shriek before a heavy, final thunk echoed through the entryway. The door stuck fast, leaving only a narrow passage into the stale, waiting dark beyond.

"That's not good," Fenix remarked, watching Ani take her first steps towards the half open portal.

Inside, the overhead lights sputtered and flickered, casting restless shadows that crawled along the cracked walls and warped floor. The air pressed in—thick, humid, and unmoving—clinging to Ani's skin like a fever. She paused just past the threshold, a prickle of unease running up her spine. Something was wrong here. Gone was the steady hum of old-world machines, the gentle breath of filtered air that marked a place still clinging to civilization. Instead, the silence was heavy, broken only by the faint buzz of dying bulbs. The place felt less like a shelter and more like a sealed crypt, the heat and stillness suffocating.

"The climate controls aren't working," Ani murmured, her voice barely more than a whisper as Fenix stepped up beside her. She looked up. In a nicely written font above the large central desk, was the word *Pharma Facility.* Below that. *Keeping the world a healthy place.* She drew in a lungful of the stale air.

"Well," Fenix said, eyeing the security desk. "Whatever was kept in here is long gone."

Ani turned. She could feel the air pressing into her, resting on her skin like a thin film. She felt a shortness of breath and assumed it was a lack of oxygen. If it was like that in the entrance, then she could only imagine what waited to be found further in. "We should go," she said a moment later. "Now we know where Arcan is."

"Well," Fenix replied. "If we leave now, we can be back in Brimhall by morning. We can catch the caravan from there to Corith. Judging from the map, it's only a three-day ride from there to your Arcan." He paused, contemplating the wight of his next words. "But that takes us right past Gol…"

"We don't have a choice," Ani replied flatly. "You have guns."

He scoffed, shaking his head. "Guns might not be enough."

"We don't have a choice," she repeated.

The pair made their way back out.

They left the door to the facility half open, an invitation for any that followed to make their way in. *'At least,'* Fenix thought as they rode away, *'some of the critters out here can make shelter…'*

The pair rode through the night, chatting only lightly. Above, a galaxy of stars sparkled down. Ani took notice that the lights flashing across the sky were particularly frequent that night. By the time they rode into Brimhall, she had lost count of the stars shooting past.

63

For a day and a half, Ani and Fenix rode the battered caravan rails toward Corith, the world outside their window a blur of rust and bone beneath a sky bleached white by the sun. They spoke in hushed tones about Arcan—their destination—and the dangers that might lie between Corith and the old facility. But it was the Tunnels of Gol that haunted their conversation most: a labyrinth of ancient orcish tunnels, carved deep beneath the wastes centuries ago, when the horde had tried to sweep south and claim the land for their own. That was before they'd stumbled into the forbidden zone—a place where the world itself had come undone, swallowing most of the orcish host and sending the survivors fleeing back east. The tunnels had never been sealed. Folks in the wastes learned to steer clear, for fear of running into an orc patrol checking the passages. No one wanted to be the unlucky soul who found out the hard way that the tunnels weren't as empty as they seemed. So, the Tunnels of Gol were left to the dark, avoided and forgotten by all but the desperate.

By the time the caravan rattled into Corith, the pair had settled on a plan. The driver said they'd arrive just before dawn, so they'd rest the morning in the city and leave just after midday. Fenix reckoned that if they set out at first light, they'd reach the edge of the tunnels by high sun—dangerously exposed, with no guarantee the orcs would be sleeping. But if they waited until the worst of the heat had passed and left at the tail end of midday, they could reach the tunnels just as night fell, using the darkness as their shield. With luck, they'd slip past unseen and reach the facility by the next sunset.

"I reckon we get there right around sundown. We find us a vantage point and watch for comings and goings. Based on that, is how we make our approach."

Ani pulled her gaze from the window, where she had been watching the outskirts of Corith growing closer in the distance. "You really think going straight in is the best option?"

Fenix took a moment. "I think going head on is the *only* option." He lingered on that thought for a moment. "These facilities only have one entrance. It's not like there *are* other options…"

Ani didn't like the idea, but he was right. At least they had the guns… It was a thought she found herself falling back on for comfort. It occurred to her that she may have begun relying upon the safety of the guns more than the drifter who had desired them.

The caravan slowed, snaking its way through the capital city, before coming to a gentle stop at the station. Then the driver stepped out from the front car and made his way to the passenger car door. "I hope you all had a pleasant journey. Welcome to the capital." And with that, he pulled the door to the car aside and stepped out.

Fenix and Ani waited for the other passengers to make their exit before standing and making their way out. They made their way to the cargo car and retrieved their horses. Fenix didn't bother securing his gun bags as they were only going a short distance to the nearest inn.

As they made their way through Corith, Ani marveled. The capital was the closest thing she had seen to the photos of the pre-world in her books. It had concrete streets, complete with painted lines. Long sidewalks lined the road, and every shop was lit up inside. There were arc streetlamps that illuminated the road and walking paths, and a bustle of business. People made their way to and fro in a hustle and she watched in amazement as a motorized bicycle buzzed its way past, the sound coming from it like a swarm of angry insects. "It's so big," she said a moment later, watching as another motorized bicycle zipped past, the man atop leaned forward in urgency.

"That's why it's the capital," Fenix replied. "Supposedly this was the first settlement established in the wastes after the flame. "Though I doubt it. I'm guessing hundreds came before it, all suffering the same fates as those abandoned outposts between Brimhall and Aberdyne. Hell," he scoffed. "I even heard they tried to build a settlement in the crater before the reapers took over. Guessing that didn't last long either. I think Corith just happened to outlast the rest. That's why it became the capital. The rest sprung up after."

Ani walked along. She had only heard the first half of what her companion had said. Her attention had been tugged a hundred other directions by the time he stopped speaking. "Mm-hm," she responded, a flash of light catching off a swirling metal sculpture hanging in the window of a shop. *Curios and Hardware,* a sign read above.

A short time later the pair were seated at a back table in one of the multitude of inns offered by Corith. This one just happened to be the first they saw that didn't have a brothel or drunk-filled noisy tavern accompanying it. They needed their rest. It was likely the last they were going to get until this whole thing was over.

"What's the farthest you've gone," Ani asked, peering at Fenix over the top of her glass.

Fenix took a sip from his glass and set it down, lifting his sleeve to wipe the foam from his moustache. "Well. There was a recovery job I took quite a few cycles back, maybe fifteen. You were probably just a baby at that point. That job took me out of the wastes and out past the rusted sea."

"Recovery job?" she asked in an accusatory tone.

"Yes, recovery job," he remarked back with a smirk. "Man's wife had run off with their infant son. I was hired to bring them back."

Ani stared at him, not liking the feeling his comment brought.

He smiled slightly. "There's a city, far to the west. Beyond the wastes and past the rusted sea. It's built atop the ruins of an old, pre-world city. Newvada." He paused, offering a moment of praise and recognition of the name. "Newvada's kind of like those pictures in your photographs. The type of place all manner of folks would make a pilgrimage to" He smiled. "They still have old photos of the city it was built atop; grand palaces that reach up into the sky, pyramids and monuments. It was one of the greatest cities ever built, pre-world." He pulled images from the deep recesses of his memory. "You can see the lights of the settlement from miles away. The lights are so bright that they all but blot out the stars above."

"Really?"

"Really. Not the safest of settlements, but if you're into gambling and whoring, then one of the best…"

"Oh."

Fenix smiled. "It's more than that though. Those just happen to be the focal points. Tradition from the city it was built atop I suppose."

"We have the caravan," Ani said, a frown tugging at her cheeks. "Why haven't they added to it? They could have it go all the way to Newvada, even further. Why do they keep transportation so isolated?"

"Easier that way I suppose. Safer maybe. A lot of things can happen out there. Reapers, scavengers, orcs. Worse… Plus, they have to maintain the rails, and could you imagine trying to do that out beyond the wastes, in the uninhabited lands where there are no settlements… I'm guessing the trouble isn't worth it. Besides. Most folks just settle where the work is. No sense leaving once you're established. Only drifters and scrappers live that life. Most folks scrape out a living in the city, like Corith or Aberdyne. Hell. Even Serenity and Heirako rotate most of their residences throughout the cycles. Business folk stay, but that feeds into that again. They have their shops or trades, and they settle there. Exactly my point."

Ani took another sip. "I don't know why anyone would *want* to stay in the wastes. Why stay in a place like this if there's an entire world out there?"

"It ain't as easy as all that," Fenix replied. "It ain't easy to just uproot and move on. You think the folks living in the wastes *want* to be here? Every person I've ever met is here because there's nowhere else for them to go. You have this fantasy built up in your head about Europa, and places like that. But have you ever tried to leave? Did your family?"

She shook her head. "No."

"Then you really don't know how hard it is. Trust me. I've seen plenty of folks try to leave the wastes. And guess what? Mont don't."

"I will," Ani replied flatly.

"And you know what?" Fenix responded across the top of his glass. "I'm inclined to believe you."

She smirked, setting her glass down and glancing around the room. "I just want to finish this. Finish this and leave. I want to forget that I ever lived here. I want to forget everything."

"I really hope you can," Fenix said, setting his glass down. "I really do."

The pair finished their drinks and made their way upstairs, boots heavy on the warped boards. Their rented room was small and spare— just a battered bed and a single, dust-choked window that looked out over the restless city. They barely spoke as exhaustion pressed in, the weight of the road and the day's worries settling over them like a blanket. Before long, sleep claimed them both, deep and dreamless. It wasn't until the first pale light crept through the window, painting the walls in soft gold, that either of them awoke.

64

Fenix had just finished pulling his boots on when he glanced over at Ani. "There's a stop we need to make before we leave. Something we need to get for you."

Ani, still tugging her vest into place and adjusting the sleeves of her sun-bleached shirt, shot him a wary look. "What?"

"You'll see," Fenix replied, standing and hefting one of the heavy gun bags over his shoulder. "One thing's for sure—I'll be damned glad when I don't have to lug these things around. I feel like a pack mule out here." He grunted as he shifted the weight, grabbing the second bag and slinging it over his other shoulder.

Ani watched in dry amusement, then followed him out. The early morning light spilled across the street, painting the dust in gold and warming her face as they stepped outside. Their horses waited, tied to the rail, heads low and patient.

They left the animals and walked a short distance down the boardwalk to a squat armorer's shop Fenix had eyed the day before. As they stepped inside, a bell chimed overhead. The shop smelled of oil, leather, and old steel. From a back room, a burly man with a thick, grey-streaked beard emerged, wiping his hands on a rag.

"Morning, folks," the man greeted, moving behind the battered counter. His eyes flicked to the duffel bags slung across Fenix's shoulders. "What brings you in this morning?"

"Need a vest for the girl," Fenix said, stepping forward.

Ani frowned. "A vest? I'm wearing one…" She tugged at her own faded leather.

Fenix shook his head. "Not that kind." He turned to the armorer. "Got something that'll stop a big round?"

The man's lips curled in a knowing smirk. "Think I've got just the thing." He started toward the back, pausing to size Ani up. "Guessing a… small?" Without waiting for an answer, he disappeared through the doorway.

"A vest?"

Fenix looked at her. "Look. You need some type of protection. Things are about to get real, and we can't have you running in there with no protection. At least if you're wearing a bullet stopper, it'll increase your chances of coming back alive. So, suck it up and get the damned vest."

"Okay, *dad*," Ani remarked, regarding him with a smirk.

A moment later the man emerged from the back. "Think this one'll work," he said, stepping up and setting a black vest on the counter. "You can replace the one you're wearing, or just slip it on underneath. Either way, it'll stop anything up to a forty-five caliber. Works well against blades too. It's steel fiber over Kevlar. Perfect blend of pre-world and new."

Ani eyed the vest in slight dismay.

"Gotta warn you though. Ain't cheap…"

"Ain't worried about that," Fenix remarked, tapping the bag across his shoulder. "I got good trade." He turned to Ani. "Go on. Try it on."

Ani grunted, stepping to the counter and hoisting the vest. It was heavier than she had anticipated by the look, but with steel fibers, she should have assumed.

She slid her arms through the vest and lifted the zipper up. There was a coolness to it, and a slight weight that she somehow found a gentle comfort in.

"I think we got a fit," the man behind the counter mused. Then he turned his attention to Fenix, and the bag. "You made mention of trade?"

Fenix eyed Ani approvingly, then turned and set the bag in his hand down. He unslung the one from his shoulder and set it on the counter. "You can pick two of these," he said, beginning to pull the guns out and setting them on the counter. The man behind eyed each of them as he pulled them out, his gaze getting wider with each one.

"Where did you get these?" the man asked, astonished.

"Doesn't matter," Fenix replied, his voice low and steady. "They all work." He nodded to two of the weapons on the counter. "Those right there—just pull the trigger and they'll empty the whole clip in a heartbeat. Each comes with a box of ammo."

The armorer lifted his gaze, weighing Fenix and Ani for a moment before reaching out, hefting the shotgun with practiced hands. He tested the weight, then cycled through the rest, finally settling on the shotgun and a stubby submachine gun. Fenix fished two boxes of shells and cartridges from the bag, setting them on the counter before starting to pack the rest away.

The armorer lingered, eyes narrowing. "You need to be careful," he said, voice dropping to a hush. "They're looking for you. And your daughter."

Ani bristled, about to protest the word daughter, but Fenix cut in, hand raised. "Who's looking for us?" he asked, then, suspicion sharpening his tone, "And how do you know who we are?"

The man shrugged, glancing toward the window. "Not sure, exactly. Couple fellas came through here the other day, asking after a man and a girl. Said one was a drifter, the other a witch. I told 'em I hadn't seen anyone like that, but I watched as they made their way to every shop on the street. Whoever they are, they want you bad. Big reward on your heads..."

Fenix paused, the last rifle in his hand. He set it down on the counter, then added two more boxes of ammunition for good measure. "Well. I guess it's a good thing you haven't seen us then, isn't it?"

The armorer looked down at the rifle and ammo, a sly grin flickering across his face. "I suppose it is."

Fenix turned, gesturing for Ani to follow. As they stepped out into the morning glare, the man called after them, "Ya'll stay safe out there." There was a glint in his eyes—something between warning and farewell.

Ani waited until they were halfway down the boardwalk before speaking. "What are we gonna do?"

"Nothing," Fenix replied, a hint of relief in his voice as he shifted the lighter bags on his shoulders. "We're gonna save them the trouble of looking."

Fenix made his way back into the inn. He headed upstairs and back into the room. There, he sat at the small table and pulled out the book he was still working through. "Might as well get comfortable," he said. "In light of this new information, I think it's best if we stay out of sight until we're ready to leave."

Ani nodded, dropping her side bag on the floor and making her way back to the bed where she flopped down, the extra weight of the vest pulling her down harder. She stared up at the ceiling, then turned to see Fenix already consumed by the story she'd read twice already. "You wanna know how it ends?" she teased.

Fenix lifted his gaze, a squint pulling at his eyes. "You wanna test out that new vest?"

She smiled, lifting her gaze back to the ceiling. *'Daughter,'* she thought, before letting her gaze fall to the window.

They waited out the morning in the hush of their rented room, Fenix hunched over a battered paperback while Ani lingered on the last ten pages of her own book. She had a habit of drawing out endings, savoring the anticipation, letting the story stretch just a little longer before the final page. Out here, in a world where so much was uncertain, the slow pleasure of a good ending was a rare comfort.

Midday crept by, the heat pressing against the shuttered windows. When the sun finally began its slow descent and the shutters lifted, they gathered their things and stepped out into the fading light.

Fenix tied the guns to his horse, this time keeping them close at hand—each one checked, loaded, ready for whatever the wastes might throw at them. All it would take was a single bad turn, and he'd need to be quick.

They rode north, leaving the city behind, the world stretching out in a haze of dust and dying sunlight. By Fenix's reckoning, they'd reach the Tunnels of Gol just as the sun was slipping beneath the horizon—if luck held. But in the wastes, luck was a fickle thing. The tunnels were old orc territory, and the shadows there were thick with stories of things best left undisturbed. If they were lucky, they'd pass through unseen. At least that's what he planned. And that was in the perfect scenario, where they didn't wind up coming face to face with a warband of orcs or goblin horde.

65

Afternoon slithered past, the sky painted with a thin vein of poppy-hued ochre just above the horizon—a last, stubborn trace of color in a world gone rust and bone. They rode in silence, the wastes stretching endless and empty, the only sound the steady clop of hooves and the faint rattle of gear. The facility lay less than half a day ahead, the Tunnels even closer—ancient scars in the earth, haunted by stories best left unspoken. Shadows grew long as the sun bled out behind them, and every mile brought the promise of danger closer, the air thick with the hush of things waiting just out of sight.

Ani's thoughts drifted back to the stories her father used to tell— tales whispered over the glow of a campfire, the wastes stretching silent and endless beyond. The Tunnels, he'd said, were more than just a scar in the earth—they were the gateway to the forbidden zone, a place where the world itself had come undone. South of the wastes, nothing was as it seemed. When the Merge happened, two worlds— two realities—had collided, and for a moment, the boundaries between them blurred. Creatures and wild energies from Corithia bled into the earth, the two realms overlapping before the Merge faded. Some things crossed over, but something else lingered—a residue, an invisible haze that warped everything it touched.

The forbidden zone stretched for hundreds of miles, an unseen cloud that twisted whatever entered. In the early days, folks wandered in and simply vanished. Later, a few returned, but they came back wrong—mutated, broken, their minds shattered or their bodies twisted in ways that defied sense. Ani remembered the term her father used: environmental dissonance. It stuck with her, a warning etched deep. Scientists had sent teams in, hoping to understand, but none ever returned. The best guess anyone had was that the Merge had left a wound in the world, a place where anything—human, animal, Corithian—would be torn apart and rebuilt, never quite the same.

Everything inside was in flux, constantly shifting, coalescing with whatever else drifted through.

Eventually, they'd tried to fence it off, but that was a thousand cycles ago, before the flame. Now, nobody went near it. Folks just called it the forbidden zone, and left it at that—a haunted border at the edge of the world, where the rules of life and death no longer applied.

"You're awfully quiet," Fenix said, after riding for the last thirty or so minutes in silence.

"Oh," Ani replied. "Sorry. I was just, thinking about what my father had told me about the forbidden zone, and how close we're gonna be to it."

Fenix glanced over to her. "We'll be plenty far away, don't you worry about that. There are more pressing things to worry about at the moment though. Like how we're coming up on those Tunnels." He nodded to a small cluster of hills rising up in the distance.

Ani swallowed hard, looking across to the mounds of earth.

As they drew nearer, they began to notice the faint traces of battle. Bannered pikes lay sun-bleached and faded on the ground, rusted armor and bones, discarded weapons.

"What happened here?" Ani asked, looking down at a half-buried skull sticking out of the dirt.

"Orcs," Fenix replied flatly. "And it would have been a lot worse if they hadn't made the mistake of trying to go south first…"

Ani looked at a broken sword lying next to a pile of scattered bones.

"I reckon that's the only thing that kept the wastes from turning into horde lands," Fenix said, his voice low as the horses picked their way through the dust. "Most of the orc army vanished into the forbidden zone. By the time they realized what was happening, it was too late—they'd lost half their numbers, and the rest turned tail for the east. That gave the settlers just enough time to band together and push back, but it cost both sides dearly. Wasn't much left but bones and ghosts when it was done." He paused, the weight of memory settling in the hush between them. "But I think the orcs learned from it. They've had three hundred years to rebuild, and that's what keeps me up at night. If they've thrown in with that mad prophet..." He trailed off, the silence stretching. "Well. That's a future I'd rather not dwell on."

Ani let her gaze fall back to the path, folding her memories back around her. For the next few hours they fell back into silence, the wasteland wafting past as they rode.

"I need to stop."

Fenix looked over at his companion. It was the first words she had spoken in hours.

"I have to pee."

He slowed his horse, smirking as she brought her horse to a stop and climbed down.

Fenix lifted his arms up, stretching. His backside was sore from riding, and he could see the thin layer of perspiration across Dirtweed's neck. He reached down and patted his neck. "You're doing good, buddy. Thanks for carrying all this for us."

A short distance away, Ani had made her way behind a rather large sagebrush. She had lowered her pants and was squatting, enjoying the beauty of a small cluster of desert flowers as she relieved herself. When she was finished, she stood, brought her pants back up and buckled her belt.

She made her way back to where Fenix was sitting atop his horse. As she approached, she saw his gaze locked to somewhere further down the path. At the same time, she noticed the look on his face. "What?" she asked, turning her head to see a small cloud of dust coming up. Four orcs and a small band of goblins led the cloud, approaching quickly. "What do we do?" she barked quickly, looking back to Fenix in desperation.

"Nothing we can do," he replied flatly, his gaze not leaving the approaching group. "We've already been spotted." Then he pulled his gaze away, locking it to her. "You fight. Don't let them take you alive." And with that, he leapt from his horse, pulling three guns from the bag. One he slung across his shoulder, the other he tossed into the dirt nearby, the third he took up, cocking it and bringing it to the ready. He took a deep breath and exhaled sharply.

Ani stepped back two paces before stopping.

The lead orc fixed its gaze on them, eyes burning with a feverish, hungry light. Saliva gathered at the corners of its mouth, anticipation twisting its lips into a snarl. This one was fresh from the Tunnels— still wild, still starved for blood. As it thundered forward, a guttural war cry ripped from its throat, echoing across the barren land. In that moment, there was nothing in its mind but the promise of death.

Fenix, cursing himself for letting his guard slip, leveled the automatic rifle and squeezed the trigger the instant the orc closed the distance. The weapon spat fire, and a spray of dark green blood burst from the orc's side, spinning it off-balance. Still, it barreled on, relentless. Fenix fired again, rounds sparking off battered armor until two shots found the soft flesh of its neck, punching through and spraying a sickly green mist. The orc staggered three more steps before collapsing, heavy and final, into the dust.

The three orcs flanking it howled, axes raised, and charged even faster. Ani's hand trembled above her pistol, breath caught in her throat as she watched the first orc fall and the others surge forward, war cries splitting the dusk. Behind them, a knot of goblins fanned out, blades and pikes glinting in the dying light.

Fenix swung the rifle to the next orc, firing in short, controlled bursts. The clip ran dry just as the second orc tumbled, rolling through the dirt, its stomach and face torn open and leaking onto the earth. The last two orcs were nearly on top of them. Fenix tossed the empty rifle aside, yanked the shotgun from his back, and fired from the hip. The shot caught one orc low, tearing its leg away in a spray of blood and bone. It dropped, screaming. Fenix barely had time to rack another shell before the final orc crashed into him, a wall of muscle and rage, sending him flying through the dust.

Ani stood frozen, her hand hovering just above the grip of her pistol, as if some unseen force had locked her in place. She watched, wide-eyed, as the second orc crumpled to the dirt, then the third. The fourth barreled into Fenix, sending him ragdolling through the dust, a good fifteen feet before he hit the ground. The whole world seemed to slow, every detail stretched thin—the roar of battle fading, replaced by the hush of the wind brushing her face.

Her gaze snapped to the goblins, a snarling pack bearing down on her, weapons raised and eyes wild with bloodlust. In that suspended moment, Ani felt the heat rising—first in her fingers, then her palms, then surging up her arms and into her chest. The air around her shimmered, energy crackling as she drew the warmth from the world itself. She could feel it building, vaporous and electric, until the goblins were nearly on top of her, blades poised to strike.

She raised her hands and let go.

Fire erupted from Ani's outstretched palms, splashing against the lead goblin and then blooming outward in a wave of searing heat. The flames stopped the goblins in their tracks, incinerating hair and flesh in an instant. Charred skin crackled and split, eyes boiled and burst, armor glowed red-hot and then blackened, studs melting to slag. Ani screamed—a raw, primal sound—her voice lost in the roar of her own magic as she poured every ounce of pain and fury into the inferno. For a heartbeat, the world was nothing but fire and vengeance. Then, as suddenly as it began, the flames died, leaving only scorched earth and silence.

Fenix fought to breathe, the world a blur of pain and dust. He clawed for air, chest heaving beneath his battered duster, hands fumbling for the pistol at his side. His vision cleared just enough to see a hulking shape looming over him—an orc, axe gripped tight, half its face torn away by the desperate blast of the shotgun.

Fenix stared up at the orc looming over him, fighting to draw a second breath. The creature's face was a ruin—one lower tusk snapped at the root, its left eye clouded and leaking a viscous green trail through a ragged hole in its cheek. Half its jaw was stripped of flesh, exposing a row of yellowed teeth, and one ear was nothing but a torn stump. The other eye, black and wide, was fixed on Fenix with a predator's focus.

The orc growled, a guttural snarl bubbling through shredded lips. It hefted its axe, muscles bunching for the killing blow. Fenix's lungs seized, and he twisted away, bracing for the end.

A thunderous crack split the air. The orc's chest armor exploded outward in a spray of bone, steel, and dark blood. Its single good eye widened in shock, then drifted down to the gaping hole in its chest. Fenix scrambled backward, rolling clear as the orc toppled forward and crashed to the dirt.

Ani stood just behind, shotgun still raised, smoke curling from the barrel. For a moment, Fenix just lay there, breath coming in ragged bursts, pain radiating from his ribs. He figured at least two were cracked, and it'd be a long while before he could lift his arm above his head again. But he was alive, and as he looked up at Ani—dust and fire in her eyes—he managed a crooked, grateful smile.

Ani dropped the shotgun to the ground and rushed over to Fenix. "Are you okay?" she asked, stopping short.

He nodded, clearing his throat with a groan. "That was good," he replied, looking past her to the charred remains still smoldering in the dirt. "Oh, shit," he exhaled, leaning back with a groan.

"Yeah," Ani replied, glancing back at the dead goblins. "Um…"

"Help me up," Fenix choked, holding his hand out. "Let's see how I stand."

Ani helped her companion to his feet. As she did, she took another glance at the orc that lay dead, the one she had put a shotgun blast through. She wasn't sure what she was doing, she had just reacted. She knew that if she didn't, her companion would be dead and the thing would have turned to finish her off next, so she had simply picked up the gun, pointed it at the thing's back, and pulled the trigger. The kick from the gun had nearly thrown her from her feet. She hadn't been expecting the gun to kick back like it had. In that moment, she had been worried that she had missed completely. It hadn't been until she looked back and was able to see the trail through the dripping hole in the thing that she knew she had hit its mark. Then she watched it fall forward, landing with a heavy thud in the dirt.

"Ugh," Fenix groaned. "I feel like I got hit by the caravan…"

"Almost," Ani replied, holding the shotgun out for Fenix to take.

"Hold it for a bit, yeah?" he asked, taking the first few steps towards Dirtweed that stood watching warily from the side. "Thanks for the help, buddy," he said stopping and looking down at himself.

Fenix took a few moments to steady himself, running careful hands over his ribs and limbs, checking for anything broken or worse. Satisfied he was still in one piece—if a bit battered—he limped over and gathered up the scattered guns, sliding them back into the pack. He took the shotgun from Ani, slinging it over his shoulder with a wince. "Think I'll keep this one a little closer from now on," he grumbled, hauling himself up into the saddle, every movement a reminder of the hit he'd taken.

Ani watched him the whole time, worry etched across her face. She'd seen him spin through the air, landing hard and rolling in the dust. She couldn't imagine the pain he must be in.

Fenix, for his part, cast a glance at the blackened goblin corpses, a flicker of gratitude passing through his eyes. He was glad the girl was on his side. "We should probably get moving," he said, looking over to where Ani still stood, concern written plain on her face. "There might be more. I'd rather not go through that again so soon. And we're likely to see more of the same when we reach the facility. Let's take a minute to regroup."

Ani nodded.

"I'm fine, Ani," he said, hoping his assurance would get the girl's feet moving.

She nodded, taking the first steps toward her horse.

66

The sun had dipped just beneath the horizon when Fenix broke the silence that had taken residence in the space between them. He looked out to the deep purple indigo that clung just above the hazy blue horizon. "That was good back there," he said, watching the stars above twinkle in approval. "Seems like you're getting a better grasp of it. Your *abilities*."

Ani rode in silence, thinking an entire almanac of thoughts before responding. "Yeah. I guess I am."

"What's your plan?" Fenix asked, squinting against a small tuft of sand lifted by a twirl of heavy breeze.

"I'm not sure I know what you mean."

"What do you want to do in your life?" he clarified. "What do you want to be? Where do you want to go? How do you envision your future?" He gave her a moment to ponder. "I mean. This can't be it. No offense, but you ain't exactly cut out for this life. And I really don't see drifting being at the top of your list."

Ani thought on it. Really thought on it. It was a question she'd had from the moment their father hadn't returned. It was a question that had grown even more prevalent since the loss of her brother. Where she sat now, it was one that hovered just behind her at every moment. "I don't know," she replied flatly. "I don't."

Fenix accepted the answer, though he was hoping for something more. She was a smart girl. She was book learnt, knew her history, knew all about the pre-world from her time in Belcor. She knew magic… That girl was special, that much he knew. He supposed she just hadn't had time with everything going on to truly sit and digest it. "Well, let me ask you in a different way. If you could be anything in the world you wanted, anywhere you wanted to be it, what would that be?"

She smiled thinly, looking over to a towering saguaro cactus, the night sky a portrait behind. She drew in a lungful of warm, night air and exhaled slowly. "Scrapper, maybe. Like my father." She pondered that for a moment. "He truly loved what he did. He loved finding old bunkers, and pre-world facilities filled with historical artifacts. It was a good life." Her horse snorted softly beneath her, and she reached down, patting it on the neck.

"Yeah," Fenix said, nearly interjecting. "But we're not talking about your dad, we're talking about you. What do *you* want to do with your life."

Her brow furrowed deeply for a moment. "I don't know. I think…" She pondered if what she truly wanted to be was even a thing, and how to articulate it. "If I could do anything in the world, it would be the study of pre-world artifacts and history. I'm fascinated with how things were before, the cities, the civilizations, the societies. I love every bit of it. So, if I could be anything in the world, that's what I'd be."

"So, a historian," Fenix remarked. "Sounds like a good profession. You let the scrappers do all the heavy lifting, and you put it all together." He smiled. "Smart."

"What about you?" Ani asked in response, a second wind coming on. "What would you be?"

"Me?" he asked, surprised. He thought of his wife, and their little homestead, the conversations about children. Then he thought about Royce and the plethora of jobs he'd pulled over the cycles. He thought about his childhood and his travels in the wastes. "You know. I think I'd probably do security." He pondered that thought. "I think I'd be pretty good at it. I got plenty of practice."

"Security…?" Ani asked, slightly puzzled by the response.

"Yeah," Fenix responded with a smirk. "Find me some wealthy do-gooder in some far-off settlement, far, far away from the wastes. Act as a private security guard, following them around and keeping all the wanting ladies off him." He smiled, ear to ear.

"I'm being serious!" Ani snapped. "If you could be anything, what would you be?"

He chuckled for a moment. Then he drew in a deep breath and exhaled in a sigh. "I'd like a family," he responded, much to her surprise. "Almost had one. I really liked that feeling."

Ani rode in silence for a moment, feeling the sadness in his tone. "Then we finish this," she said a moment later, a hint of absolution in her voice. "We go somewhere far away from here, and I'll become a historian, and you can find a nice lady to start yourself a family with. How's that sound?"

"It sounds perfect," he responded, complete honesty behind it.

"Then it's settled," she concluded. "We finish this job, and we start our new lives."

Fenix rode on, a flicker of warmth settling in his chest at the thought of something beyond the wastes—something better, maybe even a future. He liked the sound of it, even if he knew better than to trust hope out here. The truth was, leaving wouldn't be as simple as packing up and riding west. There was a good chance neither of them would make it out alive. They'd survived a handful of scraps, but what lay ahead wasn't just another dust-up. They were riding straight into the viper's nest, into the heart of every nightmare the wastes could conjure. Fenix's jaw tightened as he glanced at Ani. "Then it's settled," he said, voice low and steady. "Our last hurrah—and we're out."

67

Ani and Fenix stood atop a low rise, boots planted in the dust, staring down into the hollowed earth below. The conversation they'd shared hours earlier was gone, swept away by the sight before them. In the crater, the Arcan facility crouched like some ancient beast, its entrance ringed by banners and pikes that fluttered in the night breeze, moonlight glinting off battered metal. All around, dozens of campfires burned low, their glow painting shifting shadows across the scarred ground.

Fenix counted at least two dozen orc banners, and nearly three times that number of goblins—an army scattered across the crater floor, restless and waiting. The air was thick with the distant clamor of voices, the clang of weapons, the low rumble of something terrible gathering strength.

He stepped back from the ridge, turning away from the sight and glancing at his horse, who grazed quietly a few paces off, oblivious to the storm brewing below. Fenix wiped the sweat from his brow, his voice low and grim. "Well, shit," he muttered. "I have no idea how we're supposed to get through that..."

"What about the guns?" Ani asked, looking over to him.

He scoffed. "You just saw how well those guns worked, and that was against four of em. There's gotta be at least two dozen down there, judging by the lean-tos. "This is somethin' else..."

"We can't give up," Ani pleaded. "Not now. Not after everything."

"I'm ain't saying we're giving up," he responded, looking over to her. "I'm just saying, we gotta figure out how to get through that. Who knows how many are inside... That's a whole other can of scrap." He thought about it for a moment. "It's pretty obvious they haven't figured out how to release the flame," he said, struggling to formulate any semblance of a plan. "If they had, then we wouldn't be standing here having this conversation. So, we have time. Though, how much…? That's indeterminate at the moment."

"He can't," Ani remarked flatly.

"Can't what?"

"Release the flame."

Fenix stared at her, a squint flashing through his eyes as he waited for her to elaborate.

"Not without a second key."

Fenix stared at her through the darkness.

"He can't release the flame, because two keys are needed to make the weapon work. You need two keys, at the same time. Without two, there's no fire."

"And you know this, how?"

"I told you. I watched nearly all the videos and read all the files and papers in Belcor. Remember, I would spend weeks locked in that facility with nothing other than the terminals to keep me company. I'm telling you, that's why they haven't released the fire yet. Because they need this." She pulled her key out and held it up.

"Then why the hell don't we just destroy that thing and be done with it. Hell. We could have just done that a long time ago and been on our way." A flare of irritation fanned up in him.

"Because," Ani replied sternly. "You think these are the only two keys in the wastes? You really think it's gonna take that, *monster*, much longer to find another?" She stared at him in the silver glow. "No. All he has to do, is spend a little longer searching the other facilities, or wait until your friend gets one with the right clearance level, and then, *boom*. We're all dead." She let that thought sink in. "No. We have to destroy it."

"And just how do you plan on doing that, huh?"

Ani stared at him, the smile that wanted to creep to the surface staying forced away. "With the third key."

"Third key…?" Fenix asked, nearly exasperated at this point. "What *third* key…?"

"The one that was buried with my mother."

Fenix stared at her, another squint flashing through his eyes. *"That's* why we had to go to your home?" he said, a thin realization wafting past.

Ani's voice was quiet, but steady. "That's why we had to go to my home," she said again. "When we buried my mother, my father slipped the program key into a pouch in her pocket. That's what I needed—and why I had to do it alone. I couldn't have you trying to stop me from digging up my own mother, or making me explain why I was doing something that hurt more than anything I've ever felt." She held up the small, battered key. "Because on this third key, there's a program. If we can get inside Arcan and plug it into the main terminal, it'll destroy the place. The weapons in that facility will never be used again."

Fenix stared at her, searching her face for any sign of doubt. "And you're sure it'll work?"

"Yes," Ani replied, her voice flat and unwavering. After a moment, she added, "I hope."

Fenix let out a long breath, shaking his head. "There it is."

Ani pressed on, her gaze distant. "My father believed it. He believed it enough to bury the key with my mother. That's why he left—he knew it wouldn't be long before someone came looking, and he wanted to throw them off his trail. He told Jarek and me that if anyone ever came, asking about the third key—the artifact—we were never to say it was buried with her. Because if we did, all life in the wastes could be wiped out. He was dead serious. He said if anyone came, no matter what, we weren't to say a word. We were to wait, and when it was safe, take the artifact, find Arcan, and destroy the weapon."

Fenix stared at her silently for a moment. "Why didn't he do it?" he asked, his gaze narrowing in suspicion. "Why didn't he just take that *program* there, and go destroy the facility himself? Why run away and leave it for his kids to take care of? Doesn't seem like the very *responsible* thing to do, does it?"

"I don't know," Ani replied. "I think." Her gaze drifted to the side for a moment before returning. "I think he knew someone was on to it. I think he knew he was being followed, and that if he took the key to the facility, that he'd be bringing them just what they'd need to start the fire."

"You think he knew about the prophet and his damned goblin army?" He paused. "How?"

"I don't know," she replied, her words low and filled with a sorrowful loss. "He never got the chance to tell us. But he had to. Somehow. Or why else would he have buried the key, and told us to take it to the facility ourselves?"

Fenix brought his hand up to his mouth, rubbing his moustache and beard heavily. Then he turned his hand and slid it across the back of his neck, squeezing tightly. "It's all too convenient, isn't it?"

"We—he was being followed," Ani said after a long, heavy pause. "Somehow, that prophet knew. The keys, the program, the facility. All of it. He was tracking my father, hunting him for what he carried. He said so himself." She stood silent, letting the weight of it settle between them, the hush of the wastes pressing in. "I don't know if he ever caught up to my father, or if he had him killed. But I do know my father wouldn't have put this burden on Jarek and me if it wasn't as important as life itself." Her jaw tightened, eyes shining with the ache of loss. "My father disappeared. My brother died just trying to find someone willing to help us reach the facility. The whole world's at risk of burning. So, yes—I believe my father. And I believe if we can get this program into that terminal, we can stop it all. We just have to figure out how."

"God damnit," he growled. "Shit…"

"What?"

Fenix rubbed his eyes, groaning as he did. "Ugh," he sighed, not opening his eyes. "This is fucking stupid…"

"What?" Ani asked, watching her companion struggle through his thoughts.

"It might just be one of the worst ideas I've ever had," Fenix said, finally opening them to look across at her. "But it might just be crazy enough to work…"

Ani stared at him, her face dropping. "What are you thinking?"

68

Up close, the encampment sprawled like a lake of fire—orc tents and goblin hovels pressed tight together, thin, winding paths snaking between them. Dozens of fires burned low, their glow painting the ragged canvas and scrap-metal walls in shifting gold and shadow, flickering up the crater's rim where the Arcan facility crouched in the earth. The air was thick with the stench of fresh-cut meat, sweat, and sewage. Grunts, shouts, and the clang of steel echoed up from below, a constant, restless noise beneath the bruised sky.

Fenix kept Ani just ahead of him, studying the chaos for any sign of order, any weakness in the mass of bodies and banners. When they were about twenty yards from the edge of the camp, he drew up short, boots grinding in the dust. The heat of the fires and the press of so many bodies made the air shimmer.

"You sure about this?" he whispered, eyes fixed on the back of Ani's battered hat, voice barely more than a breath lost in the wind.

Ani nodded softly. "Last hurrah."

"Okay." Fenix shook his head, taking a deep breath before shouting. "Hey! I brought the witch!"

A ripple of commotion stirred through the camp. Two goblins appeared first, shock flickering in their wide eyes, short blades trembling in their hands. They stared, uncertain, as if their minds were struggling to catch up with what they saw. One barked something sharp in goblin-tongue, never taking its gaze off Ani and Fenix. The answer came in the form of heavy, thudding footsteps.

Ani listened, heart pounding, as the footfalls grew louder. The goblins shifted aside, uneasy, just as a towering orc shouldered through the tents—a decorated brute, skulls swinging from its belt, a fringe of scalps strung across a thick leather strap. The orc's war axe gleamed in the firelight as it came to a halt, studying the newcomers with a predator's suspicion before growling something guttural in its own tongue.

"I brought that witch your prophet's been hunting," Fenix called out, his voice steady but his hand resting on the worn grip of his pistol, waiting to see just how foolish this plan might be.

The orc's stare lingered, then it bellowed a command. Three more orcs emerged, weapons drawn, forming a wall of muscle and steel. Behind them, goblins crowded in, ears perked, shoving for a better view. In moments, the whole encampment was alive with anticipation, every eye fixed on Ani and Fenix.

The orc took a deep breath, exhaling with a growl. Then, in a heavily accented human tongue, it spoke. "Bring her."

"Here we go," Fenix said, his lips not moving as he spoke. "Be ready for anything. And, sorry."

Ani was going to ask, *sorry for what*, when Fenix shoved her hard from behind, sending her nearly sprawling out on the ground. "Move," he barked, shoving his hand into her back again.

Ani risked a glance over her shoulder, the look angered and scared.

"Keep moving," he barked.

Fenix closed the space between them and what were now five orcs waiting at the entrance to the encampment. "I tied her hands," he said as he approached. "She can't use her magic."

The orc who'd spoken grunted, apparently unconcerned whether Ani was bound or not. "This way," he growled, swinging his massive arm and pawing three goblins aside in a single, violent sweep.

Fenix followed, keeping Ani just ahead of him as they pressed through the crowd of hissing goblins. He kept his eyes locked on her back, but every so often, he stole a glance to the side—catching flashes of yellowed teeth snapping at the space between them, hungry eyes gleaming in the firelight, blades gripped tight and ready. He knew the only thing keeping them alive was the towering orc leading the way, with two more—only slightly smaller, but still nearly eight feet tall— flanking close behind.

The orcs marched them to the front of the facility, where the entrance yawned open beneath the crater's rim. The whole encampment buzzed with excitement, word of the witch's capture and her delivery by a drifter spreading like wildfire through the ranks.

At the threshold, the lead orc raised his axe, signaling them to halt. Framing the massive doorway stood four human guards, faces hidden behind heavy helmets, only their eyes and a sliver of painted skin visible—black as pitch to match their armor. Each man cradled a pre-world rifle, not so different from the ones Fenix had stashed in the bags tied to Dirtweed, grazing somewhere up on the hill.

The men eyed them suspiciously.

"The witch," the orc growled, staring down at the men.

One of the men looked around the orc to get a better view. Then he turned and made his way to a small device next to the door. He pressed a button, and a moment later a voice fell out. "What is it?"

The man glanced back at Fenix and Ani. "There's a drifter here. He claims to have the witch."

The intercom fell silent for a moment. Then a reply crackled back. "Bring her. Lock her in the pen. The prophet is on his way."

"Understood," the guard replied, turning to face them. "Bring her," the man said, looking at Fenix.

Fenix shoved Ani forward, following after. "Nice place you got here," he said as they were making their way down the main corridor that led further in.

The guard didn't reply.

"Cozy," Fenix added for measure before falling silent.

Fenix had left the ropes around Ani's wrists just loose enough to give her a fighting chance. The knot at her waist, tied off at her back, made it look like her hands were pinned low—helpless, unable to rise above her belt. To their captors, it was the illusion of safety, enough to keep them from binding her tighter. At least, that was the hope when Fenix had explained his half-mad plan. He knew they'd be taken in— likely both of them, and likely separated. He just prayed they wouldn't bind her further before the inevitable interrogation, and that, by some luck, they'd be held close enough for her to use her magic to break them both out.

They'd talked it through: Ani would free herself when the time was right, and Fenix—if he could get his hands on his pistols or the shotgun—would fight their way to the terminal. After that, most of the heavy lifting would fall on her shoulders, at least until he could get to more guns. If they made it outside, he figured they could hold the horde at bay just long enough to skirt the edge of the facility. If they could get that far, one sharp whistle would bring Dirtweed running, the arsenal of weapons strapped to his saddle. They'd left both horses at the rim, just for that reason.

For a moment, everything seemed to be going according to plan. Then something heavy crashed into the back of Fenix's skull, and the world exploded into a shower of black stars before fading to white.

Ani moved in silence, Fenix just behind her, when one of the guards up front glanced back and gave a subtle nod. A heartbeat later, she heard a dull, meaty thunk—turned just in time to see Fenix crumple face-first to the floor. She sucked in a sharp breath. "No!" she shouted, watching as a guard stooped, slid the shotgun away, and wrenched Fenix's arms behind his back, binding them tight with a length of cable before stripping him of his pistols.

"What are you doing!?" Ani barked, panic and anger twisting her voice as two men hoisted her unconscious companion and dragged him away down a side corridor. "Fenix!" she cried, only to be cut short as the butt of a rifle slammed into her stomach, knocking the air from her lungs and dropping her hard to her knees.

"Shut up!" the man barked, allowing her a second to regain herself. "Now get up and let's go. The prophet is waiting."

Ani strained, the pain in her stomach radiating deeply. Then she forced herself to her feet, the tingle of heat working though her fingers.

The men led her further into the facility, each now holding one arm.

Three corridors later, they stopped at a door with a sign above that read, *Control Room.* They stopped, the man in the lead pressing the button on the intercom. "Prophet. We have her."

There was a momentary pause, and then a soft *thunk* indicated that the door had been unlocked.

The men glanced at each other briefly before one pressed the door open and they shoved Ani inside.

She staggered into the chamber, pain still twisting in her gut, every step a reminder of the rifle stock that had dropped her to her knees. The urge to vomit and the pressure in her bladder made it hard to stand straight, but she forced herself to focus, to take in every detail. Ahead, a row of curved seats arched around a narrow aisle, leading down to a sunken floor and a sweeping console aglow with the cold light of a dozen monitors—each one flickering with cryptic diagrams and ancient folders.

At the heart of it all, standing with his back to her—almost theatrically, as if savoring the moment—was the prophet. His heavy cowl had been thrown back, exposing a pale, bald scalp that gleamed in the electric light. Both hands were splayed across the console, fingers spread wide, as if he could draw power from the old world's bones just by touching them. Ani paused at the top of the stairs, forcing herself to steady her breath, and watched as the prophet stood in silent communion with the ghosts of the past, plotting the world's end in the hush of the facility's heart.

One of the guards pushed her forward and she took two steps more before coming to a stop.

"I've been looking all over for you," the man said, not turning to look.

Ani didn't see the smile spread across his lips.

"Do you miss your brother?" he asked, his voice low, barely above a whisper.

The heat in her fingers rose into her palms. "Don't you speak of my brother," she hissed.

"How about your father?" the man continued. "Would you like me to speak of him instead?"

Ani glared at the back of the prophet's head, hatred swirling inside her like a dust storm. She could feel him trying to bait her, to draw out the fire she kept barely contained beneath her skin. But she held fast, refusing to give him the satisfaction. If she lost control now, everything they'd fought for would unravel—every plan, every desperate hope. Both their lives hung on her restraint.

She bit down hard on her lower lip, the taste of blood grounding her, anchoring her rage to something solid. She would not give in. Not here. Not now.

"Mmmm," the man sighed. "I suppose you should know. He did not die quickly."

Ani lunged forward, immediately being grabbed by both arms from behind and restrained. Though with her hands bound, she wasn't sure what she was hoping to accomplish. It had just been a reaction. Again, she reminded herself to stay in control.

Then the man turned, the smile still lingering across his lips. "And neither will you if you do not give me that which I seek."

Ani stared at him for a moment, centralizing the liquid in her mouth before leaning forward and spitting the crimson tinged saliva in his direction.

"Actually, I think I'll start with your drifter friend first. "Fenix, I believe his name is?"

"Fuck you," Ani spat.

"No," he sighed in response. "I think I'll save that pleasure for my men." He eyed each of the guards who exchanged an unseen smile beneath their helmets. "Then we'll throw you to the orcs. Though," he lingered on the thought. "I'm not sure how long that tiny body of yours will last against their girth…"

Ani felt an icy chill run through her veins at the thought.

"Where is the key?"

Ani stared at him in hatred. "I don't know what you're talking about."

The prophet smiled, lowering his gaze for a moment and scoffing lightly. Then he lifted his gaze, his expression changing, and charged forward, his hand clasping around her throat. "Do NOT, toy with me, witch!!!" he shouted, his face just inches from hers.

Ani felt the man's grasp tighten around her throat, the air and blood flow stifled just enough to make her swoon.

He released her, stepping back, drawing in a long, steady breath before letting it out through clenched teeth. "I apologize. My temper gets the best of me sometimes..." His eyes fixed on her, cold and unblinking. "There are only two ways this can go. The first is the lesser unpleasant option. You hand over the key, and I finish the work we've spent so long preparing for." A smirk twisted his lips. "Mind you, you and your friend won't be around long enough to enjoy it. You'll be let loose—allowed to leave. But you'll be the first to witness the flames." He waited, searching her face for any sign of surrender. When none came, his voice dropped, turning hard as steel. "The second option is far less pleasant. We start with your friend. My men will flay him, strip by strip, and toss the pieces to the goblins outside. When there's nothing left but bone, we'll move on to his limbs. If you still haven't given up the second key, then we begin with you. My men will search you—again and again—every inch, inside and out. And when your flesh is worn raw, we'll let the orcs have their way."

Ani stared at the man. How calmly he described the horrors, how casually he spoke of the things that would happen to her. She knew that she could fight back, that it would only take her a few moments to wriggle free of the ropes binding her hands, but if she failed. If she woke up, bound and gagged, her hands useless behind her back, the men already taking their turns. If they killed Fenix first... "Stop," Ani whispered, her gaze dropping to the floor. "Stop."

"Then tell me. Where, is, the key?"

A small sob escaped her lips, tears working their way down from the inside corners of her eyes. She swallowed heavily, sniffling back to the moisture that was working its way into her sinuses. A shuddered breath escaped, followed by a second. "I have it," she said in a hoarse whisper. "My necklace."

A smile spread across the prophet's face, and he gestured with a single nod to one of the men, who stepped around and fished the necklace from inside her shirt. The man yanked the chain hard, breaking it from her neck and then turned, handing it out to the prophet.

Ani winced as the chain was yanked free, the thin metal biting into the back of her neck. She watched the man hold it out, the smile lingering as the prophet took the key. She watched as he studied it, turning it over in his hand and analyzing the difference.

"This is not the key," he growled, the smile fading.

"No," she replied flatly, another stream of tears falling down her cheeks. "But without that, the second key won't work."

He eyed the third key again. "And where, is the *second* key?"

Ani swallowed hard. "The drifter. Fenix. He has it."

The prophet stared at her for a moment before looking to the men. "Take her away," he said. "Lock her up and bring me that second key."

The men grunted in agreement, grabbing Ani by the arms and spinning her. She glanced once over her shoulder to see the prophet staring at her as she was led from the room.

69

The prophet turned the program key over and over in his trembling hands, eyes wide and wild, lips moving in unspoken thoughts. He stared at the artifact as if it might whisper secrets only he could hear. Until that moment, he hadn't even known a third key existed—of course, of course, the ancients would never make it so simple. Paranoia and vindication tangled in his mind: they had tried to hide the true path, but he, the chosen, had seen through their lies. The girl— foolish, terrified, so sure of her own cleverness—had brought him exactly what he needed. She thought herself a player in this game, but she was only a pawn, a trembling offering to his vision. And the drifter—ha!—the drifter's greed was as predictable as the sun's rise. All drifters were the same: faithless, hungry, desperate for scraps. He would awaken soon, expecting a reward, but the prophet would give him a reward beyond imagining. He would let them both witness the dawn of a new world—let them see the cleansing fire with their own eyes before the end.

He clutched the key tighter, knuckles white, a feverish grin splitting his face. He could already see it: the horde, his horde, pouring into the Tunnels of Gol, the world above set ablaze, the screams of the unworthy rising like incense to the heavens. He would be the architect of the new age, the one who finally broke the chains that bound his kind. No more would the Corithians be spat on, hunted, burned at the stake by trembling, jealous humans. No more would they cower in the shadows, forced to beg for scraps at the tables of their oppressors. No—he would remake the world in fire and blood, and when the ashes settled, only the worthy would remain. His followers would emerge from the darkness, reborn, and all who survived would kneel or perish.

He began to mutter, voice rising and falling in a manic chant, words tumbling over each other—half prophecy, half curse. "They thought they could stop me. They thought they could hide the flame.

But I am the flame. I am the end and the beginning. I am the prophet. I am the prophet. I am—"

With a shuddering breath, he snapped back to the present, eyes blazing. He turned and stalked toward the console, key in hand, the weight of destiny and madness pressing down on him like a crown of thorns. The world would burn, and he would be there to watch it, laughing as the old order crumbled to dust.

70

Fenix came awake to the sound of boots echoing down the concrete corridor, the heavy door at the end groaning open. He sat up, wrists bound tight behind his back, the cold bite of steel digging into his skin. From somewhere close—a cell just beyond the thin, rusted wall—he heard the scuffle of feet and a voice, raw with fear and defiance.

"Ani!?" he called, forcing himself upright, heart pounding. "Ani!?"

Her reply came, muffled but urgent, strained with desperation. "Fenix! They have the third key!"

He tensed, jaw clenching as the reality of their situation settled like dust in his lungs.

The door to his cell screeched open, spilling harsh yellow light across the cracked floor. Two guards stepped in, faces hidden behind battered masks, rifles slung low. One advanced, voice flat as the wastes. "Where is it?"

Fenix met the man's gaze, wishing—just for a moment—that they'd had the decency to bind his hands in front. "Where's what?" he shot back, eyes flicking between them, searching for any sign of mercy.

The answer was a fist, hard and merciless, slamming into his gut. He doubled over, breath stolen, pain blooming through his ribs. "Where is it?" the guard repeated, voice colder than the desert night.

From the next cell, Ani's voice broke through, trembling but clear. "They know, Fenix. Just give it to them, or they'll kill us both."

Fenix snarled, defiance burning in his eyes. The second guard drew a knife, pressing the blade to Fenix's throat—a whisper away from ending it all. "It'd be easier to take it from your corpse."

Fenix swallowed, the taste of blood sharp in his mouth. "Okay. Okay. It's in my pocket."

"Which one?"

"The front."

The guard reached in, coming up empty. Fenix managed a crooked smile. "Guess it's in the other one."

The next blow caught him across the jaw, sending him crashing to the floor, the world spinning. He barely registered the guard's hand digging into his other pocket, fishing out the key.

"Buy me a drink first?" Fenix hissed, voice thick with pain.

The guard's boot slammed into his gut, curling him into the dust. Then the men turned and left, the door slamming shut behind them, the lock clicking home.

Fenix lay there, listening to the footsteps fade down the corridor, the silence pressing in. From the next cell, Ani's voice rang out, frantic and afraid. "Fenix!? Fenix!?"

He forced himself upright, wincing as pain lanced through his jaw—felt the sharp edge of a broken tooth. "I'm here," he called, voice ragged. "I'm here…"

"We don't have much time," Ani said, her voice tight with urgency, the sound of her struggling against her bonds echoing through the gloom.

71

Back in the control room, the prophet drifted through the gloom like a ghost, the echo of his boots lost beneath the low hum of ancient machines. He paused before the console, the battered key trembling in his hand—a relic of the old world, heavy with promise and madness. The socket waited, nearly dead-center on the console, flanked by the twin keyholes like the eyes of some slumbering beast.

A feverish smile crept across his lips as he pressed the key home. For a heartbeat, nothing happened. Then a small light flickered to life—yellow, uncertain, stuttering in the shadows. The prophet's breath caught, suspicion and anticipation warring in his eyes. The light blinked, once, twice, then steadied to green with a sharp, mechanical click. A chime echoed through the chamber, cold and final.

Above, the monitor flared white, bathing the prophet in a ghostly glow. A single message appeared on the screen, stark against the darkness, as the world seemed to hold its breath around him.

ENGAGE PROGRAM?

<YES> / <NO>

The prophet stood transfixed, the pale glow of the monitor painting his face in ghostly light. He read the words once, twice, then again—each time his eyes growing wider, his breath coming faster. It was almost laughable, how simple the ancients had made it. Of course they would. A species so obsessed with war and ruin would never trust their legacy to anything but the press of a button. The flame was meant to be unleashed, and he—he alone—was chosen to do it.

A feverish grin split his lips as he reached out, hand trembling, and moved the cursor over YES. For a heartbeat, the world seemed to hold its breath. Then he pressed the button.

The screen flickered, the message dissolving into a new command as the machinery deep within the earth began to stir.

PROGRAM ACTION CANNOT BE HALTED ONCE ENGAGED

FULL SYSTEM RESET IMMINENT

ENGAGE PROGRAM?
<YES> / <NO>

A twisted smile pulled at the prophet's lips. "Full system reset imminent." He read the words, then read them again, the meaning sinking in like a fever. The smile grew, stretching too wide, eyes shining with a madman's certainty.

Behind him, the heavy doors hissed open and his followers entered, boots echoing on the cold concrete. "We have it, sir," one announced, holding the second key aloft.

The prophet didn't even turn, his gaze still fixed on the glowing screen. "Bring it," he said, voice low and trembling with anticipation.

The man approached, hand outstretched, but the prophet only regarded him with a feverish gleam. "You," he said, voice echoing in the chamber, "have proved your worth. Your loyalty. You will stand at my side while the world above burns. And when the ashes settle, you will help me shape what comes next."

The man stiffened, a flicker of awe—or perhaps fear—passing through his eyes. At a gesture, he moved to the console, slotting the key into the second box. Both lights flickered green, casting an eerie glow across the prophet's face.

The prophet's smile widened, almost inhuman. "The time has come," he whispered, stepping back to the console. "Let us purge this earth of the unworthy."

With a trembling hand, he pressed YES.

As if fate itself had spoken, the screen changed once more, a final message blooming in the ghostly light—a silent, irreversible judgment, the culmination of every nightmare and every fevered dream that had brought him to this moment.

THE FOLLOWING ACTION CANNOT BE REVERSED
PURGE FACILITY?
<YES> / <NO>

The smile grew upon seeing the affirmation. Then he reached out and clicked *YES*.

72

"Ani," Fenix called, voice rough as gravel as he moved to the door. "We don't have much time. You need to get those ropes free and get us out of here. My hands are tied—I can't help you."

Unseen by him, Ani had already slipped her bonds, the ropes lying in a loose coil on the floor behind her. She stood with her hands outstretched toward the door, heat building in her chest, magic thrumming just beneath her skin.

Fenix flinched back as a sudden burst of heat flashed through the narrow seam of the door. A metallic thunk rang out, echoing down the corridor as the door to the next cell slammed open. A heartbeat later, the lock on his own door clicked, and the heavy slab swung wide.

"Ani," he breathed, relief and disbelief tangled in his voice. "Thank God."

Ani rushed into the room, throwing her arms around him. He winced, pain flaring in his battered ribs. "I'd love to hug you back," he managed, "but you're squeezing the life out of me."

"I'm sorry," Ani whispered, her voice trembling as she worked at the knot binding his wrists. "I'm sorry."

"Don't be," Fenix said, eyes darting to the open doorway. "We planned for this. Let's just hope—"

As if summoned by his words, the lights overhead dimmed, flickering to near darkness before flaring back, now burning a sickly yellow. A klaxon wailed through the halls, the sound bouncing off concrete and steel. Then a voice crackled over the ancient speakers, cold and mechanical: *"Self-destruct sequence has commenced. Please evacuate the building. Repeat: self-destruct sequence has commenced. Lockdown to commence in t-minus twenty minutes. All personnel must safely evacuate the facility."*

The pair locked eyes, a thousand silent words passing between them in a single, desperate glance.

"My turn," Ani said, the heat already rising in her palms as she turned toward the door, ready to carve their path to freedom.

73

No sooner had the prophet stabbed the YES button, the world seemed to lurch. The lights overhead guttered and died, plunging the control room into a sickly twilight. Two jaundiced bulbs flared above the console, casting long, feverish shadows across the battered steel. Then came the sound—a siren, shrill and merciless, splitting the silence like a bullet through bone.

He stared, caught in a daze, the edges of his mind unraveling. A smile twitched at his lips as a countdown timer flickered to life across the cracked screens. He watched the numbers tumble, each second a promise: when the clock hit zero, the world would belong to him. The prophet's grin widened, madness glinting in his eyes.

Then the speakers crackled, the voice of the old world echoing through the bones of the facility: *"Self-destruct sequence has commenced, please evacuate the building. Repeat: self-destruct sequence has commenced. Lockdown to commence in t-minus twenty minutes. All personnel must safely evacuate the facility."*

The smile slid from his face, replaced by a cold, creeping horror. "No," he whispered, the word barely more than a breath. "What have you done...? No..." He stared at the screens, the klaxon wailing, the timer ticking down. "No. No. NO. NOOOOOO!"

He lunged at the console, slamming his palm against the buttons, desperate to undo what he'd set in motion. Nothing happened. The words replayed in his mind, twisted now by dread: The following action cannot be reversed. Purge facility? Yes. No. Purge facility...

"No! NO!"

He'd misread the warning. Misjudged the ancients. In his arrogance, he'd doomed everything. Rage and panic boiled up, hotter than any fire he'd ever conjured. He smashed his fists against the console, heat shimmering from his skin, the air around his hands warping with wild, uncontrolled magic. Then, with a howl of fury and shame, he spun and staggered toward the door, the siren's scream chasing him into the dark.

74

Ani stepped out into the corridor, Fenix close behind, the ghosts of fear and sorrow left behind with the ropes that had bound her. Now, only fury and vengeance burned in her veins. She stalked down the dim hallway, boots echoing on cracked concrete, the fire beneath her skin begging for release.

Fenix shouted, "Look out!" His words split the hush as two guards rounded the corner, rifles half-raised, eyes wide with the shock of seeing their prisoners free. But hesitation was fatal in the wastes. Ani's hands flashed up, and in that heartbeat, fire leapt from her palms, roaring down the corridor in a tunnel of searing heat.

The guards screamed, armor melting to their flesh as they collapsed, the flames fading to leave only two smoldering heaps in the blackened hall.

Fenix stepped over the first body, catching a glimpse of charred flesh beneath the helmet. He spat, then reached down to snatch up a rifle—only to curse as the barrel scorched his palm. "Ow, shit!" he barked, shaking his hand, but Ani didn't even register the words. Her focus was locked on the door at the end of the corridor, where vengeance waited.

A moment later, the door swung open and an orc, flanked by two more guards, stepped into the gloom. Fenix watched as Ani—no longer timid, but something wild and wrathful—stepped forward, hands raised. A wave of heat flared, a plume of fire erupting from her fingers. The lights overhead went dark, plastic and glass housings melting away as the blast filled the hall. The speakers that had blared warnings and klaxons gurgled and died. At the end of the corridor, the orc's eyes went wide as the inferno rushed toward it. In a blink, it was engulfed, flesh and muscle melting away, the two guards behind it vanishing in the firestorm.

When the flames faded, Ani lowered her hands. The hallway was scorched black and smoking, the only light now a dim, yellow glow from emergency bulbs that had survived the heat. Deeper in the facility, the warning repeated, echoing through the bones of the old world as Ani and Fenix pressed on.

"Self-destruct sequence has commenced, please evacuate the building, repeat. Self-destruct sequence has commenced. Lock down to commence in t-minus seventeen minutes. All personnel must safely evacuate the facility."

"We should go," Fenix said, removing the rifle's clip and checking the ammo. Contented that it was full, he slapped it back in place and followed after.

The pair continued down the corridor, reaching the intersection. To the left was the control room, their exit to the right. No sooner did they step out, than they heard the cracked scream.

"YOOOUUU!!! What have you done!?!?"

Ani turned to see the prophet standing a short distance down the hall, two of his guards at his flank.

"What did you do!?" he demanded once more.

"You killed my brother," she growled. "My father. You took *EVERYTHING* from me!"

A glowing heat began to waft from the prophet's hands. The same glow flared from Ani's.

"You think you have won!?" the prophet shouted at the space between them. "You think the disciples of the flame will EVER—"

A single gunshot cracked through the corridor, cutting the prophet's words short. For a heartbeat, time seemed to freeze—then Ani stood, ears ringing, watching as the heat faded from the prophet's hands and a dark bloom of crimson spread across the front of his robe.

The prophet's gaze dropped to the hole in his chest, then lifted to meet Ani's eyes—defiant, wild, and burning with something unholy. His hands twitched, as if to conjure one last curse, but Ani was faster. She unleashed a torrent of fire, a long, unrelenting plume that roared down the hall, swallowing the prophet and the two men behind him in a storm of heat and vengeance.

Fenix ducked behind her, using her body as a shield against the scorching blast. He heard the short, desperate screams of the prophet's followers, then nothing but the gentle crackle of flames licking at the blackened walls and the warped remains of old photographs.

When the heat finally faded, Fenix straightened, peering past Ani at the charred remains at the end of the corridor. He placed a steadying hand on her shoulder. "Come on," he said, voice low and rough. "Let's go."

Together, they turned and started toward the exit, leaving the silence and the ashes behind.

"Self-destruct sequence has commenced, please evacuate the building, repeat. Self-destruct sequence has commenced. Lock down to commence in t-minus fourteen minutes. All personnel must safely evacuate the facility."

The pair reached the entrance to the facility as the timer bled down to ten minutes. The air inside was thick with the scent of scorched metal and fear. As they stepped in, a massive orc blocked their path, flanked by a knot of sword-wielding goblins, their eyes glinting in the dim, flickering light.

Ani halted, Fenix at her side, rifle raised and ready. The orc's gaze swept over them, lingering on the corridor behind as if weighing the odds.

"Your prophet's dead," Fenix called out, his voice flat as the wastes, finger tightening on the trigger.

A ripple of unease ran through the group. "Dead. He's dead. The prophet is dead," came the murmured echo, disbelief and dread mingling in their guttural tongues.

The orc stared, unmoving, the timer ticking down—eleven, then ten. Fenix met its gaze, unblinking. "Your move," he said, the words hanging in the charged silence.

For a long moment, the orc's lips curled back, fangs bared in a snarl, muscles tensing beneath dark green skin. Then, with a single guttural growl that reverberated off the concrete, it turned and stomped out through the entrance, boots pounding like thunder.

"Dead! The prophet is dead!" the goblins shrieked, panic blooming as they turned on each other, confusion spreading like wildfire. In a flurry of motion, they rushed outside, their voices carrying the news to the rest of the horde.

Fenix and Ani exchanged a glance—worry, relief, and urgency all tangled together. The timer counted to ten.

"We gotta go," Fenix said, already moving for the door.

75

The world outside the Arcan facility had erupted into a maelstrom of violence and confusion. The crater, once a staging ground for conquest, was now a cauldron of madness. Goblin clans, stripped of leadership and purpose, turned on each other with feral abandon. War banners that had once flown side by side were now trampled in the dust, their colors muddied by blood and ash. Screams and war cries tangled in the air, echoing off the crater walls—a chorus of rage, fear, and betrayal.

Everywhere, goblins clashed in frenzied skirmishes, blades flashing in the firelight, armor ringing as rival clans fought for dominance. Old grudges, barely held in check by the prophet's iron will, now exploded into open warfare. The ground was littered with the fallen—some still writhing, others already claimed by the dust. War horns blared, their mournful notes rising above the din, only to be drowned out by the shrieks of the dying and the clash of steel on steel.

Orcs, grim and disciplined, wasted no time on the chaos. Their chieftains barked guttural commands, and the warbands fell into tight formation, marching away from the carnage with heavy, thunderous steps. They left the goblins to their blood feud, knowing that without the horde at their backs, any hope of conquest was lost. The orcs' retreat was not a surrender, but a promise—a silent vow that their march would come again, when the time was right.

The air itself seemed to vibrate with violence. Smoke from a dozen campfires mingled with the dust, swirling in the wind and stinging the eyes. The crater's rim was alive with movement—goblins fleeing, others giving chase, arrows whistling through the gloom. In the confusion, a few desperate souls tried to break away, only to be cut down by their own kin, the law of the wastes written in blood.

Fenix tapped Ani, gesturing for her to follow, his eyes never leaving the roiling chaos beyond the facility's shadow. The crater had become a battlefield—goblin clans, stripped of leadership, had turned on each other with a savagery born of old grudges and fresh betrayal. War banners that once flew side by side now lay trampled in the dust, their colors muddied by blood and ash. The air was thick with the clang of steel, the shriek of war horns, and the guttural cries of goblins locked in a frenzy for dominance. Smoke from burning tents curled into the bruised sky, mingling with the dust kicked up by stampeding feet.

Fenix's plan was simple: use the spreading violence as cover, moving low and fast along the battered wall of the facility. The goblins were too busy tearing each other apart to notice two more shadows slipping through the gloom. Every step was a gamble—one wrong move, and they'd be swept up in the storm. But the horde's attention was elsewhere, each clan desperate to carve out its own future from the chaos.

By the time they reached the corner of the building, the battle had reached a fever pitch. Goblins darted between fires, blades flashing in the firelight, armor ringing as rival clans clashed. A few stragglers caught sight of Fenix and Ani, but found only a quick death at the muzzle of Fenix's rifle. The ground trembled beneath their boots, the distant rumble of the facility's impending destruction adding a new note of terror to the night.

A cloud of dust was rising in the air, the crater's rim alive with movement—goblins fleeing, others giving chase, arrows whistling through the gloom. In the confusion, desperate souls tried to break away, only to be cut down by their own kin. The law of the wastes was written in blood tonight.

The pair edged their way around the side and, with a final glance at the chaos behind, broke into a full sprint for the back of the facility. Inside, the timer had reached four minutes and counting. Fenix sucked in a gulp of air, brought his fingers to his lips, and let out a sharp whistle that cut through the din. Then he ran, Ani just behind, boots pounding the earth.

By the time they reached the back, Dirtweed was already barreling down the slope, gravity lending speed to the old horse's desperate charge. Two minutes later, they were scrambling into the saddle, Fenix kicking him stiffly in the side. "Go! GO!" he shouted, slapping the reins. Dirtweed lunged forward, hooves tearing at the dust, as behind them the countdown reached one.

At the facility's entrance, the massive door shuddered and began to close, inch by inch, as the timer bled away its final seconds. The goblins outside were too lost in bloodlust to notice, locked in a battle for clan supremacy. The promise of greater lands had been the only thing keeping them from killing each other before; now, with the prophet gone, all bets were off. The crater was a cauldron of violence, every clan fighting to be the last left standing.

The door sealed shut, tungsten rods locking into place. When the timer hit zero, a single warhead deep within the earth went critical. The ground rumbled with the explosion, the polycrete walls of the facility straining to contain the blast. Everything inside was incinerated, leaving nothing but a hollow, scorched shell. The rods in the door snapped, the mechanism melting into place, sealing the tomb for all time.

Outside, the shockwave rolled across the wastes like an earthquake, sending flocks of desert birds screaming into the sky and every creature scurrying for cover. On the crater's lip, Dirtweed lost his footing, collapsing to his side and sending Fenix and Ani tumbling down the slope. They slid a dozen feet before catching themselves, dust swirling around them.

For a moment, the goblins paused, stunned by the force of the blast. Then, as if nothing had changed, the battle resumed—war cries and the clash of steel echoing into the night. Ani turned to Fenix, their eyes meeting in the haze, the world burning and broken around them.

76

Fenix had just finished securing the gun bags in place when Ani stepped up, Dusty's reins in her hands. The crater behind them still smoldered with the echoes of chaos, but here, in the hush before dawn, the world felt strangely new.

"What are you going to do now?" Ani asked, her voice soft, eyes searching the man who had become something more than a companion. The word friend flickered through her thoughts, bright and unexpected.

He smirked, shaking his head slowly. "I don't know," he said, honest as the dust. "If I'm gonna be honest, I didn't think we were gonna walk out of there. I just ain't had time to think about it." He patted his horse on the neck, the gesture gentle. "Probably make my way back to Royce. Sell him these guns. Use those credits to go, I don't know. Somewhere, not here."

Ani nodded, the weight of the past weeks settling on her shoulders.

"What about you?" he asked, remembering their old conversation, but letting her take the lead. "What's the plan of the great Anika Summersong, unknown savior of the wastes?"

She smiled, a soft scoff escaping her lips. "I don't know. If I'm gonna be honest," she said, "I didn't think we were gonna walk out of there, so… I didn't have much time to think about it."

Fenix smiled, warmth moving through his chest. "Whelp. I've heard there's a decent-sized settlement in the Calexico Republic out west. Might be worth checking out. I mean. Unless you wanna stay here."

Ani smiled, a similar feeling stirring inside her. "I don't know. Could be kind of peaceful with the orcs gone and most of the goblins dead…"

Fenix shook his head, a real smile breaking through. "You know, I'm betting they could probably use a good history teacher in Calexico. Maybe even someone with first-hand knowledge…"

Ani laughed. "I don't know. I was just getting used to the thought of being a wasteland drifter."

Fenix made his way around his horse, climbing up into the saddle. "Would you shut up and get on your horse…"

Ani grinned, locking her foot into the stirrup and hoisting herself up. For a moment, they sat side by side, the battered wastes behind them, the unknown ahead.

Fenix clicked his tongue twice, gently tapping his heels into Dirtweed's sides, nudging him forward. "Come on," he said with a loud sigh. "Let's get the hell out of the wastes…"

Ani nudged Dusty after him, the two of them riding out together.

Across the horizon, a pale yellow edged its way upward, a thin line of gold scattered just beneath, a quiet calm spreading across the desert on the breath of a warm breeze. The morning's heat had already begun to work its way up, and behind them, the last of the goblin clans fought their exhausted battle. In the distance, a single crow made its way across the sky, cawing out to the rising sun.

For the first time in a long while, the future was unwritten. And as they rode toward it, side by side, the wastes behind them and the world ahead, it almost felt like hope.